Morgan 512

H.C. Schaffer

ISBN 978-1-943650-23-1
Library of Congress Control Number 2016909155

Cover design by David Bahm.
Published by BookCrafters, Parker, Colorado
www.BookCrafters.net

This book is dedicated to

Two angels in my life

You believed me

and

You believed in me.

Shackled by who you are

Bound by what you think you are not

Better to lie to someone else

Than to lie to yourself

~ Excerpt from *Adieu* by

H. Schaffer / Beyond Classy Music

Chapter 1

IT WAS A SUNNY DAY in early May at a little past three in the afternoon. It was soon to be half past hell. North Hollywood High School had just adjourned for the day but the highlight of the day would begin shortly in an alley that ran behind the school. This alley had seen all kinds of life experiences since its existence in the mid-1940s. It tended to be the students' easiest place to meet as there was only one alley. It had been the site of many groups, rallies, deals of all sorts, kisses, and even a couple of killings. But today it would serve as the fighting ring where a large portion of the student body would turn out to see what they perceived as justice to a student who had more people who disliked him than liked him.

Lewis Morgan was a straight A student who was also the student body president and the captain of the football, basketball and baseball teams. A tremendous athlete and scholar, he was also very giving and tremendously helpful. Lewis had been this type of person since the first grade. All of his teachers believed Lewis was their student of a lifetime.

All year long Lewis had been fielding over thirty full ride scholarships to some of the most high profile colleges and universities in the United States. They wanted him not only for his perfect 4.0 grade point average but also for the leadership and talent he displayed in leading his high school football team to a national high school title and two state divisions the two previous years as quarterback and captain. As his father Charlie said, "Not bad for a school that had never won anything of any kind." His high school football stats looked remarkably similar to the high school stats of one John Elway.

If that wasn't enough, Lewis had led his respective basketball and baseball championship teams the three years that he had played varsity. At six feet four inches, he had the height, but he also possessed an unbelievable quickness that was usually associated with much smaller athletes. His career batting average of .428 had a number of pro-baseball teams trying to get him to pass on a college career. He could easily throw a fastball in the mid-90s without much effort.

His basketball prowess was equally impressive. He broke a California state high school record of sixty points scored in the state championship game that propelled North Hollywood High onto a national championship stage against perennial champion schools from the northeast like New York, New Jersey and Boston. To top it off, Lewis sunk the game winner at the final buzzer at the home of the New York Knicks, Madison Square Garden, with a national television audience watching. The pro offers hadn't stopped coming to the Morgan family's mail box since Lewis's junior year.

And if all of this was not enough, Lewis had been dating the absolutely gorgeous Sarina Burke, who had been a professional model since she was six years old. She was a fellow classmate and they had been an item since the tenth grade. It was already pre-ordained that they would marry after their respective college careers. Sarina was also an equal to Lewis in the academic realm and was as popular as he, being runner up to Lewis as student body vice-president.

There had been a lot of talk that the two would try to go to the same college so they would not be parted from each other. They had been inseparable since the tenth grade, to the delight of both families.

Lewis was not only much taller than his parents, but he embodied the best of both gene pools in his physical good looks. Charles Morgan, aka Charlie, was descended from a line of Morgans that traced all the way back to County Tipperary in Ireland. The fair complexion and the classic Gaelic good looks were passed unsparingly to Lewis.

Angeline Morgan was a Mediterranean mixture of Italian and Sicilian ancestry. She was of dark complexion, deep dark bewitching brown eyes, and a very petite build. Charlie, her husband, described her many times as being five feet four inches of "pure dynamite."

From the time he was a little boy, girls had used the same adjective in describing Lewis: hot.

Lewis's temperament was again the perfect balance. He had been described many times as soft spoken, resolute in not only character but physically, calculative and controlled, and with intelligent fury. Both Charlie and Angeline had supplied various doses to this genetic blueprint. Charlie was a controlled and soft spoken individual, while Angeline was the resolute and the fury, or as her husband would say, "Hell, fury and damnation."

The Morgan family consisted of four children. Lewis was the eldest, followed by Paul, one year younger than Lewis. Then came sister, Ashley, two years younger than Paul, and finally, the baby of the family, Claire, two years younger than her sister Ashley.

The Morgan family was Catholic on both sides of the equation. They all attended church every Sunday at St. Charles.

Lewis was an altar boy and sang in the choir. The two girls were involved in various choir groups. The lone exception to this family tradition was Paul.

Paul Morgan was a junior. Born son number two, Paul lived in the shadow of his older brother in many ways. Where Lewis was described as a great student, fabulous athlete and good looking, Paul was a good but not great student, a pretty intense athlete, and very good looking but from another aspect of his genetic pool. He had more of his mother's Italian/Sicilian physical looks. In other words, he was more of a darker handsome than his older brother. He did not have the height, build or strength of Lewis, but he more than made up for these perceived shortcomings in focus and intensity.

"Paul can overcome anything he puts his mind to," his mother would say. He could also get himself into an unbelievable amount of trouble with very little effort. He was outgoing and very funny. He sometimes gave the impression that he was going only at half speed or half caring but that could change with the flip of a switch. It was said he could go from the speed of a turtle to a cheetah in a blink of an eye.

Paul questioned many of his family's long held tenets, beliefs and aspirations. He did not want to grow up to be a servant to anyone or anything. He very decisively let his parents, family, and anyone who would listen to him, know that he had no plans to pursue work that had small money and manual labor attached to it. He was directly on the path of a highly paid executive.

His father Charlie had been a longshoreman for over thirty years and was very proud of that fact. What Charlie lacked in education was more than made up for in singular focus on hard work to provide for his family. His sons inherited their leadership qualities from him in that he headed his local union for many years; as many times as he tried to step down he was re-elected by a landslide of votes.

Each son's leadership qualities were exhibited in very different arenas. Lewis's forte was the classroom, the athletic field, and being a natural born leader among whomever he was with. Lewis did it silently and from within. A person you always felt you could trust. Paul, on the other hand, led a completely different set of individuals using the opposite approach. If he told you to do something and you failed, he used the corporal method; he would physically make you do it. His belief in what he was doing was unwavering and God help you if you were found to be doubtful. His tenet was all in or all out warfare.

While they were growing up, Lewis tried many times to show Paul that there were better ways to interact and lead. Paul would have none of it. Focus on the prize and go get it with as few interruptions as possible. Paul was a street fighting man from the time he was in grammar school. With no concern for size or weight, he was going to do his damnedest to either convert you to his side or physically convert you to his perspective.

Whereas Lewis never saw the inside of a dentition hall, Paul spent a great deal of time there. His sisters, Ashley and Claire, began to call it Paul's home away from home. His parents' approach was to tell Paul that his behavior shamed the family and reflected badly on their parenting skills. Paul was oblivious to their remarks, saying that it was his way and he was not going to be a kiss ass, like his brother.

The comparisons to his brother had obviously left a burnt patch on Paul's psyche. But looking at the two boys as a third party bystander, they both had a world of talent and intelligence; it was just exhibited in opposite pathways of life.

Many times, as brothers do, Lewis and Paul would get into physical skirmishes, usually with size and strength (i.e., Lewis) being the victor. But victory over Paul always came with a cost, sometimes a very painful cost. No matter how injured Paul was, he would continue to extract a measure of either vengeance or a sudden turn of events in his favor with absolutely no care or concern with amount of pain being inflicted on him.

Angeline's father, Carlos Catania was born in Sicily's largest town, Palermo. Carlos's family had left the province and city of Catania, which about half of the residents used as their last name. Catania is located on the south side of the island but most industry and commerce would be found on the north side of the island, namely Palermo. When Carlos's family sought a better life they, as many immigrants before them, left the old world to seek a better future. The Catanias left Sicily by ship and three year old Carlos would not see his native country for another seventy years.

The ship docked in New York City where, even though there were many fellow Sicilians, the Catania family did not want any part of the harsh winters and humid summers. They headed west to California, where the weather was more like home. It gave them the opportunity to have vegetable gardens and a life style that generations of Catanias had been accustomed to.

Carlos was made to attend school and he mastered the English language ahead of anyone in the family. He didn't think of himself as a Sicilian. He was an American first, a Californian second, and if someone persisted in asking him, he was a former Sicilian. He whole heartedly adopted his new country. He was very popular at school and was a decent student.

He learned very early and very quickly how to participate in American sports but his passion was baseball. He followed it, played it, and some said he loved it. He was not very tall at about five feet eight inches, but he was tremendously quick and agile. His coaches called him a natural second baseman.

Carlos was ambidextrous and switch hitting came naturally to him once he figured out which hand went where. He was easy going in most circumstances, but throughout his growing up, Carlos showed a mean streak that could get ugly fast. The generations of Catanias that had preceded him had yielded various boxers and wrestlers. Carlos was very territorial when it came to family matters and was well known for once going after a couple soldiers on leave who whistled at one of his sisters and his mother. He gut punched one and kicked the other in the groin. He was ten years old.

Carlos continued playing baseball throughout high school but any thoughts of college were quickly put aside. The family operated a produce supply business and harvested various farms that were actually leased pieces of vacant land where they grew vegetables.

A couple of small colleges were willing to give partial baseball scholarships but, again, Carlos was brought back to reality by his family's need of physical labor to keep their enterprise afloat. Carlos spent the better part of weekdays with school, baseball and working on the family's produce business. His usual day lasted between sixteen to eighteen hours.

In his high school junior class of World History, he met the love of his life. Her name was Carmen Razza, and in her, the best of eons of Italian genes now infused his class. Carlos was smitten, more like shot. Carmen's family had emigrated from Venice, Italy, and was in the grocery business. Not suppliers like the Catanias, but store owners. The three Razza brothers owned and operated about twenty small grocery stores. The middle brother, Carlos, was Carmen's father.

The Catanias lived in the basin of North Hollywood. The Razzas lived in the foothills among the other nouveau riche of California consisting of movie and recording artists and various

other professionals who found California a great place to hit
the proverbial gold rush.

Chapter 2

THE STUDENTS BEGAN to fill the alley behind the school for the meeting between Paul Morgan and the very intimidating Peter Duffy. The Duffys were a very well-known and long established family in the valley that operated a chain of liquor stores. The men of the family were classic Irish bog farmers or mountain men in appearance, being very large and heavy. The nurses who assisted in their deliveries at birth said they needed a crane to get them out and they were big enough to pull a plow. They tended to be very pale in complexion and whatever hair they were born with would soon go into "balding" mode. Before most of the male Duffys were out of middle school, they were prematurely bald.

On the other hand, the female side of the Duffy clan tended to be petite and fair haired. In most of their respective households, it appeared that there were actually two distinct species of humanity residing together—the males being almost Neanderthal in their appearance and manners and the females being their complete opposite.

The Duffy girls were very popular at school as they were outgoing and rumored to be always looking for a good time. The family was never going to produce a female who was going to become a nun. Their reputed promiscuous behavior was a backlash to their family's support and devotion to their local parish, St. Charles Catholic Church.

The men of the clan tended to grunt rather than speak and the girls never stopped talking.

Lisa Duffy was a junior at North Hollywood High School. She was a very good student, a cheerleader, and had been the previous year's sophomore class president. As in the Duffy female tradition, Lisa was the star of the debate team for three years and her verbal barrages were legendary. It was noted that Lisa could talk you to death before proving a principle in debate. With her family's money and success, Lisa believed there wasn't anything she could not attain. With that conviction she set her sights on Paul Morgan. There was just one problem. He had absolutely no interest in her.

Paul, in contrast to his brother, was quiet and detached. Lisa had taken notice of Paul while watching her brother Peter practice with the varsity football team. Peter was the anchor of the varsity line and had been an integral part of the championships that the high school had won. Peter was listed at two hundred eighty pounds but many believed he was over three-hundred. He was still the Little Duffy at home at six feet, because the clan topped three hundred fifty pounds and six feet four as a starting point. When lining up against him at right guard, it was rumored you couldn't see the opposing backfield. Most of the school's running success was with Big Pete leading the way. He was frequently referred to as the big cat, not for being feline or quick, but in reference to a Caterpillar bull dozer.

Making varsity this year, Paul was roughly about half the size and weight of his right guard. His five feet nine and one-hundred and forty pounds were adapted to only one function on the team—speed. Since he'd been very young, brother Lewis had thrown the football and Paul had caught it. Paul lettered in track in sprinting and distance. He was quick, but more important, he was fearless. He also was a talented baseball player at shortstop or second. He was very much a throwback to his maternal grandfather, Carlos.

Just as Lewis was a composite of both families, Paul was a carbon copy of the Sicilian side of the family. If Carlos had been younger, Paul could have been his clone son. Growing up, Paul listened to his grandfather's sage advice about being fearless, reserved, and focused. His grandfather taught him to fight as he had been taught. Paul's temper was something that Carlos worked on with him as it was a common theme of trouble at school and socially for Paul.

Very early in middle school, the girls began to notice Paul. Though not very talkative, the natural attraction to him was his brooding good looks. His rebellious nature as a bad boy was even more solidified because the ladies found him interesting. Rumors about him circulated that he had been seduced by older women, and that he actively sought out older, more sophisticated bad girls put even more fuel to the fire of his dark and mysterious dating career. In reality, it was very much false advertising. He was forward but discreet in his dating activities and kept his affairs as his own business.

Lisa began to ask her friends about Paul and where he hung out. Her friends warned her that he was part of a group of misfits who ran the gauntlet of convicted felons to nerdy brains that had very little in the way of social skills. Paul felt at home with this array of people, while Lewis, though amiable with everyone, was drawn to the upper social strata of the school that he and Sarina Burke ruled as king and queen. The more Lisa was warned, the more she focused on Paul.

Lisa found out that there was a party on the north end of town on Friday night and she was assured that Paul would attend. She made it her mission to be there and ensnare her prey. The only way to describe what she changed into after leaving her house was seductive. And that might have been an understatement.

She had to have Paul. He was all she thought about and dreamt about, and she was going to make it happen. She also brought along what she called the 'great persuader.' She had stolen a bottle of very expensive Irish whiskey from her father's locked liquor cabinet. If she couldn't get him sober, she would get him by way of being smashed. She dragged along a couple of her cheerleader friends for support. They weren't bothered by the fact that they stood out at the festivities because of the knowledge of the Duffy family's penchant for physical violence, which might occur with a misstep toward Lisa.

At ten o'clock, Paul and a couple of misfits entered the party house. A number of female eyes targeted him. Lisa saw Paul was drinking a beer and mentally noted that her Irish whiskey was going to be effective in her seduction. Up to this point her coat concealed the bait of her lack of clothing. She moved in and tried to start a conversation with Paul, who was a little more than one can of beer into the evening. Lisa took Paul by the arm as she spoke to him. He rambled on about nothing in particular and when she got him outside, she opened her coat and revealed her lack of clothing and the bottle of whiskey. She told him that she had an idea and he followed like a lamb follows its mother. She had taken her mother's compact station wagon and had intentionally parked it a block over from the party, near an open space with plenty of foliage for cover. Before Paul knew what hit him he had a couple of swigs and began to fondle her. The next thing he knew, his pants were off and she had him.

Paul began to focus on what had just occurred as he pulled his pants back on. He had a lot of thoughts running around in his head but one that he would have never thought of was that Lisa's central focus of existence was she had found the man of her dreams, and they would marry, have kids, and live happily ever after. She wanted to talk and he wanted to leave and go home as his post alcohol headache began to be his central focus. Lisa realized that he wasn't feeling well and wanted to mother him, but Paul just wanted leave. He left still trying to piece together what had just occurred. Sure it was fun and satisfying, but it seemed to be out of reality to him.

Lisa immediately got dressed, put on her coat and retrieved her friends. She spoke incessantly about Paul and how he would be a great addition to the Duffy family. They looked at her as if she was nuts, but because of her status among them, they quietly agreed. They knew of her other sexual conquests but never had she acted like this. Usually she was as casual about them as if she was checking off a grocery list of liaisons.

On Saturday morning Lisa fumbled through her brother's list of phone contacts for the varsity football team. She found Paul's telephone number and tried numerous times to contact him over the next two days. She needed to hear his voice and if she wanted something to occur, in her mind, it was going to happen.

Lisa caught a glimpse of Paul at Sunday Mass as he was going out of the side exit as soon as services started. She was told he liked to go to the donut store on the corner during Mass and visit with other sinners like himself. He said he never saw any value in sitting on a hard bench, hung over and sleepy on a Sunday morning. Lisa was forced to stay through Mass as her family sat together in front of the church and her absence would be very evident. As soon as the service ended, she made a beeline to the donut store. To her dismay, Paul had left about twenty minutes before with no word of where he was going.

As Monday morning dawned, Lisa was in her bed thinking of how she and Paul would talk and laugh and walk around arm in arm during the day at school. It was as if she had entered her dream world on Friday night and wasn't going to be brought back to reality. She went to school early, which was unusual for her, and waited at Paul's locker like a cat waits for a mouse.

He appeared about two minutes before first period and was greeted by Lisa, verbally and physically. He recoiled from her hug. He was not one for physical touch and this open behavior was very foreign to him and not in the least wanted. She used that opportunity to broadcast to everyone in sight that Paul now belonged to her. He told her not to touch him and she very loudly reiterated some of Friday night's events to make the public point that he had wanted her then, and for a whole lot more than a hug. What was wrong now? Paul started to walk toward class and Lisa, to save face, called him a wop pile of crap, saying that he would pay for taking advantage of her.

She immediately left the school and went home in fuming silence. She stormed by her mother without a word, slamming and locking her bedroom door like a small child having a temper tantrum. Her mother knocked and was told to go away. Her mother could hear muffled crying and wondered what had upset her daughter so much. All day and into the evening her mother continued trying to get Lisa to open the door, to no avail.

When her father arrived home, he went upstairs and demanded that she come and out and sit at the dinner table with the rest of the family. Two things occurred for certain in Duffy households when the patriarch either spoke or arrived for a meal: the patriarch was obeyed and the family prepared to eat. The large size of Duffy family meals required a copious amount of preparation and quantity. When Mr. Duffy arrived home, he was ready to eat. Period. No melodrama of his daughter was going to keep him from his dumplings.

Lisa refused to open the door, so with a slight flick of the wrist, the door knob latch was broken. He saw his daughter's condition and realized that she was truly distraught. He sat down with the ever present meal on his mind to deal with this as quickly as possible.

The story that Lisa told was obviously vastly different from the occurrence. Mr. Duffy was known to stop off at the local Irish pub for some libation before heading home. Combining that with an empty stomach resulted in something that resembled a drunken grizzly bear, not only in mood but in stature. The story unfolding by the now vengeful Lisa had her being seduced and raped, rather than the actual course of events. Mr. Duffy was ready to call the police but she persuaded him that it would not be beneficial to either his or her reputation if this got out. He agreed but only with a plan for retribution for the disgrace and deflowering of his little girl. They would reconvene at the dinner table after she made herself presentable.

By the time Lisa made it to the table, both her father and brother had devoured enough food for ten hungry adults, and that was only the first course. In short audibles, with his mouth often full, Mr. Duffy instructed Peter to right this wrong against his sister, their name, the church, and even the universe. Peter wondered if there would be some kind of school or police action against him for injuring another student. His father said he would take care of any actions, but he wanted Paul taught a lesson and to be physically reminded of his actions with his daughter for the rest of his miserable life. He asked if Peter understood and then told him to pass the gravy. "Obliterate the little Italian bastard. Got it, son?"

Between mouthfuls, Peter grunted, "Yeah."

Chapter 3

Tuesday morning arrived with Peter on a mission to right the Duffy family's good name. He had already tipped his football friends of his intent to damn near kill pretty boy Morgan. It was supposed to be a secret but word of an event that could be the biggest thing to happen during the school year spread like a wildfire.

Paul and his older brother arrived at school about thirty minutes before first period. Lewis was well known for being early for class and totally prepared. If Paul had his way, he would arrive as the bell rang for class. A couple of Paul's friends met him at the school gate and told him that his tryst with Lisa the past Friday was well known all over the school and that her brother, Peter, had been chosen by the family to redeem his sister's honor. Peter was wandering around the halls of the school looking for Paul. His friends warned Paul to be on the alert.

First period came and went, and Paul spent the entire time considering a way to diffuse the situation. The notoriety of an event like this would be sternly dealt with by his parents, especially the carnal side of the matter along with the use of alcohol. Paul had track practice in the afternoon but with the high volume of calls from Lisa, he hoped to use that time to talk to her about the events of Friday evening.

Paul stood at his locker gathering his books for the next two periods, when Peter and his entourage came down the hall. Peter was obviously very irritated and the words coming out of his mouth were anything but coherent. In fact, he stuttered through the threats he leveled at Paul and came across as the buffoon that most knew him to be, not the white knight out to avenge his sister's disgrace.

Paul was not at all rattled by the encounter. He was very collected as he spoke calmly to Peter. He was sorry for the misunderstanding with Lisa and intended to speak to her that day. Paul's soft spoken apology so surprised Peter that he actually began to soften his approach to show compassion for Paul. That is until the rest of his offensive-line friends interjected with comments about not being duped as his sister had been by Mr. Suave. Their verbal persistence raised Peter's ill temper to a boiling point again and he told Paul to meet him in the north alley behind the school to settle the matter like men. Paul asked if he could speak to Lisa first and perhaps settle the matter between them.

Peter's friends suggested that Paul was chicken and gutless, and that he was afraid of the punishment he would receive for taking poor Lisa's virginity by way of a drunken stupor. Paul could see that this was steamrolling out of hand so he shut his locker door and headed to second period. Peter repeated his command to be in the alley after last period as Paul walked through the group. Right tackle Jack Danelle made the mistake of asking how Paul would feel if one of them had raped one of his sisters.

The words were barely out of Jack's mouth when Paul dropped his books and planted an unsuspected right upper cut to Jack's jaw. This was followed by a couple of additional punches to his mid-section that caused poor Jack to vomit his breakfast on all of those within puking distance. The non-puked upon members of the group finally sprang into action and grabbed Paul as the bell for class rang and the vice principal came around the corner to inquire what was going on.

The group broke up with poor Jack remaining on the floor, blood flowing out of his nose and mouth, and the real need to alert the school janitor to come and clean up the mess. When the vice principal asked Jack what had happened, he muttered that he had slipped and fallen and it was his own fault. Mr. Martin, the vice principal, was very aware of the true circumstances and made a mental note to contact the city police about what he had heard was going to happen after school. John Martin was not only the vice principal but he was the football receivers' coach and the track coach. He had seen firsthand the toughness of Paul Morgan and knew that someone could really get hurt if they ignited Paul's temper.

Chapter 4

THE FINAL BELL rang for dismissal but it may as well have been the starting bell for a championship boxing match. The majority of the student body headed for the north alley to watch big Pete Duffy beat up pretty boy Paul Morgan. Paul had friends, but the consensus among the males was that they wanted to see some handsome beaten from his good looks. The feminine side of the group was split between those who hadn't ever been noticed by Paul and wanted him to be punished for his aloofness, to rooting for David to bring down Goliath.

Peter's football friends spent the rest of the day stoking his anger by saying anything they could to make him even more aggressive than he already was. By the time school was out, Peter was in a blind rage and nothing short of killing the little son of a bitch would be considered acceptable. Peter's one major oversight, for there was no question that he could beat Paul, was that he was defending the Duffy good name. He never believed for one minute that the decision was not already known; he only considered how much ruin and degradation he could rain down on his opponent.

By the time Paul arrived with a couple of his track friends, the crowd had grown into a mob. He handed his belongings to his fellow 440 relay partner Tom Fogerty and asked him to keep them safe. Concerned, Tom asked him to be careful, to which Paul replied that he would diffuse the situation quickly so they would only have to run laps for an extra half hour for being late to track practice. Tom was amazed at how calm his friend was with the mass pandemonium going on around him.

Paul approached Peter, saying he wanted to apologize again for the misunderstanding and would still like to talk to Lisa about Friday's events. Lisa stood off to the side and yelled to her brother that Paul had seduced her with alcohol and taken her against her will.

Peter lumbered up to Paul and pushed him backward. Peter planned on a short bout, finishing up his opponent with a couple of punches and a bloody nose. Paul came back at him as if on a spring and a surprised Peter continued pushing. The third time Paul bounced back, Peter met him with a body blow punch, taking the air right out of Paul. He was bent over when Peter landed a two-handed blow on his upper back that sent Paul to his knees, to the cheers of about half of the crowd.

Peter felt very confident and was verbally rallied by his teammates to teach Paul a lesson. The much smaller Paul was down and considered how much more punishment he would need to tolerate to appease Peter before they would shake hands and move on. But Peter made the mistake of taunting Paul that he should get off the ground because he reminded him of Paul's mother when she got on her knees for Peter. That remark drew cheers from Peter's buddies.

In a flash, the remark about his mother took Paul from zero to explosion. From the ground, he punched Peter in the groin area so hard that Peter fell backward. As he hit the ground, Paul was already on top of him, punching alternately in the face and the mid-section. The crowd quieted immediately and heard Paul's punches hitting bone and flesh with the sound of a hammer hitting a piece of wet wood. The savagery of Paul's attack made it obvious there wasn't going to be a loser, there was going to be a corpse.

Momentarily the crowd was stunned and then Peter's friends decided to intervene to save him by trying to stop Paul. The first person to grab him met with a lightning speed snap of his forearm by a leverage technique that Paul's grandfather, Carlos, had taught him. The screams of the injured only drove more of them to restrain Paul.

Coach Martin was waiting about a hundred yards away from the crowd for the police sirens to give notice that the bout was over. When he didn't hear them, he realized that something was horribly wrong and called 911. He then proceeded to the center of the fight to stop it. A mob was trying to stop Paul from continuing to attack Peter and another was hurt trying to break it up.

At about that same moment, Lewis left the library and asked a passing student what was going on with the students running toward the north alley. Not realizing that he was Paul's brother, she said that the football team was going to beat up Paul Morgan because of what he had done to Lisa Duffy on Friday night. Lewis dropped his books and went into an immediate wind sprint to save his younger brother. He heard sirens blaring as he ran.

By the time he got to the alley, he was winded but shocked at what he saw. His bloodied brother was sitting up and staring intently at the carnage that lay before him. Paramedics worked on Peter, who looked like he had been in auto accident with a semi-truck. They were giving him oxygen and trying to find a clean vein as it appeared he had extensive internal bleeding from the vitals they took. Lewis's focus widened and he saw other medical emergency staff tending to about six others whose injuries ran from broken noses to a compound-fractured arm.

He approached his brother, who seemed to be in a daze, but when Paul saw Lewis he began to smile. Lewis leaned over and asked, "Are you alright?"

"Yes. Grandpa Carlos was right."

Coach Martin met the police who had failed to show up at the school at the time that had been arranged with the captain earlier in the day. When the captain approached the battle site, Coach Martin shouted in anger that the fight wouldn't have escalated if he and his men had arrived when they had agreed. The police captain, an old fraternity brother, pulled Coach Martin aside and told him that he was ordered by the commander to wait an extra fifteen minutes before dispatching, even after the 911 call.

"Why?"

"The Duffy patriarch asked the commander to delay as a special favor to him."

Chapter 5

THE AFTERMATH OF the fight was not pretty. Five ambulances were required to transport the wounded. When Paul was examined by a paramedic, he was told that he had suffered a concussion and had some swelling in the region of his neck and upper back. He was advised to go to the hospital but he refused, even with Lewis pleading with him to go.

The commander of police force showed up about fifteen minutes after the conclusion of the events. He was on his cell phone when he arrived. He got out of his car and surveyed the injuries and went back to his car and resumed talking on his cell phone. With the windows up, it was impossible to hear his conversation but from the commander's gestures it was a heated discussion.

He finally ended the conversation and called the captain away from the scene to discuss something with him. After a very heated exchange, the captain approached Paul and Lewis and told Paul that he was going to be placed under arrest for attempted murder.

Coach Martin spoke up loudly. "This is absolutely outrageous. If you persist, I'll publicly ask on television why the officers were detained for over fifteen minutes after a 911 call. I'll ask the press to investigate whether the commander is taking orders from Richard Duffy in this altercation."

After a huddle of the captain and the commander, they decided to forego the arrest.

John Martin and Tom Fogerty, who had stood by holding Paul's clothes and books, helped Lewis get Paul into his car and away from the scene as the news media from various television stations were setting up to broadcast the aftermath of the event.

As Lewis drove Paul home, he told him to let him speak to their parents and he would try to diffuse the matter, especially with their mother. When Lewis opened the back door and helped Paul into the kitchen the first of successive yelling and screaming began. Angeline spotted her wounded son and simultaneously questioned Paul about his welfare and accused him of uncivilized behavior. Lewis assured her Paul was fine and led her into an adjoining room to talk to her while Paul's younger sisters attended to him.

Lewis explained the entire situation including Lisa Duffy's false accusations against Paul. She gasped a couple of times and said that they needed to call his father immediately and have him come home. Lewis also told her of the remark that made Paul snap and go ballistic to defend her and the family's name. She calmed down and wore a slight twinge of a grin after that. Paul had become his mother's champion.

Charlie arrived home and the events were recounted to him and he was especially angered over the police being delayed. Coach Martin and Tom Fogerty showed up about a half hour later to see if help was needed. The discussion was again ignited when the coach recounted his phone call earlier that day and the delay in the police response.

Angeline worried about how her father would react when he heard what happened. He arrived at the house in record time, not to hear the stories but to check on the wellbeing of his grandson. While everyone was in the kitchen talking loudly, Carlos spoke very quietly to Paul. Had Paul used the techniques that he'd taught him? He wanted to know the sequence of events during the fight. He bowed his head and grimaced at what had been done to his flesh and blood but smiled at the carnage Paul wreaked upon his adversaries. Paul didn't tell him the remark that flipped his switch. Carlos would find out later and would not be angered but proud of his grandson for defending his mother and the family name.

After a couple days when things had calmed down, Carlos, who had been Paul's constant companion in the aftermath, told Paul of his pride, saying that he wished he had told him of an event that happened many years before. In the past, Richard Duffy, the patriarch of the Duffy family, and he had had their differences. Carlos related one such incident to Paul.

Richard had been drinking, a very normal circumstance for the Duffys with their ready supply of alcohol. Carlos and Paul's grandmother, Carmen, had been out on a Saturday night and had run into Richard and his cronies at a bar. They were minding their own business and enjoying the evening when Mr. Duffy decided to intervene and make some remarks about Mrs. Catania's beauty. The remarks went from flattering to derogatory very quickly in Richard's attempt to entertain his friends at the bar.

Carlos politely asked him to leave but when the remarks went negative, Carlos gave Richard Duffy an uppercut that had him swaying, hitting him in the face with a full broadside sweep of his left hand. That sent poor Richard falling out of control, unconscious. His face hit the side of a table and he required a number of stitches. For a moment, Richard's friends contemplated retaliation but when they saw the Sicilian fire in

Carlos's eyes they collected their drunken friend and took him to the emergency room.

The bartender came to the table with a free round of drinks for Carlos and Carmen to thank Carlos for shutting up the 'biggest pig in town.' He told them to stay and enjoy themselves on the house, saying that garbage like Duffy never came back to the site of a defeat. Others in the bar sent over drinks and desserts for Carlos's heroics, as Duffy had been abusive to others in the same manner.

Carlos told his grandson that this was where the bad blood started and reminded him to look for a large scar if he ever saw the man again.

"Your grandmother said from that day on I seemed to become grander in stature and demeanor. Paul, you know women think they see things that maybe aren't there. I don't know if what she saw is true, but I do know that I enjoyed letting her observation wash over me.

"Maybe I should have told you about this before, and if I'd known about this fight before it happened, I might have done so. But it didn't make any difference to the outcome. You won. And you, my grandson, I think you look more grand and self-confident than before."

A full-of-pride grin swept across Carlos's face.

Chapter 6

THE FOLLOWING DAY, the school took on a silence reserved for church or a court room. The principal and the vice principal had spoken extensively the night before and both had made obligatory trips to the hospital to check on the injured students. Peter's friend with the broken arm had had surgery late Monday evening. The surgeon needed to insert screws due to the severity of the break. Four football teammates had injuries ranging from a broken jaw to a displaced knee cap that had to be treated.

Peter had obviously taken the worst of it. Paul's groin shot had ruptured one of Peter's testicles. He had internal injuries with a possible ruptured spleen, but his two internists could not agree on what other vital organs were involved. His nose was broken and his jaw had been displaced, but the most concerning of his injuries was the head trauma that he had received. The medical team hoped that it was just a severe concussion, as there was real concern that he had suffered a severe brain trauma. A neurosurgeon was called in by the family to make sure their son's injuries received the best treatment that money could buy.

When Richard Duffy was not at his son's bedside or conversing with the doctors, he was on the phone with his attorney and the police commander. He insisted that Paul be arrested, saying that he was going to pursue him legally however he could. His attorney advised him that a civil case would be impossible to pursue if there was not an arrest or if Paul was not charged with a criminal action. Richard was not going to have his son injured at the hands of some Italian hoodlum and not be punished for his actions.

The police commander was apprehensive about any further interference by Mr. Duffy in his official duties as the police commander. The time delay of dispatching the police to the high school could be grounds for his dismissal and it in all probability had added to the injuries of Peter and his friends. He could only imagine how news that he didn't perform his duties as a favor to an old friend would read in the papers and sound on the television. He blamed Richard Duffy, telling him that it was his fault that Peter and his friends were injured as badly as they were because the commander was honoring Mr. Duffy's request.

The Duffy family attorney agreed, reminding them that if any action was taken against Paul there was also the problem of Coach Martin, who had somehow had connected the dots of the delay in dispatching the police and the relationship of Richard Duffy and the police commander. Mr. Martin's outburst at the scene of the impending arrest of Paul had led the police chief and the commander to not go through with his arrest. Richard Duffy and his attorney wondered how the coach had realized what had happened.

Paul stayed home as he was not in any condition to go to school. His parents wondered what was going to happen next. The vice principal inquired on the phone about Paul's condition. He and the principal wanted to know when they could come over and discuss Monday's events. The Morgans agreed to see them that afternoon.

Paul's statement was recorded and after the tape recorder was shut off, they both agreed that Paul was only defending himself against Peter and his friends. They also stated that Richard Duffy had been on the phone earlier trying to persuade them to expel Paul from school for grievous bodily injury to five of North Hollywood High's best student athletes. After reviewing the facts along with very interesting comments by Coach Martin, they decided that no action would be taken. The Morgans were relieved that Paul would not be kicked out of school, which would hamper any chance at a good college and possibly of a good career later on.

Richard Duffy's reaction was the complete opposite. With all of his team telling him that he had no chance of any legal reprisal, he still contended that he would get even with that little bastard, Paul. That was until his wife got into the fracas. She told Richard in no uncertain terms that it was his own damn fault that their son and his friends were injured, and if he persisted in this vendetta, she would notify the school, the press, and the police department of his involvement.

Mrs. Duffy would report Mr. Duffy's instructions to Peter "to obliterate the little bastard" for his alleged assault on their daughter. She would also notify the liquor licensing board of his actions, which would preclude him from renewing his stores' licenses.

Finally, Mrs. Duffy told him she would retain the best divorce attorney that his money could buy for her and render him penniless.

This verbal barrage from his normally very quiet wife made Richard reconsider his venomous actions. And for one final kick in the butt Mrs. Duffy said, "You never have gotten over the fact that you got your ass kicked by his grandfather Carlos in that bar for making remarks about his wife."

Chapter 7

Paul returned to school the following week. Peter remained in the hospital for an additional three weeks. School had recessed for summer break by the time he was released from the hospital. He did not return to North Hollywood High the following year but transferred to an all-boys private high school. None of his other accomplices returned for the rest of the school year due to either injuries or downright fear.

Graduation was set for about three weeks after the incident. Lewis was the valedictorian and class president. He would lead his graduating class into their next adventure in their lives. The source of conversation at the school after Paul's incident was what college Lewis would accept a full ride scholarship from.

Major universities and colleges with world caliber academics chased him, in addition to schools with major athletic programs that had courted him since spring for a decision. Of course, in addition to his education being paid, there were all kinds of incentives added to help him make the right decision.

Lewis immediately scratched schools that did not play by NCAA rules off his list. He knew he could get anything he wanted with his 4.0 GPA and a triple threat in football, basketball and baseball. He made them all wait for his decision.

One quiet Sunday afternoon, when their parents and grandparents were at a church picnic, Lewis and Paul sat in the backyard making small talk. Paul asked Lewis point blank, "Where are you going to go to college, and why are you waiting to make the announcement when you probably decided months ago? Are you and Sarina going to get married and go to the same college, or wait until you finish college to marry?"

Lewis gave Paul a somber look. "Slow down a minute. I want to talk to you about something that's been bothering me." He paused. "I'm having mixed emotions about the direction of my life. I've made a decision."

Paul said sarcastically, "What's wrong? Did Mr. Perfect only get a 99.9% day today?"

Lewis shook his head and asked Paul to be serious with him because he valued Paul's opinion. That statement shut his younger brother up as Lewis had never complimented him like that before. Paul had never seen him ask for anyone's help or advice—ever, especially his younger, not-so-perfect brother. Paul had a feeling that a bombshell was imminent that was going to change everything as they knew it.

Lewis confided in Paul that he wasn't happy with his life as it was. He wanted something more from it than what he had known to this point. After much private consultation with their father's brother, Paul, a priest who was called Father Paul by everyone in the family, he had come to the conclusion that he wanted to pursue a career as a priest for a higher calling from God. If Lewis's voice and demeanor had been any different, Paul would have accused him of pulling his leg or making up a total science fiction story. But Paul understood that his brother was at the crossroads of his life and he told him he would support Lewis in any decision he made.

Paul asked when he had been in contact with Fr. Paul.

Apparently their uncle had come from Rome twice to privately confer with Lewis. His advice to Lewis had been to listen for what God wanted him to do and follow that path. Lewis was convinced that this was what God wanted him to do.

"Does anyone else know about this?" Paul asked.

"Only the two Pauls in my life that I admire know about it."

Again, Paul was struck by his brother's words. Lewis's sincerity hit Paul squarely in the head and the heart. Paul asked Lewis when he intended to let everyone know. Lewis said he would tell them at graduation during his valedictorian speech. Everyone who meant anything in his life would be there and they can all hear at the same time. Lewis went on to say that he had been accepted into the Jesuit seminary in Santa Barbara and would be leaving for it immediately after graduation.

* * *

That was the exact same path that Fr. Paul Morgan had taken over twenty-five years ago to the chagrin of his family, who thought he was very likely to be successful in any career he undertook. Fr. Paul's love and his forte was mathematics. Anything with numbers fascinated him. He found that numbers' best application in the real world was accounting. After finishing the seminary, Fr. Paul had been sent to Yale to get his doctorate degree in accounting. He accomplished his degree in record time and was immediately dispatched to the Vatican to be a part of their worldwide accounting system.

He rose very quickly through the ranks and in a mere five years, he was completely in charge of the accounting division of the Catholic Church. He was instrumental in the computerization of the department. He foresaw that technology was the direction of finance so he completed another doctorate in computer science, this time from Harvard.

In addition to his remarkable mental capacity and his advanced degrees, Fr. Paul was a very handsome man. When he announced his intention to become a priest, there were many young ladies who were disappointed at his decision. He had been quite the ladies' man during high school. But he felt as though the secular world was not enough for him so he sought direction from God and, after much prayer, he believed he had received it.

Although Fr. Paul was a priest, there had always been rumors that he was a bon vivant. He traveled and stayed in the best places on earth. His expense account was unlimited and there were those who thought Fr. Paul didn't honor all of his vows as a Jesuit priest, namely the vow of celibacy. Through the years, there had been whispers of mistresses and illegitimate children. There were even hints that Fr. Paul maintained a couple of marriages and children throughout Europe and the Caribbean. His position in the church was absolutely vital and he answered to no one, except possibly His Holiness the Pope. No one would ever suspect him if they met him in person. Fr. Paul was very quiet and unassuming. He gave the impression of a man with a total devotion to his faith.

Fr. Paul visited his family at least annually and when any of his church finance travels brought him close to California he stopped by. Paul knew that his uncle's secret meetings with Lewis were something out of the ordinary. His family knew him as a warm and generous man who would do anything for his family.

His nephew would one day discover that none of what they believed about their uncle came close to describing who his uncle really was.

Chapter 8

Graduation was fast approaching, with the second Saturday in June being the usual day for the system to kick its students into either upper education or into the real world of life. Paul saw no indication that Lewis had let anyone know of his intent to announce his life's new direction before the big day arrived. Lewis's steady girlfriend since middle school, Sarina, acted as she always had through the years. Paul began to wonder if Lewis had a cruel streak he'd never observed before that made him want to drop this bomb on everyone in such a public setting. He couldn't even begin to understand how Sarina would feel. It was a foregone conclusion that she and Lewis would attend the same college followed by marriage and a family.

Sarina's father, Chuck Burke, was also a member of St. Charles Parish and frequently met the Morgans on Sunday to attend Mass together. They had brunch afterward at his Toluca Lake Country Club. This ritual had gone on for years and he also thought it was understood that his only daughter would be Lewis's bride one day. She was the light of his life and he gave her anything she wanted.

Lewis worked on his class president/valedictorian speech with his usual focus on preparedness. There wouldn't be even one letter out of place. He worked tirelessly to perfect every nuance of every word to make it seamless. He was on a mission from God. It was important for him to expertly express every thought and point that he wanted to get across to all in his audience. Lewis knew there were going to be recruiters from colleges and universities in attendance, not only for sports but also from the upper strata of the academic world. And he had made them all wait for his decision about which college he was going to attend. He had told them he would announce his decision in his graduation speech.

Since he was one of the most sought after student athletes in the entire country, this was going to swell the already large crowd expected at North Hollywood's graduation ceremony. With about four hundred fifty graduates, the annual attendance always numbered three to four thousand. The football bleachers held about six thousand so there was no worry about overflow capacity, or so the school administration thought. Lewis was a triple threat as a student athlete. He was a high school all-American in football, basketball, and baseball. All the leading schools in these sports hoped to entice Lewis to attend their school and take their respective teams to national titles. The offers were akin to what a top college prospect entering the pros would receive only they needed to be disguised as scholarships to maintain the school's amateur status. Lewis had never let any of these colleges think that they were out of the running for him to attend their respective schools.

To Paul, it seemed that Lewis was playing games with his suitors, which was out of character for his brother, who was always very open about his intentions. But it was also true that recently Lewis had been disgusted with the recruiters for trying to sway him with inducements that, at best, could be described as illegal bribes. Paul knew that this bothered his brother for, more than once, Lewis had remarked that he felt as if he were a commodity on the open market.

Paul wondered if this was just another justification for his brother to flee from the secular life of education, sports and the all-mighty pursuit of money. Paul believed it was self-centered of Lewis, even cruel, to surprise those closest to him with this impactful decision in the most public of settings, a school graduation. But Paul kept his thoughts to himself, even though his brother had confided in him, asking Paul for a serious answer because he valued Paul's opinion.

Two days before graduation, Fr. Paul showed up at his family's house unannounced. The family had expected their uncle but had no idea when he would appear. He arrived in a limousine. Fr. Paul always traveled first class. He told them that he had just flown in and made a beeline to see his family, whom hadn't seen him in almost a year. Paul knew his uncle had seen Lewis twice in the past six weeks and he observed how well his uncle fabricated his story of not having seen the family for so long and how good it was to finally be back in California.

Paul found it strange that a priest, a man who was ordained and supposedly lived his life to emulate Jesus, could so easily fabricate and mislead his own family about not being in the country or even the state of California. Paul thought his uncle was a professional liar. But after all, Paul reasoned that he was his uncle who had always treated him well. What did it matter if he didn't tell the truth?

After Fr. Paul distributed the always expected gifts from Rome, he asked if he could take the soon-to-be-graduate to dinner. Of course he wanted his namesake to attend as well. Fr. Paul delighted in watching his family open the very expensive but well thought out gifts. For his sister-in-law, Angeline, he annually added to her very expensive collection of Dresden figurines. She had looked up the pieces and their cost was in the thousands for each piece.

"How can a priest afford such luxuries?" she asked her husband.

"Well, my brother is a big shot in the Vatican and is probably paid a lot for his job."

Fr. Paul's nieces, Ashley and Claire, were treated to the newest and most expensive electronics. Some of the gifts were prototypes that hadn't been released to the public yet. In addition, he always presented them each with a handmade classic doll from a country he had visited the previous year. Cost seemed to be no object and again his sister-in-law wondered how a priest could spend that kind of money. His brother defended him, saying who else did he have to spend his money on but his family. The Vatican paid for all his other living expenses.

After the presents were unwrapped, Fr. Paul and his nephews retreated to his waiting limousine to go to dinner. To their surprise, he told the driver to take them to the Beverly Hills Hotel where he was staying. The boys protested that they were not suitably dressed. Fr. Paul reassured them that he would see that they were outfitted appropriately for dinner. The trip took about an hour. Fr. Paul divided his time between speaking with Lewis and Paul and using his cell phone to bark commands in various languages to obvious underlings. The boys tried to guess whether their uncle was speaking French, Russian, or another language. One thing was obvious, regardless of the language spoken. Their uncle was the person in charge and giving the orders with little regard for tact.

They arrived at the hotel, where valets escorted them to an on-site tailor. Fr. Paul excused himself, saying he would see them in his suite in a little while. Two tailors immediately went to work on the boys to outfit them in attire appropriate to their dinner reservations. No expense was spared and Paul almost choked when he saw that the shirt that he was about to put on cost over $500.00. His first thought was of returning his attire and using the money for his car but he thought twice about it. Fr. Paul would be insulted.

When the boys were suited up, they were led to Fr. Paul's suite. It was one of the most expensive in the hotel the valet told them. There was an armed guard stationed on this particular wing of the hotel. When they entered his suite of rooms, the flower arrangements from various well-wishers seemed more than your average florist shop would likely have on hand. Fr. Paul was still dressed in his Jesuit attire and he was famished and ready for dinner.

The dining room was very private, with a waiter to hover over each of them. Fr. Paul remarked, "They always take good care of me here." He had gone to the liberty of ordering wine and the main entrée but told them if they didn't like lobster and steak, they could order whatever they wanted. Paul viewed the menu and gulped when he saw the $300.00 price for that entrée.

Fr. Paul eventually steered the dinner conversation toward Lewis's decision to become a priest. He asked Paul what he thought.

Paul answered, "I support my brother, no matter what his decision is."

But their uncle was seeking a more decisive response. He wanted to know Paul's opinion, not hear about his undying loyalty to his brother.

Paul was uncomfortable with this questioning but decided to continue to support Lewis. Fr. Paul did not relent in his pursuit of his nephew's true feelings and, finally, Paul's temper broke through with the short remark, "What difference does it make what I believe? It's his life."

Fr. Paul realized he'd pushed his nephew too far and effortlessly changed the subject to baseball. Paul noted the smoothness with which his uncle changed the subject when things got too intense for the person being questioned or, as Paul felt, interrogated. Paul wondered whether Lewis's decision had been manipulated or steered by Fr. Paul but he quickly dismissed the thought because of his brother's always self-assured nature.

After dinner, Fr. Paul told the boys he would see them tomorrow for lunch and instructed the limousine driver to take them home. On the way home to the real world, Paul noticed a woman's small purse by the jump seat door. He picked up the car phone and told the driver about the purse. The driver said he would return it to their uncle. Paul thought, he knows who it belongs to. Paul wondered how his Fr. Paul could know whose purse it was. Paul had never seen a nun with a Louis Vuitton purse.

Lewis was strangely quiet on the drive home. Paul asked, "Everything all right?"

He looked at Paul. "I just hope that I've understood God's wishes correctly.

Chapter 9

GRADUATION DAY DAWNED as most Southern California mid-June mornings do, sunny and clear, headed toward hot and hazy. Paul had spent a restless night playing out various outcomes of his brother's announcement this afternoon at graduation. He wondered how his parents would take the news that their eldest son, of whom they were so proud, was forsaking the real world for a spiritual calling.

His father had seen this first hand when his brother, their Uncle Paul, had done the same thing. For Catholics, having a family member give himself to the church was something to be proud of. But for a son and brother who showed unlimited potential in anything they undertook, there would always be questions of "what if?"

Paul wondered how many of his generation would follow the previous generations in unquestioned faith in their religion. He thought at times of how the church had lost step with the average person who believed that the Catholic way was a little outdated. It crossed his mind that Lewis was joining a sinking ship.

Of course, he worried about what would happen if Lewis was searching for something that didn't exist or was unattainable in his pursuit of a career as a priest. Would it be possible for Lewis to return to what he'd given up if his decision turned out to be a mistake? His chance at athletic pursuits would be gone. His academic aspirations would still be viable but without athletic scholarships, Lewis would bear the cost of his education.

Then there was the question of Sarina, his brother's constant love interest since middle school. How would she take this change of course that would affect the rest of her life? This would crush her, Paul thought.

She had been a member of the Morgan family since junior high school. Their mother treated her as if she was her own daughter. She and his sisters, Claire and Ashley, frequently spent time together when she wasn't attached to Lewis's arm. The Morgans and the Burkes were like one family now. Both sets of parents got along great together and frequently wondered out loud about what their future grandchildren would be like.

Paul's sleepless night came to an end when his brother knocked on his door. "Are you ready for my big day?"

Paul couldn't help asking his older brother if he was sure of what he was doing. Lewis answered in the affirmative and reminded him Fr. Paul was picking them up to take them to the graduation and wanted his namesake to sit next to him during the ceremony. That was fine with Paul as he didn't intend to sit anywhere near his family and endure the repercussions of Lewis's speech.

As extended family members arrived at the graduation, Charlie and Angeline were visibly nervous. It felt to Paul like his parents were preparing to deliver the commencement speech themselves.

Fr. Paul left with Lewis and Paul ahead of the family in the chauffeured limousine. Fr. Paul worried that he might need to calm Lewis down before the speech because about halfway there, Lewis expressed some doubts to his uncle.

Fr. Paul reassured him that God had made His wishes known to Lewis and that he would have to follow them. Paul looked very closely at his brother and thought he had never seen him in such a vulnerable way. Lewis looked like a lamb being led to slaughter, not the super star that had never had a weak moment in his life that they all were familiar with.

Fr. Paul suggested that Lewis consider what it must have been like for Jesus before going to his crucifixion on the cross. He reminded Lewis to think of what Jesus gave up to redeem the world of its sins—His own life for the good of millions, not for the good of Himself. Lewis seemed to relax and the color came back to his face as he felt better.

What a load of propaganda, Paul thought. It was the same kind of nonsense used by nefarious leaders like Hitler to convince their citizens to behave badly toward others. Pep talks like these made Paul even more skeptical about his uncle's actions in leading Lewis to his uncle's decision. It reminded Paul of the Japanese kamikazes on their suicide missions, getting into their planes thinking of the instant eternal reward for their sacrifice for the empire.

His thoughts were interrupted by their arrival at school. A massive group of humanity converged on the limousine as it pulled up—the star of the show had arrived. The crowd consisted of various special interests groups that Lewis had either been involved in or was being courted to become a member of, along with the school band, faculty members, students, and Lewis's fans. Recruiters from colleges and universities were the most visible. Some of the larger schools had enlisted various sports figures, both collegiate and professional, to attend along with the recruiters, to meet their school's prospective star who would lead their school to a national title.

Fr. Paul's limousine driver and valet helped move the well-wishers out of the Morgans' way. When the small group made their way to the library doors, Paul knew that Lewis would go in alone to prepare for the procession. Paul pulled him aside and whispered in his ear that he loved him and would support him in any decision that he made and not that someone else had made for him. They fought back tears as they hugged each and went their separate ways—Lewis to the library and Paul toward the bleachers with Fr. Paul in hot pursuit.

Fr. Paul finally caught up with Paul asking him what the hell was his hurry?

He stared defiantly into his uncle's face and declared, "If you pushed my brother into this and it turns out badly for him, I will make your life hell on earth before I send you to your just reward of eternal damnation."

Fr. Paul collected himself before addressing his nephew's insolence. He informed Paul that it was God's calling and not his that had led his brother to his greatest decision, one that he had made many years earlier, and that maybe one day Paul would understand this. And with a final stab at his nephew he said, "Perhaps one day you can replicate a decision of this magnitude and sacrifice."

Paul glared back at him and told him to go sit with the family as he didn't want to sit by him or them.

The announcement by Lewis came and went. The shock was felt by everyone who was present. The hope and promise for Lewis was annihilated by his decision. As Paul listened to his brother in those packed stands, away from anyone who knew him, his mind replayed a vision of the mushroom cloud that hung over Hiroshima after the atomic bomb was dropped. The immediate devastation was obvious but the subsequent ramifications would not be known for generations. Something in Paul's heart told him that this was bigger than anyone could imagine and that somehow he would be involved in a way that he couldn't now fathom. Worse, he also felt he couldn't escape this destiny even if he tried to.

Chapter 10

PAUL LEFT THE graduation as soon the gasps started from the large assembly. He heard various comments that ranged from complete and total disbelief to this must be a joke or a prank that Lewis was playing on the entire audience. When his brother's voice began to crack with emotion he knew it was only a matter of time before Lewis would be in tears and that was something that he didn't want to witness. As Paul walked away from the school grounds, he asked himself if he was missing something in trying to make sense of what his brother was doing with his life. Lewis had it all, and with one decision it was all gone. The thought that kept rolling around in his head was why?

Paul did not see Lewis afterward for he didn't believe he could stomach another gut-wrenching scene between them. Lewis left for the Santa Barbara seminary with Fr. Paul in his limousine. Fr. Paul thought it was best for Lewis to evade the questions and the drama that would be plentiful after his announcement. Fr. Paul also thought it prudent that Lewis avoid a confrontation with Sarina for both of their sakes. It could only be an ugly scene so it was best to not have it occur.

Once the shadow of his older brother was removed from Paul's world, he had to make some decisions. He had secretly wanted to be like his brother in academics and sports but always believed he would come in second best. Now with that barrier gone, he seamlessly stepped into to the spotlight that previously had been only his brother's. He made a vow: nothing would stand in his way of mastering whatever he wanted to do or didn't want to do. No compromise, he thought. I am making this happen come hell or high water.

Paul began to ponder who, when and where he wanted to be. He calculated the how of achieving it all. He began to think about his future—not just what college and what career, but what he wanted to accomplish with his life. He was certainly not going the route his brother took.

As he formulated his strategy, he also wondered whether his brother just might have taken the easy way out by retreating to an organization where not many would see the result. Maybe Lewis chose the church because in the secular world, as you go up the ladder of success your faults are amplified. Perhaps his brother could see that he wouldn't be what everyone thought he would be so he changed course.

As his reflections turned inward, Paul wondered if might be trying to justify the pain of not having his brother around with thoughts of an ulterior motive on Lewis's part. Whatever it was, Paul believed it was now his time to show what he was made of. He would not let anything or anyone stand in his way or to try to convince him otherwise, especially not some Uncle, who Paul felt was basically a highly paid hypocrite.

In a complete about-face, Paul contacted his high school counselor and requested an appointment with him to discuss his academic options. His counselor resisted saying he wanted to take the summer off. Paul insisted, and the two of them mapped out a strategy to accomplish what Paul wanted in the way of positioning himself for as many scholarships as possible. His advisor informed him that he would not get offered anything close to what his brother had.

Paul looked him intently in the eye and said, "Watch me." The affirmation was startling in its intensity.

Paul's next stop was to sit down with John Martin, his receiver and track coach. He wanted his advice on how to athletically improve himself in football and track to align himself with a better chance of getting athletic scholarships to Division I colleges. Mr. Martin, who had always had a good relationship with Paul, asked him if he was chasing his brother's ghost or doing this for himself.

Paul emphatically replied, "For me. What Lewis did is no barometer for me."

His coach constructed a training regimen that in his heart he didn't think Paul could handle. He scheduled twice a week wind sprints with a copious amount of strength training in the weight room. And he started Paul with such intense receiver training that it later was said that he could have caught a football upside down with six defenders hanging on him.

As the intensity grew, Paul did not lose any of his ambition but continued to push himself to attain an even greater level of performance from himself. His speed and agility very quickly improved and were noticed by not only Coach Martin but the head coach of the football team. The head coach wondered if Paul was trying to achieve Lewis's level of excellence, from which Coach Martin had received much notoriety. Or was Paul showing what had been there all the time but now, with the monkey off his back, could be seen.

Both coaches hoped that the younger Morgan would pick up some of the slack left by his brother's graduation.

Paul's intensity continued into summer practice and his teammates were in awe of his dedication and improvement.

The coaching staff couldn't have been happier. Paul served as a real field leader to his team. Lewis had led by example and compromise, where Paul led them by example tempered with an intensity that left his teammates with a bit of fear and a lot of respect, in that order. They didn't have to worry about their coaches' comments; they performed so as not to have Paul in their grilles. They all remembered the rumble in the alley, as it was referred to, and saw what Paul could do to five or six people who were at least twice his size. Three of the linemen that Paul had beaten up were returning to the team as seniors. They had all been All-Conference players in their junior year.

The forecast for the next season began to leak out. While there was a good chance that the varsity team would follow in the footsteps of the past four championship seasons, there were still many doubters until North Hollywood played its first game against Van Nuys High School, the team that was the runner up in the conference to them the previous year. That championship game had been very close and the final the score was in favor of North Hollywood by only ten points.

The first game of the season began with the rematch of the final game of last year. North Hollywood was facing a Van Nuys team where the vast majority of players were returning juniors. Many in the San Fernando league believed that with the graduation of Lewis Morgan and a large portion of his team, Van Nuys stood a chance. How wrong they would be.

Game one was a complete decimation of a very good football team by their opponents. North Hollywood's execution could only be described as flawless. Van Nuys didn't stand a chance. The score of 63 to 3 didn't even begin to tell the story. The stretcher crew was busy shuttling injured Van Nuys players off the field.

Paul's field leadership was very impressive in all aspects. The coaches decided during summer drills that Paul should play middle linebacker in addition offensive wide-out, but only if it didn't compromise him on the offense. Paul liked the idea, as even his brother hadn't accomplished that.

As North Hollywood's varsity football team rumbled its way to an undefeated fifth straight championship title, the inevitable comparisons between the Morgan brothers were the talk of not only the students, coaches, and parents, but also the local and national news media. When Paul was interviewed he downplayed all the comparisons as just luck, great coaching, and any other explanations that would detract from a Lewis versus Paul comparison. But in his heart, he believed he was the victor in the comparison with his older brother. Paul's sense of pride was only matched by his confidence that was spurred on by his intense resolve.

Paul became a completely different person during his senior year. On the academic side there was no less than a complete metamorphosis as Paul, always a good student, now became a perfect student. He pushed himself to the point of perfection. Nothing else was acceptable. Paul took courses some of his teachers thought might be beyond his comprehension or skill level, especially in the mathematics curriculum. He routinely proved them wrong. His intensity was unyielding. If he put his mind to it he would accomplish it. Period.

Paul had been on the honor roll all through his school years. He now led the school's honor roll. The faculty were astonished that he was able to accomplish so much. They believed Paul never slept—spending every hour of the day with school work and athletics. They were wrong.

Paul was popular with the girls, but he was discreet about that part of his life. He wasn't out to win a popularity contest; he just wanted to have fun. He focused on the best looking girls in the area schools. With his newfound stardom, many beautiful coeds sought to be seen with Paul. In private, he was everything they had been told and more. He had an amazing ability to play the entire field while keeping them all as friends. There was no animosity among his conquests. They were just a group of good friends who all happened to be in love with Paul Morgan. It was as if he had all these girls under a spell or hypnotized. At this point in his life, Paul seemed incapable of making a mistake.

At home, where he was rarely found, his grandparents, parents and sisters marveled at the transformation. They'd believed he would be a leader one day, but this was way beyond any of their wildest expectations. "Who is this person our second son has become?" his parents asked themselves. And within a week, two people who were very close to Paul had a very similar conversation with him.

* * *

Paul's grandfather Carlos sat with him in the back yard one Sunday afternoon before the weekly dinner that brought the family all together. "Is everything all right? Are you happy? You know, I always believed you would be the equal to your brother in time. Don't drive yourself too hard. Don't allow life to overwhelm you."

"What do you mean?" Paul asked.

"If you leave nothing in reserve to use when needed, then a stumble might become a fall, and sometimes we never recover from a fall. Do you understand me?"

"The will to overcome will take me successfully through life," Paul answered.

Carlos said he thought the same, adding that sometimes a life force is greater than any will or resolve we might have. "Too much arrogance can take a person down to his knees. Don't forget the old adage: pride comes before the fall. Remember my grandson, adversity is put here to test you. To make you, not kill you."

Paul tried to be respectful of Carlos, but his words only irritated him rather than were counseling to him.

Carlos, knowing his grandson better than probably anyone, said, "I am telling you these things not so much for now, but more for the future, when you may need them the most." He ended the conversation with, "You know you have always been my favorite because everyone else seemed to fall at your brother's feet. That's one of the reasons I spent more time with you than I ever spent with him. He looked like he would get what he needed. You, on the other hand, were the one I wanted to help by imparting some of my life's lessons.

"I taught you how to fight. I tried to instill in you the importance of being your own man. And you appear to have learned your lessons well. I also saw a great deal of me in you. You look more like our side of the family. The day you were born, I thought this little bambino came straight from the heavens above Sicily.

"Paulo, just remember to slow down and not to drive yourself to the point of no return. Seek to be a good man, a good human being. Nothing else is more important. And know that I love you, and we are all very proud of you." And with that they adjourned for Sunday dinner.

Paul thought he saw his grandfather staring at him throughout the meal, and when their eyes met, a smile came across his lips and a twinkle shown in his eyes.

Chapter 11

The other close relative who approached Paul was his sister Ashley. Paul's relationship with his sister had always been close, not only in age, but in outlook on life. He was very protective of her even when they were very young, and she was equally as supportive of him. Because of his extraordinary accomplishments, their brother Lewis had always received a great deal of attention. He was the best and brightest with seemingly very little exertion. Achievement came harder for Paul, Ashley and Claire. They all did well in school but, even with extreme effort, they often felt as though they were chasing a phantom of perfection in their oldest brother.

Paul sat under the large walnut tree in the back yard taking in the rays of the warm sun. He was totally exhausted but didn't let it show. He acted like he was sunning himself, not resting.

Ashley approached. "Okay if I sit with you? Would you rather be alone?"

"Sit down and don't be stupid."

"If I'm stupid, then you're retarded." They both laughed.

She told him that she wanted to ask him a question if that was okay.

Paul said, "You're going to even if I don't want you to, so go ahead."

Ashley asked if he was all right. "You seem to be burning the candle at both ends and in the middle."

Her conversation was very much in the context of their grandfather Carlos the week before. Paul asked her if she'd been prompted by Carlos to continue his train of thought.

"No," she replied. "I'm worried that you'll annihilate yourself while trying to be even more successful than Lewis."

"I'm the same person I've he always been. I just decided to actually do something with my life—"

Ashley interrupted him. "You mean like our brother Lewis didn't do? I think you believe he got it all too easy and went out of the game on top, a legend before the reality of life turned him into just another man, rather than someone special."

Paul stared at her. He realized his sister knew him as well as he did himself.

She continued, "You must know the family's always known how special you are even when Lewis was in the limelight. When Mom and Dad talk about their conversations with Lewis from seminary, you seem to turn off the volume in your ears or ignore their excitement."

Ashley stared intently at her brother. "Don't knock what you don't understand. It's his life not yours. Maybe his void allowed you to expand. I think you and I share the same opinion about at least one of the reasons Lewis went in the direction he did.

"We're also on the same page about Fr. Paul. I've always had a feeling that he was two very different people in the same body: the man who spouts fake holier-than-thou crap and the guy with the wandering eye. I've seen the way he looks at my girlfriends and it's not with faith, hope and charity on his mind. Hell, I've caught him looking at me like a school boy with bad intentions. And no, I don't think Lewis will become Fr. Paul. He is much too honorable for that. Mom and Dad did too good a job raising us. And you know something? I think that even they're wise to Fr. Paul, especially Mom. She's good at making accurate observations. She sees what's going on. Maybe that's where I get it from.

"My advice to you is to lighten up and have a good time, but be you and don't try to be perfect. Remember, even though you are a jerk, I love you. You've always been my favorite because I know how hard it's been for you. But, still, you give it your all every time. I also know you are one of the meanest people I've ever met when you're pissed off. Remember, I still can kick your ass. Grandpa taught me some moves that he didn't teach you because you aren't a girl . . . or are you?"

Paul laughed and hugged his sister, then gave her a bruiser on her arm. She retaliated with a pinch on his ear lobe that was so sharp he thought she'd cut his ear lobe in half.

In spite of his family's good wishes and praise, Paul knew he would not be distracted from his goals. He had his chance to be in the family limelight and after all these years, he would take full advantage of his brother's defection. He approached his studies with full resolve and not only got straight A's but seemed to have a grasp of his courses that was beyond the scope of average high school students. He asked in-depth questions of his teachers. In his Math classes he looked for clarity of applications that were far from the usual understanding of his peers, especially considering that he was a student athlete. His college algebra teacher told him he should pursue a degree in mathematics and possibly a career in teaching.

This was a complete turnaround from Paul's junior year where it appeared that his only academic goals were to just get by. Now, he was doing well for himself and he had his sights on reducing the financial burden of going to college.

In the absence of his brother, Paul's athletic abilities began to get more notice. The one person on the coaching staff who truly understood his talents was John Martin. He knew about Paul's intensity and his ability to shrug off pain on the football field and on the track. Coach Martin's inventory of players and runners were mostly young men who were either trying to get the girls to notice them or build a resume to enter a college or university that was not within reach based on their grades. But in Paul, Coach Martin saw someone who was competing with himself as if he didn't consider his contemporaries equals. To Paul they were just markers that he used to push himself to be better. And the talk around school was that Paul was using that same technique in his academic studies as well.

His football receiving skills greatly improved over the off season and Coach Martin worked with him on a daily basis. Paul's influence on his fellow teammates was infectious. They all wanted to try as hard as he did, and to his surprise, the team voted him captain. He told the assembled team he'd rather turn down being captain but that he'd accept on the condition that they committed to excellence on the field as he had. Their vote was unanimous. The team would follow him into hell if he wanted. He accepted the honor.

The void at quarterback was a major issue. Paul approached his friend and fellow track runner, Tom Fogerty, and convinced him he would be a great replacement at the position, possibly even better than his brother Lewis. Tom had been Lewis's backup for three years and had never had the opportunity to play in a game as quarterback. Tom's confidence soared with his friend Paul's endorsement. They practiced every day for hours on end to develop that sixth sense between quarterbacks and their receivers. That telepathy is a major ingredient in all great sports partnerships.

The first part of the season was not very difficult. The team was undefeated, and as committed as they were, they could have won those games with just their attitude. The real challenges emerged during the last three games where they had to dig down deep to keep their perfect record intact. North Hollywood rose to the occasion, playing with an unbreakable will that would not be denied. As the competition rose, so rose Paul's leadership and the team followed.

Two incidents occurred during the season that represented North Hollywood's resolve to exceed the coaching staff's expectations. The first was against an inter-conference rival, Reseda High. Reseda's coaching staff realized the only way to stop North Hollywood would be to take out wide receiver Paul Morgan. They knew he was the team's heart and soul, so they instructed their players to cheap shot him on a passing play. They went so far as to say that if one of their players was thrown out of the game, it would still be a victory for Reseda if they could stop Morgan. Reseda's shift of much larger players off the line and into the backfield became obvious to North Hollywood's coaching staff. The big middle defensemen were playing to "maim, not cover" their opponents.

Coach Martin spotted the tactic early in the first quarter and called Paul over on a time out, telling him Reseda was bouncing him around on the sidelines. He warned Paul that they were trying to take him out of the game as it was probably the only way for them to win it. Paul shrugged it off as just rough play. "I'll tire their fat asses out chasing me."

Coach Martin wasn't so sure of that. His doubt was confirmed early in the second period when a two hundred forty pound lineman was converted to a safety and covered Paul on a deep sideline route. Tom Fogerty lofted a perfect spiral down the sideline to Paul. As he reached to catch it, his cover sent all of his weight flying at Paul's head. Paul caught the ball but was knocked unconscious.

Paul lay on the field with the ball in his arms but knocked out cold as the team ran to their fallen leader's side. While he was lying on the ground unconscious, the referee tried to remove the ball from Paul's arms, but he couldn't pry it loose. The team physician administered smelling salts to restore consciousness. Paul refused the stretcher; he preferred to leave the field under his own power.

North Hollywood's coaching staff screamed at the officials that this could have been avoided if they had done their jobs. The officials turned a deaf ear to the staff. In fact there was no penalty assessed against the lineman, who smiled as he was congratulated by his fellow teammates. Paul was taken to the locker room with what looked to be a concussion; he was disoriented and woozy.

The outcome that Reseda's coaches had hoped for blew up in their faces. Tom Fogerty rallied the team and they agreed to seek revenge for the cheap shot on their team captain. Their dial was turned up to a place that none of these young players had ever experienced. Now it was war with no survivors.

Paul's replacement was Bill Begley, the punter who doubled infrequently as a wide receiver. The second play after their leader fell replicated Paul's same route, and when the safety cover lumbered over to maim him, Bill went airborne like a hundred fifty pound missile straight for the lineman's head. Bill succeeded in not only knocking him out but in breaking his jaw with his helmet. He was assessed a fifteen yard penalty for unnecessary roughness. One of the smallest players on the field had just taken out one of Reseda's largest and fastest players. That was the first of five incidents in the quarter where opposing players were injured and were removed from the game.

Reseda's coaching staff realized they had awakened a deadly demon with their cheap shot on Paul. The quarter ended with North Hollywood amassing a 24 to 3 lead. Reseda's coaches wondered what kind of beating awaited them in the second half.

The team gathered around their fallen leader in the locker room. He seemed a bit groggy. He told his teammates he was proud of them and that he would lead them to victory in the second half. The team physician put an immediate stop to that saying that Paul had suffered a concussion and he was declaring him out of the game. Paul resisted but the doctor won. This inflamed his teammates even more. They decimated Reseda in the second half with a final score of 56 to 3. Reseda lost four more stretcher cases in the half.

The second incident of the season took place in the championship game between North Hollywood and Notre Dame, a perennial championship team from the powerhouse Catholic High School League. This was the school that Peter Duffy, Paul's old nemesis, had transferred to in order to escape the degradation of the beating he received from Paul.

Paul had an idea that he ran by Coach Martin. Peter was offensive lineman and Paul was on offense so they would not be on the field at the same time. Paul wanted to try being a defensive back, namely middle linebacker, so he could face off against Peter, not for revenge but for fun.

Paul and his teammates built up a 42-7 lead. Late in the fourth quarter Paul's wish was fulfilled. He trotted out onto the field on defense and when offensive guard Duffy realized what was happening, he didn't know what to do. The significance of Paul's appearance on the field was lost by many in the stands, but for the Morgans and the Duffys it took on very different meanings.

Paul played right up on the line and acknowledged Peter with a nod. As soon as the ball was snapped Paul shot the gap between Peter and the center and sacked the quarter back for a ten yard loss. North Hollywood's fans went berserk.

The same result occurred on second down. Peter's teammates exhorted him to stop Paul and they would at least walk off the field with some sort of pride at the beating they were taking. So on third down, Peter decided to stop Paul from getting to his quarterback. As Paul came across the line when the ball was snapped, Peter stepped into Paul as did the center. North Hollywood's right-side linebacker shot the gap and sacked the quarterback for another ten yard loss.

Chapter 12

PAUL MORGAN HAD a very good senior year. Because of his grades and athletic prowess he was the beneficiary of more attention than he had ever known in his life. The state football championship and the track awards were a testament to his commitment to excel athletically. Academic achievements were even more satisfying to him as they gave him a solid base for a stellar career in an esteemed profession. When his brother Lewis sat atop the honor roll every quarter of his high school classes, Paul wouldn't or couldn't bring himself to see that name as number one. Everyone at school complimented Paul about Lewis being number one on the honor roll to his total dominance in any sport he undertook.

In the winter of his senior year he met with his counselor who just happened to be John Martin, his coach. They discussed what schools Paul was interested in applying to. Paul wanted to stay in California, not far from home, for a couple of reasons. His brother's departure left his parents and grandparents with a void that Paul felt the need to fill. Staying in close proximity to his family would allow them to visit each other and share in Paul's college exploits. And lately, Paul had noticed that his grandparents had visibly slowed down and he worried that he wouldn't get enough time with them if he was out of state at a school.

Coach and counselor Martin knew which schools were interested in his star receiver and runner and would give Paul the best financial incentive. After weighing the various options, Paul mailed applications to the schools with the best match for his college needs and his future.

Very surprisingly, the offers were not as lucrative as student and counselor anticipated. Though Paul had been a decent student in the past and now excelled, the academically focused schools did not offer full scholarships. Neither did the athletically centered schools. Their cumulative belief was that Paul, while very good, was not as great a prospect as his brother had been the year before. So now another challenge was thrown at Paul. He would have to work part time while going to school. No full-ride offers were extended to him. While it was disappointing to them both, for Paul it was just a shift to another gear to get what he wanted.

Upon committing to attend UCLA, Paul learned of another factor that affected the schools' decisions. It was mentioned to Paul in passing by the recruiter. Lewis had disappointed several programs by stringing them along for months until his announcement at graduation. There seemed to be a consensus among the schools, especially those in the Pac-12, that after their experience with Lewis, the Morgan name was not held in high esteem. Paul couldn't help feeling that he would be paying for his big brother's decision for a long time.

Graduation came and went without the aftermath of the previous year. Paul was asked by the football team to speak on leadership, which he did by deferring all credit to his teammates, taking none for himself. He graduated third in his class and had a number of awards presented to him. The most important award was given to him by Coach Martin, who tried to relieve some of the disappointment he knew raged in Paul's heart but was only known by those closest to him.

Coach Martin spoke about Paul's intensity and his absolute commitment to excel and his ability to ignore any obstacle that stood in front of him. Paul's family had their heads bowed, hiding the tears streaming down their faces. Only they knew how hard he had tried.

After the ceremony, the Morgans adjourned to Charlie and Angeline's home for a small party to honor their second son. The party grew as well-wishers from school stopped by to see their leader—on and off the field. Unbeknownst to Paul, a number of students and athletes had been inspired by Paul to follow the example of his commitment to be someone.

As the house swelled with people, Sarina worked her way toward Paul. They had only seen each other a couple of times through the year as she had decided to go to UC Santa Barbara, which required her to live on campus. She continued to visit his parents and was still very close to his sister Ashley. She frequently sent oceanography material to his youngest sister Claire.

As Sarina got closer, Paul was reminded of what a beautiful young woman she had matured into. He thought Lewis had been a fool to forsake her and become a priest. When their eyes met, he felt a pull toward her. When she was near, an undertow dragged him close to her. He shrugged it off, but when they finally met she hugged him and kissed him on the cheek. She wore his favorite perfume and his heart raced as he hugged her back.

His grandfather noticed the embrace and remarked to his wife that his grandson might be continuing where his older brother had left off. After their somewhat long embrace, Sarina whispered that she would like to talk to him after things quieted down. His eyes followed her as she talked to his parents, who received her as if she was still going to be their daughter-in-law. They loved Sarina and her family and had not yet recovered from Lewis's decision. They were not upset by his calling, but of what it had done to Sarina and her family.

After several hours, the well-wishers began to leave. When Grandpa Carlos was ready to leave, he gave Paul an envelope with a check in it. Paul said, "Grandpa, you don't need to give me this."

Carlos looked him in the eye with that twinkle that seemed to appear every time he looked at his grandson and said, "Take it and shut up. You have given me a million times more in the satisfaction of watching you grow up to be an honorable representative of the Catania name. Your grandmother and I couldn't be more proud of you."

Paul blinked back the tears. He'd always considered Carlos his favorite and most admired family member. As Carlos turned away he said, "I saw the way you hugged your ex sister-in-law to be. Don't be stupid like your brother. Get her before someone else does. She would be a great addition to the family."

Ashley walked up to Paul and told him Sarina was on the patio waiting to talk to him. Paul didn't know whether to go join her or run and hide.

He sat down next to Sarina and made small talk until she turned to him and asked, "Is there something wrong with me that made your brother want to become a priest?" Tears streamed down her face as she spoke.

Paul assured Sarina that there wasn't anything wrong with her. He confided that he believed his brother was the one with something wrong. He also told her about his suspicion that Lewis had been put under a trance by his uncle, Fr. Paul. He went on to tell her that she was a much better a human being than his brother, who had proven himself to be a self-centered jackass who only cared about his goals and needs not anyone else's.

Sarina gave Paul a look he had never seen before. "There was always something about you that I couldn't quite figure out. It's something that I tried to tell myself your brother had, but he didn't. I always felt that that you were genuinely more interested in others than he was; more aware of other people's feelings.

"I'm going to admit to you something that no one else knows. I had a feeling that Lewis was going to go sideways. I wasn't sure if it was me or something or someone else. He gave me that impression and I didn't press him about it in case I was misreading my feelings.

"And on the subject of your Fr. Paul, I've felt your brother was being influenced by him for a long time. I also confided in him that Fr. Paul looked at me like a dirty old man. But what bothered me most was that he had dead eyes like a shark."

Paul felt he was sinking with their conversation and decided to change its direction. He looked at Sarina. "Forget about them and tell me what's going on in your world. How did you like your freshman year? Are you doing as well in college as you did in high school?"

"So many questions of so little importance," Sarina said.

Paul saw her eyes lock on him again and he knew where this was going, so he leaned in to embrace and kiss her. Not the kiss of an old friend but a fusing of lips and a deep, long embrace that he wished would go on forever.

A hand on Paul's shoulder interrupted this pleasant interlude. With a shock, Paul saw it was Lewis, just arrived from the seminary to congratulate his little brother on his graduation and all of his accomplishments. Paul had never experienced a more awkward moment in all his life.

Sarina stood up, looked at Lewis and walked away without saying a word. Paul started to explain what had just happened but Lewis interjected that no explanation was necessary. He had left that part of his life behind to find real meaning. Lewis said, "Don't think twice about this, little brother. Matters of the flesh and humanity don't concern me anymore."

The two brothers sat in the backyard of their childhood while Lewis talked about Paul's senior year and how proud he was of his little brother. He spoke very sparingly about his first year in the seminary. Paul observed that even though his brother seemed to be secretive about his new life, he appeared to be happy. Lewis was very interested in Paul's goals. He knew Paul was going to UCLA, but did he have a direction or a career path picked out? It had been almost a year to the day since they had last seen or talked to each other.

Their parents and Ashley looked out the kitchen window on the Morgan brothers. Charlie and Angeline were very proud of both of them. Ashley shocked them with the comment, "I love both of my brothers, but Paul will be the brother who will do more for humanity than Lewis ever will."

Her father turned her and asked, "What do you mean by that?"

"Paul is a very old soul who really cares. He's had to fight and struggle for his accomplishments. Lewis has had it much easier; he is softer and more pliable. He would rather be a chameleon than stick up for what is right."

Charlie and Angeline looked at their daughter and immediately understood that she knew what they had always suspected.

Chapter 13

WHEN THE LETTERS of acceptance from various colleges began arriving at the Morgan household, Paul had a sense of remorse that he had not applied himself more in his first three years of high school. It wasn't that he didn't try; it was that he only went at "half-speed." As Paul read the letters of acceptance, it was very apparent to him that he could have worked harder and it would have paid dividends to him at the start of his college career.

A great many schools wanted Paul, but not on full rides. His football and track resumes were excellent but the scholastic side was not on the same par with his athletics. Paul believed that his altercation with Peter Duffy hurt his chances and wondered what comments from some of his teachers might have been made about his almost killing a fellow student.

Paul chose University of California at Los Angeles, or UCLA. One of the benefits to UCLA was that it wasn't mandatory that he live on campus if he was willing to commute. UCLA also gave him the advantages of in-state tuition and some fellow high school graduates attending the same university. The closest person to being his best friend, Tom Fogerty, would be at UCLA also. Paul reasoned that with Tom there, he would know someone on the freshman football and track team that he could trust. They could commute together and help each other in their academic studies.

There seemed to be only one drawback: transportation. Paul's Junker was on its last fumes and his fellow carpooler, Tom, had just blown his clunker's engine. To repair his car would cost Paul in the neighborhood of $5,000.00. With a new engine and transmission, the car in pristine condition was worth $1,500.00. As Tom liked to say it doesn't take a math major to know that it would be moronic to fix it.

When Paul opened the graduation envelope from his grandparents, he was shocked to see a check for $10,000.00. He again tried to give the very generous gift back to Carlos and Carmen with no luck. Paul had gone to their house with that intent, but his grandfather would have none of it. He told him to use it for school. When Paul said that he had his education paid for and didn't need it, Carlos saw right through his remark.

"Well then use it for a better car than that 'crap can' you drive. How can you expect to meet nice girls with a heap like the one you own now?"

Paul thought about his grandfather's remark, not for using it to attract women, but to have more dependable transportation for him and his paying commuter, Tom. He told Carlos that if it was truly okay for him to buy more dependable transportation then he would do it. Carlos agreed fully with Paul's decision. Naturally, Grandma Carmen threw her two cents in that she always worried about him in that car and with something safer she would rest easier. Paul was overwhelmed with gratitude, and thought how lucky he was to have such great grandparents. He reaffirmed to both of them that he would make them proud of him.

Paul settled on a late model Volkswagen that he and Tom could work on if necessary. With his transportation issue settled, Paul met with his freshman counselor at UCLA. He quickly realized that his financial shortfall would be even greater than he'd anticipated. The deficit was in the neighborhood of $12,000 a year. He could finance some of it but it was obvious that he needed a job to augment his shortfall. He began considering his options. He wanted to work at something that was on the path toward his future profession.

Paul began to browse the want ads. After about a week into his search, he ran across an advertisement for a tax preparer at a Certified Public Accountant practice. Paul had not settled on any path or profession but he knew his strong suit was mathematics and he'd always enjoyed numbers. He remembered that Fr. Paul was in charge of some type of financial unit at the Vatican and that the church had sent him to some very prestigious universities to study accounting.

Paul called Mr. Lawrence Vandermeer's office and secured an appointment with him for the next day. He donned his best suit and brought a number of letters of recommendation from his teachers. The office was not far from UCLA. When Paul walked in he was impressed with the office and the very attractive receptionist who greeted him. Mr. Vandermeer's diplomas hung on the walls and Paul was elated when he realized that his prospective employer had also attended UCLA. He hoped this might help.

When he was led into Mr. Vandermeer's office, Paul was struck with the enormity of it but his eyes fixed on the resident CPA. Paul stuck out his hand and said he was pleased to meet him. Mr. Vandermeer immediately told Paul that there were no formalities in his office and to call him Larry and nothing more. Paul noticed that when the receptionist left the room she turned and saw Larry wink at her. She giggled.

Larry motioned for Paul to sit down. His first words were, "Why the hell do you want to prepare tax returns? It will turn your hair gray, ruin your eyesight, and give you hemorrhoids."

"I'd like to pursue something with mathematics and am considering a career path in accounting like my uncle," Paul said.

"Did your uncle tell you this was an admirable pursuit?"

"Well, I haven't had much input from my uncle but he seems to enjoy what he does and it looks like he is very well paid for his efforts."

"Then why don't you get a job with him?" Larry asked.

Paul explained that his uncle is a priest in the Vatican and is in charge of accounting.

Larry whistled and said, "Those bastards don't make enough being a charity so they have to have accountants to screw the books even more to their advantage. Hell, I wouldn't be able to take that job for all the money they have. There is no way I'd ever give up women. There ain't enough money in this world for that."

The dumbstruck look on Paul's face invited Larry to caution him. "Hey kid, you look a little shocked. You better get used to it because between the swearing and me hard driving you to do the returns correctly and quickly, you might find a direction for your life. One thing you will learn is that you never worked harder than when you worked here. Do you think you're tough enough?"

Paul was simultaneously insulted and challenged. He felt that Larry could make him into something but he also was intrigued.

Larry blurted out, "Do you want the job or not? I can't sit here all day. Time is money, my money."

Paul stuttered, "Yes, I want the job." He realized later that they had not discussed money or the amount of time that was involved. Paul felt that anything he learned would surely make up for money he hadn't asked for up front. He later learned that if he had asked for anything, he would have been unceremoniously told to never come back. Deep in his heart, Paul had a feeling that this was the opportunity that he was looking for and needed.

Paul thanked Larry for the chance to work with him. Larry retorted, "Thank me in a month if you last that long. By the way, keep your eyes and hands off my receptionist. She's mine." Paul was just about to leave when Larry called out to him and asked if he knew anyone else like himself who wanted to learn about tax preparation.

Paul answered, "I have a friend named Tom Fogerty. He's a teammate and friend and a damn hard worker."

Larry fired back, "Bring him with you when you start on Monday morning at eight."

As Paul got into his car he wondered if Tom was at all interested in learning about tax preparation. He called Tom from his car telling him he'd gotten him a job and describing the beautiful receptionist who would be working with them. Years later Tom would admit to Paul that he could not have cared less about accounting; it was the description of the receptionist that convinced him to take the job.

Chapter 14

ON MONDAY MORNING, Paul rose at five. There was no way he was going to be late for his first day at work and he had to pick up Tom, who was not very punctual at times. Paul smiled to himself, thinking of how Tom turned out to be a better runner because of all the extra laps he had to take for not making track and football practice on time.

Today Tom was on time, though probably a little over dressed for Larry's taste. No doubt Larry would take care of that in short order. Paul had an instinct that Larry's no-nonsense, straight to the point style would be of value in his career.

When the two new employees at Larry Vandermeer CPA strode through the door, they felt as though they were no longer students with part time jobs but were on their way to becoming adults and professionals.

Larry greeted them. "Glad to see you got your asses here before eight. If there's one thing I can't stand, it's someone being late. Hell, I give my clients grief if they're late and they know I will charge them accordingly." Larry took a second look at Tom and yelled, "Don't ever out dress your employer. It makes me look bad and makes you look more important than you are. Got it?"

Paul had clued Tom to keep his focus from the receptionist, whom he had described as drop dead gorgeous. In the years that Tom had known Paul he'd never heard such a lofty description from his usually understated friend.

When Dianne, the receptionist, made her appearance about twenty minutes late, Larry smiled, completely ignoring her tardiness. She produced a bag of croissants and coffee for all the employees including Tom and Paul. Paul tried not to stare, and Tom uncharacteristically became speechless. He later told Paul he thought he had died and gone to heaven. His daydreaming was interrupted by Larry who barked orders to all of the staff, except Dianne.

Before the two new employees could take a breath, they were standing in front of Larry in his office. His manner was abrupt and to the point. He had watched Tom and Paul during the entire prequel and noted the expressions on their faces when Dianne entered the room. Larry barked, "Listen you two sons of bitches, I don't have time to be your babysitter, mother, father, or confidant. You are here to work your asses off, not ogle my secretary and play executive. If you think otherwise, leave before I shoot you." At that moment he produced a weapon that put Dirty Harry's piece to shame. The two boys looked at it and each other and nodded simultaneously. They were ready to go to work on Larry's terms. No matter what he told them to do and how high he said to jump, there would be no questions asked. Larry offered them a streetwise education in a career that each would be able to use as the roadmap for their future successes, but all they could think about was the cannon he kept in his desk drawer.

The first stop in their accounting apprenticeship was IRS form 1040. Larry instructed them as if he was lecturing surgical students while standing over a patient who'd been prepped for surgery. He explained that they held a client's financial life in their hands, comparing them to surgeons whose patients' survival was in their hands. At first, Larry's description felt like overkill to Paul and Tom, but they quickly learned that was the dogma of Larry's practice. It was soon obvious that this was one of the main reasons he also was as successful as he was. There was no bigger champion of his client base than he—pure and simple. He was the client's white knight who went up against the tyrant, the Internal Revenue Service.

Their first day was a whirlwind of knowledge dumped on them and their concentration was totally on the content and processes taught. They both retained an amazing amount of their lessons for two reasons, the cannon in the desk and the unbelievable opportunity that had dropped in their lap. And their interest only fueled Larry's zealous instruction.

Before they realized it, it was two o'clock in the afternoon and six hours had sped by. Dianne interrupted them to ask Larry if he needed reservations for a very late lunch. "Yes," he replied. "Make the reservation for three people."

Paul and Tom followed Larry through the back door of the office and were amazed at the number of people scurrying around in the very large back office area. They'd assumed that Larry had about ten to fifteen employees but it was closer to three times that. He nodded at his staff as he walked through and noticed a form that was slightly out of order. His reprimand came more in the form of a nod and quick couple of words rather than belittlement. It seemed that once you became Larry's employee, he was less combative. They thought that was something to strive for.

Their next shock was the car that was waiting for them.

Tom looked up the price of the Mercedes later on and learned that that particular model was a special order with a starting price of $350,000. Larry's model was anything but a starter.

Once in the car, their mentor, employer, and task master relaxed and asked them to tell him what their first impressions were. Paul said he was impressed and that he was very eager to learn more of the process. He continued, saying that he found the work interesting and more like problem solving than just inputting a series of numbers. Tom tried to echo his co-worker's feedback when Larry pulled him up short. "Tom, no one wants to hear carbon copy remarks. Tell me your own personal thoughts. And do it now!"

Tom said he was amazed at the power of Larry's position, but was blown away by how thoughtfully Larry had handled his employee's mistake."

"That's very observant of you, Tom," Larry remarked. "Remember, once someone has proven himself or herself to your organization, let the little stuff slide. It's only a big deal if I make it a big deal. My employees would go to hell and back if I asked them to. That's what I look for in others and in return I do the same for them. I pay my staff about forty percent more than my competitors, but they can out-work and out-perform my three largest competitors combined."

They pulled up at the very famous and exclusive Beverly Hills restaurant, Cicero's. Even the boys, who knew nothing of high society haunts, had heard of this restaurant. The valets were immediately on all doors and welcomed Mr. Vandermeer by name.

They were ushered into a private dining room. The boys were impressed and noticed the very ornate brass plaque imbedded at the end of the table that proclaimed this was the table of Larry Vandermeer, Padrone.

From all directions the table was bombarded with waitresses with a collection of entrees and appetizers that Dianne had called ahead to preorder. They both would learn that Larry preferred his meals to be ready when he arrived, to give him more time to focus on the day's challenges. To put it in Larry's terms, "Efficiency rewards her proponents with more time and, hence, more money."

It was a meal and setting that neither of the boys had ever experienced or even conceived of. It was beyond their comprehension. During the course of the meal, two very large men entered the room, followed by an elderly gentleman who was obviously the owner of Cicero's. Larry stood and hugged them and between English and some Italian, which Paul could barely overhear, the owner asked Larry if the meal was satisfactory. Larry thanked him, saying he appreciated everyone's efforts and that as always, the food was prepared to the highest standards—Cicero's standards.

The next thing they knew, they were once again in the car and headed back to the Vandermeer office. Paul and Tom repeatedly thanked Larry for the lunch. Larry commented positively on their courteous behavior and remarked that it was obvious they had been raised in homes where manners were stressed. He told them to thank their parents for giving them that social advantage that so many young people lacked. Larry pointed out that this shortcoming compromises many careers.

The rest of the day was spent in Larry's office, observing. The boys were at amazed how easily he could go from one issue to another seamlessly and efficiently. There was no down time or hesitating. He handled one task after the other. Again, they were shocked when Dianne appeared to ask Larry if he was ready to go home to prepare for a fund raiser at the Beverly Hills Hotel, reminding him that it was already seven o'clock. Dianne said she needed time to get ready and Larry joked, "Ridiculous. How can you improve on perfection?" Larry winked at her as she left and she giggled.

"Well boys, that's it for today. If I haven't worn you two out with this monotonous day of pencil pushing, I'll see you tomorrow at eight sharp. Oh by the way, today was not a typical day. I usually work until nine or ten in the evening or until Dianne tells me we need to go home. I don't want you to expect that we don't put in the hours here."

As Paul and Tom drove home, they looked at each other. It was Tom who blurted it out first. "Now that's what I'm talking about." And so it was that the two new employees became hooked on becoming a part of Larry Vandermeer CPA and ultimately the successors of the firm.

Chapter 15

For as little sleep as Tom and Paul got, they would have been better off just dozing in the firm's parking lot. Their excitement was not easily contained. To have jobs in a prestigious accounting firm was an experience they would not have thought possible considering it was their very first job ever. And to be under the guidance of such a knowledgeable and respected CPA who was willing to teach and mentor them, was beyond all expectations.

The boys made it a point to arrive early each day to take on extra tasks that needed to be handled. No one ever had to call to find out where they were or what they were doing. As Tom would say, "We are on it."

Larry later admitted that when he met Paul, he felt he had found his successor in the firm. He routinely dismissed applicants for entry level job interviews. Larry was very quick to show them the door and not to waste his time. He believed part of his success was due to making quick decisions based on a combination of experience and intuition.

Larry was immediately struck with Paul Morgan's character and work ethic. He also sensed there was a burning passion in the young man to be both successful and coachable. Those traits were a rare combination and that combination was sitting in his office wanting a job and ultimately a career.

Tom Fogerty, according to Larry, was similar to Paul—every bit as coachable, just not as intense on the success curve. Whatever Tom initially lacked, Larry believed Paul would help his friend overcome. Larry was going to use Paul as his bell cow to shape Tom into a duplicate of himself. That was Larry's theory of two for the price of one.

Larry believed Paul's central focus on success was for the sake of success and that the monetary reward was not paramount for him, much like Larry. Larry felt Paul wanted the accomplishment and that the money was an afterthought. He thought that the philosophy was a necessary ingredient for a high level performer. Larry believed that mediocrity was fostered by a money-first focus. He believed in the accomplishment first, then the reward, and not the reverse.

Throughout the summer, the two new employees learned how to work in an accounting office. They were taught the importance of asking questions and making sure they absorbed the answers so they could learn accounting processes and procedures inside and out. They discovered what it was like to feel like valued employees. At first, they were surprised to find their opinions sought. Paul and Tom quickly learned that Larry actively sought their opinions and was not very amicable when he received what he called lip speak. According to long time employees, Larry's modus operandi was: if you're going to give input, it better be constructive and insightful, or don't open your mouth.

Larry looked to his employees for any way to improve office processes. This resulted in the employees feeling that they had a voice and a vested interest in the firm, which naturally fostered loyalty to Larry and the firm. One legendary story went: Years ago, Marilyn, a longtime tax preparer who had been with the firm for over twenty years, had given Larry an idea that cut about two hours off tax preparation time for their corporate clients. Her idea was rewarded with a check for $50,000 and a brand new car. Years later, she still drove that car as a testament to Larry and the firm. Upon hearing this story, Tom made a remark that was adopted into the firm's vernacular. "Now that's some serious money."

While Larry was relentless in the boys' training, he was never perceived to be unjust or unfair. He prepared them to be exact and efficient in order to feel comfortable about not having to check their work. He was ultimately striving for clones of himself, and his hands-on training would achieve something very close to that. He challenged them to be their best, that's all he wanted and that's all he would accept. Paul and Tom flourished in this environment.

The summer drew to a close and their freshman year at UCLA was about to start. Paul and Tom told Larry that they both wanted to continue in their apprenticeship at the firm while attending school. That was agreeable to Larry on the condition that he had access to their grades and that they both continue with their athletic endeavors. If he found them lacking in either of those pursuits, there was a good chance they would be terminated at the firm. They accepted Larry's terms but were a little unnerved when he asked them to sign agreements to that effect, witnessed and stamped by a notary. Larry wasn't going to allow either of them to be mediocre in any facet of their lives.

Their work schedules were adapted to give the boys the flexibility they needed to take care of their academic and athletic responsibilities and also continue earning at the firm. They both felt they were indeed lucky to work for someone like Larry.

Chapter 16

By the time Paul met with his freshman counselor for the first time, he had settled on his course of study and major. Larry had helped him and Tom with their electives and coached them on how to fast track to degrees in accounting without short-changing themselves on the university experience. It helped that as an alumnus, Larry had ties to the school and the faculty. He knew a lot of the professors and understood where the best value was hidden in the curriculum.

Paul and Tom both tried out for freshman football and in short order, both were red shirted on the varsity team. Some of their former high school opponents were also on the varsity team. The enemy became the comrade in this varsity team setting. Coach John Martin had sent glowing letters of recommendation to one of his own former teammates, UCLA receivers' coach Matt Fulmer. This helped immensely when they were promoted from their freshman squad. Paul did not disappoint as he had perfected his laser focus at work and could now use it to his advantage in academics and athletics. The accounting position had proven to him that the only limit he had was the limit he placed on himself.

Tom was not as gifted as his friend in his focus, so Paul worked to help him overcome his shortcomings in that area.

When Paul felt Tom wasn't giving it his all, he helped Tom refocus on the professional opportunity that was theirs for the taking. If that didn't fully get Tom's attention, reminding him of having to meet with Larry and the large caliber gun that was in his desk did the trick. Tom knew the magnitude of what was ahead; he just wasn't at the same stage of laser focus as Paul.

The two of them learned the balancing act of multiple pursuits with trial and error. There was not much in the error column as Larry quickly retuned their priorities. They were amazed that after a full day of academia and football practice, when they dragged themselves to the office for a few hours of paid work, they almost always found Larry there. No matter what the hour or day, he and a great number of staff were knocking out the hours. Exhaustion was not something he allowed himself or anyone around him to succumb to. His motto was, "If you're upright, you are working."

With the flexible working hours, financial worries were non-existent for them, unlike some of their college friends. Paul and Tom had money in their pockets, money in their bank accounts, and very little spare time on their hands to get into trouble with. A number of fellow teammates seemed to be either practicing or partying and the carnage on the team's freshman class was brutal. You name it, someone did it and got busted for it, which got them kicked off the team, kicked out of school and/or arrested. That was never an issue for Paul or Tom with their strict upbringing, but they didn't have time anyway.

They each had some playing time in the varsity games their first year which was unusual but they were competitive on the college level. When track season rolled around, a juggling of their schedules ensued with tax season in full swing until April 15. It was not unusual to see Paul and Tom on the school's lighted track at three or four in the morning running laps and training. They were willing to do whatever it took to keep all their balls in the air. Their performances in football and track as freshman brought renewal of their athletic scholarships for the following year.

Larry and Dianne made unannounced appearances at a couple of games and track meets and were very supportive. Paul's family, especially his sister Ashley, was present for most of the events. After one football game, Paul had the pleasure of introducing his parents and Ashley to Larry and Dianne. The parental roles seemed somewhat reversed with Larry speaking of Paul in glowing terms as though Paul was the son that Larry never had. Charlie and Angeline were pleased that their son had someone in his corner that was every bit supportive as they were.

Dianne spoke to Ashley about their admiration for her brother and how much he had come to mean to them in such a short time. Larry offered Ashley a position with his firm if she ever desired it. The entire Morgan family was, in Charlie's words, "Over the moon" at the opportunity their son had earned with Mr. Vandermeer.

It was a special meeting when Paul's grandfather met Larry and Dianne. Carlos had heard from everyone how much of a benefactor Larry had been for Paul. Carlos wanted to let him know of his gratitude for giving his favorite a chance to prove himself and to guarantee that Paul would not disappoint him. Paul and Tom almost fell over when Larry and Carlos hugged and embraced Italian style. Carlos kidded Larry after that there was more Sicilian in him than most people knew. Larry laughed and said he had been found out; his heart and roots were in Sicily.

Larry was reserved in his interaction with Tom's family but was effusive of their son. He told Tom's father that he ought to be the one being paid because he was doing his best to keep Tom out of trouble, which caused everyone to laugh.

To cap off the boys' freshman year of college, both of Larry's protégés attained the Dean's List, a feat that was not considered out of the ordinary, but that was expected.

* * *

Summer was upon Paul and Tom, bringing with it full time employment. They felt as though they were on vacation with the lessening of their workload. The reprieve left them both with some time to conduct their social lives. They had been hermits during their freshman year, always keeping first and foremost in their minds where they were heading, not where they were presently.

After work, Larry and Dianne occasionally had a cocktail or a beer with Paul and Tom at the more classy establishments in the Westwood area of Los Angeles. They were introduced to a number of celebrities at the clubs who Larry knew or who knew him. The owners of the clubs often were clients of the firm and nearly every check was complimentary at these establishments. Larry appeared to have admittance into every high ranking club or restaurant in the area. When the group migrated to high end places in Beverly Hills and Hollywood the reception was the same.

If Dianne was not with them, beautiful women were all over Larry, or "Mr. Cool," as Tom described him. Larry lectured the boys on social graces and etiquette but, more importantly, he urged them to think of the repercussions of their actions. It was obvious to them that he loved Dianne and that he would never do anything to jeopardize that relationship. Nor would he compromise his professional rank in anyway.

Paul felt that he sat at the feet of the master when it came to accounting, but Larry's lectures and snippets on life and living were just as invaluable. Paul wondered how Larry had gained his wisdom about life. Larry would share his wisdom and experience with Paul for the rest of his life. Some of those lessons, Paul came to find out, had cost Larry a great deal in his younger years.

Chapter 17

As the summer wore on, Paul and Tom found they had time on their hands in the evenings after working all day at the office. They often went out with Larry and Dianne but they also had the opportunity to see friends from high school and college at places below Larry's social strata of restaurant or bar.

One warm August night found the two undergraduates at an old bar on Ventura Boulevard in Studio City not far from where they both were raised. Ernie's was far from a dive but it was not on the caliber of drinking holes on the other side of the mountain in Westwood or Beverly Hills.

Paul and Tom were talking to old friends when the arms of a woman reached around Paul's neck suddenly and she kissed him. Startled, he turned to find Sarina standing over him. He immediately jumped up and embraced her. Tom knew who she was from afar and he was amazed how beautiful she was up close. Paul introduced her to Tom and asked her to join them. Paul and Sarina began talking about old times. Tom felt out of place so when he spotted an old high school girl friend with a couple of her friends, he excused himself to go over and say hello.

As soon as Tom left, Sarina and Paul's conversation took a more intimate direction. She asked him if he was seeing anyone and he told her not anyone on a regular basis. He asked her the same and the reply was the same. Out of the blue, Paul asked Sarina if she had been in contact with Lewis. She hadn't and hoped that he would never try to contact her. Paul was taken aback with the abruptness of the answer and decided not to pursue it further.

He focused on Sarina, thinking she was more beautiful than ever. It was a warm evening and the tank top she wore revealed more of her than he'd seen before. She wore shorts and her bare legs were long and lovely. With a couple or three beers under his belt, he rummaged through his mind and realized he had never looked at her this way because she was always going to be his brother's wife. It was clear, now, what he had missed and what a fool his brother was to give up someone as beautiful as she.

Questions had nagged at Paul over the past year and he waited for the chance to merge them into the conversation. When the small talk subsided, he asked Sarina why she had decided to go to UC Santa Barbara.

"Well, the curriculum is more in alignment with my major. And, I didn't want to be that close in proximity to Lewis at the seminary. In fact, I thought about changing schools when I realized that they both were in the same city. But I refused to change my plans because of him. When he never gave me any indication of his change of heart and his feelings about a future with me, I truly thought, to hell with him," she finished angrily.

Paul was surprised by how quickly Sarina became white hot about the whole episode. He realized that his brother had not only hurt her, but had embarrassed her as well, in front of her family and friends.

Sarina continued, "You may not have known this, Paul, but Lewis and I were going through a rough patch in our relationship toward the end of our senior year. He was distracted and distant. I thought it was the pressure of deciding which college to attend, but looking back now, he seemed to get colder and colder, not only with me but in other areas of his life. It was as if he was detaching or unplugging himself from everyday life and was more an observer than a participant.

"In the past, he was always very attentive to those around him and as our senior year went on, he went from sympathetic to others in need to more judgmental of people. The person he became before my eyes was not the person I had fallen in love with. At times, he was condescending at best. That was something that I could not accept or understand.

"The day you had that fight in my senior year is when I first noticed you as someone other than the younger brother of my boyfriend. There was something different about you after that. I knew you were intense from your demeanor, but the whole incident made me realize that you were very different from your brother. It was quite an eye opener for me and I began to study you from afar.

"Your sister Ashley filled me in on certain details about you when I asked her about you. It was during those conversations that I began to see Lewis differently. Ashley was very candid in her views of how easy life had been for him. She wondered what Lewis would do when life's pressures became too much for him. How would he react?

"She told me long before graduation that she thought he was going to do something stupid. But looking back now, it was the best thing that he could have done for us. It freed me from a commitment that I would never have been able to go through with based on how he changed. It freed him to go into the priesthood, to a position your Fr. Paul sold him on. It's like he's delaying entering the real world by entering into a world where he won't be an active participant, but a casual observer sitting in judgment.

"So my freshmen year I spent a lot of time reflecting on my life and its direction. Hurt, yes, but not broken. Ashley kept me abreast of what you were doing and I actually came down and watched some of your football games. I attended some of your track events as well. Your actions and focus were very attractive to me. If I could design the perfect guy, it would be you. What haunts me is the thought that everyone will say that I'm on the rebound so I'm moving on to the next Morgan brother. That's not true and it wouldn't be fair to you. Not that I think anyone would ever confront you with that statement. You have a reputation for not taking remarks like that.

"When your graduation came around last year, Ashley invited me to attend. I would have come anyway to see you walk. What's funny is your sister was aware of my attraction to you even before breaking up with your brother. It must have been subconscious because I wasn't aware of it, but she said she saw my eyes following you and look at you in a way that I didn't look at Lewis. So your sister had it figured out before even I realized."

Paul's head was spinning with the revelations. He ordered another round of drinks for them. He tried to take it all in and make sense of where all this was going. He looked at her in a purely lustful way and again he realized how truly beautiful she was. He didn't give a damn what anyone said and if there were those, including his moronic brother, who thought they wanted to debate it, he would take them on with no reserve.

His next question seemed like a stupid one, but he asked anyway. "Did you plan or intend to kiss me at the house?"

Sarina visibly blushed. "No. It wasn't planned, but I couldn't stop myself from doing it. I was drawn to you and like being caught in the ocean's riptide, the more I fought it, the weaker I got. It was a pure accident that Lewis showed up but fitting justice for how he had treated me. But his treatment of me was not the catalyst for my attraction to you, Paul. It's been developing for quite some time."

Paul leaned over and kissed her and she threw her arms around his neck. Tom, sitting at the other table, saw the embrace and thought, you lucky son of a bitch. We come here for a couple of beers and you are leaving with a beautiful woman.

It was obvious to both Paul and Sarina that the evening had just begun so they decided to find a hotel and make up for lost time. On the way out, Paul gave Tom the keys to his car and told him to call him in the morning and he would tell Tom where to pick him up. They left in Sarina's car and checked into the El Portero on Ventura Boulevard. It was the first of many nights the two of them found love and solace in each other's arms.

Chapter 18

THE NEXT MORNING Tom's cell phone rang. It was Paul. Sarina had given him a ride to work and Paul hoped Tom wasn't going to be late. When Sarina dropped Paul off two events occurred almost simultaneously. She kissed him and asked him to call her later, and Dianne came around the corner to witness it all.

Paul responded emphatically. "I'd love to see you again tonight if possible and I'll call you later."

Paul walked through the parking lot as Dianne got out of her car. She gave him a pleasant, but all-knowing smile as she greeted him, "Good morning."

He was working at his desk when Larry asked to see him in his office. Larry made some small talk and then said, "Dianne tells me that you have a real looker for a girlfriend. Is that true?" Paul blushed, so Larry quickly added that he thought it was great that Paul was dating someone because all work and no play means you are a moron. He added, "If this is a serious relationship, Dianne and I would love to meet her. Maybe we can double date some time, if that's okay."

"That would be great," Paul said.

Larry then put on his fatherly hat and told Paul that if there was anything he needed to let him know and he would do what he could. Paul knew he meant what he said. As he was leaving, Larry said, "Remember kid, if there is a chance of this being the one, don't screw it up."

As Paul came out of Larry's office Tom approached him to ask about last night. Knowing his friend as well as he did, Tom was careful in how he brought the subject up. "So did you have a good time last night with the best looking woman to ever grace Ernie's bar?"

Paul uncharacteristically smiled and said, "It was perfect, brother."

Tom suspected what Paul already knew. Sarina was "the one." Not the one for a week, a month, or a year. The one for life. Tom again thought, you lucky son of a bitch.

He was still mulling over the Paul and Sarina situation when his phone rang. He heard Dianne's voice saying that Larry wanted to see him. Tom wondered, what the hell did I do wrong this time? He said to Paul as he passed him, "On my way to gallows to pay for everyone's sins."

Larry greeted Tom uncharacteristically warmly, which immediately put Tom on alert. Larry was always friendly to him, but not as friendly as he was to Paul. Tom had no problem with that because sometimes it was best to be second favorite than to have more expected of you. After a little shop talk, Larry asked Tom about Paul's girlfriend. Tom told Larry everything he knew and even reiterated Paul's comment about her being "the one." Larry smiled. "I suggest you follow your friend's example. You'll be a much happier man." Then Larry added, "And it will make me happier, too, because you'll be more focused on school and, more importantly, work. It'll even save me from paying for a trip to the veterinarian for you.

Tom asked, "How so?"

Larry answered, "By not having to pay for you to be castrated to get you to focus on your responsibilities instead of skirts."

Tom said he would take it under advisement. Larry smoothly opened his desk draw where he kept his Dirty Harry-sized revolver and remarked, "There is a less expensive way to have you neutered without the use of a veterinarian.

As he left Larry's office Tom said, "I'm on it."

"So, how'd it go? Paul asked Tom on his return.

"Larry gave me a lecture on veterinarian procedures. Don't worry about it. Do you need a ride home tonight?

Paul replied, "Nope, I've got it covered."

Tom began to ponder in earnest what Larry had suggested to him and thought, I have to find a girlfriend and be in a relationship that is going somewhere or I am going to be whole lot lighter in a certain area.

Summer football practice started up in earnest the following week putting Paul and Tom's time for social life at a premium. Occasionally, Tom showed the strain of having too many balls in the air at the same time, but Paul always seemed to manage the stress and his activities with very little problem. His relationship with Sarina was now an integral part of his life and he would allow nothing to interfere with it.

A couple of weeks into their relationship, he decided to break the news to his family. He asked Ashley for advice on how to handle it since she knew more about it than anyone.

She said, "Just tell Mom and Dad. They'll approve, I guarantee it. It's a natural. They've never stopped loving her and want what makes the two of you happy."

Paul decided to make the announcement at Sunday dinner with his grandparents present. All Paul had said was that he was bringing a girlfriend to dinner on Sunday. He was a bit nervous as he'd never brought anyone to Sunday dinner, let alone a girl, let alone his brother's ex-girlfriend. He was nervous as he walked up to his parents' house arm in arm with Sarina.

Imagine his surprise when the door opened and not only his family, but hers, were standing in the hall to congratulate them. Everyone was pleased. Paul wondered how it was possible that everyone was there, but he had only to look at his sister Ashley. A Cheshire cat smile adorned her face. Ashley had always been Paul's champion. Later in life, Paul would learn that Sarina had shown up at Ernie's bar not by chance, but by the design of his younger sister who wanted two people she deeply cared for to be together. She spotted their fondness for each other long before they spotted it. This Sunday dinner was an affirmation of her design.

Chapter 19

Paul's second year at UCLA was much more rewarding than his first. Although Sarina attended UC Santa Barbara as a junior, she seemed to be with Paul as much as she was at school. She arranged her schedule so she could be with Paul from Friday afternoon until Monday morning. She got up early every Monday to drive the two hours to Santa Barbara in time for her first class at ten o'clock. She also maneuvered her class and workload so that she was finished with school in time to have lunch with Paul every Friday. She never missed his football games or his track meets on the weekend.

Paul continued to thrive in his studies at UCLA and his varsity playing time increased. Even with all of the academic and personal distractions, Paul's speed and strength training showed in practice and was noticed by the head coach and his assistants. It was apparent that late night training sessions yielded results. Tom's playing time increased also as his commitment to a greater training regimen brought results that were noticed by the coaching staff.

Paul was eager to finish his required classes and start his major-specific courses in accounting. Larry had taken painstaking efforts to prepare Paul and Tom for those courses.

He wanted them pre-educated in all facets of accounting. He not only taught them every what, where, when and how, he drilled the why of every nuance into their heads. He wanted them to know their courses inside out before even starting them. Their attendance would be mere formalities to getting the grades and the credits. Flawless was the adjective he burned into their brains. Anything else was unacceptable to Larry. He quoted the Mercedes slogan over and over to them, "The Best or Nothing."

Larry knew a number of the professors in the university accounting department. They were either friends or former classmates; strangely, very few were both. Larry had been very competitive at the university, and if you were a classmate, you were an adversary that he needed to decimate scholastically. According to his friends, Larry had built his practice while still in pursuit of his degree. He'd wanted anyone and everyone to know who was the "accountant's accountant." His theory about the importance of being known before graduating would become essential to graduates who wanted to be known as successful by the time they left school. There was no question who they would call when they started their careers as professionals. Larry was fond of saying, "I planted the seeds when they were nobodies, then the idea flowered when they became somebodies."

Among Larry's client base were doctors, dentists, lawyers, and a vast array of various sports celebrities. In addition to that portion of his client base, Larry had some interesting clients who were mainly in the restaurant and distribution businesses like liquor and tobacco. Not all of these clients had sprung from Larry's higher education days, but it seemed to Paul that every high end restaurateur in Beverly Hills and Westwood were clients and friends of Larry. And the more successful they were, the more likely it was that a bodyguard or two were always present.

Larry was warmly met by the owner of any establishment where he took his protégés for lunch or dinner. Invariably the proprietors embraced and hugged Larry in greeting. There were snippets in Italian or Sicilian that Paul picked up in the Italian restaurants. When he heard a term he didn't know, he would later ask his grandfather what it meant. Carlos explained that some of the exchanges were terms of respect used in his native Sicily for a highly regarded person of the community. On more than one occasion Carlos asked Paul if Larry was Sicilian. Paul didn't think so.

The name Vandermeer was as Dutch as it comes but Larry's complexion was a little darker than most of the people Paul had met from the Netherlands. Carlos was convinced that with Larry's command of the nuances of his native language, he must either have Sicilian blood or have been raised there. Paul didn't know, nor did he know of a way to bring it up with Larry. So he filed it away in his mind as a possible question for Larry if the opening ever presented itself.

Carlos took the initiative himself when he saw Larry at one of Paul's football games. When the two met, they shook hands and Carlos told Larry, in Sicilian, how happy he was to see him and how well he looked. Seamlessly Larry countered in Sicilian that it was his pleasure to be in the company of the patriarch of the family he so respected.

Carlos immediately asked Larry if he had spent a lot of time in Sicily and Larry replied that he had been born in Palermo and had been raised there until he was about six years old. Carlos asked if his parents had immigrated to Sicily from the Netherlands and Larry laughed.

"No," he said. "My parents were both from Sicily, as were all known generations of my family on both sides."

It was Carlos's turn to laugh. "I've never heard of a Sicilian family name like Vandermeer."

"The name was changed from Paluso to Vandermeer when we immigrated to the United Sates. My father discovered that if you wanted the doors of opportunity to open for you in the accounting or bookkeeping world, you had to be either Dutch or German. My father couldn't bring himself to being thought of as German due to what the Nazis had done during the Second World War. And, my father was a self-proclaimed connoisseur of fine art and was crazy about the Dutch Masters."

Carlos said he understood the bias against Sicilians and added that he had followed his parents in the grocery and produce arena, where it was a plus to be of that nationality.

The two made small talk about the upcoming football game and how well Paul was doing. Larry asked Carlos if Paul had shared his thoughts on the outcome of the game. Did Paul think UCLA would beat Oregon State? Carlos relayed that Paul thought UCLA would dominate their opponent. Larry nodded, saying that Paul had told him the same thing. The flag ceremony was about to begin to start the game so Larry excused himself to go sit with Dianne in their season ticket seats, which Larry had owned since graduation. Carlos looked over to them before the game started and saw Larry intently typing on his phone, finishing just before kickoff.

The Bruins trounced the Beavers and beat the spread by twelve points. Carlos met Larry and Dianne after the game. Carlos remarked that Paul had nailed his forecast of the game and Larry nodded with a smile. Dianne remarked to Carlos that wasn't it wonderful that Paul and Tom had caught a couple of passes each for about eighty yards between them. Carlos felt they were truly happy for his grandson, but the smirk on Larry's face told Carlos that he had made some money on the outcome.

Another thought crossed his mind. Had Larry been confirming what he had been told by Paul prior to making a bet?

Carlos told Paul about the incident the next day and Paul just took it in stride saying Larry was always interested in what was going on with his alma mater's sports programs. Carlos asked Paul if he thought Larry was betting on these events. Paul said he didn't know and really didn't care.

Later that evening, Carlos and Carmen were talking at home and he wondered out loud if Larry had hired his grandson because of his Sicilian roots. Did he get the job because he was on the football and track team? Did Carmen think that Larry was gambling on information he got from Paul about how the team would perform? Carmen answered him directly, saying that it was no one's business but his. She only knew that he was helping her grandson as a mentor and had been very good to him in giving him the opportunity of a lifetime. That was the end of the conversation for Carmen.

Chapter 20

Lewis made once a month calls to his parents from the seminary in Santa Barbara. He was vague in his comments about how things were going, but he said he was happy with his decision. His mother kept him informed of his brother and sisters' accomplishments and asked him repeatedly when he would come home to visit. It had been almost two years since they had seen him.

On one of his monthly calls, Lewis told them his days were very full and he was part of an accelerated program the church was trying out on a trial basis. Fr. Paul had used his connections in Rome to get Lewis in the program. Basically, he was cramming four years of education and training into two intense years.

Lewis said the program was very tough on some of the students and that it had not yet yielded the results that Fr. Paul and the church had hoped for. He, on the other hand, was doing quite well, which gave his uncle hope that the program would become a long term success, especially since it was called the Morgan Curriculum.

Lewis seemed to know about Paul's accomplishments already and he asked for additional details about his brother's academic pursuits. Was he really that interested in accounting?

Why was his employer taking such a personal interest in him? Was his inexhaustible pursuit of his goals beginning to wear on him? To his parents, Lewis seemed more interested in his younger brother than in any other family member.

Angeline and Charlie were concerned about Lewis finding out that Paul and Sarina were seeing each other. They thought someone should tell Lewis about the relationship, thinking that if they didn't tell Lewis about it he might feel as though they were hiding it from him.

It was Charlie who unexpectedly dropped the news on his oldest son, "You know that Sarina and your brother have been going out."

Angeline had her ear to the telephone to hear what her son's reaction would be.

With little or no emotion, Lewis replied, "That's nice."

They could have been talking about two rocks in the yard, for all the emotion he displayed.

When his father pushed the point to get Lewis to exhibit some sort of emotion or further comment, Lewis calmly stated that he had found everything he needed in his pursuit of being a priest and knowing God. The robotic way he said it gave his parents a shock. They both worried that their eldest had been brainwashed.

During a call in late May that year, Lewis informed his parents that he would be coming home for a couple of days to see his family before he left for his assignment at the Vatican. Charlie and Angeline were shocked that he was so soon to be a full-fledged priest and traveling so far away for such a lofty position in the church.

Of course, Angeline wanted to have a large reception with neighbors, family, and friends. Lewis immediately declined that offer. He wanted to see them and his brother and sisters, and no one else. He repeated that his stay would be brief and that he had no interest in anyone else. He also mentioned in passing that there was a possibility that Fr. Paul would be in town and would want to see his brother and family also.

His parents pressed their son about his ordination or investiture that would be coming soon. They wanted to attend. Lewis bluntly informed them that no one outside of the order would be allowed to attend.

The more his parents, especially his mother, asked for details the more emphatically Lewis responded that there were no details or information that would be made available. Pure and simple, it was a private ceremony for only the order of the seminary to attend.

The conversation ended, and his parents sat speechless and motionless trying to absorb what had just transpired. They had never heard of an ordination ceremony that was closed to the family of the ordinand. They later agreed that the only good thing to come out of the telephone conversation with Lewis was that they would get to see their son after almost a year. Charlie remarked that Lewis's demeanor was reminiscent of his own brother, Paul, when he was in the seminary years ago. Charlie commented on how, for some reason, the religious order thinks of itself as above the rest of us. Like they're above us plain, ordinary human beings.

After catching her thoughts and breath, Angeline let her daughters and son know that their brother was coming home for a couple of days and was about to become a priest. When Paul received the news he was a little shocked at how fast his brother was to be ordained.

Paul brought up the subject of Sarina. Angeline told him that Lewis wanted a "family only" visit and dinner. Paul immediately stated that if Sarina wasn't invited, he wasn't coming either.

Angeline knew her youngest son and when his voice carried a certain tone, it was fruitless to do anything but relent. She said, "You're right, Sarina is family to us."

Paul told Sarina of the coming visit and she said that it might be better if she didn't attend. Paul said if she didn't go, he also would not go. They finally decided that it would be best for them to be together when Lewis arrived. They wanted no secrets about their relationship.

The big day came and Lewis Morgan, the newly minted Catholic priest, walked through the door of his parents' home. His mother believed that he was a little taller and thinner but still the same handsome young man that she and Charlie had raised and were so proud of. Lewis hugged his mother and father and then went down the line of sisters and grandparents.

Paul and Sarina were a little late to the homecoming. They entered through the back door to came face to face with Lewis. He warmly hugged his younger brother and shook hands with his past girlfriend. There was a complete absence of any animosity among them. It was a meeting of two brothers and one old friend. Lewis commented that Paul was taller and better built than the little scrawny rat he used to be.

Of course everyone in attendance watched Lewis's every move and reaction. His confidence and warmth was evident. He had become a man since they had last seen him but with his confidence was also the feeling that he was at peace with himself. He seemed to know exactly where he was and where he was going and for what purpose. No question of it.

The only doubter of the family was Carlos. He obviously was Paul's biggest champion, but he later told Carmen that he believed Lewis was hiding his true feelings. He put on a good face for everyone. She reiterated, "Can't the boy be completely happy serving the Lord?"

Carlos answered, "Show me someone who is holier than thou and I will show you a world class hypocrite." Knowing her husband's bullheadedness, Carmen let the conversation drop, but her husband had put some doubts in her head.

During his visit, youngest sister Claire never seemed to be more than two inches from her oldest brother. Ashley, on the other hand, was friendly yet apprehensive. She had watched her brother destroy her good friend Sarina with no warning and no emotion. She noticed that the interaction between Paul and Lewis was no longer two boys in discussion but two very different men who talked.

She was also aware of the difference in the facial reactions of her parents and grandparents. Her mother and father's faces shone with had pride and adoration. Her grandparents were congenial but more reserved, especially since her grandfather Carlos had always been a little wary of his first grandson. Carlos believed that Lewis had everything just a little too easy. The grades, the athletic success and the girlfriend that walked into his life. Carlos didn't believe that he ever had to scramble, fight or try. His interest now was to see if anything had changed in him that he could discern. There wasn't. He was still Mr. Charming. Carlos battled with himself over his opinions about Lewis, but it was what he felt.

The reunion could not have been going any better when there was a knock at the door. It was Fr. Paul. He walked in and hugged his sister-in-law and brother, asking, "Has Fr. Lewis Morgan arrived yet?"

Chapter 21

ONCE FR. PAUL arrived and exchanged the usual pleasantries, he made it clear that he wanted to have a meeting with just his nephews. Charlie and Angeline weren't going to let that happen. A feast of food had been prepared to feed her sons and Angeline would brook no before-dinner conversation with her brother-in-law, who would take over the itinerary. Paul concentrated on watching his uncle to see if he could catch him in a lecherous stare at Sarina. Sarina had once compared Fr. Paul to a hungry animal staring at sustenance.

Sarina walked into the dining room and, out of the corner of his eye, Paul saw his uncle fix his gaze on her in that very manner she had described. When Fr. Paul realized his nephew was watching him, he quickly refocused and asked for the potatoes to be passed to him. Paul now knew that what Sarina had told him about his uncle was true; he'd seen it before with other women when he and Lewis were on an outing with the good priest. Paul filed the knowledge of it for future reference.

Dinner progressed with the usual family banter about friends and neighbors. Lewis seemed much more engaged than he'd been at his brother's graduation and he teased his sisters as he had done before his decision to enter the priesthood.

Angeline remarked to Charlie that it seemed like a weight had been lifted off their son with his graduation from the seminary. That pleased her, but at the same time, Charlie wondered what spell his brother and the other priests had cast on his son. Charlie still had trouble coming to grips with the fact that Lewis, who seemingly had everything going for him, had forsaken his advantages to become what his uncle had become.

Charlie always wondered why his brother had "quit" the real world. Deep down he very much thought his brother would regret the decision to become a priest in his old age But with the success and wealth his brother had achieved in his position with the church, Charlie had to now consider that he'd been mistaken in his original assessment of his brother's career path. For some reason, Charlie had thought that all who took the religious path also took the vow of poverty. His brother was proving him wrong on that misconception also, as evidenced by the chauffeur and the very large diamond ring he wore. Charlie thought he could pay off his mortgage with just half the carats in that ring.

Unbeknownst to Charlie, Paul was observing his father's study of his uncle. Paul noticed how his father's facial expression flashed from admiration to contempt. Paul wondered what wheels were turning in his father's head and he realized that he would never fully understand what his father and uncle thought of each other. Paul began to think that Lewis and he had a similar relationship to his father and his uncle. Interestingly, when growing up, Paul and Lewis knew most of the time what the other was thinking, giving them a tremendous advantage in team sports. But now, with some adulthood upon them, that had almost totally faded away as they grew older and more apart.

Fr. Paul had a couple of glasses of his favorite Italian wine which he had brought with him from Rome for the dinner.

Nephew Paul took notice of the fact that the alcohol had gone to his uncle's head a little more than he had ever seen in the past. The relaxation in his manner and speech was discernible, possibly more to his nephew than to others at the table. Paul thought to himself how valuable the lessons taught to him by his mentor Larry Vandermeer were in his life.

Larry, time and time again, in the beginning of his apprenticeship at work, encouraged him to watch and observe whenever possible. He told him that the better he got at this, the better his professional results would be. Larry repeatedly said, "They're transmitting. You've just got to watch and note." He credited his powers of observation as one of the major reasons for his success in the business world.

For the first time, Paul noticed that his uncle was showing a little wear and tear. Age was finally catching up to Fr. Paul. His father, through the trials and tribulations of taking care of a family and working to support them had shown his age faster than his seemingly ageless brother. Angeline often commented to Charlie that it looked like her brother-in-law never seemed to change physically or to age. Charlie always retorted he wouldn't age either if he didn't have the real world stress of life and family.

Paul observed that there also seemed to be even more of a lifeless demeanor about his uncle. He was putting on a good face for his family, but something was weighing him down. It was unlike anything Paul had seen in the past. He wondered if his uncle had a health issue that he was hiding. In Fr. Paul's wine-induced state of relaxation, his nephew was able to glimpse many previously hidden chinks in his uncle's armor.

After dessert, Fr. Paul convened his nephews for a meeting in the back yard. That had been his plan before he had even entered the house. He had something on his mind and wanted to proceed after being sidetracked by his brother and sister-in-law and the wonderful dinner.

He immediately kicked the conversation in gear with a series of questions for Paul. "Well, what do you think of your brother getting through the seminary so quickly and being assigned to the Vatican? Aren't you proud of him? Don't you want to know what he's going to be doing at the Vatican?"

Paul was taken aback by the directness of his uncle's questions, so rather than blurt out a knee jerk response, he turned the questions back at his uncle with, "What do you think?"

Fr. Paul then broke the news that Lewis was leaving for a permanent assignment at the Vatican to study the original roots of our faith. He would spend his time with countless and priceless artifacts of the foundation of the Christian faith. Lewis was hoping to come up with a definitive plan to unite all Christian faiths as one under the holy pontiff. If Lewis was successful, his name would be forever known in the same realm as the other great religious minds in history. Immortality in the world of Christianity. What did Paul think?

Paul was surprised by the fervor of his uncle's verbal barrage. He thought to himself that his uncle missed his calling. Fr. Paul reminded him of some of Larry's sports agents he had met who claimed that their clients were the greatest at what they did and no amount of money should prevent them from being acquired.

Paul then asked his uncle if this would be the basis for his brother to rise to the position of Pope of the Catholic Church. Fr. Paul was very dismissive in his reply. "Why would Lewis want to be a figurehead when he could be the real power in the church?" Fr. Paul obviously was not in awe of the Holy Father. He said, "Throughout history, popes have rarely been anything more than photographs for the populace. They don't run or control the direction of the Vatican. That's done by very educated men who specialize in various areas. Specialists rule the church not the spiritually blessed. The church is one of the largest enterprises in the world. To be at its most effective and profitable, it must be directed as a CEO and Chairman of the Board would direct a public company. The Pope is used as a front man for the masses. Nothing more."

Paul was shocked at his uncle's revelations. The great spiritual entity that he had grown up with, and that at times had given him comfort and solace, was nothing more than a tax-free mega corporation that was in business for its own financial gain. Dealing with the faithful was a sideline. Now Paul understood his uncle's haggard appearance, which was akin to that of a division head trying to maximize his unit's profits than that of a man under the strain of the world's redemption.

Fr. Paul, under the influence of the wine, began to boast and to bemoan the world's condition. He said, "As Machiavelli wrote, if you win their hearts and their allegiance, all else is possible." So his uncle was quoting the author of *The Prince*, the architect of great rulers and despots, as his litany as to how the church operates basically above the law.

Paul interjected that today's world seems to be less church and faith oriented than at any time in history. Did Fr. Paul believe this to be true?

Fr. Paul then said in a voice so cold-hearted that his nephew would never forget it, "The faithless and non-believers will experience a holocaust that will make the Nazi treatment of the Jews during World War II seem like a picnic in the park. Hitler was a moron. He, too, was a figurehead who started to believe his own nonsense. The Nazi regime was a financially based empire. They needed capital to operate. The Jews supplied the capital and at the same time gave the German state a rallying point to right all wrongs since the time of Christ. It's bigger than just a group trying to take over the world. Religious fervor and faith will take raw nationalism far beyond the boundaries that have been set. It's like a mega-world corporate doctrine that becomes the religion of its shareholders. The Nazi's major failure was that the jackass, Hitler, began to believe his own press. He soon found out that the Fuhrer was not God the Father. The Vatican repeatedly tried to tell him that to no avail. Hell, if he hadn't taken his life, it would have been ordered."

Paul was in state of shock. Dumbstruck. In a matter of minutes, his Uncle had disemboweled the whole ideal of faith and church. As he came to his senses, he realized that he was hearing this from a "major" player in the Vatican. His lack of emotion when talking about humanity and human lives was akin to a corporate raider contemplating a hostile takeover. There was nothing personal, it was just business.

Paul thought he was going to be sick to his stomach so he excused himself to use the bathroom. His head was spinning and not because of the wine as he'd only had a couple of sips. As he left the back yard, he ran into Sarina who grabbed his hands and asked him what was wrong. He was pale and sweating and his hands were wringing wet. He told her they would talk later and proceeded to the lavatory where he vomited his mother's fabulous dinner. He sat by the toilet in a state of shock and tried to collect himself. It would take a while before he could return to his uncle and his brother.

Chapter 22

As Paul collected himself, he realized this might be a once in lifetime opportunity to get insight into an organization that was so unbelievably secretive and yet as powerful and affluent as any nation in the world. He also wondered why, other than the wine talking, his uncle would begin divulging information to him? Paul knew his uncle never did anything without an agenda. Was he part of that agenda? Larry had taught him to think of life as moves on a chess board. What seems of no consequence is of consequence and those consequences will affect you, the player. Any move should be noted, no matter how minute or seemingly unimportant.

Paul walked back through the kitchen where his parents, Sarina, and Ashley sat. He grabbed the almost full open bottle of his uncle's Italian wine and proceeded out the door to the back yard. Ashley asked, "Do you need my help brother?"

Paul answered, "Nope. Got it."

He headed outside another thought hit him. What the hell does my brother think of all of this? Is this the first time he's heard this revelation or is this the business as usual philosophy at the Vatican? Paul was determined to flush his brother out of the bushes on his personal point of view.

As soon as he appeared with the bottle of wine, protests arose from Lewis and Fr. Paul and he was greeted with a chorus of, "Oh no, we've had enough!"

Paul had equipped himself with a fresh glass and said, "We can't let this fabulous wine go to waste. It's already opened. It would be a shame to cork something this good." He continued, "You know, some of my accounting firm's clients are wineries. I've heard the owners and vintners say that an open wine bottle should be finished. Corking the remainder destroys the flavor." He poured his brother and uncle each a generous goblet.

Small talk ensued about the family and what his sisters were doing in school and in athletics. Lewis remarked that the parents looked good and didn't seem to have changed in the last couple of years, but Grandpa Carlos was looking a little older than usual. Lewis also remarked that he didn't think his grandfather liked him much as he always looked at him with a scowl. They laughed and said it might be the "old country" way of showing affection. Fr. Paul said that if he gave him a fished wrapped in newspaper and kissed both his cheeks, then that scowl would be confirmed Sicilian style. They all laughed.

Paul waited for an opening to reconvene the conversation. He was never given the chance. Lewis started it right back up, "What did you think of the real philosophy of the corporation we like to call the church? The expression on your face told me that you were both shocked and intrigued. Did I read that right, brother?"

"Well, it was certainly interesting to hear that particular explanation of the church. I suppose there are those who find it very alluring to think that people have that much power and money with no oversight or human boundaries placed on them. It very much fits the definition of a god."

Fr. Paul, who began to sip his favorite wine in earnest, laughed and said, "We supposedly serve Him when, in fact, we are trying to be Him. As history shows, we have done quite well at it. One only has to look at the balance sheets and income statements to realize the success of the philosophy. As an accountant in the making, you, of all people, should realize that."

Lewis interjected, "Whatever you want in this world can be yours if you are in the right organization. Anything and everything. Whatever the world has to offer can be gained. Where else can someone say that? I want to pursue something that will be historically significant for time immemorial. Something that will give me significance in the world and, at the same time, further the goals of the church.

"There are manuscripts and documents that could irrefutably unite almost all faiths on this earth. Where does that put the church then? As part of a single unit of church and state? And the world would be a better place. No more wars or despots, and many diseases would be eradicated. Almost a heaven on earth."

"What about free choice and the ability to make mistakes and then work to improve?" Paul asked.

Fr. Paul said, "My nephew knows his catechism well. I expected that but let's not be idealistic. The church portrays its followers as sheep for a reason. They need to be guided and they want, or should want, to follow. They never want to lead and if by chance they do, disaster will surely follow. Remember that Christ was pictured as a good shepherd."

Paul replied, "The current flavor in the world today is of erosion of marriage, free love, lack of faith and not going to church. The questioning of old guard ideals, geo politics and the now ready availability of instant knowledge and truth when before, stories could be made up and sometimes it could take years if ever to find out that the public was being lied to.

Wouldn't that be something that would have to be changed or manipulated to accomplish your goals?"

"Refocus and retooling can be accomplished much easier today than in Hitler's time, said Fr. Paul. "Communications can be used as a positive for anyone's goals. Knowledge can be made to breed fear among the sheep. When a flock thinks it hears a predator like a wolf, what does it do? It closes up ranks and lets the shepherd and his dogs guide it through the ordeal. And it does this unquestioningly. Most humanity is a glorified herd of sheep. When you understand this it makes living in it a little more palatable."

As his uncle spoke his words, Paul realized more than ever how much he disliked him. He was an egalitarian and had given himself a lofty status akin to God. He and his comrades were some sort of super humans with god-like attributes. Paul thought maybe his uncle should have studied catechism a little closer as it sure reminded him of when Lucifer, the archangel, was cast into hell. Hell, he thought, would be a fitting place for his uncle. He chuckled to himself that many of his uncle's friends and predecessors would be in attendance and his days would be spent shaking all of their hands."

Fr. Paul then abruptly changed the conversation. "Are you still going into the accounting practice after graduation? From what I hear you have a knack for it and you seem to be very involved with the owner of your firm. I have heard nothing but good things about him and your time there is not being wasted. Your parents have kept me abreast of his wanting you to take over which is a godsend in disguise.

"Though I always saw myself becoming a priest, I've thought about what a big hurdle it would have been if I had kept to the secular route, to start a practice and get it off of the ground. It's like raising a child, 24–7." Fr. Paul laughed and added, "Being a priest absolved me from the rigors of parenthood. Although there are some single mothers out there who believe I should have been a part of the pain of parenthood, not just the pleasure of the start of parenthood."

Lewis chuckled like a person who was privy to some inside joke. Paul put on the facade of a smile but inside he was even more appalled by this hypocrite. He actually felt the need to strike him, he was so disgusted.

Fr. Paul continued that when his brother Lewis got his footing and career going at the Vatican, he would like Paul to join the two of them in Rome to see firsthand what a church career had to offer. Also he would like to show Paul, as a fellow accountant, some of the programs he had invented and implemented as the Chief Financial Officer of the Vatican. "From strictly a corporate standpoint, the financial underpinnings of the church have no equal. None. It might make for a fun and informative vacation for the future tax preparer. Of course, all expenses and transportation would be supplied by me and my employer."

Fr. Paul had obviously had too much to drink and had let down his guard. Paul had never heard anything like this before. If he hadn't been sitting in the back yard and hearing it for himself, he would have never believed it. Fr. Paul was truly a chameleon. But his true character of evil and power was something that was hard for Paul to understand let alone digest. He again thought he was going to be sick to his stomach. He excused himself and retreated to the house. His brother and uncle followed him in short order.

Chapter 23

Paul arrived at the kitchen door before his brother and uncle. Sarina and Ashley were still in the kitchen talking and waiting for Paul despite the late hour. As he pulled open the screen door they both immediately noticed that Paul was pale and looked like he was going to be sick to his stomach again. He told Sarina that if she was ready to go home, he would take her.

Ashley said she wanted to accompany him. Paul agreed, but only if she would drive. The girls looked at each other as if to say, "What's up with him?" Something was wrong if Paul, who always had to be the driver, was relinquishing his keys.

Paul tossed his car keys to his sister and opened the front door for Sarina. At the car, he climbed into the back by himself. As soon as the car left the driveway questions from the front seat bombarded him. Paul weakly protested that he didn't want to discuss it right now. After continued prodding by Sarina and Ashley, he promised to fill them in soon.

As they rounded the first corner, his uncle's limousine appeared on its way back to his parents' house no doubt to pick up his uncle and take him to his hotel. Paul now understood where all the money came from to pay for these amenities. It blindly angered him all over again.

Sarina saw an expression on Paul's face that she had seen only once before. She and Lewis had run to an alley behind their high school to find Paul nearly decimating half of the varsity football team over a remark that had been made about Paul's mother. His eyes were wide and wild as if he was about to destroy anything and everything that got in his way.

Paul's eyes tonight were not the eyes of the man she had fallen hopelessly in love with. She knew in her heart that he would do anything for her. Anything. And from his expression, it would take anything and everything to stop him from whatever destruction he had on his mind.

Ashley looked in the rearview mirror and spotted that same wild look on her brother's face. She tried to make small talk to diffuse the palpable tension in the air. Very quickly they arrived at Sarina's parents' house. As Paul escorted her to her door, she grasped his hand. It was sweaty and clammy. She whispered to him to let it go saying, "Whatever was said has been said. There's nothing you can do to change any of it, so please be at peace and don't let yourself be aggravated over it."

Paul regained some of his composure with her soothing words and voice that he so loved to hear. "I'll try to not think of what was said but it's going to be very hard to be civil to Lewis and Fr. Paul the next time I see them," he conceded.

They arrived at her doorstep and he grabbed her and kissed her and told her that he loved her and she repeated the same thing. She made him promise to call her when he got up the next day. Paul said he would. They embraced again and she went inside.

When Paul returned to the car, Ashley, to break the mood of the ride over, said, "I didn't realize you wanted me to drive to a necking session between my best friend and brother. Awkward. I guess it could have been worse. The two of you could have been in the back seat together and I could have taken on the role of a taxi driver like in that television show Backseat Confessions. I guess I should thank you for *that* not happening."

Paul wore a very detached look and while he was physically present, Ashley knew that mentally and perhaps emotionally, he was very far away from the front seat of the car.

Ashley said, "Are you going to tell me what was said or are you going to just poison yourself on their venom?"

Paul answered, "Not right now. I have to collect my thoughts to give you and Sarina a totally unbiased and unemotional accounting of what was said. I will say, if you haven't figured it out by now, it was truly bad. The absolute pinnacle of evil."

Ashley's curiosity pushed her to see if her brother would at least relate some of it now. Paul emphatically said, "Absolutely not." They pulled into the Morgan driveway. Only the porch light was on. They both headed to their bedrooms.

Chapter 24

Paul took a shower to wash away the stench of what he had heard that evening. If he had hoped to stop his brain from running his brother's and uncle's comments at warp speed he had another thing coming. He got into bed and closed his eyes to release the choke hold of the evening. Again, no luck.

It was a couple of hours later around two in the morning that the analyst in Paul got the upper hand and the questions that would be key to his understanding all that he'd heard came to him. It was an analyzing process that Larry, his mentor, had taught him. Why is this being done? Whom does it profit? What happens isn't important until a person can see the start, middle and finish of the event. How does it work? Where is it going to occur?

After tossing and turning throughout what was left of the night, Paul finally fell asleep. Soon he heard the Morgan household stirring with the usual Sunday morning activities. His mother and father attended nine o'clock Mass with his youngest sister Claire. Once their children were out of high school, their attendance at church was something that neither parent thought was their business. It was left up to each individual child and his or her own conscience. The Morgans had watched many a family divide and relationships end over children's attendance at Mass.

Today was going to be especially important for Charlie and Angeline as their son Lewis, a newly ordained priest on his way to his assignment at the Vatican, was attending Mass at their longtime parish church. This was the church where Lewis and his siblings had been baptized, received first communion, said their first confessions, and had been confirmed. So it was with obvious pride that the Morgans would be joined by Fr. Morgan in their usual pew.

Through his closed door, Paul heard Ashley say that she was going to a later Mass because of the headache she had from the night before.

Then came the inevitable knock on Paul's door. It was Lewis asking when Paul would be ready to go with the family to Mass. Paul gave Lewis what sounded to his own ears like a lame excuse, saying that he Sarina had already made plans to go to a later Mass with Ashley. For a brief moment, Lewis considered debating this with his younger brother, but the expression on Paul's face told him that he was in no mood for discussion of any kind. Case open and closed. They left for Mass in Angeline's minivan. They were meeting the grandparents at church for this noteworthy event.

Ashley came in to see her brother right after the family left. She had just texted Sarina not to go to the nine o'clock Mass as she and Paul had said they were planning to go to a later service with her. Sarina was just about to go out the door expecting to meet up with Paul and Ashley at the church.

The change in plans further fueled her curiosity about what had happened the previous evening. She texted Ashley to let her know that, since the house was empty, she was heading over to hold Paul to his promise from last night.

When Ashley informed Paul that Sarina was on her way over, he jumped in the shower to get cleaned up before his girlfriend showed up. By the time Sarina arrived, Paul and Ashley had made themselves presentable.

Ashley offered to make coffee but Paul asked Sarina to make it. He said he preferred Sarina's coffee to Ashley's, even though he had raved about Ashley's coffee for years. Ashley was a bit put off when she heard this, but decided not to make a big deal about it. She watched Sarina, looking for some secret ingredient or process that was different from her own The ingredients and process were identical. If these two people in the kitchen with her hadn't been her two favorite people in the world, she would have made an issue of it, but she refrained.

The three sat down and Paul was given the floor. He had thought about what he could say that would not make either of the girls a target later on. By the cold blooded way Fr. Paul had spoken, Paul wondered if his family was also a target of the Vatican. He relayed to the girls, all the controversial views expounded by Fr. Paul about the church, the Pope, and the façade by the "real" leaders of the church to put forth the belief that it was all about helping humanity find God when in reality, it was all about money.

Sarina and Ashley agreed that Fr. Paul had his head up his ass, but both wondered if Paul had misunderstood what his uncle had said. Paul defended himself, saying that if they'd been there, they would realize the full impact and venom of his verbal barrage. Paul then realized that his Cliff Notes version hadn't accurately reflected the full meaning of his uncle's diatribe but he wasn't about to endanger either one of them by allowing them to know too much. Paul didn't trust either his uncle or the church.

The girls asked the same question almost simultaneously. "How did Lewis react during Fr. Paul's rant? He couldn't have possibly agreed with him, could he?"

Paul had thought about how he would handle this question before it arose. Would he make Lewis out to be the genius or jackass? Would he throw Lewis under the bus? Paul decided he would lie. He said he thought Lewis was only being respectful of his uncle and, more importantly, his superior in the church, and those couldn't possibly be his brother's views. Paul wondered if the girls were convinced. He had an idea that they knew he was lying. They did.

They talked a bit more and then Paul asked if they wanted to go to noon Mass. It would probably get them out of the house before everyone came back and would give them the opportunity to miss Sunday lunch which seemed to appeal to them all. Then Paul suggested they cut Mass and go out to lunch instead. All agreed, but Sarina wanted to go home and change out of her church clothes.

A plan was hatched to say they went to a nearby church to hear Mass in a more casual setting. They did their due diligence about the other church and full-proofed their charade in case they were questioned about the services. It was more likely they would not be.

Paul was also pleased that this plan helped him avoid seeing and talking to his brother, which was a good thing after last night. Little did he know Sarina and Ashley thought the same.

Chapter 25

THE THREE SINNERS went to lunch at a Mexican restaurant about three miles from their parish church and about a mile further from their home. They knew there was no chance of any family members showing up there since it was mandatory after mass that the Morgans congregate for Sunday lunch. With the exception of Paul and Ashley, the Morgans weren't much for Mexican food with the grandparents not liking it at all.

They agreed that since they had committed a sin for missing mass there was no harm in compounding their transgression with a round or two of margaritas. As Ashley said, if you're guilty on one count, why not throw in some more on the same incident. The conversation was light and joking and everyone had the good sense not to bring up the previous evening.

Sarina noticed that Paul looked extremely tired at times during lunch and that his thoughts were not totally on where he was. She knew that whatever had been said had deeply hurt him and wondered if she would ever learn the full story. Ashley observed the same and vowed to herself that somehow she would get the full story out of someone.

As the second round ensued, Ashley's cell phone rang and their home phone number came up on the display. She almost didn't answer but figured that if she didn't there would be a message and follow-up calls until she did.

She took the call and her mother asked where she was. Ashley explained that they'd gone to a restaurant after mass. Her mother had thought that she and Paul would have known there would be lunch after mass at the house. Lewis was leaving in a couple of hours. Didn't they want to spend some time with him? Who knew when he would be back from Rome?

Lewis wanted to know if Paul could take him to the airport. Of course, Angeline and Charlie wanted to ride along but Lewis wanted to spend some one-on-one time with his younger brother.

Angeline went on to say how proud she and Charlie were of their eldest. "Everyone at church wanted to shake his hand and congratulate him on becoming a priest. Even the very old Monsignor John came out of retirement to supplement the sermon with a congratulatory message that lasted over five minutes and received four standing ovations from the parishioners."

Angeline said the experience was like a movie star winning the Oscar instead of a Sunday Mass. She started talking about Lewis being mobbed after the service when Ashley interrupted saying she had to go and that they would be home in a little bit.

Ashley quickly ended the call and looked around the table. Anyone with half a brain would have been able to ascertain the conversation.

Ashley said, "What a lousy way to end a great meal." She was getting a buzz from the margaritas.

Sarina glanced at Paul and saw the face of a man who looked like he had been captured and was en route back to prison.

They arrived at the Morgan home to find it filled with well-wishers, neighbors, and family friends. It wasn't a Sunday lunch as much as it was a gigantic buffet. The number of people was startling. Paul welcomed them as it took the pressure off of him having to listen to select family members praise his older brother.

Charlie spotted the three of them at the door and asked, "Was the mass you went to conducted in a bar?"

They were prepared and Ashley took the lead. "St. Bonaventure takes a more casual approach."

Charlie retorted, "It looks like you're dressed more for St. Adventure's than St. Bonaventure.

Paul and Sarina searched out where Lewis was holding court and headed in the opposite direction. Ashley wasn't as lucky. Her mother snagged her into helping in the kitchen.

Lewis was in the den so Sarina and Paul headed to the back yard. Sarina told Paul that he needed to think about what he had and not risk it for anyone.

"Your brother and uncle are not worth it. Trust me. I, of all people, know that about Lewis. They are damaged, you are not. Don't you make a mistake that makes you damaged goods as well. Besides I love you and don't even like them."

Paul smiled. "Sarina, as always your logic makes perfect sense to me. I promise I will not blow it, but you should know there is something going on with them that relates to the Vatican that I am really curious about. I don't know if I can let it go, but if I proceed, I'll do it 'Larry Vandermeer style.' They'll never know what I am up to."

They both laughed. It helped break the mutual tension of being back at the house.

Angeline appeared to tell Paul it was time to take his brother to the airport. Paul dreaded the two plus hours each way to LAX and the thought of being a captured audience sickened him. Lewis appeared asked, "Are you ready for some brother-to-brother time, little brother?"

Claire and Ashley had been enlisted to carry their eldest brother's suitcase and carry-on bag to Paul's car. Sarina waited in vain for the invitation from Paul to come with them. Lewis received a call on his cell phone and learned that the travel arrangements had been changed. Fr. Paul's private jet had been diverted to Burbank Airport and they would make the flight to Rome on his plane. A town car would be at the house in five minutes to bring him right to the plane. Lewis would not need to go through security. Fr. Paul would see Lewis in about twenty minutes.

Paul felt like Christmas had just come. He'd been given a reprieve on spending unwanted time with his brother by, of all people, good old Fr. Paul.

Lewis ended the call and said to Paul, "It looks like you just dodged hours on the San Diego freeway. Fr. Paul is picking me up in his private jet in Burbank. He also said there is a town car en route to pick me up so I can go directly to the plane. It's funny. I thought he left for Rome last night. Maybe after drinking all that wine, he decided to go today. This makes things a lot easier for everyone."

Paul thought to himself, you have no idea.

Lewis said to Paul, "Let's get the bags out of your car and I'll say my goodbyes on the way out. I want a couple of minutes to talk with you in private."

He leaned over to hug Sarina goodbye and she recoiled from him, thrusting her right hand forward to shake his hand instead. Paul thought, now that was awkward but that's my girl. Lewis looked a little dumbstruck.

Lewis embraced his parents and sisters. Paul had cut around to the side of the house to meet him. Before he left the back yard, he grabbed Sarina and kissed her passionately in the hope that Lewis would turn around at just that instant.

Sarina gave him a look. "What are you doing? Are you using me to show up your brother?

Paul smiled. "No. I kissed the most special person in my life out of sheer love. Now I have to go listen to his brother-to-brother talk, but I promise I'll be good."

By the time Lewis got to the front of the house, the driver had already stowed his bags and was waiting for him. Lewis walked over to Paul and the driver, who were making small talk.

Before Lewis could say anything, the driver said, "Your uncle has been calling to make sure you're on your way to the plane. He doesn't want to have to change the flight plan, especially on a Sunday afternoon in a small busy airport."

Lewis looked at Paul. "This will have to wait."

"Yes, but you and Fr. Paul should know that I am very interested in what was said last night, very interested. When I graduate, I will come and spend some time with you and Fr. Paul in Rome."

They hugged and the car was gone in flash. Paul congratulated himself on being spared the agony of being in the same car with his brother during the long drive to LAX, and on having planted a very fertile seed that would germinate in his uncle's brain.

Chapter 26

PAUL HAD LITTLE time to mull over the weekend's festivities as he drove to work early Monday morning. Tom needed a ride, not so much because he didn't have a car, he did, but because if Paul picked him up he knew he would be on time. They were very close friends and Tom kept no secrets from his friend. Paul on the other hand, did not let Tom into certain parts of his life. He did not believe in full disclosure except to Sarina, and even that had some caveats. Larry knew a lot about Paul but not all. For over two years Paul's mentor had gotten really good at reading the emotions and mind of his heir apparent.

Larry was already at his desk working on this mid-June morning. There were no deadlines or due dates to be met, but this was how he'd become successful, and to his credit he loved it. When Paul and Tom walked in and greeted him, Paul studied Larry briefly and thought that Larry could retire at any time or take a lesser role in the firm that he had painstakingly built from the ground up. This thought was immediately followed by a remembrance of Fr. Paul's remarks on Saturday night about not having the guts, for lack of a better word, to build a private practice on his own. And so his uncle had taken the easy route and became a member of the clergy, being educated at the world's best schools at the church's expense. Not Paul's idea of a challenging career and life.

Within a couple of minutes, Larry handed Paul a cup of coffee and shut the office door. They chit chatted about the weekend and Larry asked, "When do you and Tom start the serious two-a-day drills for football."

Paul replied, "They start after the first of July."

Larry asked what Paul thought of this year's team so far.

"It looks a lot like last year, with a lot of returning players. But the majority of the good players are seniors. I sure hope that we have existing or new players that can step up and fill the void next year, or it's gonna be a bad final year for me and Tom as seniors.

Larry laughed and said, "That's always the way. It starts to work and it has to be changed. I heard your brother was in town and the good reverend accountant from the Vatican was with him."

"Yeah, it was just great," Paul answered sarcastically. Larry could tell by the look and sound of Paul that it had not been a great weekend. Larry began to probe and dig for more details.

Paul knew exactly where this was going so he told Larry, "Let's just cut to the chase and lay the cards on the table."

Larry chuckled, "You know me way too well."

Paul told Larry the whole story with no holds barred and no information omitted. Paul trusted Larry and knew that Larry would know right away if he was not telling the whole story. Paul was still tired from Saturday night and was eager to offload some of the burden of what he'd heard.

As Paul talked, Larry nodded. "I knew those holier-than-thou bastards were no damn good. Beware of people who claim to do good for others; often they're in it for themselves. You know, I would love to run a forensic audit on those bastards. Wouldn't that be an interesting study?"

Throughout their conversation, Paul's cell phone had continually buzzed. Larry said to Paul, "You better see who's trying to reach you. It sounds like it might be an emergency."

There were a number of texts from Ashley with the same message: Call me ASAP. Paul said, "It's Ashley. She needs to talk to me. I better call her back and see what she's so excited about on a Monday morning."

Paul dialed her and she answered on the first ring. "I got it! I got it! I got it! I got accepted to UCLA and got a scholarship! Are you proud of me?"

"What? I didn't know you wanted to go to UCLA. Of course I'm proud of you!" Paul exclaimed.

"Well, I was afraid I wouldn't be accepted and I didn't want to disappoint the family.

By this time, Larry had gotten the gist of the conversation and asked to speak to Ashley. They had met briefly a number of times when she'd come to the office or when they attended her brother's football games.

"Congratulations," Larry said. "It's a great school as you well know. I'm a proud alumnus and your brother will do his alma mater proud when he graduates." They made some small talk and Larry asked, "I realize it's too soon to really know, but do you have any idea what your major is going to be?"

"I'm not a hundred percent sure," Ashley replied. "But I'm fascinated by what Paul is doing. I've been considering accounting. I like numbers and I can see how much Paul enjoys what he's doing. It sounds very interesting to me."

Larry laughed. "Don't believe everything he tells you. Remember he plays football and more than likely has impaired judgment due to the head blows he's sustained from playing."

They both laughed and then Larry asked if she needed a job for the summer, possibly as an intern as her brother had done two years before. He would make sure she was paid better than he'd been. Was that of interest to her?

"Oh, yes. Thank you very much, Mr. Vandermeer."

"When can you come in and look over the job description and get a feel for the position? Are you as good a worker as your brother?"

She immediately responded, "Oh, I'm much better and smarter. I can come in tomorrow if that works for you, Mr. Vandermeer."

"Perfect. See you at eleven o'clock. We'll have lunch afterward."

He handed the phone back to Paul who looked as if he was in a state of shock. Ashley was hysterical on the other end. Paul told her he would talk to her later and hung up.

He asked Larry, "Are you sure about this?"

Larry was quick to explain. "In the future, this will be your firm. But for now, I'm still in charge and running the show. Yes, I'm sure. I've been inquiring about Ashley's grades and aptitude tests. I have a friend in the registrar's office at UCLA who told me they planned to accept her as an incoming freshman. What's not to be sure about? She comes with a better recommendation than you did and look how well you've worked out.

Paul realized that he shouldn't have been surprised. Larry was thorough in his decision making process. He said, "I guess I should thank you for helping my sister."

Larry waved Paul's thanks off. "It's a business decision to improve the firm and it just happens that she's your sister. And that brings me to another topic I wanted to discuss with you. Do you have a problem with your lady friend Sarina working here too? I have a client who runs a top notch employee placement business that Sarina has registered with. She listed you as a reference and the owner of the business called me about her. She mentioned that you worked for me. I told him that I've met Sarina a number of times and that she is charming and intelligent, and that her only flaw, one that could be fatal to a good career, was her association with you. I took the liberty of asking him to hold the placement because I might have a position for her, and I wanted to talk to you about it first. What do you think?"

Paul stammered, "I don't know what to say." Again Larry's generosity was way beyond anything he ever could have expected.

"It's not generosity or a gift. You earned this and we need someone to take over for Dianne when she and I ride off into the sunset. You will need a Dianne to keep the firm running at the necessary pace. I know she is the only distraction in your life, as well she should be. It's a win-win for everyone. So do I have your blessing or should I just override you since I'm the boss?"

Paul again stuttered, "Thank you."

Larry, noticing his stuttering, jokingly said, "If that speech impediment continues, I have a client who's a speech coach who could help you with that stutter." He laughed uncontrollably.

Larry concluded the meeting with, "I'll call my client and tell him we want Sarina. Then I'll have Dianne call her and set up the appointment at the same time as your sister's tomorrow.

"Maybe you should tell your sidekick, Tom, to dress better than he usually does because we have two important job candidates visiting tomorrow for lunch. Don't tell him who they are. Let's see how he handles this surprise. My guess is he pisses on himself.

"Oh, and isn't it about time he started driving himself to work and being responsible for getting here on time? He's a big boy. He should be able to handle that instead of having to depend on someone else. Don't tell him I said this, but his skill and work level have greatly improved as of late. He's much more focused than he was in the beginning. I also like the fact that he is scared shitless of me. The gun in the desk trick worked well with him. Remember, say nothing."

Chapter 27

PAUL THOUGHT HE had it all. He worked for someone who appreciated him for his work ethic and loyalty and who wanted to teach him everything about the business.

Larry, on the other hand, had found the kind of employee he'd been seeking for quite some time—a worthy successor to take over the accounting practice that he'd worked so hard to create. His criteria were very exact and for a long while he had doubted that he'd ever find the perfect candidate that he had now in Paul. Larry would ensure that Paul would learn every aspect of the business. It would not be easy for Paul and nothing would be handed to him.

Paul wondered why Larry had been so generous with him. Was he the son Larry never had? The family he didn't have? Other than Dianne, there wasn't anybody in his personal or family life. Paul had the impression that this was an area Larry didn't want to discuss and so they never went there. Paul knew what a calculating business mind his employer had so he tried to look at it from Larry's point of view. He made sure that Paul had his sister, girlfriend, and friend working there. He knew that Larry felt it would solidify the firm, and in turn, make it a better running machine. More revenue would follow. Everything he did was ultimately for this end result.

Paul was not surprised when Sarina phoned to tell him the big news and wanted to know if he had anything to do with it. And wasn't it great that Ashley would be working there as well?

"I think it's great, Sarina, Paul said. "He wouldn't have made the offer if he didn't think you would make a positive difference in the firm. Larry's extremely generous, and he knows that he'll get our best efforts in return.

"Ashley caught me completely off guard. I didn't know she had an interest in accounting. But when I think of Larry's other moves, it makes perfect sense to keep the 'family' talent in his firm. Ashley will be a success in whatever she pursues. She makes Lewis and me look like lightweights in the focus and accomplishment department. But you would know that better than anyone, Sarina, since she's your best friend. Yes, it's going to be fun to have you here, but it'll also be a lot of work. I know the end result will be more than worth it. I'll see you tonight."

Ashley texted Paul to come by the house before he went to see Sarina. She needed his opinion on something very important. He dropped Tom off, deciding to save telling him of Larry's belief that Tom should drive himself to work for a later date, and he headed home. When he arrived at the house, his parents and Claire greeted him from the dinner table and told him that Ashley had missed dinner and was busy in her room. Paul headed up the stairs to see her. When he opened the door, her entire wardrobe was on her bed.

She ran to her brother and hugged him. "Paul, I'm so excited to be given this great job opportunity. As you can see, my biggest problem is what am I going to wear? It has to be business-like and professional. I need your opinion. I don't want to look out of place. I have to look perfect for my interview tomorrow."

Paul said, "The best barometer of what to wear in the office would be Dianne. You have to ask yourself, would Dianne wear this? If not, don't do it. I've seen staff come and go for various infractions but I think the number one infraction for a pink slip is attire that's not appropriate for the workplace. So if you want my opinion, watch what she wears and you'll be okay."

Ashley's next question was, "But first I need to get through the interview and I don't know what Dianne wears to the office. Which of these do you think she would wear?"

Paul looked at the mess of dresses on the bed and pointed. "That one looks like something she would wear." The decision was made.

Next, Paul went to see Sarina. Low and behold the same scenario was played out with her wardrobe decision. Paul only hoped he was right in his selections. He was no "fashion maven."

He picked Tom up the next morning and to his surprise found him looking quite dapper in a sport coat and tie. Paul always out-dressed Tom, but this morning it was a dead heat. Paul took the opportunity to delicately relay Larry's desire for Tom to show up in his own vehicle, on time, to show that he could do it on his own.

Again Paul was surprised when Tom responded, "I think that's a great idea." I'm sure I can get there on time, and driving my own car gives me options in the afternoon when we don't have football or track practice, to go places that are not on your agenda. But, I do think it would be stupid not to car pool when we have practice. Maybe we should split the travel between my car and your car."

Paul thought, Larry's right, Tom is getting more mature. Paul said, "Sure that works."

Tom continued the conversation. "Say, do you know who these new people are who are coming in at eleven?"

"I'm not sure, "Paul said.

"I knew the firm was growing but Larry seems committed to growing it even bigger." Tom commented.

"You know. Tom, Larry says that you should always be five years out in your planning and thinking. If you are, your firm will look and produce how you want it to. If you wait to have the receivables pay for it, your opportunity to grow will be lost. He always preaches this to his clients and to me. Hell, don't you remember it from our last management meeting, or were you asleep?"

Tom laughed and said he remembered. "Larry is the only guy I've ever met or worked for who practices what he preaches. He tells his clients what he does that makes his practice successful and in turn he helps them with their growth. That's why he's a great mentor to us. He knows and does what it takes to grow a business."

Paul remembered back to one of his first conversations with Larry about how long he intended to continue to work. Larry said that he didn't think he could ever retire. "But in six to eight years I'd like to slow down and work when I want to and start enjoying my success by taking Dianne on those trips we couldn't take while I was building the business." He then went on to say, "I want someone to not only maintain the firm but to keep growing it. Someone who, whether I am lying on a beach in the Bahamas or Rio or wherever, I can be assured is managing the firm as I would."

That's why Larry's hiring Ashley and Sarina right now, Paul thought. Genius, pure genius.

In five years, Paul would have finished school and completed his CPA certification. He'd have two years as a fully productive accountant in the firm. The same for Tom. Ashley would be finished with school and have or just about finished her CPA certification. Sarina would have graduated and have four years learning the ins and outs of the firm from Dianne.

They arrived at the office and immediately went their separate ways; both of them were busy. The morning flew by uninterrupted until ten minutes to eleven. He had told his sister and Sarina that arriving at an appointment ten minutes early was something that would be noted positively by Larry.

They came together and no doubt tried to calm each other down. Dianne met them and had tea brought in. They went to the conference room, affectionately known as the glass palace, which had recently been redecorated. She spoke to them in a motherly fashion, rather than the interviewer talking to prospective job candidates. From the expressions on the girls' faces they were relaxed and were enjoying themselves within five minutes. This made Paul feel even better about Larry hiring both of them.

Tom managed to find an excuse to walk by the conference room to see who the job candidates were and was shocked to see Ashley and Sarina. He nodded to them as he went by and Ashley waved at him. He smiled and then headed to Paul's office.

"Did you know about this?" he asked Paul.

"Yes."

"Why didn't you tell me when I asked you about it this morning?"

Paul told him that Larry didn't want him to know who was coming in.

Tom wanted to know why.

"I'll tell you but first, stand up." Tom stood up and Paul laughed.

"What's so funny?"

"Larry said you would probably piss on yourself and he

specifically asked me not to tell you what was going on. And as you well know, when he asks you to do something, it better be done."

"Okay, so the two of you have had your fun. Great. What do you think of his decision?" Tom asked.

"What were we discussing on the way in? Larry is looking five years into the future. Enough said."

Larry appeared at Paul's office and asked if there was a meeting going on that he was not aware of.

"Of course not," Tom replied, "We can't have a meeting without the boss there, boss."

When Larry asked Tom what he thought, Tom gave him the thumbs up signal.

"Glad you're on board," Larry said, half joking. "Not that it matters if you're not."

Larry looked at Paul. "Did Tom wet his panties?"

Paul grinned. "Amazingly, he didn't." They all laughed.

Larry checked his watch and told them that the town car would be there at noon. "We're dining at Mama Lisa's so if you have any work to finish it would be a good idea to get it done before then.

Chapter 28

THE CHAUFFEUR APPEARED in the reception area dressed as if he was going to drive the President of the United States to a formal dinner. Of course the owner of the town car and limousine company was a client of the firm and he and Larry had been close friends since their childhood.

From overhearing snippets and short remarks from Larry over the last two years, Paul gathered that Larry had bailed Tony out of trouble a number of times. Tony's penchant for automobiles had begun with multiple grand theft auto violations. His focus on cars, especially other people's high-end cars, started when he was about fourteen years old. He 'borrowed' cars that didn't belong to him for his various errands and speeding contests. So it seemed only natural that Tony ended up in the auto business.

Paul knew from Tony's tax returns that he had done very well. Tony commented every time he met with Larry, "Who would have believed that a two-bit hot-wiring hustler could ever have a business that does this well? It's a blessing."

Dianne, Ashley and Sarina were waiting in the reception area when Paul and Larry joined them. Dianne and Paul knew of Larry's obsession with punctuality. Naturally, Tom was the last to arrive prompting Larry to make his obligatory remark, "Tom is always the caboose of the train or the ass end of the mule." Everyone laughed.

Together, they headed to the stretch limousine parked in front of the office. The new recruits were duly impressed as the chauffeur opened the door for them. It was only a couple of miles to the restaurant, and Larry immediately launched into its history. Lisa Storey, the proprietress of the Italian restaurant, was an east coast transplant to California. According to Larry, she had been operating the restaurant in Westwood for the past year, but in no way was she a neophyte in a commercial kitchen. Larry surmised that she was probably born in one in New York. She was a daughter of Angelo Carmine. The Carmines, for the last eighty or so years, had operated every Italian restaurant of note on both sides of the Hudson.

Lisa's great-grandfather had worked at the original pizzeria in Little Italy in New York as a chef. He was a legend for his coal fired pizzas and other Italian dishes. Lorenzo Lombardi, the inventor of the pizza pie, had taught him to master the art of a great pizza. The restaurant, started by Lombardi in 1899, still exists today. It is the only restaurant in New York that uses a coal fired oven. Larry joked that either the politicians personally knew how good the pizza was or they didn't want to piss off some Sicilian who eats there, thereby shortening their life. The tradition continues undisturbed.

When Lombardi began to slow down, Angelo and family were ready to step in and purchase the business. When not busy at the restaurant, Lorenzo was busy at home procreating his own company. The children began to arrive almost like clockwork and in eleven years there were ten children, eight girls and two boys. Lorenzo loved his family and it was expected at an early age that they would help out in the kitchen.

His kids could toss the now famous pizza dough high with artistry and skill most experienced chefs couldn't master in a lifetime. With the next generation of grandchildren, Lorenzo began to accumulate restaurants in both New York and New Jersey. It was easy to see why; their food had no competition. Not only did they make the best pizza on earth, they also prepared Italian courses that made imported Italian chefs cry and throw their hands up in surrender.

The Carmines usually took the opportunity to enlist those chefs into their ranks with the promise that they could learn the art from the master. Most took advantage of the offer and almost none of them ever left. Their allegiance to the Carmines was unwavering. They stayed until they retired or died. The Carmine empire had done well enough that they had a pension plan for their longtime employees unlike anything in existence at the time. In addition, the working conditions were so family-like that most employees had to be driven out of the restaurant. It was truly a unique multi-generational business that continued to prosper.

Larry finished his history lesson just as they pulled up in front of the restaurant. They were met by the doorman who escorted them to a private booth that had been prepared for them. The physical premises were something one would expect to see in one of Rome's greatest gastronomes. Both the exterior and the interior of the restaurant were classic and rich but not lavishly overdone. No cheesy gold and flash here, as in the Las Vegas-type establishments that tended to flourish in Southern California. Strangely, that gaudiness was only a hit there and in Las Vegas.

The six of them were immediately aware of the two wait staff and their four assistants. From the manner in which they were greeted and spoken to, it was obvious they were very well trained but not stiff and robotic. Larry ordered wine and appetizers. He and Dianne had been eating here since it had opened. Sarina and Ashley, who sat side by side, kneed each other under the table and mentioned to Larry and Dianne how nice the restaurant and staff were.

Larry said that in New York they know how to run a great establishment because if it's not better than great there, the competition will eat you alive. "The Carmines have always run a top notch establishment," Larry finished.

Lisa appeared at the table as if on cue. Larry stood and kissed her hand and she hugged Dianne. Larry made introductions around the table. Paul was impressed both with her beauty and her sheer presence. She was someone you would not only like to meet but would love to talk to. Larry insisted that she sit down. She said for just a minute, because she wanted to oversee their lunches after they ordered. She described the menu and asked each of them their likes and dislikes and then made suggestions. Paul thought, most people aren't asked this many questions before they have major surgery. It was obvious that she wanted her customers to enjoy an unforgettable dining experience in a beautiful atmosphere.

Now Paul began to study Lisa in the analytical manner that Larry had taught him. She was typically Italian or Sicilian. He thought it would be difficult to guess her age, which was not usually the case. She gave the impression that she was very happy and content to be a master chef and owner of this restaurant, but at the same time he suspected she would probably be happy cooking in a cheap diner because it gave her satisfaction to feed people.

Paul's observations continued. Her face was something out of a Botticelli painting. Her nose was not the classic parrot beak but a much more subdued high fashion classic euro nose. The last name of Storey was probably an infusion of some English line into the Carmine equation. It was obvious that Lisa's mother was a Carmine.

The waiters reappeared to take the lunch orders and Lisa used the opportunity to excuse herself. Paul's interest was piqued and he waited for his chance to ask Larry about her. Before Paul could begin, Ashley prodded Larry with a myriad of questions about Lisa and her family. She wanted to know how old Lisa was and why she'd come to California. Paul thought, there's a lot of my sister in me and she's going to be like a duplicate of me working at the firm.

Larry explained, "Lisa was raised in the Carmine tradition."

He continued. "Starting with Lorenzo's offspring, it was expected, no, it was mandatory to go to college. Carmine wanted his family to be educated artisans in the kitchen. The Carmine way was the Carmine way. You never changed the formula or the recipe. You just didn't. It works, so don't mess with it. Just work with it, not on it. Lisa went to the University of San Diego for a business degree. Dating back to her grandfather Angelo, Catholic college was preferred. The church had been instrumental in keeping the doors open in the beginning years at Lombardi's due to the patronage of their fellow Catholics. Lorenzo Lombardi supposedly got the idea for pizza because it was a portable Italian dish that was perfect for church functions. A box and dough. It was that simple.

"So Lisa graduated and returned to be a master chef at one of the many restaurants the family owned. One day she had a wild idea. Why can't we bring Carmines to the west coast? And after extensive research with the family, she opened her restaurant here in Westwood."

Ashley asked, "Is the restaurant hers or the family's?"

Larry assured her that the restaurant was owned by Lisa

but with the family's support. He said, "I should know, I'm her accountant."

Ashley continued, "Why isn't it called Carmine's?"

Larry turned to Paul. "She already has my verbal client questionnaire method perfected before she even starts."

To Ashley, he said, "The Carmine family, even with their extensive number of establishments, never wanted the family name to be associated with anything that remotely resembles a chain. Their model and success is built upon the premise of individual restaurants that use the Carmine family formula."

Lunch arrived and drew everyone's focus to the food and drink. No one reached for the wine until Larry and Dianne had taken a couple of sips. Then Larry said, "It's okay to sip some wine at lunch, Tom and Paul. Just don't meet with clients with it on your breath." Everyone poured either a white or red wine that was complimentary to what they were eating. The food was fabulous.

About halfway through the meal, Ashley continued with her questions to Larry. "What is Lisa's age?"

Larry laughingly said he couldn't divulge client information.

"She was married once, but not anymore."

"She is very beautiful," Ashley remarked.

"Yes she is. And you ought to see her mother, a knockout."

With the main course now served small talk ensued among them, only broken up by repeated remarks about how good the food was. Forks of the various meals were exchanged as they tried each other's entrees. Lunch was excellent for all. As if on cue, the waiter arrived to remind them to leave room for a dessert that was especially prepared for them by Lisa herself. They glanced at each other as Tom asked the waiter what the dessert was.

With a smile on his face, the waiter replied, "The restaurant's specialty and most noted dessert, Lisa's cannoli. Everyone loves them." All silverware and nibbling ceased instantly. Not because everyone knew of them, it was the manner in which the waiter had described Lisa's specialty. You knew it was a winner before it touched your lips.

Shortly thereafter Lisa and the waiter appeared with a large platter of cannolis. Tom looked like a small kid on Christmas morning. "Wow!" he exclaimed. Once they had been served and were enjoying them, Larry motioned to Lisa to sit down with them.

She again said only for a moment. She was showered with compliments on the cannoli. Ashley, of course had questions. "Where did you get the recipe?"

"It's an old Sicilian family recipe."

"Did your mother teach you how to make them?" Sarina asked.

"No. My grandmother taught me."

"They're delicious. I mean, it may well be the best thing I've ever eaten," Sarina continued.

"Thank you." Lisa rose and thanked them for visiting.

Larry looked at his watch and said to Lisa, "Thank you for the great meal, as always. It's time I get us back to the salt mine." And just like that the maître d arrived at the table to let Larry know that his car was waiting.

The short trip back to the office was not as talkative as before. Ashley asked Larry if the firm did the accounting for the entire Carmine family of restaurants.

Larry chuckled and said to Paul, "Maybe we ought to put Ashley into marketing and promotion."

To Ashley he answered, "No. We don't handle all the accounting for the Carmine family. We do a small portion. The main crux of the work is done in New York. I would have to be five or six times larger to be able to handle just them. It's not in my business plan to be a firm that large and have only one major client. I like a diversified client base. Anyway, I declined the family's offer."

"The Carmines offered it to you?"

"No, the Mafia did," Larry said. It was very quiet the rest of the way to the office.

Chapter 29

PAUL MORGAN'S JUNIOR and senior years at UCLA were at the same time eventful and predictable. Larry's generosity continued when he gave both Paul and Tom sizable raises at the start of their junior year. In fact, their pay scale was equal to a journeyman certified public accountant. Tom was shocked in a pleasant sense and spoke to Paul about it. "Why is he being so generous with our pay checks?"

"We're the definite future of the firm, so Larry wants to tie us to the firm in every way he can. Generosity and good business practice, all rolled into one. Larry is the consummate business man," Paul explained.

One of the first orders of business for Paul was to look for a condo to purchase that was in close proximity to the office and school. He started with the idea that renting was the way to go, but Larry set both boys straight. He told them that buying was a better financial investment. Larry also advised them each to get their own place as the responsibility and image would improve their professionalism.

He went even further to say that they should look into the purchase of new vehicles as well.

"I already have a good car," Paul said.

Larry fired back immediately that he should give his car to his sister, so she and Sarina would have reliable and safe transportation to go to school and work. With the job opportunity and wanting to be near Paul, Sarina had made the decision to transfer to UCLA her senior year. Larry felt his two future partners should drive vehicles that spoke of their success at the firm. He told them that to be successful, one must first look successful. He had a great realtor and car guy to help them with their purchases. As he was leaving Paul's office, he cast a barb at Tom, "Living near the office will help you get to work on time."

Tom and Paul looked at each other and Paul shrugged. "If Larry says it's the right thing to do, then we damn well better do it. He knows our financial situation better than we do. What he said makes a lot of sense and it would cut out a tremendous amount of travel time between here and North Hollywood."

They began looking at condos near the office. Paul immediately enlisted Sarina's opinion and input. They agreed that their relationship had only one destination—the altar at St. Charles—when they were financially stable. They tossed around the idea of moving in together, but they scrapped that idea because their conventional Catholic families would frown on it. Their relationship was very intimate but very private. They loved each other a great deal but gave the outward appearance of nothing serious. The people close to them knew how crazy they were about each other.

Paul finally settled on a two bedroom condo not far from the Egyptian Theatre, within walking distance of most of his classes and the office. Tom looked in the same complex and settled for a one bedroom on the opposite side.

Tom did something that struck Paul as odd. Tom asked Ashley to look at the condo. When Paul asked him about it, Tom just shrugged it off as needing a woman's input on his future purchase. Paul wasn't convinced, but he was too busy to meddle in his best friend's purchase. The thought crossed his mind that he should be more attentive to the interactions between his sister and his best friend. He wondered if there was something going on between them.

The car purchases followed the same process except for Larry having the firm lease them for the future partners. When Paul protested that it was too generous Larry responded, "I either lease the cars and help two of my most trusted employees or give the money to the god damn treasury department. No choice, my colleague."

So Paul opted for the high-end Audi sedan and Tom acquired the sportier BMW coupe. Larry jabbed at Tom, "Once a player, always a player."

Paul silently thought to himself, maybe not so much anymore.

Ashley was overwhelmed that her brother was giving her his car. He had kept it in great condition but when he transferred the title to it to her, Larry stepped in and asked to borrow it for the day.

Ashley thought that was odd. "Sure," she agreed. When she finished her work for the day, Larry presented the keys to her and walked her and Sarina out to the parking lot as if he was leaving at the same time.

Ashley almost fainted when she saw the transformation that her car had undergone. What was once a traditional black paint job was now a dark navy blue. The car sported new tires and the interior had been completely redone in dark blue leather that was complimentary to the new exterior color.

"Well, what do you think? Do you like it?

Ashley was so excited she couldn't contain herself. With a bear hug for Larry she cried, "Yes, yes, yes! How did you know that the new paint is my favorite color for a car?"

Larry explained that he'd overheard her talking to one of the staff about the color and decided to surprise her with it. He added that the car had been overhauled from bumper to bumper and was as good as new. Ashley had really liked the car before but now she loved her car. Larry turned to go back into the office.

Ashley thanked him again and he said, "I want two of my most important employees in something safe and reliable."

Larry and Paul had met on the car issue the day before and Larry had asked Paul to keep quiet about it because he wanted to surprise his sister.

In her short tenure at the firm, she and Sarina had shown a great work ethic. They genuinely cared about the firm's clients and treated them courteously and professionally. Larry received numerous compliments about the two of them and some of his most difficult clients gushed over them.

Larry bragged that his biggest car dealer client threatened to steal the two of them out from under the firm with offers of much more money than he was probably paying them.

Larry had good-naturedly threatened that client. "If you do that, I'll have the Department of the Treasury so far up your ass for income tax fraud, you won't live long enough to get out of jail." They both laughed at this and the car dealer said he was just trying to make sure the two of them were rewarded for their actions because they were the kind of people you just didn't see much anymore.

While Larry and Paul were meeting so Larry could unveil his plan for Ashley's car, Paul asked him his opinion about taking some courses on computer code writing. Paul thought it might be beneficial in the future. The firm could design its own software or tweak existing software to be more conducive to its needs without having strangers rummaging around in the firm's client records. Larry was in total agreement with the idea.

Paul enrolled in a number of computer programming courses over the next two years, which ended up being his degree minor. It proved not only invaluable to the firm but was a great personal asset to Paul.

He had gotten the idea about getting skilled in that area when he thought about some of Fr. Paul's remarks on how invaluable that expertise was in the business world. He said the Vatican had spent millions of dollars on educating both secular staff and clergy in this area. To date they had never had to bring in outside consultants and technicians, which would have made Fr. Paul and the church very uncomfortable.

Fr. Paul had indicated that the church was now actively recruiting prospective computer programmers and code writers who were thinking about a career in the church. He had said, "Paul, the best servants of the church have been those with exacting skills in a particular area or discipline and a complete devotion and commitment to the church and its principles.

"It would never have been acceptable for the Vatican to have strangers looking at its books. We are a very private organization and we want to keep it that way."

His uncle's remarks had planted a seed in Paul's head. Computer programming and code writing was the outgrowth of that conversation, and the birth of Paul's plan.

Chapter 30

FOOTBALL PRE-SEASON DRILLS started in mid-July. Paul and Tom thought they had stayed in pretty good shape in their off-season between track and the start of football drills. However, each year the physical exertion seemed to become more abusive and it was more difficult to get in shape. Although they were only juniors, they were on the trainers' tables more often and spent a significant time in the whirlpool tubs this year. Ice packs were almost body extensions for them.

In spite of this, they were determined to not only make the team again but to get more playing time in than previous years. A number of the firm's clients were UCLA alumni who asked the boys several times a day how the team was going to do this coming football season?

The stock answer was that the team would do even better than last year. The first two years they had been on teams with winning records but had failed to get to the second season, otherwise known as a bowl invitation.

The team had a few sophomores this year that looked like they could not only make varsity but be key components. The seniors were light; this class hadn't been very successful due to a number of injuries and players dropping out of the program.

UCLA was one of the first colleges that held its athletes to a higher standard than some other schools, especially in the Southern California area. Students' first and foremost responsibility was to secure graduation, and then students could be athletes who competed for the greater glory of the school. There were no exceptions to the rule: "No pass, no play."

Coach Martin, who had been hired by UCLA as a receivers' coach and a track coach as he had been at North Hollywood High, had been with Paul and Tom since their freshman year. He made them comfortable from the start and they joked that it still felt like they were still in high school. Coach Martin made it clear to them at the start of the season that the receivers would get a lot of passes this year because the new quarterback, a junior, promised a high scoring offensive type of game.

His name was Matt Whaley. He was from Colorado and had been a high school legend there. Every college and university had been after him since he was a sophomore in high school, but he opted for UCLA because of their outstanding theology and philosophy departments. He was a great athlete but also a tremendous student who had his eyes firmly fixed on his educational pursuits.

When Matt started the mid-July two-a-day drills, there were three older quarterbacks ahead of him. Within two weeks they had all been relegated to backups. The funny thing about him was that he was not that big. He was short at five foot nine and about one hundred sixty pounds but he had an arm like a cannon. He could easily loft a ball seventy-five to eighty yards with pinpoint accuracy. He quickly befriended Tom and Paul, but on the practice field his rockets caused them to be a little bruised and battered.

Both the entire school and the alumni were buzzing about the Colorado junior, who bore a striking resemblance to Dustin

Hoffman. His teammates called him Mr. Hoffman, the graduate, the good reverend, or father. Matt had made it well known that upon graduation he planned to enter the seminary to become a priest. That made coeds even more attracted to him. A number of them made it their personal mission to dissuade Matt from becoming a man of the cloth. A bevy of girls could be found hanging around the football field before, during, and after practice for the chance to talk to Matt. He didn't ignore them or treat them rudely. He always displayed the manners of a gentleman.

UCLA's first home game was against the Cougars from Washington State. They were not a powerhouse team but they had a pretty effective pass defense. Matt picked it apart. The Bruins won 63 to 6. Paul caught all six passes that were thrown his way for a total of one hundred and eighty yards and two touchdowns. That was almost half of what had taken him an entire season to do the previous year.

Tom caught a seventy-four yard pass for a touchdown in the first quarter which primed the Bruin scoring machine. It was his first game of over one hundred yards since high school. The team, the school, and the community were very excited about the team and it was the topic of conversation everywhere in Westwood.

With such a talent calling the signals, the quarterback and receivers' coaches came up with plays that could only be accomplished by a very skilled quarterback and well-trained offensive unit. The team rolled through its first eight games without really taking a deep breath.

With both wideouts, Paul and Tom, being on the small side of a typical receiver in football today, their unmitigated absence of fear gave the entire team a lack of fear or intimidation. The consensus belief was if those two small guys were fearless then so should they be. And it worked. Every player to the man outplayed himself and, therefore, being outweighed on both lines was not a consideration.

Their first real test was the home game with the Stanford Cardinal. They outweighed the Bruins on the line by over fifty pounds per person.

The coaches told the UCLA team how proud they were of them and reminded them to keep their heads in the game and to focus on the goal. They were playing their chief rival; a team that had repeatedly beaten them over the years. As had become the custom since Matt had taken over as quarterback and leader of the team, there was a prayer before the game and at half-time. Everyone took part even though it was a junior leading the team.

Quarterback Matt Whaley was always accurate but the Stanford game was probably his best to date for pinpoint accuracy. He threw passes like a neurosurgeon operates, with complete skill and focus. He put balls in places that were only seen on the professional level. The Stanford Cardinal very quickly fell behind to the Bruins 24-0 in the first half. The defense had risen to task of holding Stanford's high powered offense to a goose egg.

After the kickoff to UCLA by Stanford, Coach Martin noticed there was a shift in the defensive backs. One of Stanford's sophomore defensive ends shifted to strong safety. He was probably forty pounds heavier than the average safety and from scouting reports, this kid was fast. A number of schools had tried to entice him to attend. He was a product of Compton High, a proverbial powerhouse from the inner city of Los Angeles. They turned out a great number of very good players that eventually made it to the pros. If you could cut it in Compton, you could cut it anywhere.

The Achilles heel of the program at Compton was that most of their players had run-ins and issues with the law. It wasn't unusual to see police cars removing students under arrest for assorted crimes, most of them connected with some sort of felony activity. Murder arrests and convictions, minors tried as adults and imprisonment in adult facilities were not uncommon among its student body. Gang violence was very prevalent in their system. Some educators and coaches believed if they could channel their energy toward something positive like sports, it might change the course of their lives.

Coach Martin was familiar with the player, Jeff Gatwick, from scouting reports but he wanted to know about the personal side of this player. Coach Martin relied on his computer to discover that Jeff Gatwick had had some minor skirmishes with the law but nothing that was a felony. The Bruin's scouts had put a "pass" next to his name because of a tendency toward being violent, which had come about wrestling in high school. He had broken a number of opponents' arms and other bones in school tournaments. He was very strong and knew how leverage could be used to not only defeat his opponent but decimate him at the same time. Being the only white player on Compton's teams, he had a chip on his shoulder. So much so that even the meanest and toughest gang members gave him a wide berth.

His only skirmish with the law had been when his former wrestling coach at Compton wanted to test how tough Jeff truly was. He took him to the railroad tracks in East LA where the reputed meanest and toughest hobos congregated. The coach then sent Jeff to practice his wrestling moves by hurting live targets. Jeff was immediately jumped and he held his own with four or five vagrants beating on him at the same time. In his anger he snapped, breaking arms, legs, knees, and collarbones of those who assaulted him. The carnage was unbelievable. It was an orthopedic nightmare.

The police were called and even the seasoned veterans on the force had never seen anything like it. Jeff was arrested. An attorney for the district plea-bargained Jeff's foray down to a number of misdemeanors rather than felonies, because his wrestling coach had thrust him, a minor, into a life-threatening situation to fend for himself. The coach was rightly fired from his position but Jeff's assault on the train track bums in East LA was legendary in the Southern California school system.

And now, Jeff lined up to guard Tom Fogerty in the second half. Receivers' coach John Martin fixed his eyes solely on this matchup when the Bruins were on offense. Tom was knocked around on almost every passing route he took. After the second series of plays, Tom came back with a bloody lip and nose, but certainly not intimidated. He told Coach Martin that the guy was just trying to scare him and that it wasn't working.

Paul asked his friend if he needed any help.

Tom was emphatic. "Hey, if I keep him busy it'll open up more lanes for you. This big jackass is going to get worn out chasing me all over the field. One thing I know for sure is, he's no track star unless it's throwing the javelin or the discus. I think he's getting tired. No worries, just keep catching the passes."

As the game progressed the Cardinal and the Bruins exchanged touchdowns leading to a score of 31-7 heading into the fourth quarter. To the amazement of the crowd, Stanford dropped back Jeff Gatwick to receive the Bruins' punt. The head coach of the Bruins immediately called a timeout to huddle with the players and the coaches.

The Morgans and the Burkes attended all of Paul's football games. The Burkes viewed the Morgans as family. First it was Lewis, and now it was Paul that the Burkes had adopted as their own son playing on the field. Three generations of Morgans watched the game, with Carlos being the most vocal on all of the plays, especially when the referees called infractions against the Bruins.

The Fogertys had also been adopted into the extended family. Tom's parents had been part of the 'family' since his senior year in high school. This large contingent sat together and cheered and moaned as a single unit. Sitting next to each other, Sarina and Ashley occasionally covered their eyes when Paul or Tom were involved in a play. Those two players were not only family, but fellow co-workers whom they spent more time with than anyone else. And, there was the romantic relationship between Sarina and Paul.

Grandpa Carlos led the discussion of why the opposing team had put some white hoodlum in to run back punts. Ashley and Sarina both had binoculars so they were aware that Tom was getting bloodied by Jeff Gatwick on every series.

After an uneventful series of downs, the Bruins set up to punt and the punter was instructed to kick away from Jeff Gatwick. The coaches told the punter to kick it into the bathroom before directing a ball toward him. He punted the ball about thirty-five yards to an up back who started to run the ball back, then immediately pitched a lateral pass back to the trailing Jeff Gatwick, who ran it back for a touchdown.

When the last player to have a shot at tackling him was the punter, Jeff did not try to avoid him, instead taking aim and running into him with a vengeance. He deliberately tried to mow him down and he was successful. All eyes were fixed on the Cardinal running into the end zone for a touchdown.

Then the eyes backtracked to the fallen kicker who was writhing in pain on the field. The bottom of his right leg was at a ninety degree angle from where it had been. It was badly broken and severely displaced. The huge crowd fell silent and heard his screams of pain. The team physician ran out with the medical crew, assessed the situation quickly, and gave him a sedative to prevent him from going into shock. The entire Rose Bowl crowd was stunned.

After the initial shock was absorbed, Larry and Dianne, sitting near the Morgan contingent, went to talk with them. Larry was as vocal as Carlos. During the last three years they had become football analysts for each other.

Larry asked Carlos if Stanford had recruited this Gatwick player out of San Quentin to play today. Carlos was equally animated and wanted Gatwick thrown out of the game for the physical abuse that he dished out on every play. Amazingly, he had not been called for a single penalty since entering in the game. Through their binoculars they all watched what he was doing to the Bruin players, especially Tom. Just before the medical timeout was over, Larry remarked to Sarina and Ashley that he wanted his boys out of the game. He was afraid that 'convict' might kill one of them. All this remark did was add to the already over the top anxiety that they felt. Ashley looked at Sarina with tears in her eyes and said nothing. They both understood and were afraid.

As the punter lay on the field, Matt Whaley knelt near him, leading some of the players in prayer. Some players held hands as they gave up their thoughts and prayers. Most of the Cardinal players just stood watching.

The Bruin coaches met with the referee and expressed their concern over the brutal assault of their player by Stanford player Jeff Gatwick. After the stretcher was removed from the field, the head referee threw a flag on the field for unsportsmanlike conduct against Jeff Gatwick on the runback. The officials gathered with the Stanford head coach to let him know in no uncertain terms that this behavior would not be tolerated. Bruin fans wanted Jeff Gatwick ejected for his play. The referee told the respective teams to ready themselves for the kick off. The score was now 31-21 with about eight minutes to go in the game.

The coaches huddled with their players. Receivers' coach John Martin told his players that the referees would be watching Jeff Gatwick closely and he believed Gatwick would now play within the rules.

Tom spoke up and said, "We need an additional touchdown to put the game out of reach of Stanford. If we can get a couple of first downs and burn about three minutes off of the clock, they can't catch us." His idea was to send him, Paul, and the tight end deep on each play and open up the middle for short passes and the running game. Tom told Coach Martin, "I think Jeff Gatwick is getting tired from running all over the field so if I can bait him into about three or four all out sprints going long, it will soften up the big son of a bitch."

Coach Martin agreed.

Paul looked at Tom and warned, "Be careful. This guy is an animal."

"Yeah, but he ain't no machine."

That was the immediate game plan. After the second all out sprint, Jeff Gatwick took a cheap shot, pushing Tom after the play ended. He was immediately flagged and then warned by the referee. Tom returned to the huddle and told the quarterback, "One more long, Matt, and Gatwick will be out of oxygen. He's puffing light like a broken accordion."

Tom ran a straight sprint down the sidelines. It was obvious that it took all Jeff Gatwick had to stay reasonably close in his coverage. Gatwick muttered something to Tom, who only laughed without breathing hard as he returned to the huddle. Matt asked if the strong safety was softened up for a bomb.

Tom was confident. "He'll be out of air twenty yards off the line of scrimmage. Let's end this thing now."

It was first down and about forty-five yards to the goal line. Tom took off down the sideline like he had been shot out of a cannon. True to his prediction, Jeff Gatwick started to falter after about twenty yards but Matt's throw was off and up. Tom went airborne to bring down the pass for a touchdown but the elapsed time gave Jeff Gatwick the opportunity to catch up to the play. Gatwick knew he was beat but decided to inflict as much punishment as possible on Tom as he came down with both arms around the ball leaving him completely exposed and defenseless. He hit Tom with the full force of a two hundred twenty pound projectile moving at full speed. The whole scenario unfolded as if in slow motion. All eyes were fixed on the catch and then seeing the defender go parallel for the hit. Tom landed with a thud but with the ball still in his hands as the official signaled a touchdown.

Players and viewers stood in silence as Tom lay completely still. The entire bench and team ran to their fallen teammate's side. Tom was unconscious and not breathing. The team physician was on the scene immediately and got him breathing. He then addressed the blood coming from Tom's eyes and left ear.

The physician told the referee to have the paramedics bring the ambulance in immediately. "We have to get this boy to a hospital as soon as possible. I think he has a traumatic brain injury. Alert neurosurgery at the closest hospital what we're bringing in."

Paul was on the opposite side of the field when the hit occurred but he was there to hear the unbearable remarks about his best friend's possible condition. Matt knelt, along with players from both teams except Jeff Gatwick, and prayed. Paul noticed and he thought, you unfeeling animal.

Among the players, coaches, and officials trying to reach Tom was Paul's sister Ashley.

The ambulance made its way onto the field. By the time they had Tom on the neck board and strapped down, Ashley had pushed and shoved her way to his side. She grabbed his hand and squeezed it, and to her amazement he squeezed it back. She immediately told the doctor.

"Thank God. Who are you?" asked the physician.

"I'm his girlfriend." She looked up to find her brother standing over them.

Paul winked and smiled. He mouthed the words, "I knew it."

As the paramedics and the doctor administered smelling salts and other injections, Tom opened his eyes. When he saw Ashley at his side a smile came across his blood splattered face.

"Can you wiggle your toes?" the doctor asked Tom.

Tom complied. He then looked at Ashley and asked faintly, "Did I keep possession of the ball for the touchdown?"

"Yes you did, you idiot."

Ashley turned to the doctor and announced that she was riding to the hospital in the ambulance with Tom. From the expression on her face the doctor knew that it would best not to debate the issue. When they raised the stretcher up on its legs, Ashley asked Tom if he could raise his arms to let his parents know he was okay. He did and the crowd erupted with a cheer.

Paul leaned over his friend with tears in his eyes and said, "Very dramatic. Not bad for a theatre major."

Tom whispered, "I meant to tell you about Ashley and me."

"Be quiet and remember if you ever mistreat her I will give you a dose like I gave Peter Duffy. I couldn't be happier for the two of you. It shows I did a good job raising you. See you at the hospital. I've got some unfinished business to take care of."

Tom, even in his injured state, didn't think for one minute that Paul's parting remark had anything to do with finishing the football game. When he'd seen that look a few years back he had thought, I pity the poor bastard he goes after.

Chapter 31

As the ambulance left the field, the Bruin and Cardinal players knelt together and were led again in a prayer by Matt Whaley. Paul had his eyes fixed on Jeff Gatwick who, again, did not kneel or hold his head down during the joint team prayer for Tom.

The referee threw the penalty flag and signaled personal foul against Jeff Gatwick for unnecessary roughness and also that he was expelled from the game. No one on the Stanford sidelines made any protest to the referee's call.

Gatwick protested vehemently that his tackle was delivered cleanly and was not intended to injure. His protests to the officiating staff met deaf ears. He was clearly becoming excessively agitated, prompting the referee to call for police assistance from the sidelines to lead Mr. Gatwick off the field. That was when national television decided to cut to a commercial set.

As the head referee turned to walk away, Jeff Gatwick loudly yelled, "Football is a game made for men, not little weak girls." He added, "I didn't know I was playing a game of bitch ball with a weak sister."

The referee wheeled back around to direct the police who had just arrived. Paul knew in his heart what he was going to do, so he put his helmet back on, cinched the straps, and put his mouthpiece back in.

He had planned to avenge Gatwick's cheap shot on his best friend after the game but with Gatwick's derogatory rant about Tom, Paul couldn't wait any longer.

Paul took off about ten yards from Gatwick at a dead run. Gatwick didn't spot him until he was almost on him because his attention alternated between the head referee and the police who were approaching him from the sidelines. In the last second, he saw a powder blue missile closing in on him, but he didn't have enough time to react.

Paul went airborne right before impact. Gatwick did not have his helmet on. Paul's helmet struck Gatwick's jaw with an upward thrust. The crack of his jaw sounded like a thick stick being broken in half. Gatwick staggered backward from the hit. Paul then took his right hand and hit him as hard as he could in the rib cage. Paul felt the bones snap. At the same time he lifted his left knee into Gatwick's groin with all the knee thrust he had in him. Gatwick fell backward on the field unconscious and Paul landed on top of him.

Paul immediately jumped back up before anyone could react and started to walk back to the Bruin locker room. He knew he was going to be thrown out of the game and didn't wait around for the officials to come to their senses to expel him. The head referee ceremoniously dropped the yellow flag and signaled a personal foul as the paramedics ran to the field to attend to Gatwick, who was still unconscious and bleeding from the mouth.

It happened that at the instant of Paul's attack on Gatwick, national television had finished its commercial break, allowing millions of viewers to witnesses Paul's brutality. The police, who were just about to escort Jeff Gatwick off the field stood motionless and in shock, just like the crowd.

The referee conferred with the balance of the officiating staff while the police turned their attention to Paul for his blatant assault of another player. The police ran after Paul, who was almost to the locker room entrance.

Recognizing the savagery that they had just seen, the din of the crowd grew louder as the events of the past few minutes were discussed. The head referee called for a game delay of ten minutes to regain order. National television cut to an unscheduled commercial break so the announcers could later plausibly explain what the audience had just witnessed.

Amazingly, none of the Stanford players went anywhere near their fallen teammate. They stood in shock as did all of the UCLA team and staff.

When the paramedics and the attending physician got to Gatwick, it was obvious that in his unconscious state, he was clearly choking on the blood in his mouth. An emergency tracheotomy was performed to allow Gatwick to breathe. Upon further examination by the doctor, he wasn't sure if the blood coming out of Gatwick's mouth was from the several broken ribs or his jaw which was clearly shattered. The Stanford player looked like he had been hit head-on by a truck. A second ambulance arrived on the scene and picked up what remained of Jeff Gatwick and transported him to the hospital.

In the first ambulance, Tom was in stable condition. He asked the paramedic if the radio could be turned up so he could hear the rest of the game. Ashley knew in her heart that Tom was going to be okay after that request. The paramedic working on Tom gave her the thumbs up on his vitals.

Following Paul's attack of Gatwick, the radio announcer tried to explain what he had just seen. He seemed to be struggling to make sense of it. Tom looked at Ashley and said, "I knew your brother wasn't going to stand for that hit and that he wouldn't be able to stop himself from avenging me. You know, for being raised Catholic, he sure follows the Old Testament in the eye for an eye thing."

Ashley ordered Tom to lie there quietly and to get that stupid smirk off his face. She was worried about what would happen to her brother for his actions.

Her fears had already reached the grandstand where Paul's family and employer were sitting. Larry immediately headed for the locker room, hastening further when he saw the police pursuing Paul. As he ran down the stairs to the locker room, he encountered defense attorney, Ellen DePaolo, an alumnus who was a client. She, too, was headed in the same direction as Larry after seeing what had occurred on the field. She wanted to make sure Paul didn't say anything that could damage him in court. As they descended the Rose Bowl stairs, they just looked at each other, each knowing what the other was thinking.

When they arrived at the locker room door, Ellen stated that she was Paul's attorney, immediately gaining admittance to see Paul. As she entered the locker room, she promised to keep Larry informed. She closed the locker room door behind her, leaving Larry waiting anxiously in the hallway.

The police sergeant arrived out of breath from his pursuit of Paul. He ordered his men to put Paul under arrest for assault. Ellen seamlessly produced a business card and said that she would be representing Paul Morgan and that the hand cuffs which they had just placed on his wrists behind his back were to be removed. As the sergeant tried to exert his authority over the situation, the Los Angeles Police Chief arrived on the scene. He knew Ms. DePaolo very well. He asked his sergeant if the handcuffs were necessary.

Paul had a dazed look on his face and the team doctor confirmed that he had suffered a concussion. The doctor placed smelling salts under Paul's nose to clear his head. He told a paramedic to order a third ambulance.

In the corner of the locker room, defense attorney Ellen DePaolo and the police chief, another alumnus of the powder blue were in deep conversation of how to handle what had just occurred. They both were in agreement that Gatwick's actions were despicable, but Paul's reprisal was unlawful. Ellen, of course, said she believed the savagery of Gatwick's intent to really harm Tom provoked Paul into an uncontrollable rage. The police chief didn't agree fully, but said they would talk later when things had calmed down and discuss possible actions.

Chapter 32

THE PARAMEDICS DELIVERED Paul to the emergency room where Tom was undergoing tests. Ashley ran to her brother when she saw him and asked him if he was okay. Paul's concern was for Tom, not himself. Ashley said Tom was fine and they just were finishing some tests. Her concern was now for her brother.

The doctor examined Paul's eyes with an ocular scope. He ordered the nurse to call a neurological specialist immediately. Within moments, the neurologist appeared and upon examination ordered an IV and some injections for shock and a concussion. Paul's headache left him with little resistance to what was happening around him. The medical team suspected that Paul suffered from a blunt force concussion. This was later confirmed to be the diagnosis. The doctors ordered that he be admitted for further tests and evaluation.

Because Tom was spending the night at the hospital, he and Paul were asked if they wanted to share a room. They both agreed.

By now, the family had arrived at the hospital and on learning of Paul's concussion and admittance, the reassurances and incessant hugging of each other began in earnest.

After Paul reached his room, he asked to see Sarina. She had come with Paul's parents to make sure he was okay. Paul told his folks that he was all right and that he loved them. He held Sarina's hand through the entire conversation and didn't take his eyes off of her. The intensity between them was palpable.

Angeline interrupted the interlude. "Thank God you're okay. Your father and I were so worried. Is it all right if your grandfather comes in to see you?"

Paul nodded as his mother leaned over and kissed his cheek. His father squeezed his son's foot under the covers as he left. Paul looked at him and he winked.

Paul's grandfather was very emotional at seeing his grandson in the hospital bed. He glanced at Sarina, but his eyes were fixed on his pride and joy, his grandson. Without words, the two of them looked at each other and Carlos knew his grandson was going to be okay. Paul saw in the older man's eyes and facial expressions not only concern, but extreme pride. He had taught Paul how to defend himself and to be the man that he had become. He squeezed Paul's arm repeatedly without speaking, leaned over and kissed him on both cheeks, and winked at Sarina as he left without uttering a word. He didn't need to.

Family and friends left the hospital to go home. Tom and Paul in adjacent beds in the semi-private room said their respective goodbyes and kissed their girlfriends. Ashley and Sarina left hand in hand. A little while later Larry, Dianne, and attorney Ellen DePaolo arrived unannounced. They were checking in on them before they left. They'd been at the hospital for hours waiting until the families had confirmed for themselves that their loved ones were okay.

As always, Larry took the initiative, telling the boys that he didn't expect them to be at the office on Monday, but that he would meet them at their respective condos. He went on to say that he had retained Ellen as Paul's attorney and that the firm would cover all of Paul's legal fees. He looked at Tom specifically and told them both he was proud of them.

"Ellen had the police chief station two officers outside your door here to make sure nobody bothers you," he told the boys. Then he laughed, looking at Paul. "Anyone who saw you hit that jackass Gatwick will be afraid to set foot in this hospital, let alone bother you." As he left the room he added, "Oh by the way, we won. Your teammates were so inspired they marched down the field and scored another touchdown with the clock about to expire."

As Tom and Paul were about to fall asleep, Tom quipped, "Man you are one bad ass. Remind me to never piss you off."

Paul laughed and replied, "If you ever hurt my sister, what I did today will be nothing compared to what I will do to you."

Chapter 33

The aftermath of the Stanford game would be felt for some time. Paul's attorney, Ellen DePaolo, and the police chief agreed in principle on what should happen to the assault and battery charges filed against her client. With multiple delays and bargaining, the charges were dismissed and community service of forty hours and some anger management classes were the only punishment metered to Paul. The head referee lost his position for not removing Gatwick after the first personal foul for roughing the receiver. That action and the loss of control of the game spelled the end of his twenty year career as a head referee in college football.

After much debate with the NCAA Board of Directors and their officiating staff who ultimately lost control of the game, Paul's punishment was a suspension under special circumstances beyond his control for the remainder of the season. The Bruins would play without one of their best receivers for the "civil war" game against arch rival USC and any subsequent bowl games they might be eligible to play. The alumni appealed the decision, but to no avail. UCLA's loss to USC left them without a bowl bid with national championship ramifications.

Stanford conducted a thorough investigation into what occurred in a very important nationally televised game. Before the NCAA could initiate their own investigation, Stanford fired the entire defensive coaching staff. A university of their standing was not going to put its reputation on the line for some two-bit hoodlum and a coaching staff that was supposedly in control of him. Stanford showed their true colors and beat the NCAA to the punch. They were a class organization that won games because they were the best. Period. Their longtime head coach was put on warning for the first time in his twenty-five years at the helm of Stanford. The university wanted to give everyone a wakeup call to zero tolerance.

The Chancellors at UCLA met and interviewed all parties concerned regarding what had happened during the Stanford game. Some believed this was just an attempt to mirror what Stanford had done, but the Chancellors wanted to show some due diligence in the matter. In order to keep up appearances for the NCAA and the media, the Chancellors issued some directives to Paul. He was placed on probation and before he would be allowed to play, he would have to go through a number of evaluations next fall to see if he was not only physically able to play football but also if he was able to control his temper.

Paul and Tom were wheeled out of the hospital the day after the game and went by the open door of Gatwick's room. He saw them and they saw him. Nothing was said. Unfortunately it wouldn't be the last time Paul would hear Jeff's name.

In the end, neither Paul nor Tom was in any condition to play football in the immediate future. Tom was badly bruised in his chest cavity; breathing deeply was very painful and out of the question. He had a variety of other ailments as well that ultimately led to him missing the entire track season.

Paul's concussion proved to be even more of a problem than the disciplinary issues. He suffered from severe headaches and was sick to his stomach on a regular basis. He tried to downplay it as much as he could but those closest to him knew he was trying to mask his pain. He didn't want his health issues widely known in the event they might prevent him from competing in the future. He had also missed track season due to his injuries.

Jeff Gatwick's future was not as promising as Paul's and Tom's. He wasn't able to speak or eat solid foods for over six months. His multiple rib fractures would prevent him from competing in football or wrestling ever again. Gatwick lost his athletic scholarship to Stanford. He was a borderline student and his main value to the university was his prowess as a wrestler and temporarily retooled defensive back.

After the first of the year, Ellen got permission for Paul to be on the sidelines of the Bruin's Fiesta Bowl appearance against Nebraska and both injured warriors attended the Fiesta bowl in Phoenix. Tom was on crutches and Paul looked as though he had just gone ten rounds with a grizzly. But both were there to support their team. Quarterback Matt Whaley asked Paul to lead the team prayer before the game.

The team rallied with the appearance of their teammates and in a very close game, the Bruins prevailed over the Nebraska Cornhuskers. Tom and Paul helped receivers' coach John Martin with spotting the opposition's weaknesses and formation opportunities during the game. The entire UCLA student body was excited about the bowl victory. However some bemoaned the fact that UCLA had been missing two of its stars in the USC game due to Tom's injury and Paul's revenge on the field. Many fans felt that if Tom and Paul had played against USC, they would have prevailed, propelling them into a possible national championship.

The firm's client base was composed of a number of UCLA alumni and Paul had gained some unwanted notoriety. Everyone who knew Paul professionally liked and respected him.

Once the two partners were able to be somewhat functional at the firm, Larry called a meeting in the glass palace with Tom and Paul. Dianne, Sarina and Ashley were also present. Tom halfway expected a lecture but he and Paul heard only the concern of a person who truly loved them.

Larry told them he was glad they would not compete in track and was very worried that their injuries would be debilitating to them for the rest of their lives. In all of the glory that they gave to UCLA and the firm, Larry made it clear that none of it was worth seeing them injured. Nothing. He made it clear that he would prefer them to think about not competing in football or any contact sport again. They needed to realize that they were much more important to the firm and their families as professionals in the accounting field than they were as football players.

The two upcoming UCLA seniors couldn't help but disagree. Tom and Paul had already discussed what they wanted to accomplish the following year for their team and no one was going to stop them from achieving what they both had strived for since they were kids playing Pop Warner football. However, out of respect for Larry, both remained silent.

With no track practice and the ability to concentrate more fully on the tax season ending on April 15, the young partners were able to take on an even heavier load of clients. Paul and Tom came to realize how much energy and time it had taken to compete in the spring after the grueling football season.

Larry was grateful for the extra help, which gave him the opportunity to expand some of his corporate clients, adding significantly to the firm's bottom line. He anticipated the day his two apprentices graduated and receive their CPA designations and he and Dianne could finally enjoy the fruits of their hard labor over the years. That had been his grand design since Paul had first walked into the firm.

Eagerly Larry began to think about what his and Dianne's lives were going to be like in a couple of years. Larry had plenty of money on which to retire. His major concern was his clients and the continuation of the firm that he'd built. The firm would also give him an excuse, when he needed it, to retreat back to what he knew best, accounting.

Chapter 34

As the summer break came to a close, Paul and Tom had high hopes for their senior year.

Tom's injuries had healed nicely and he had embarked on a strength building regimen to improve his stamina. After his injury-enforced vacation, he was considerably stronger and faster.

Paul mirrored Tom's program with the intent of bringing home a national title to UCLA in their senior year. The team coalesced with the same focus and were in tremendous condition well before the two-a-day drills commenced in July. The coaching staff knew of the extra work their players had taken on voluntarily but their sharpness and conditioning surprised even the veteran coaching staff.

At the end of the last school year, UCLA's All-American middle linebacker had graduated and become a first-round draft pick of the Denver Broncos. His departure had left a gaping hole in the middle.

Tom had an idea and suggested that the coaching staff call a football camp friend of his who was the star and anchor of the Penn State defense, middle linebacker Patrick Ritchie. UCLA's coaches used their best sales pitch on Patrick to entice him to leave a school he dearly loved. The convincing element was UCLA's offer of a full ride his senior year, including a job to offset his living expenses. And, upon graduation, he would be admitted into the school's very prestigious and unbelievably expensive graduate school in computer programming.

Tom knew that Penn State was currently on probation for their recruiting practices, so all athletic scholarships had been stopped starting in Patrick's senior year. He and Tom had talked about what a financial burden this was going to cause him and his parents. Patrick also wondered where the money was going to come from to attend graduate school in Pennsylvania. Therefore, UCLA's offer would be a godsend to Patrick if he could close the deal.

Even after his initial fears about his partners playing another year of football, Larry jumped on board and enlisted the support of a number of alumni for the Penn Stater to become the Bruins' middle linebacker. UCLA invited Patrick to California for an all-expense paid trip to look over the school and hear the pitch of the university coaches, chancellor, and the computer programming department heads to convince him to switch schools.

The icing on the cake was noted author and professor emeritus, John Dunne, who held a two hour one-on-one with Patrick. Professor Dunne was Patrick's idol and catalyst for wanting to pursue computer programming. The professor agreed to be Patrick's mentor in graduate school, which he informed Patrick would also be a full ride. Patrick called his parents and told them what he was being offered. His dad advised him not to think twice about Penn State. He believed that this was a chance of a lifetime for his son.

On his first visit, Patrick met Paul. Paul had heard about him through the years from Tom but they had never met. With Tom as the common denominator, they both felt that they knew each other very well. It was instant chemistry between them. Tom was very pleased the two of them hit it off so well. Now it was going to be the three amigos.

When full contact practice started, it became very obvious why pro scouts followed Patrick to the west coast. He was like hitting steel. He had worked as a day laborer in Pennsylvania each summer since his junior year in high school and was dead fit.

Paul and Patrick took a couple of classes together in Paul's minor, Computer Programming. Paul was fast at writing code but he was no match for Patrick in deciphering, and it was well known that there was no computer which Patrick couldn't crack. His nick name in the department was the safe cracker.

Larry quickly became fond of Patrick and offered to help him find employment when he finished his schooling. Larry offered Patrick a position in the firm if there was one in his chosen field, saying that if his firm didn't have a position, he'd contact alumni who did.

Paul continued to experience occasional headaches even though he had passed every post-concussion test. This was the only remaining area of concern for UCLA's football season. When Patrick noticed that Paul had an especially bad headache one day, he refrained from telling anyone. Keeping this secret bonded the two of them even more.

The team breezed through their first six games. Their average winning margin was three touchdowns. They were as impressive on defense as they were on offense. Tom and Paul had become very cagey in their complicated pass patterns that Coach Martin improvised. This was intended to not only put points on the scoreboard but also to protect the two of them from any further injury. It worked on both fronts.

Game seven that year was at Stanford. No hometown advantage. Both teams were undefeated. The winner of this game would definitely be the Pac 12 Champion and there was a very good chance that one of the teams would advance to the national championship game. Standing in either team's way was the other team and their upcoming "civil war" game.

The intensity on the field was palpable. All eyes were fixed on the field for every play. Both teams were well matched and it became obvious that the contest would end with either a singular error or a phenomenal play. It would be the latter. The scoreboard went tit for tat as every touchdown was answered. At the half, the score was 21-21. In the fourth quarter, tied up at 42 all with three minutes to go, the Cardinal offense was marching and it looked like the Bruins would have very little time left when they got the ball back. The nervousness of the teams was felt even in the stands, but no mistakes had occurred so far.

On second down and three, an obvious run play, Patrick shot the gap from the middle linebacker position. He knew he had milliseconds to get to the ball before the back ran right into the space he had just voided. It was a brazen move and the entire stadium held their breath. Patrick got to the quarterback almost before he got the ball from center. He was that fast. He stripped the ball and ran the fumble back sixty-five yards for the winning touchdown. The UCLA fans erupted; no one had ever seen such speed. The Bruins' sideline exploded in celebration. When Patrick got back to the bench, he was mobbed. Paul asked him, "Where did that play come from?"

Patrick, gasping for air, answered at the same time as the national television broadcaster announced over the air waves, "Lawrence Taylor."

Next, the Bruins went on to defeat the Trojans in a rout.

They were the favorites for the BCS Championship Game, which this year happened to be the Rose Bowl at UCLA's home stadium, where they manhandled the Wisconsin Badgers. The Bruins were up three touchdowns and a field goal late in the fourth quarter when Paul caught a pass. He had already scored two touchdowns and Tom had caught one. Matt Whaley, the quarterback, was on fire in his final game as a collegiate.

Paul went up to catch the ball and the defender couldn't get to him. Paul landed with the ball and the Badger back touched him while he was down to end the play. Paul could not get up. He had such a severe headache he couldn't get to his feet. First on the scene was Patrick, who pulled him up and helped him to the bench. Patrick stated that Paul just had the wind knocked out of him. They both knew it was a lie. It was Paul's last play of his football career.

UCLA was crowned national champion and finished the BCS poll number one. The celebration in Westwood was over the top. Paul didn't feel well so he and Sarina stayed in and watched the festivities from his condo that bordered the campus. Sarina knew Paul was hurting but her patience prevailed and she didn't question him. A couple of days later, he told her what had happened, adding that he was finished with sports. "Sarina, I'll never keep a secret from you again, he declared.

Sarina smiled at Paul. "Ditto. I love you."

There was only one sporting event left on Tom's and Paul's schedule. The boys had a heart to heart conversation about Paul's headaches and Paul retired from the track team. He had been the anchor of the 4 x 400 relay which UCLA had dominated since their freshmen year. The final leg man was retiring. Tom wondered who would fill the void.

Patrick called Paul at the office about a week later inviting him for coffee. They met at a coffee shop around the corner from the office. Patrick, ever blunt, cut to the chase. "Hey man, do you have a problem with my taking your old position on the track team?"

"Are you kidding me? That would be such a blessing." Paul looked both relieved and happy. "I've been wracked with guilt about letting the team down. Thanks, man."

Patrick's transition to Paul's position on the team was seamless. It was though Paul was still sprinting and relaying, only it was Patrick. The final meet was at USC. The Bruins held their own, as in the past. Paul and Sarina came to offer support for the team.

"Do you miss it?" She asked Paul before the start of the four by four.

"No. Instead of being down there sweating, nervous, and sick to my stomach anticipating my leg, I'm sitting up here with the best looking woman in the stadium." They both laughed.

Tom and Patrick's four by four set a new collegiate record. UCLA won the meet and when Patrick was presented with his gold medal for the record breaking final leg of the race, he jogged over to the stands and tossed it to Paul.

"This belongs to you, brother."

Paul felt in his heart that Patrick and Tom had taken the place of the brother he'd lost. He chose them, not biology. Paul stood and bowed and thanked Patrick and turned and put the gold medal around Sarina's neck.

"You can tell our kids about this one day."

The rest of the team had followed Patrick over and stood applauding Paul, the real leader of the team, who couldn't be on the field with them.

He leaned over to Sarina and whispered, "I will never forget this day or these guys for this."

Chapter 35

GRADUATION DAY WAS upon them in the blink of an eye. The ceremony was held at the Rose Bowl, the setting of so many memories for Paul and Tom and their families. The assigned seating lasted only until after the first speech, followed by jockeying for seats of the attendees' choosing. Paul, Tom and Patrick sat together in the business major section.

Matt was seated in the theology section of the philosophy graduates. Over five thousand students were graduating and most departments had hundreds, if not over a thousand, respective graduates. Matt's theology degree had only two others like him, who were going to be a priest, pastor or preacher. His friends joked with him about the scarcity of graduates in his major. He corrected them by pointing out that it was selectivity not scarcity.

Paul was unaware that Fr. Lewis and Fr. Paul had flown in that morning from Rome on the private jet that was always staffed and at his uncle's disposal. He didn't notice them until he spotted his parents in their seats. From a distance they were like two black spots next to the rest of his family. Paul had been hoping that something of far greater importance than his graduation would keep them in the Vatican, but here they were.

Because of the large number of graduates and the immense size of the Rose Bowl, the various majors were segregated into their own sections for efficiency. It was a hot day and the regents didn't want to prolong the ceremony. Each of the eight department heads presented diplomas to their respective graduates separately and simultaneously. The four largest majors were set up at the four corners of the stadium and the others, based on size, were situated on the sidelines. UCLA had used that formula for the past couple of years to great effectiveness.

At the announcement of Paul's and Tom's names, great applause and cheering erupted. Patrick, Rose Bowl national championship hero, received a similar ovation even though he had only attended the university in his senior year. Several pro scouts were in attendance, hoping for the chance to talk to Patrick about opportunities that may await him at their respective professional football teams.

Patrick had made it clear that he intended to forego a pro football career to continue his master's and, possibly, doctorate in computer programming at UCLA. Patrick's parents hadn't seen him since he'd headed to California the previous summer, and eagerly traveled to California from Pennsylvania to see him graduate. They were happy to see him graduate with no student loan debt.

Patrick's father was proud of his son and told anyone who would listen about his son's MVP award in the BCS Championship. Patrick followed his parents' advice on finishing his master's degree rather than enter the football draft. He was candid with the pro football scouts and coaches and the media about his decision to not play professional football. His future career was foremost on his mind and agenda. Even with his public statement, he was drafted third in the first round of the draft to the Pittsburgh Steelers, his favorite team since childhood. Patrick wasn't swayed, even by the Steelers and the millions of dollars that were discussed. The consensus of the pro teams was that he was one of the best middle linebacker prospects to come out of college in the last decade. Still, Patrick didn't budge.

Matt Whaley was another player who was not interested in the glamour and money offered to him. He was determined to embark on his life's dream to be a Catholic priest. The coaching staff believed he could have a professional football career if he wished. His lack of height was never an issue because of his quickness and the accuracy and distance of his passes. But Matt's life declaration had been made early and nothing was going to deter him.

* * *

Charlie and Angelina, along with Tom's parents, held a joint graduation party in the Morgan's back yard so that both families and Sarina's parents could all celebrate together. The boys' mothers, with the help of the girls, had prepared all the food making the event low-key and close knit. Paul and Tom had agreed that if there had to be a party, this was their preference.

When Paul made his way over to his family Sarina greeted him first with a big hug and kiss. Paul wondered if her affectionate display was for Lewis and Fr. Paul, to let them know her and Paul's true intentions. She was central to Paul's life and he didn't really care what the Vatican refugees, as Charlie called them, thought. His hard work and focus had put him on the doorstep of a great career as the successor of a very successful firm.

Lewis pushed ahead of everyone else to embrace his brother. "So, little brother, you're finally a college graduate. Congratulations."

Angeline and Charlie waited for their youngest son to get to them and with tears in their eyes, hugged him and told him how proud they were.

Ashley ambushed him next, but only briefly, as she saw Tom and his parents enter the backyard. She kissed his cheek and said, "Congratulations. Don't think being a college graduate is going to get you any special consideration at work on Monday. Same time, same grind. Oh, gotta go. There's Tom."

Since Ashley had started working at the firm, Larry had christened her Ball Buster. She was twice as tough as he ever was. Dianne and Larry credited Ashley for making a very efficient machine even more so. Everyone liked her but they knew she wouldn't hesitate to critique them or their work if she thought it necessary. Even though she had two more years of college left, she acted as though her name plaque was already on the managing partners' door.

Larry and Dianne engulfed Paul next. They both appreciated how hard he had worked with school and sports, and they hoped he would have an easier time at the firm now. Larry and Dianne had become like a second set of parents to Paul and Tom, partly because they spent so much more time with them than their own parents did. Both Tom and Paul realized Larry had presented a unique opportunity in a professional career that few others would ever see, let alone be made a part of. They knew these two people cared as much for them as their own parents and loved them as if they were their own.

When the greeting line dwindled, Fr. Paul stood there with a grin on his face. He thrust his right hand forward and said, "Congratulations. You bring honor to the name Paul Morgan."

"Thank you." Paul wondered if his uncle was talking about himself or his nephew.

He thought how much his uncle had aged in the last couple of years. Although he had always been on the thin side, he'd appeared to be in the best of health. Now he wore the gaunt look of someone who was very ill, or had been. Paul decided to get to the bottom of it later with Lewis.

Toasts were made that lauded not only Paul and Tom but Patrick and Matt, who were at the party. Their respective families knew how much their sons meant to the people there.

Larry waited until the end to speak. When it was his turn, he and Dianne walked hand in hand to the front. Dianne carried two legal size envelopes in her hand. Larry began his speech by describing what it had been like to raise and develop two rag tag high school graduates who had walked through his door four years ago. He went on to say they and Ashley and Sarina had become the children that he and Dianne had never had. They wanted the four of them to know they had rekindled an interest in the firm that had dwindled before they came and made them refocus their commitment to not only their business but to their new family. Larry took the envelopes from Dianne and handed them to Paul and Tom. With tears in his eyes, he finished with a toast to Paul and Tom, "To the two sons I wish I had. At least I was spared having to change their diapers."

Larry explained, "In these envelopes are the legal documents that Dianne and I signed making Paul and Tom full partners of the firm on the condition that they both pass the CPA exam."

Paul rushed forward with tears in his eyes and hugged and thanked them. Tom was right behind him and hugged Dianne but put his hand forward to shake Larry's hand. Tom was still a little afraid of Larry after four years. Larry pushed it aside and bear hugged him. Tom started to cry.

The toasts continued and the celebration kicked into high gear. Sarina was welded to Paul's arm. When Charlie and Angeline surveyed the party's landscape, they were not surprised to see Paul, Sarina, Tom, and Ashley off to the side talking to Patrick and Matt. Angeline turned to her husband, "Charlie, I think we did okay with this one."

Chapter 36

The party continued until about eleven o'clock that night before it started to wind down. The guests thanked the hosts for such a great time in the Morgan back yard. The Burkes handed an envelope to Paul as they hugged him. Sarina was going home with her parents so he walked them to the car. As he leaned over to kiss her cheek good night she grabbed him and kissed him passionately on the lips.

Paul's blush was obvious, even in the moonlight. Mr. Burke said, "I think the two of you had better start making plans for a church date."

Paul walked over to his side of the car. "Sir, I plan to ask you for her hand in marriage later this summer, after I've gotten on bended knee to officially ask her."

"Well that is the traditional order for proposing, but you know you have both my and her mother's approval when you do," Mr. Burke said.

"I suppose I could go back to the party and announce it right now, but I just want the immediate family to know first, if that's okay."

"Sure, I fully understand. Though you might consider asking Sarina first and, if she consents, get her a little ring."

"It will be done before the summer is out, if she'll have me."

He went around to the other side of the car and kissed Sarina again. She whispered, "You already know what my answer is, but you are ever the stickler for proper etiquette."

"My mother didn't raise a heathen." Paul gently shut Sarina's door.

They drove off and he saw Lewis standing at the side gate waiting for him. Lewis completely ignored what he'd just witnessed. "Our uncle wants a word with you. He has been waiting to talk to you about something important."

"He doesn't look good. Is he sick or recovering from being sick? He doesn't look well."

"He'll talk to you about it himself,"

Fr. Paul had ensconced himself at the farthest table with a couple of new bottles of his favorite Italian Pinot Grigio. "My namesake, sit down with your uncle."

As Paul sat down, Matt and Patrick came up to say their thanks and goodbyes. Paul introduced them to his brother and uncle who were very gracious to the two graduates.

Fr. Paul said, "Matt, I understand that you have heard God's calling and are heeding it."

Matt politely nodded.

"Congratulations my son. From what I know of your college sports and academic career, the priesthood is getting a winner. Your example may help lead those to salvation who might not follow a lesser man. You might consider talking to my other nephew, Fr. Lewis. He can give you further enlightenment into what it takes to be a priest today. It has been many years since I was in your or his shoes. What seminary are you attending? I would have thought the seminary would have sent at least a monsignor, or bishop possibly, to show support for their newest rank and file."

"I'm planning to attend the monastery outside of Fresno, St. Martin's," Matt answered respectfully.

"Have you considered the accelerated Morgan program that is being taught at the Santa Barbara seminary in Montecito?"

"I applied, but never heard anything from them, Father."

"That is absolute nonsense." Fr. Paul's posture was now very upright in his seat. "The director of Santa Barbara should have been in touch with you immediately."

Within seconds two of his attendants, also priests, appeared out of nowhere. No one had seen them the entire afternoon or evening until now. Fr. Paul whispered to one of the priests to get the Santa Barbara seminary director on the phone immediately.

The college grads sat transfixed as the two priests scrambled to speak to the director on a satellite phone that was different from anything they had ever seen.

Paul asked his uncle about the phone.

"It's a special kind of satellite phone that gets a signal wherever you are and scrambles the signal so it can't be hacked. The Vatican had them developed. In fact, the Vatican now markets downgraded versions of this model to just about every president, chancellor, and high ranking official and despot in the world."

The priests returned quickly with the phone, and the director on the line. It was eleven thirty at night. Fr. Paul commenced speaking in fluent Italian to the director and it was obvious from his inflection that he was aggravated. Five minutes after the conversation began he switched to English and the mood of the conversation changed to one of agreement and less strain. Fr. Paul concluded the conversation with, "Matt Whaley will call you tomorrow to set up a time to visit the seminary and if he finds it to his liking, you will take care of the other arrangements and the other seminary. Gracias." He then hung up the phone and turned to Matt.

"Here is the personal number of Monsignor Angelo Moretti. He is expecting your call tomorrow. Go up and visit. If you like what you see and hear, your enrollment is guaranteed in the Morgan accelerated program. You could be a practicing priest in two years, not the customary four. I know from your education records that there is no doubt you can handle the program. I know you also have an interest in the furthering of your study of theology. My understanding is that you are nearly a scholar on the subject with only basic training. The Catholic Church in Rome is always looking for scholars, like my nephew Lewis here, to further investigate the scholastic side of our faith. If that is of interest to you, then it will be available."

"Thank you very much, Father. I don't know what to say." Matt was dumbstruck.

Fr. Paul replied, "I am embarrassed that you weren't given this opportunity when you applied. I am a lowly accountant and if I can spot a great candidate then what are the morons doing who are supposed to be experts at recruiting top quality priests?"

Paul watched this exchange between his fellow graduate and his uncle and noted that Fr. Paul evidently had done his homework on Matt, having investigated his scholastic and his athletic achievements. He thought about how he'd known his uncle was thorough, but it seemed there was nothing that he couldn't find out about somebody.

Now Fr. Paul turned his attention to Patrick. He paused as he sipped his wine and studied him intently. "Are you sure you don't want to play professional football? I have watched a number of your games and you could be the next LT."

"No sir," Patrick said politely. "I have some thoughts about programming that could really change the way computers function in the future. That's more important to me than being a warrior on television. I've often thought that I have been phenomenally lucky not to be seriously injured. It's time to count my blessings and move on to really important work."

"Impressive, very impressive," Fr. Paul said. "I told my nephew Paul the last time we visited, that the church needs computer experts to help master our worldwide interests. We've tried bringing them up from our ranks but we haven't gotten the results we want. We suggested to the Holy Father that we employ the best, no matter what their faith. I know that you are a good Christian, whose church is very close in its beliefs to Catholicism. On behalf of the Vatican, I am offering you an opportunity, once you have perfected your computer programming ideas, to come to work for us. We may be the only interested parties today, but by the time you're ready, there will be many. Remember we were first to see your genius and I will personally up the ante on any offer and circumstance that you require to work for us. Do you understand my offer?"

"Yes, Father, I do. I may just take you up on it one day. I do have one question. Do I need to convert and become a priest?"

"That's two questions." Fr. Paul laughed. "And no to both. The Vatican employs all colors, faiths, and beliefs at its top levels. Remember, we are the most successful business the world has ever known. Keep that in the back of your mind."

"All I can say is thank you." In the space of a few seconds, another of their party was dumbstruck.

Paul, standing off to the side, was hit with two thoughts: Fr. Paul is being unbelievably generous to my best friends, and what does he have up his sleeve? Fr. Paul had done his research and clearly he knew what he was talking about. Paul wondered how his uncle had uncovered so much information about his friends. What was his real intent? It would be revealed to him very quickly after his friends left with their respective families.

Chapter 37

PAUL WAS FILLED with both dread and anticipation thinking about the conversation he was about to have with his uncle. Past experience indicated that Fr. Paul would lead the conversation in the direction he wanted it to go.

"Those are great friends to have Paolo. Lifetime friends. The kind who will be with you through thick and thin."

He offered Paul a glass of wine and Paul knew it would be extremely rude to turn it down. As he tasted the wine, his palette remembered the fine taste and aroma as years of vintner magic and expertise danced across his tongue.

Fr. Paul took the initiative and began the conversation to gain control, as always. Paul knew his uncle always needed to be in control of the discussion, just like every previous one he remembered.

"From the expression on your face when you first saw me, I guess the best place to start would be to give you an update on my health." His stare never left his nephew's face. "I am recovering from an illness. The recovery has taken longer than I anticipated. The Vatican has access to the best physicians in the world, so my care could not be improved upon.

"There was nothing in this world that would have stopped me from being here to see my namesake graduate. It is also very heartwarming to me to see that your friends and business associates feel strongly for you. You are well loved. That is very important in the secular life that you have chosen. I would have loved to see you follow in your brother's and my footsteps on the road less traveled, but that appears, at least for now, not to be your future. From your expression, I know you have questions for me, so proceed."

Fr. Paul picked up a glass of wine and took a sip. Lewis followed his lead.

"I appreciate your coming from so far, but as you can tell, I'm concerned about your health. I've never seen you look this sick before."

"I am recovering and though I appreciate your concern, it is nothing to worry about. I am also here to remind you of the promise you made to me about my invitation to visit the Vatican as our guest. I can facilitate your transportation on my private jet and you will have the vacation you so richly deserve. I want you to see the crowning achievement of my life's work at the Vatican. With your advanced accounting and now, with your proficiency in computer programming, I think that you will appreciate what I have done. I am also aware that your education in this area is much more current and advanced than either my own or my coworkers, so any advice that you can give us will be appreciated. As an outside consultant, you will be very well paid for any help you provide."

"I think you greatly overestimate my skills and education. I took programming as a minor to my accounting degree. I had the thought that I wanted to learn how to possibly adapt the firm's software to being more conducive to continual changes in the tax code, not to ever consider being some sort of computer expert." Paul was perplexed because his uncle always brazenly bragged about the church's access to the best technology in the world.

Fr. Paul quickly finished his glass of wine. "My God, it's been a long time since I was allowed to have a drink of this divine nectar."

Paul took this as a cue to refill his uncle's glass. Glancing at his brother's glass he urged, "Drink up. How often does your little brother graduate from college?" He had already topped off his glass to give them the impression that he had finished his.

"Yes," Fr. Paul continued, "We have access to the world's talent in this area but one thing that is missing is you. I can trust you but not anyone else. You are my nephew and namesake. And I think you underestimate your skills and education. According to your professors, you were a brilliant student and scholar in both accounting and programming.

"Another question that I have for you is how many of your fellow classmates were embarking on those two subjects at the same time? Let me answer that question for you, none. Out of about nine hundred accounting graduates at UCLA this year, you were the only one who pursued both at the same time. You know, I know of only one other person who did that in their college career. Me, way back when. Do you know how many resumes we look at as possible independent contractors for the accounting department from all over the world that have those two pursuits at the same time? Maybe four or five worldwide per year."

As his uncle spoke, Paul wondered what he was up to. His uncle had always been civil to him, but this was the first time Paul could remember being praised by him. It was so unlike his uncle. He felt Fr. Paul was playing his hand at cards and was setting him up to lose.

The wine was beginning to affect his uncle. This first taste of wine since his illness was much more potent than when they previously had wine together. The last time he had visited, as Paul remembered, it took about four to five glasses to get his uncle to loosen up and begin to speak openly about the church.

He glanced over at Lewis, who wore a dumb look of admiration for his uncle. It disgusted Paul. He wondered how his brother could be so brain dead and spineless as to fall for the venom that Fr. Paul and the church fed him? Paul felt a powerful urge to punch Lewis in the face, to break the trance or spell he was under. He refocused on his uncle.

"Your brother has given his entire existence to further the church. Do not be critical of what you don't understand." Fr. Paul, though tipsy, looked at his nephew and sensed his thoughts.

Great, Paul thought, now he can read my damn mind.

"To cut to the chase," Fr. Paul went on, "I want you to consult for me and my division at the Vatican. I will make it very financially worthwhile. I will give you any access you want but make no mistake, I want Paul Morgan's fingerprint on this. Mine and yours. It will be my legacy and contribution to the church and it will you give you financial rewards that you can only dream of. And you will have the opportunity to help the church, which has always been such a focal point of our family. I'm not asking you to give up your partnership and accounting practice here. This work would be in addition to your business."

Paul was a bit stunned at the offer and he needed a little time to regain his composure. His uncle had dropped a lot on him in a very short span of time. Paul tried to come up with a plan on the fly. His uncle's offer might be his chance to really see the inner workings of the church. It could confirm or dispel his suspicions about what was going on in his faith's central nervous system. And if it was as tainted as his uncle previously described, it could possibly give him an avenue to perhaps fix it one day. It was hard to think straight with all these thoughts racing through his head.

"Well, what do you think nephew?" Fr. Paul, having almost finished his second glass of wine spoke with a slight slur in his speech. "Is this something I can interest you in, not only for yourself and your church, but also for me?"

Paul quickly measured his reply. "Yes, I'll do it as long as it coincides with my other responsibilities. Yes, I'll help you."

Fr. Paul was very pleased. "My nephew, I am very pleased and proud. Now fill our glasses with wine to seal our deal."

As he poured more wine into his uncle's and brother's glasses, Paul hoped he hadn't just made a deal with the devil himself. But he believed it was the only way he could learn what was truly going on in Fr. Paul's world. A world that once was a source of comfort and belief, but now one that seemed to be an unbelievably corrupt and merciless vehicle for manipulation of the world and its followers.

Chapter 38

The next day began a great deal earlier than Paul would have liked when he got a call on his cell phone from his brother. Lewis and his uncle were coming over to say goodbye. There was an emergency in Rome that required them to leave much sooner than planned. The limousine pulled up to the house before seven o'clock. Paul had stayed at his parents' home last night and none of the other family members had gotten up yet due to the previous day's hustle and bustle.

The passenger door opened before their car attendant could get there to open it for them. Lewis climbed out with Fr. Paul in tow. Fr. Paul and Lewis looked a little worse for wear from last night's wine consumption. To Paul's great surprise, his uncle uncharacteristically hugged him. In his memory, his uncle had never been one to show any type of affection.

When Paul recovered from his shock, he found his arms being held by his uncle. Fr. Paul said, "I am very proud of you and look forward to seeing you in Rome."

Because of what had transpired last night, Paul hadn't slept well. During the long night, he had developed a strategy to buy time before embarking to the Vatican.

Again, as if he had read his mind, Fr. Paul said, "I know you need to pass your CPA certification and you need to be at the office for the first wave of tax returns. It's exactly how I would handle it. And as with most accounting firms, I know that the majority of your clients have different fiscal years."

"So," Fr. Paul continued, "the best time of the year for you would be May or early June when the weather in Rome is not oppressive. How does that sound?"

Paul agreed.

In an instant, they were gone. It all happened so fast that if he hadn't been holding an envelope that his uncle had slipped him, he would have questioned whether he had dreamed this encounter.

In the envelope was an identification badge for admittance into the Vatican and its office. The I.D. contained all of Paul's vital information but he noticed something that puzzled him. His photo on the badge looked as if it had been taken the day before. In fact the shirt and coat he wore in the picture were identical to what he'd had on when he left his condo to walk to the graduation ceremony. This greatly disturbed Paul. It was as though his uncle had eyes on him all the time. He affirmed that he would be careful about who he talked to about his plan to visit the Vatican.

As Paul turned to walk back into the house he noticed his sister Ashley watching him from the window. She just stared at him blank faced and unsmiling. As he approached her in the front room she blurted out angrily, "What the hell is going on? Have you sold out to Lewis, the enemy?"

Paul tried to calm her as he assured her he hadn't. "He wants me to visit after I've passed my certification boards. I said I would."

"He hasn't won another Morgan to his cult, has he?"

"Hell, no," Paul snapped.

"Are you sure, Paul?"

"I'm totally sure. Now let's drop it, okay?"

Paul headed upstairs to shower and get ready to leave for his home. He was picking up Sarina on the way and they were going out to breakfast. He knew he needed to tell her at least a portion of his plan.

He abruptly turned on the stairway and said to Ashley, "You're coming to breakfast with Sarina and me. Be ready in about ten minutes."

By the tone and manner in which her brother had spoken, Ashley knew it was important for her to go. Paul was going to let the only two people in his life that he trusted be privy to something that had been bothering him for some time. Ashley sent Tom a text message to tell him she was changing their breakfast plans.

True to his word, Paul was in his car honking the horn in ten minutes. Ashley had barely gotten out of the shower and into her clothes when she ran for the car. Her brother wouldn't wait for her very long, and as she climbed in he took off. She fumbled with her purse as she tried to apply her makeup before they got to her best friend's house.

Sarina, having been given a little more notice, was waiting in front of her parents' house. She waived to Ashley to stay in the front as she climbed into the back seat. She leaned over the front seat and kissed Paul on the cheek. He seemed very detached.

"Are you mad or are you hung over from the wine your uncle and brother insisted you drink with them?"

Without answering Sarina, Paul continued driving in the general direction of the restaurant they'd all agreed on. When he spun a sharp left turn into an undeveloped cul-de-sac,

Ashley and Sarina hung on for dear life. They were still trying to recover from Paul's race car driving, when he pulled to an abrupt stop.

"I'm going to tell you something that I don't ever want repeated. Do you understand?"

They agreed and Paul described what had transpired between him and his uncle the previous night. He went on at length about his uncle and the Vatican and his complete revulsion over what Fr. Paul had told him the last time that he and Lewis visited. Paul explained how his idea of investigating the Vatican was the catalyst for taking computer programming as a minor. He thought it would help him accomplish his secret agenda to learn and maybe correct what his uncle had done. He impressed on them how creepy it was that his uncle seemed to know everything about him even though he was halfway around the globe.

Paul was ashen when he pulled out his new identification card with the photo taken the day before. The two women sat in shocked silence, unsure of what to say. Sarina broke the silence.

"You know I love you, but I am also very afraid that if you do something to the church, they will eliminate you without a second thought. The history of our church is strewn with stories of martyrs who died unspeakable deaths. Paul, please reconsider."

He just shook his head no. "I can't. But remember, Fr. Paul's reach is very long. Hell, he knows about the composition of the firm's clients and when they file their returns. You must keep this a secret and tell no one."

Ashley and Sarina nodded in unison and promised they would keep silent.

"My first visit next May will be a cursory look," Paul continued. "Maybe it's not as bad as Fr. Paul bragged. There may be no way to pierce their security shield. I'm not going to rest until I at least see what it is that I'm up against. When I do go, we need to have a code or system in place so I can communicate with you safely. I am going to have to be damn sure about what I say or write."

Again, they all agreed.

"Let's go have breakfast. This spy stuff makes me hungry. Oh by the way, how do you like my identification card? Very official, hmm?"

Paul tried to lighten the effects of the bomb that he had just dropped on his two favorite people in this world. It didn't lessen their fear for Paul. In fact, they both were sick to their stomachs.

Sarina broke the silence when they pulled up to the restaurant. "You have to swear to me you won't do anything stupid. You promised me we would grow old together. Remember?"

Paul nodded.

"I will kill or kick the ass of anyone who tries to hurt you," Ashley declared emphatically.

Paul and Sarina were speechless at the vitriol in Ashley's tone of voice. They both knew she meant business.

Chapter 38

After revealing his undercover plan to infiltrate his uncle's world, Paul hoped that he had diffused some of his girlfriend's and his sister's anxiety. He had told them so that someone would be aware of his intentions. He'd given the most vanilla version in order to downplay the danger as much as possible. Of course, neither of the two people he'd told had reacted as expected. Paul hoped it would sound more like a research project but they'd reacted as if it was some sort of international espionage, which in fact it was.

As he continued to study the identification badge Fr. Paul gave him, it appeared much more complicated than the usual ID card or credit card. It bore the obligatory holograms, but it was thicker than the others he carried. Paul called his main man on technology, Patrick Richie, to arrange to stop by on his way to work.

He handed the identification card to Patrick, who was more than a little interested in it. He was going to take it to his computer lab at UCLA.

"Do not tell anyone about this card or that I'm checking it out for you," Patrick warned.

When Paul gave Patrick a puzzled look, Patrick said, "I mean it, don't say anything to anyone. I've seen one of these cards before. I'll call you in a couple of hours."

It didn't take long before he knew why Patrick was so concerned. He got a call at the office from a phone number he didn't recognize. Patrick was curt. "Meet me in fifteen minutes at the Starbucks on the corner of Sunset and Main." The phone immediately went dead.

Paul walked to coffee shop and about a half block away saw Patrick standing in an adjacent alley. He motioned Paul to walk in his direction. As soon as they were in the alley, Patrick pulled Paul into the back of a store.

Paul laughed and said, "Hey, what's with all the James Bond spy stuff? We've both got better things to spend our time on." But the look in Patrick's eyes told him something bad was up.

Patrick looked directly at Paul. "Short and sweet, that identification card is a whole lot more than an ID card. Behind your photo is a micro camera with an unbelievable pixel count for as small as it is. There is an audio device embedded in the magnetic tape on the back along with a very precise GPS tracking mechanism. It's so damn precise that I think its coordinate accuracy is within five or six inches. It has some sort of heat sensor for radar and infrared tracking. In a nutshell, what the hell have you gotten yourself into?"

Paul was dumbstruck. He told Patrick of his plan to find out what his uncle was up to in the Vatican and explained how his Fr. Paul had given him the badge to use when he came to visit in the spring. Paul went from looking surprised to terror stricken. "Oh no, they must have heard me discussing my plan to the girls. Damn, not only do they know what I'm up to, I've gotten the girls involved."

"I knew wide receivers weren't too smart." Patrick laughed.

"But you have to be the luckiest son of a bitch who has ever walked the planet."

"What the . . ." Paul eyed him with a very puzzled look.

"They just activated it while I was doing a scan on it. It sounded like a jet taking off on an ultrahigh frequency. I immediately threw a towel over it so if they were using the camera they'd think it was in your pocket or drawer. I left it at the lab in my office, locked up. You need to put it someplace where no one will find it or where it doesn't matter if someone does see it. And keep your mouth shut about this. Understand, dummy?"

Paul nodded. "Thank you. You probably just saved Ashley's, Sarina's and my lives. I owe you brother."

"What would make a religious organization need such high tech stuff to spy on its ID card holders? What are they doing that makes them so paranoid? If they're into blackmail, wow, what a tool to set someone up with. I mean that camera is something else. Thank God I had the ultrahigh frequency mike on or I would never have known it was going hot. I've never even heard of, let alone seen anything this advanced. You need to be very, very careful. These people mean business."

Paul was shocked. He believed more than ever now that his uncle and his division must be up to something really bad to go to such extremes to watch their employees. This thing sounds so advanced that they could take you out from anywhere on earth and never leave their office in Rome. What was Fr. Paul up to that he needed this kind of technology?

As Paul recovered from his shock, another thought occurred to him.

"Patrick, remember the damn satellite phone at the party a couple of days ago? My uncle was bragging about how secure it was and how the Vatican could sell as many of them as they wanted because they were so secure. Remember he talked about the ones they sold to leaders and despots that were not as good as the ones the Vatican used? Do you think they could be using those in the same way they use the ID cards to get information that they wouldn't otherwise be able to get? Damn, this is bad."

Paul was in a state of disbelief and Patrick brought him back to his senses with a good shake of his shoulders. "Listen, tell me everything you're thinking about doing and let me help you. If it means that much to you, it means that much to me.

"I'm saying this with no intention of defaming your family or relatives. When your uncle threw out the invitation to get me into the Vatican because of my computer and code expertise, it made my heart go cold. I felt like I was talking to Satan himself and he was looking into my heart and soul with only bad intentions. Your uncle gives me the creeps. Sorry, brother. There is something very evil about the man. I told my parents about his offer and they were surprised that he knew so much about me. They wondered why he would go out of his way to give a chance to a non-Catholic."

Paul felt dizzy and hot. He realized that he might have stirred up a very large and dangerous hornet's nest. A nest that encompassed the entire world. He was worried now. Not for his safety but for the safety of everyone he loved and cherished. And by blind luck or possibly divine intervention, the ID card hadn't been activated when he told the girls of his plan. What a dumb ass he was to think he could drive down an empty cul-de-sac and be safe from anyone hearing his damn plan.

Paul expounded on his suspicions and on his plan to expose his Uncle and the Vatican. The eyes and ears of his uncle and his organization would be on him every step of the way. This was very serious business but having gotten this break, he would never let the plan slip again. In fact, he had an idea to use the Vatican's eyes and ears to his advantage.

Paul stuck his hand out to shake Patrick's. He said, "You're in brother. I'm going to need all the help I can get."

Patrick pushed his hand away and hugged him. "I'm in, brother. Let's get the bastards."

Chapter 39

THIS TURN OF events upset Paul to the point of distraction. Anytime he allowed his mind to wander, it came back to the identification card. He couldn't bring himself to tell Sarina and Ashley of Patrick's recent discovery. They were paranoid enough with the little he had told them. The girls, now entrusted with Paul's secret, never discussed his plan anywhere they could be overheard. Paul sensed that Sarina knew there was more to the story because she continually asked him what was bothering him.

He needed to focus on preparing for the CPA exam around the holidays. Larry had pulled some strings so Paul could sit for it six months early due to his working at the firm for the last four years. He just couldn't blow it after Larry had gone to all the trouble of getting him an early exam date.

Tom preferred to take the full year to sit for his exam. He said he wanted to get through the first tax season without having to think about a damn test. Larry agreed with him.

Larry could tell that something was troubling Paul. He seemed distant and distracted. And with Larry's finger-on-the-pulse style of management, it wasn't long before he questioned Paul. Early one morning about two weeks after graduation,

Larry and Paul were the only ones in the office. Larry used the time to talk to his protégé about what was bothering him. He walked into Paul's office and asked if he had a few minutes to talk.

"Sure."

"What's bothering you? Are you having personal trouble at home? In over four years, I have never seen you like this for any length of time. What happened to Mr. Happiness?" Larry bombarded Paul with questions.

Paul wasn't surprised. It was in Larry's DNA to always come straight to the point. Paul started a little apprehensively, but knew in his heart he would have to tell his mentor the entire story. As Paul recounted the incidents with his uncle, Larry tried to remain as neutral as possible, but very quickly his blood began to boil over the statements made by Paul's uncle.

As Paul finished, Larry noticed the look of relief on his face. Larry paused a moment to try to frame his next remark with something that would resemble composure.

"Paul, this is absolute bullshit. Period. There is no other way to interpret it." Larry then surprised Paul. "What are we going to do about this?"

Paul told Larry of his plan.

His mentor said, "These people mean business. I know it's useless to try to talk you out of this so let's strategize how to best attack the problem. Have you given any thought to what you'll do if, in fact, you discover any wrong doing on the part of your uncle or the church? I don't have to remind you of the risks and possible consequences if you discover some horrible plan or plot."

"I've been thinking about that possibility," Paul said in a barely discernible voice.

Larry nodded. "I know this is bothering you a great deal. I certainly hope you know I will support and help you in any way I can."

Paul looked up at his mentor. "I hoped you would say that."

"Did you have any doubts?"

"No, but when I add all of this up, it kind of knocks me off my axis."

"That's understandable. Just remember, you have to keep your focus not only so that you can remain strong for your own sake, but so that you can act as normal as possible if they're watching you. The only way to be beat these charlatans is by deceiving them. You've got to go on like you always have in order to catch them.

"I want to help you any way I can, because I care for you, but also because I have issues with organizations that operate outside of the law and human decency. Trust that I am going to be right by your side through this, son."

This talk made Paul feel a whole lot better and of course his mentor was totally right on his assessment of how to proceed.

Chapter 40

PAUL REFOCUSED WITH a vengeance on what he needed to do and perhaps just as important, what impression he wanted to give to anyone who observed him, professionally and personally. He sat for his certification exam and he knew he aced it before he pressed the result button. So now he could call himself a CPA, which was central to his practice of accounting.

He and Sarina had their first Christmas together as a couple, and to her great surprise, he insisted on attending midnight Mass with her. Paul had always been a sporadic attendee at Mass, but he seemed to be more focused on his spiritual side since he graduated. Sarina was a bit surprised by his seeming to have turned over a new leaf with his renewed attention to his faith. She and his family expressed how pleased they were with Paul's refocus on being a practicing Catholic. But Sarina had grown to know Paul nearly as well as he knew himself. In her heart she suspected he was up to something, and she played right along.

Tom and Ashley discussed Paul when he and Sarina weren't around. Tom wondered out loud what had happened to his best friend. Going to Mass had never been a top priority for him before. Ashley suggested that it wasn't a bad thing and maybe the two of them should follow his example. Now, the foursome went to Mass together each week, either Saturday night or Sunday morning.

When Matt Whaley wasn't sequestered at the seminary in Santa Barbara, he attended Mass at the same church and often ran into his former teammates and their significant others. He was very pleased that they had rediscovered their faith and he told them so.

Paul asked Matt how he liked the seminary, its curriculum, and the Morgan fast track to priesthood. Matt told him that it was intense, but he really enjoyed the total focus on his main goal in life: becoming a priest.

Paul asked his former quarterback about his ultimate goal in the church. Matt explained that although there was great opportunity to advance within the ranks of the church hierarchy, it wasn't something that interested him. He wanted to be a shepherd for his own flock, not the owner and director of many flocks. His statements solidified what Paul had always thought of Matt. He was a good man, with nothing but good intentions about wanting to help people.

Out of the blue one Sunday, Paul asked Matt about his uncle's offer to work in Rome. Matt was grateful to Paul's uncle for the opportunity at the Santa Barbara Seminary and to be a participant in the accelerated program, but after that, his interests were and would always be local.

"Of course, I'd love to see Rome and the Vatican one day but nothing more. Your uncle works on a completely different level than your average parish priest. His focus is on the throngs of Catholics all over the world, not those in the backyard where he grew up."

Paul wanted more than anything to tell Matt of his suspicions about his uncle, but felt that doing so could possibly blow his cover. He kept his beliefs about Fr. Paul to himself, knowing that some day he would have to confess the truth about his uncle.

Paul mentioned to Matt that he seemed to be home from the seminary almost every weekend. Matt asked why he thought that was odd since they had no weekend classes at the seminary.

"Well, in the two years that Lewis was at the seminary he never came home once. He always gave the impression that he couldn't come home until he completed his two year program."

"That seems strange, but who knows?" Matt answered.

Paul now realized what he had always suspected. Lewis didn't want to, or couldn't, come home to the emotional mess he had left behind. Paul wondered if his brother had been ordered not to visit his family and friends to avoid weakening his newly announced commitment to the priesthood. Paul thought it was weird how the whole scenario had played out and he filed those thoughts away to revisit at a later date.

Paul speculated about what had possessed Lewis to walk away with everything going his way—Sarina, his great athleticism, and his "free" education. He just gave up and ceded the playing field. The thought occurred to him that maybe there was more of Fr. Paul in him than he had ever noticed. Paul recalled the night when wine had loosened his tongue and Fr. Paul talked about foregoing the secular life for his calling, but in the same breath admitted his fear of failure in getting an accounting practice off the ground. Lewis also had taken what Paul considered the easy way out.

Fr. Paul became a priest who ultimately rose to the position of CFO of the Catholic Church. Paul wondered if his uncle ever thought of what he could have done in the secular world if he had taken that path and whether it ever bothered him. Did he really need the crutch and head start that the church afforded him? Paul made a mental note to broach this subject with his uncle a later date, when he had a little wine in his system to help him actually tell him the truth rather than a concocted story.

That meeting came a lot sooner than even Paul could have guessed. On April 16, the day after the first tax deadline, he received a phone call from his uncle in Rome. He was sending his private jet for Paul in three days. He was looking forward to his visit and was eager to show him the Vatican and Rome. As he was about to the end the call Fr. Paul said, "Don't forget to bring your identification card with you. It's very important."

Chapter 41

PAUL HAD LITTLE time to ruminate on what was coming. His first priority had to be getting his confidants on the same page. Sarina, Ashley, Patrick, and Larry all had to know that whatever he said to them while he was in Rome could possibly be overheard and anything that he wrote, including text messages, could be intercepted. They needed to sit down and come up with a simple code for relaying information in secret.

Paul called a meeting with all those concerned on Wednesday after work. He didn't include Tom; he felt the need to keep the inner circle to as few as possible. He trusted Ashley to fill Tom in as appropriate. The meeting started sharply at six o'clock.

In a very short statement, Paul informed them that he was going to the Vatican on Friday and he believed his communication and correspondence with the outside world would be monitored to a certain extent. He wanted to put in place a short, basic code they could use to contact each other and relay information. To an outsider, the verbal code resembled a football play with its reverse meaning, but the recipient of the message would know the true meaning with only few words.

The topic of this meeting made the danger to Paul seem more tangible now. Sarina and Ashley were more vocal than the others in their concern for Paul, which he shrugged it off in an effort to downplay the danger.

"I just want to be prepared for anything I may encounter. Because of the security Fr. Paul has put into effect, there's a real possibility that my conversations will be monitored. My Vatican ID is a surveillance device. Let's not get too worked up about something dangerous. This could be happening because of Fr. Paul's paranoia about his financial dealings. Just don't say anything that you wouldn't want my uncle or brother to hear."

Paul's confidants agreed. The meeting concluded and they adjourned.

Tom waited for Ashley in the lobby of the office and acted like he had been ostracized from the inner circle. Paul immediately spotted Tom's feelings were hurt.

"Hey Tom, I need to see you in my office for minute."

Paul asked Tom to shut the door. He told him the exact same thing that he had told the others. Tom asked him why he hadn't been invited to the meeting. Paul said something about another layer of security and told Tom of his intention to ask for Sarina's hand the next day. He told him no one knew, and he would kill him if he divulged this to Ashley. Tom promised he wouldn't.

"I'll call you from Lisa's restaurant tomorrow night and if she refuses my proposal you should come by yourself because I'll be getting drunk and will need a driver to get me home and to the flight the next day."

"I don't think there is any chance she'll refuse." They both laughed.

Sarina longed to ask Paul more questions but didn't want to mar their last two days together before he left for Rome. Paul felt a strong urge to unburden himself to Sarina but decided to keep the information as he'd left it. At the last minute, Paul asked her if she would like to go to Lisa's for dinner tomorrow night.

"You know, dessert and a drink might be just the ticket."

Sarina gave Paul a warm, tender smile.

They were met at the door by Lisa, who personally escorted them to a private booth set off by itself from the foot traffic of the restaurant. If they hadn't sat there before, that probably would have alerted Sarina. Lisa asked them if they knew what they wanted for dinner.

"Why don't you decide for us," Sarina answered, adding, "and we'd love some of your famous chocolate cake and that fabulous wine you got us addicted to."

"Okay, coming right up."

Lisa's selection of pescepescado with fettuccine in Alfredo sauce arrived along with a bottle of Chablis. Paul and Sarina took their time savoring the meal and enjoying being together. When their dinner plates were taken away, an entire chocolate cake was brought to the table. Sarina questioned the waiter.

"Lisa's orders," the waiter said with a grin.

As Paul handed Sarina a knife to cut the cake, she made a comment about how they could really get fat eating the whole thing. The sound of metal hitting metal caused Sarina to gasp.

"What in the world? This is weird," Sarina said as she carefully proceeded to slice into the multi-layered cake. When she saw the diamond tennis bracelet in the cake she glanced over at Paul who had a guilty expression on his face.

"What? You always wanted one, so I got it for you."

"Oh, Paul. You shouldn't have, but I love it. Here, you can clean the chocolate off it." They both laughed.

Paul got up as if to excuse himself. He came around to the far side of her chair and knelt on one knee. Sarina's with wide eyes gazed down at him.

"Will you—"

"Yes!"

Paul produced a very large diamond centered engagement ring and slipped it on her finger. Tears of joy streamed down her face as he lifted her up and they hugged each other. They became aware of the muffled applause from Lisa and her staff, who had witnessed the entire proposal. Congratulations began to stream in. Sarina would later recall that it had been the happiest moment of her life.

They finished their chocolate cake and drove to Paul's condo in silence. Sarina couldn't stop touching her ring. She finally broke the silence. "When can I—"

"We'll tell everyone tomorrow at dinner so they can all hear it all together. If that's okay with you." It was as if he had read her mind.

"Why do I bother? I start sentences and you finish them." She laughed and put her arms around him.

Paul sent emails and texts that evening to their parents, all their family members, and their friends to be at Lisa's tomorrow evening for a surprise dinner for Sarina. He told both his and Sarina's parents that he had ordered a limousine to pick them up at five o'clock so there was no need for them to drive downtown. This raised questions with both sets of parents, who got on the phone immediately and began to speculate what was going on.

When Tom received his text message he smiled. Sarina had said yes. He picked up the phone and called Paul.

"What's up?"

"Just wanted to confirm that Ashley and I will be there. Hey, do you mind if I bring my parents and my sisters?

"Yeah man, that would be great." The families had always been close and Paul didn't give it a second thought.

Thursday morning at work Sarina reluctantly took her ring off to save the moment for later. It was even more difficult to keep their engagement a secret from her best friend, who was very perceptive and kept asking her why she was in such a good mood.

Sarina deflected the question. "It's such a nice day for the families to have dinner together." That raised Ashley's suspicion even more.

Sarina countered the interrogation. "You look amazing. Are you exercising more, or taking vitamins or on some sort of diet? You look positively radiant."

"No just the usual stuff," said Ashley.

For all of the dinner participants the day dragged on as they watched the time crawl by slowly. Each one had an idea of what was going to transpire. What they'd hoped for so long would be announced that evening, and it couldn't come fast enough for them.

Finally it was five o'clock. Larry and Dianne had ordered a town car for themselves, Paul, Sarina, Ashley, and Tom to ride over to Lisa's. Lisa had reserved a corner of the restaurant for all of the invitees, which included the private booth that Paul and Sarina had occupied the night before.

When they arrived, they were met by Lisa and her staff and ushered to their private section of the restaurant. Almost immediately the wine steward appeared with Larry's favorite wine. They all took glasses and Larry said he wanted to propose a toast this evening, to the future of his firm. Everyone except Ashley raised a glass.

Sarina noticed. "You're not drinking?"

"I have a headache and I don't need to make it worse with wine."

Hmm, Sarina thought, you didn't say anything about having a headache on the way over.

The first guest to arrive was Matt Whaley. Paul had sent him a text invitation but didn't expect him to be there if he couldn't leave the seminary until the weekend.

"Don't look so shocked," Matt said with a grin. "We can come and go very much like we did in college. What, do you think that the seminary is some sort of prison?"

"Of course not. I just had it in my head that you couldn't come and go as you pleased. My mistake." Paul again thought of Lewis, who had told his parents that he couldn't leave the premises while he was enrolled in that very same seminary.

"You know that I wouldn't miss this dinner for anything. And when I got a second text from Tom, I knew it had to be very important."

Paul wondered why Tom had felt the need to solidify his invitation to Matt.

"I have a question for you." Paul took Matt aside and asked, "Can you perform a marriage ceremony while you're still a student at the seminary?"

"Yes, I can." Matt smiled and grabbed his friend's arm. "I hoped you were asking me to be here for the announcement of your engagement. It would be my honor to marry you two. You know what's funny? Tom asked me the same question for himself and Ashley. He's going to propose to her. I gave him the same answer I gave you. It seems my old wide receivers' minds think alike."

Paul didn't know how to react to this news but he thanked Matt for being at the dinner.

The guests arrived and mingled and when the bell was rung to be seated for dinner, all took their prearranged seats. Wine had been placed before each setting so Paul immediately stood to address the dinner party.

"I am happy you all could come. It's a very special night. To get the suspense out of the way so the party can begin, I asked Sarina to marry me last night and, unbelievably, she said yes."

There was collective sigh and applause broke out. Paul turned and helped Sarina to her feet. She had placed her engagement ring on under the table and stood and raised her left hand for everyone to see. The applause got even louder. Paul then motioned everyone to sit down.

"I'm sure everyone here suspected the reason for this dinner so let's all have fun tonight."

Paul's parents hugged Sarina's parents and the party was just starting to roll when Tom rose from his seat. He tapped his glass with his spoon to quiet the room. Paul's first thought was that his best friend was going to propose a toast to him and Sarina.

As the noise died down, Tom cleared his throat. Paul noticed that his best friend was sweating profusely; perspiration ran down his face. Paul made a mental note to suggest that Tom consider joining Toastmasters to get over his fear of public speaking. Tom looked around the room and cleared his throat again. Paul and Sarina glanced at each other, perplexed.

Tom leaned over and took Ashley's hand to bring her next to him. He began to speak jerkily. "I am very happy to propose the first toast to Paul and Sarina. We all knew this day was coming. It just took longer for Paul than we thought it should."

Paul nodded and smiled at Tom.

Tom continued, "But before we toast the soon-to-be bride and groom. I have an announcement to make." He turned and smiled at Ashley.

Paul looked at Sarina and said, "Uh oh."

Tom again cleared his throat and continued, "I have asked Ashley to marry me and she has accepted." The shocked group loudly applauded. Tom raised his hand for silence. Normally,

I wouldn't steal the thunder of this special occasion from my best friend, but I have something else to announce to this very special family gathering. I . . . I mean we're expecting a baby."

The collective inhale from all present seemed to suck the oxygen out of the room. The dinner guests glanced at each to gauge their reactions. Slowly a muffled applause began.

Sarina caught Paul's eyes as she said, "I knew something was up when she didn't have any wine. She looks radiant. Now I know why." She added, "You need to be supportive and nothing more. Got it?"

Tom's and Ashley's parents were now the recipients of congratulations along with Paul's and Sarina's parents. This was truly a "double barrel" announcement. Paul watched as Matt made his way over to Paul's sister and soon to be brother-in-law. Matt hugged them both and almost simultaneously they all turned toward Paul.

With Sarina on his arm, Paul moved quickly to give his sister a hug and congratulate her. He turned to Tom and hugged him and whispered, "It's about damn time."

As he retreated from the hug, Tom said, "Ashley and I want you to be the baby's godfather." Paul nodded, speechless, as his eyes filled with tears.

The festivities continued for the next few hours until Paul glanced at his watch. He realized it was time to go. He had a flight the next day and he wanted time to reflect on the evening's developments at home with Sarina.

The original party gathered to take the town car back to the office with Larry and Dianne. They were en route when Larry broke the silence, "I want to congratulate both couples on this magical evening. Very surprising. Very pleased. But I've got to say this at the risk of getting into trouble. We better start making arrangements with an architect to put a nursery in the firm's office." The sound of laughter filled the town car.

Larry smiled as he turned to Tom. "I knew I should have castrated you with that big knife in my desk when you started." The merriment didn't stop until they all arrived at the office.

Chapter 42

Sarina and Paul made themselves comfortable on the couch in Paul's condo. They held each other close as she said, "You have made me the happiest person on earth, Paul Morgan."

"Ditto," was his reply.

"Are you mad about Ashley and Tom?"

"Not at all. I knew it would happen sooner or later but sometimes schedules are determined in a way that we can't control."

They laughed and continued to hug each other in silence for a while until Sarina said "We better get to bed so you'll be rested for your trip tomorrow."

Neither of them slept well. In their minds they attributed their insomnia to the adrenalin of the evening but both, unbeknownst to the other, were thinking about the same thing—the trip the next day to Rome.

Sarina wondered what the trip would hold. Would Paul discover what his uncle was so secretive about? Would Paul be in danger? What was so important that Fr. Paul needed to show it to his nephew? Sarina didn't trust Fr. Paul, but the one thing she didn't fear was that he would be able to brainwash Paul as he had done his older brother. Even though she was much happier with Paul, she couldn't help wondering if she had played a part in Lewis's complete turnaround and his becoming a priest. She would never know the answer, but it still bothered her.

Paul, on the other hand, pondered what he would see and hear in the Vatican. He, too, wondered what was so very important about what Fr. Paul had been working on that he insisted he must show Paul. He knew that he still had a few details to tell Sarina before boarding that plane. He reaffirmed to himself that he would wait until the last minute so she wouldn't have the opportunity to talk him out of the trip. He knew that if there was anyone who could dissuade him from going it was Sarina, and he was determined to go through with it. Paul also considered the sick feeling he got in his stomach and heart every time he thought about what his uncle had been up to. It filled him with dread. He knew he had to go or it would haunt him for the rest of his life. He was getting on that plane.

Dawn came too quickly because neither of them had slept much. They got ready for the airport and headed out with Sarina driving. Paul joked, "Hey, you look good in the driver's seat. For a wedding present, I think I just might buy you a convertible."

They arrived at the private jet terminal at Burbank airport. Paul had to show his identification badge at the gate to gain admittance. After clearing the security check point, Paul looked at Sarina and just knew she was going to say something provocative, so he placed his finger over her lips and nodded at the badge and then shook his head no. She realized that the badge was recording their trip conversation.

He winked at her, saying he was excited to finally get to see Rome and the Vatican. He winked again and said, "It will be nice to see where Lewis lives and works, and to see Fr. Paul again. I hope he looks better than the last time. He looked rough, but he's tough as nails. I don't think there's anything that can keep him down for long." The devilish grin on his face told Sarina that he was setting up his brother and uncle with nice compliments about them.

When they pulled up to the terminal, they were greeted by a valet. Paul popped the trunk and told him which pieces of luggage to take. The valet reached for Paul's briefcase and Paul stopped him. "No, I will take care of that myself."

The valet informed Paul that the plane would be ready soon.

"No problem, more time with my girlfriend."

Sarina looked at him with a pout and said, "Girlfriend? I'll show you girlfriend, mister."

As the valet turned to leave, Paul said, "Hold up a minute." He took his identification badge from his pants pocket, placed it in his jacket and handed his jacket to the valet. "It's too hot for a jacket." The valet continued into the terminal. Paul said to Sarina, "Let's go sit on that bench over there now that I don't have the monitor listening to our conversation."

They sat and Paul pulled a large manila envelope from his briefcase. He began with, "You know I believe only the unprepared get surprised and lose, so I had some preventative measures taken to make sure I come back to you, baby."

Sarina could only stare at him. She saw in his eyes that he truly loved her but she also saw a trace of concern in them.

"I set up a trust covering everything I own or am entitled to," Paul continued. "This is yours if anything happens to me. Also, there's a five million dollar life insurance policy with you as the sole beneficiary."

She started to speak and he just placed his index finger on her lips. "Let me finish before you start. There is something my uncle wants me to see that he is extremely proud of. I know that. If I'm able to find out more about Vatican finances without triggering some sort of alarm, I will. But I will do nothing to endanger myself. The preemptive measures of life insurance and the trust were going to be done anyway, so it's money well spent. Know that I love you more than anything on this earth and will come back to you to enjoy the rest of our lives together."

Tears streamed down Sarina's face and Paul's eyes were red as they stared at each other.

The valet reappeared to announce that his plane was ready to depart. They embraced and Paul started to walk to the terminal. He turned, winked at her, and said, "Remember the code."

Chapter 43

PAUL WAS ESCORTED to the private jet by the valet, who handed him his coat as he started up the stairs to the plane. The valet said something in Italian to the pilot at the cabin door. They both chuckled, and from their mutual camaraderie, it appeared that they knew each other.

The pilot shook Paul's hand and said with an Italian accent, "Welcome aboard, Mr. Morgan. We are happy to take you to see your brother and your uncle. I am your uncle's personal pilot. He said he wants you to have the smoothest trip possible so we will do our best to accommodate his wishes. And by the way, I am sorry you had to wait fifteen minutes. Your uncle expects punctuality. My apologies. Again, welcome aboard."

Paul sat in a large overstuffed recliner on a rotating pedestal that allowed him to face in any direction. He looked toward the rear of the plane where a couple of flight attendants were standing. Both were attractive in very short skirts—almost obscenely short. Fr. Paul, the international jet setter, he thought.

He wondered how the pilot knew almost to the minute what time he'd arrived at the terminal. Did the valet tell him or did he know because the identification badge had tracked him? In his mind, he was convinced it was the latter, and again he resolved to be on his guard at all times about what he said and what he did. The badge gave his uncle, and who knew who else, access to his conversations and his whereabouts.

He looked out his portal window and saw Sarina waving at him and he waved back. God I love that woman, he thought.

His train of thought was interrupted when one of the flight attendants leaned over and asked if she could get him something to eat or drink. Her accent had a slight trace of Italian with a heavier dose of French. She was a very attractive woman in her late twenties or early thirties.

"No," Paul answered. "I am a little tired. I think I might just close my eyes and take a nap."

She smiled and said that after the plane was airborne, she would show him the sleeping arrangements in the rear of the plane. There was no need to sleep in a chair when he could lie down on a real bed.

"Thanks. I might take you up on that."

The plane was very quickly airborne and Paul dozed off. When he awoke, he didn't know where he was at first. Someone had placed a light cashmere blanket over him while he slept. He looked at his watch and realized he had been asleep for a couple of hours. As soon as his eyes could focus, the two rather provocative flight attendants were standing over him. "Did you have a nice nap?" asked one.

"Yes, very nice, thank you."

"My name is Ingrid and she is Angeline. Isn't that your mother's name?"

Paul nodded. He touched the ID badge in his pocket and wondered if there was anything the attendants didn't know about him.

"If you would like, we can show you some of the amenities of the plane. Whatever you want, we are at your service."

"Thank you, maybe later. I'd like to get some sleep right now. How long is this flight to Rome?"

"About eleven to twelve hours depending on the tailwinds. The captain informed us we are getting quite a push right now, so we might just get there in a little under eleven hours. But we will keep you posted as we are updated. Let us show you your sleeping quarters."

Paul followed the attendants to the back of the plane. He thought that if their skirts were any shorter, their panties would be showing. He could only imagine what those two beautiful women had done to get this obviously easy job. They opened a door behind the galley and walked past two closed doors toward the tail of the plane.

The door in the center of the wall opened into a spacious bed room. It had a queen size bed and was very well appointed with paneling, a large flat screen television, and lovely antique furniture. Paul commented, "Those replicas of the Louis XIV furniture are amazingly accurate from what I remember from a French period class I took at UCLA."

They both giggled and Ingrid said, "They ought to look original because they are. Your uncle does not tolerate replicas, or fakes as he calls them. These are the Sun King's original bedroom furniture pieces."

That bastard, Paul thought.

Angeline opened a door on the left to reveal a full size bathroom with a tub and shower. Paul found it hard to believe that all of this fit within the confines of a private jet. He studied the tile closely and before he could ask, Ingrid said, "Yes, it's from the original quarry that supplied the stone for Michelangelo's Pieta."

Paul was impressed with the quality of the amenities and, again, he was struck by the opulence with which his uncle surrounded himself. He thought of the poor making their weekly donations at Mass. This plane and everything about it screamed to him that his uncle was truly a hypocrite of the highest order.

"If you need anything, don't hesitate to ring for us."

Paul nodded and ushered them out of the bedroom. Ingrid turned and faced him and said, "Oh, by the way, if you want to make a phone call to anyone, you can use your personal cell phone or the cabin phone. Angeline and I thought that you might want to call your fiancé, Sarina, to tell her you are safe and sound."

Again Paul silently nodded. He thought, is there anything these bastards don't know about me and my life? He might just take them up on that invitation after he got some more rest. He fell asleep almost immediately.

Chapter 44

WHEN PAUL AWOKE several hours later, it was pitch black outside the portal window. He looked at his watch and, although it said three o'clock in the afternoon, he knew that by heading east it would be much later than his Pacific Standard Time. He turned on the nightstand light and got his bearings. He stretched and thought he would use the shower and freshen up, then have something to eat before they landed. He roughly calculated that the plane would land sometime in the late evening and he didn't want to be bothered trying to find something to eat in a place where he didn't even speak the language.

His luggage had been placed on a stand in the room and he opened it to find that his suits and dress shirts had already been hung up in the closet for him. He wondered when this had occurred—when he boarded or when he was asleep. No matter. He went into the bathroom and started the shower.

He closed his eyes and sighed deeply, enjoying the extremely hot water running over his skin. He felt a slight breeze and opened his eyes to see Ingrid and Angeline in the bathroom with him wearing only bath towels. Both dropped their towels to reveal that neither had on anything else. Paul averted his stare as Ingrid asked if they might join him in the shower.

"No, and I would prefer that you both leave this instant," Paul said emphatically. Angeline came closer to the shower glass and pressed herself against it saying coyly, "Are you sure? We could have such fun."

"Thank you, no. Please leave."

They grabbed their towels and left the bathroom. Paul was stunned by this very forward behavior but he was determined to not let anything or anyone get the upper hand on him. He figured it must be another of his uncle's temptations, to see if he could get Paul to fall, or to find something he might be able to blackmail him with.

He finished showering, and as he shaved he plotted the cool manner with which he would handle what had just happened. Another Larry Vandermeer concept: Never let them see they rattled you.

In the main cabin both Ingrid and Angeline were waiting for him. They started to apologize and Paul stopped them. "Your offer was an unbelievable opportunity with two very beautiful women, but I am engaged to marry someone who I don't think would approve of my cavorting with two lovely ladies at thirty thousand feet. But thank you anyway. I will not soon forget your generosity." And other visual images, he thought.

Paul reseated himself and they asked if he was ready for dinner. They had Maine lobsters on board because they were told it was one of his favorite meals. Ingrid further stated that they were large and succulent, as if to tempt him with the double entendre.

"That will be fine," Paul said softly.

Angeline stayed behind to show Paul how to operate the state of the art entertainment center onboard. He could access movies and any television or radio station in the world. The picture was razor sharp and the sound quality was as if the band or musician was standing in front of him playing the music solely for his enjoyment. Angeline handed Paul the remote and dismissed herself to help with dinner. Paul opted for a news channel to check the day's happenings. A carafe of wine was by his side; the same brand of Pinot Grigio that his uncle favored. He took a sip and found an American cable news channel and settled in to watch.

It was more of the same news that was recycled on every evening broadcast. But one piece caught his attention. A field reporter in West Africa was giving updates on the Ebola outbreak that had so far claimed about three thousand lives. He saw workers put their dead in white body bags and into the back of waiting trucks to take to a common grave. He thought, how sad for the families and friends watching their loved ones being disposed of as though they were trash. It greatly saddened Paul.

The next segment of the news was about a respiratory ailment occurring in all fifty states. The pneumonia type symptoms came with a cruel twist; it caused paralysis in some cases. Though all ages had been stricken, the paralysis and deaths which occurred seemed to only affect children. Paul wondered how he would react if his child was suffering and it made him sick to his stomach for a moment. All of this pain and suffering in the world and the majority of the disease's victims are innocent children or the very poor in underdeveloped counties. It just was so unfair, Paul thought.

Before he knew it, Maine lobsters were served complete with a butter bib to protect his clothing. The meal was fabulous. It seemed to be a composite of all of his favorite sides especially the large Idaho baked potato. It was followed by a decadent pecan pie that had been made that morning and picked up in New Orleans at Cafe du Monde. It was delicious.

Paul was effusive in his praise. Not only was it worthy of praise, he was wanting his eavesdroppers to feel he had dropped his suspicions about his uncle's lifestyle. Let them think that they've overrun me with the whole over-the-top treatment, Paul thought. He almost purred when he told the flight attendants he thought it was the best meal he had ever tasted.

The captain came from the cockpit to inform his only passenger that they would be landing at Aero RomaFiumicino Airport in Rome within the hour. They had picked up almost two hours with tailwinds. Not to worry, his uncle would have a driver there to meet him. He added that he hoped the flight had been satisfactory.

Paul nodded. "Excellent."

"Great," the captain replied. "We just wanted to replicate your uncle's favorite travel menu."

Again Paul just nodded. "Thank you," was all he said.

Chapter 45

THE PLANE BEGAN its descent into Rome. The landing was so smooth it felt as if they were still in the air when Paul looked out the cabin window to find the plane had already touched down on the runway. They taxied to a private terminal and Paul noticed a 777 jumbo jet parked at the same terminal. It had the papal seal on each side. It was obviously the Pope's plane.

After thanking everyone on board, he started down the stairway. He was immediately greeted by his driver and assistant. They both looked vaguely familiar and then he realized that they had been with his uncle on each of his trips to California. They must be among the permanent staff his uncle maintained. Those thoughts quickly passed as Paul's senses were bombarded with various stimuli.

Paul had both dreaded and looked forward to this trip for some time. The warm Mediterranean air caressed him and he could almost taste the salty breeze. Even though it was after midnight, the bustle of people and activity took him by surprise. He was struck by Rome's similarity to New York where, day or night, the energy ran at full throttle. Rome seemed to be another city that never slept.

Paul was escorted to a very unusual looking Mercedes Benz limousine that had the unique appearance of being heavy and weighted down, like a cross between a Mercedes and a blitzkrieg tank. Paul realized his observation was not amiss when he tried to open the door and found that it weighed considerably more than the usual automobile door. Why would an employee of the Vatican need a luxury edition tank? He could understand it for the Pope but his uncle?

He made himself comfortable in the back seat and they were in motion very quickly. Every aspect of Fr. Paul's life ran like clockwork. Punctuality and efficiency were the overriding principles of his organization. No wasted motion or time. Paul picked up the car phone and asked the driver if he understood English, to which the driver answered in the affirmative.

"How far is it to the Vatican?"

The driver said it would take about twenty minutes because they were accessing a special underground tunnel through most of the city. Otherwise, it could take anywhere from an hour to an hour and half to the Vatican.

Paul was alone with his thoughts in the back of the limo. When they arrived at the Vatican gates, heavily armed security guards approached the vehicle. One of the guards held what looked like a bar code scanner in his hand. The driver lowered the security window. "Let them scan your identification badge."

Once Paul's ID was scanned they were passed through into the inner sanctum of the Vatican.

They pulled up to a condominium complex. Paul expected a traditionally robed priest or brother to meet him and was shocked to see two stunning women at the entrance steps. One of them opened the limousine door and welcomed Paul to the Vatican. Her beauty was only surpassed by her strength. She helped him out of the car by lifting him by his arm. She was strong, very strong. A heavyweight wrestler couldn't have pulled my arm with more power, he thought

Paul was shown the way to his suite by the other woman. Speaking in a very heavy Italian accent, she told him that his uncle and brother would meet him for brunch so he could catch up on his sleep tonight. She laughed and said four or five hours of sleep would get rid of the jet lag.

Paul smiled and nodded. To that point nothing he had expected had transpired. He wondered what other surprises were in store for him.

Chapter 46

PAUL'S ACCOMMODATIONS CONSISTED of a nicely appointed suite with a living room, bedroom, and bathroom with a Jacuzzi tub, among other amenities. However, his only concern was in pulling the sheets back and getting into bed. As soon as his head hit the pillow he was fast asleep.

Paul came out of his slumber a few hours later. He'd been so tired he hadn't even looked at his watch when he arrived in Rome. He kept it on Pacific Standard Time to remind him when to call or text Sarina. He looked at the bedside clock and saw it was eight o'clock in the morning. That meant it was ten in the evening California time. He grabbed his cell and called Sarina, remembering that his badge was on the night stand next to him.

Sarina answered and blurted out, "Paul, is everything all right? How are you? How was your flight? I miss you!"

Paul recounted the details since he had departed, including the awkward shower episode, to his fiancée.

In code, Sarina asked, "Are we being listened to?"

"Yes," Paul answered. The conversation was brief and he said he was looking forward to seeing his brother and uncle in a couple of hours and that he would call her later. He assured her again that he was okay and that he loved her very much.

Paul stretched as he got out of bed. He wanted to shower, shave and brush his teeth before his upcoming brunch. He'd just completed his morning ablutions when Lewis called to say that a town car would pick him up in about thirty minutes. "How was your trip?"

"Fabulous, absolutely world class."

"It'll be great to see you," Lewis said as he hung up.

Thirty minutes later, Paul was leaving the building. He noticed that the car was the same black Mercedes but that Vatican papal flags decorated the front fender of this vehicle. The obligatory driver and valet appeared. Every time Paul saw or rode in a car that had anything to do with the Vatican, it came with a two man crew. Other town cars and limousine services he'd used in the past operated without a crew. He wondered why Fr. Paul used this setup.

The cobbled, bumpy streets of Rome were congested with traffic that traveled at a high speed. Paul felt like he was in an amusement park ride that shifted from side to side. Either there was no speed limit, or drivers motored as fast as they possibly could regardless of traffic flow. It was pure mayhem but, amazingly, he didn't spot any accidents on the twenty minute ride.

The town car turned down a very quiet and quaint street off of the main thoroughfare and seemed to morph through a time machine to a much earlier place when hustle and bustle didn't exist. In fact the town car was the only vehicle Paul saw on the road. Later he learned the Vatican flagged automobile was the only vehicle allowed to use the roads in this section of Rome. The car stopped at a small cafe and Paul immediately spotted Lewis and his uncle sitting at an outdoor table shaded by an umbrella.

Paul opened the car door before the valet could get there and made his way to his brother. They hugged and then he turned to his uncle and was unexpectedly embraced by him. They exchanged pleasantries and sat down. Paul immediately noted his uncle did not look well. The months since he had seen him had not improved his medical condition; it had worsened.

"Well, what do think of Rome so far, little brother?"

Fr. Paul spoke up before Paul could answer Lewis. "What can he possibly think of Rome? He only arrived last night. All he's done is sleep and come here. How can Paul have formed any opinion as yet?"

They all laughed and talked about the family back in California. They both wanted to know Paul's opinion about Ashley's upcoming marriage and the announcement of her pregnancy. He was very diplomatic about his comments.

"Life sometimes brings surprises to which we must adjust."

Fr. Paul observed that his namesake had mellowed with time. "As you grow older you come to realize that what was extremely maddening in your youth now doesn't seem to bear as much weight. Such is the passage to wisdom."

Paul smiled. "Your words illustrate that passage, Uncle."

Their brunch had been preordered and was brought to the table by two waitresses, both attractive young women. They were very chatty, speaking fluent Italian with Lewis and Fr. Paul. One of the young women was strikingly beautiful with long black hair and a wild look in her eyes. She became positively radiant when she spoke to Lewis, flirting shamelessly with him. Paul thought that was odd because Lewis and Fr. Paul were dressed in their black cassocks, supposedly to convey their commitment to Christ. That sure didn't deter the waitress from her attention to his brother.

As the brunch came to an end, Lewis excused himself. Fr. Paul leaned over to his nephew.

"My namesake, I can see from your surprised expression that you believe it is inappropriate for the waitress to express an interest in your brother. One thing you will need to keep in mind when you see how he and I live is that it isn't what the general public thinks or is told. In fact, it is just the opposite. Remember that before judging anyone here on the public's view of being a religious person."

He leaned even further over to Paul and said, "You and I will talk privately later. There are things I need to tell you and you alone. Lewis knows a great deal, but not the whole story. He only knows what he needs to know. I am invoking your silence because of my trust in you. Do you understand and agree to that, my nephew?"

Paul nodded.

"Very well. Our next destination is the financial center of the Vatican. Lewis is only allowed with his badge to a certain point. I am taking you well past his credentials. I know he wants to give you a tour of the city and I approve, but later. As you can see, I am not doing well. It is imperative that we make your visit as productive as possible. My original hope was that you would be my successor here when I am gone. But after all your hard work and subsequent success in the lay world, it would be ridiculous for me to ask you give it up to pursue a religious path. And now, with the announcement of your marriage, it seems that path will never be an option. That is fine. We, the church, need your brilliance. I have let the powers that be know that you can be trusted. My word and reputation have been given. There are surely others who can continue my work, but none are my blood kin. Is this acceptable to you?"

"Yes."

On the car ride to the Vatican financial center, Lewis pointed out various historical locations. Paul was impressed with the

Coliseum. He thought of all of the contests that had been staged there over the millenniums and how many lives had been lost in pursuit of triumph in the games. From the lions that were used on the newly converted Christians to the gladiators who sought freedom from slavery by entertaining the blood-thirsty crowds. In spite of all the misery that transpired there, it was still a twenty-first century attraction.

The town car arrived at a very modern building within the shadow of St. Peter's Basilica. The glossy windowed exterior made a stark contrast to the classic Roman architecture. Lewis was not joining them so he told his brother that he would call him later; they would have dinner together that evening.

Paul was astounded by the number of armed guards and the security technology he saw in the facility. His uncle directed him to a security office before they entered the building. He was electronically fingerprinted, his retinas were scanned, and his skin was scraped for DNA. A security officer held a scanner to his forehead, the purpose of which Paul didn't know and didn't ask. His badge was updated with all of the new information and handed back to him. He was surprised that all the staff spoke English.

"Only English is spoken here as you might have noticed. It seems to have become the world's official language," Fr. Paul explained, looking at Paul.

Did that bastard just read my mind? Paul thought.

The security checkpoint was infinitely more involved than the usual airport screening. All who were admitted went through three different body scans. Fr. Paul later explained it was necessary for detection of not only weapons but any type of microchip implants and computer discs. Nothing like that was allowed into or out of the financial center. Paul noticed that upon leaving the building everyone had to go through the same process.

Paul and his uncle navigated their way through security and rode the elevator to the top floor and Fr. Paul's office. As he slid his badge through the slot on his door, Fr. Paul explained that the badges were encoded to limit the access of some of the staff to certain portions of the complex.

In the ultra-modern office resided one of the largest computer screen displays Paul had ever seen. Five of them were arranged on Fr. Paul's desk in a semi-circle. Five! His uncle explained that it gave him the ability to work or look at five different processes at the same time. He could also split each screen into many sub screens if he wanted. He showed Paul the numerous divisions of the center, the most important and sensitive financial divisions being located on this floor.

After they toured the entire floor and Paul was introduced to each department head, they returned to Fr. Paul's office. A fountain in the corner of the office turned out to be a facade that moved when his uncle touched a button. When an elevator was revealed, they got in and he told Paul to use his badge and to push the button with the helicopter on it.

When the door opened, Paul was astonished to find they were on the roof where a helicopter sat ready.

"Occasionally, I need to get to the airport immediately and the helicopter is always here at my disposal. It is a special American made Black Hawk used by the US military. When I have international visitors who need to keep their identities unknown, the helicopter delivers them to the financial center to meet with me when circumstances dictate it."

Back in his office, Fr. Paul motioned for his nephew to take the chair next to him behind his desk.

"I am very sick. There is nothing modern medicine can do for me. My time on this earth is limited, very limited. I need to show you as much as possible. The Vatican needs your help to streamline many of our accounting procedures. Will you help us?" Fr. Paul looked into his nephew's eyes as he delivered this news.

"I will do anything for my family and my faith, Uncle. You know that or I wouldn't be sitting here. Let's get started."

The two of them proceeded to view the various accounting screens while Fr. Paul questioned his nephew about his opinion on certain accounting procedures. Several hours passed with only a couple of brief distractions when refreshments were brought in. Their session continued until Fr. Paul stopped work because he was very tired.

"I'm sorry. I am just not the man I used to be. This illness has robbed me of one of my best traits—endurance. It is not unusual for me to spend a day and a half working nonstop without realizing how much time has elapsed. I find the work intoxicating and fulfilling. Some would say I'm possessed or sick. Not me."

Paul got the impression from the rapid sequence of events that his uncle didn't have long on this earth. He concentrated on every detail, for it appeared that, whether or not he wanted to take on this task, Fr. Paul had put his stamp of approval on his doing just that.

Outside, the sky had darkened. An exhausted Fr. Paul said, "That's enough for you for today. There is no shortage of work and tomorrow we will take up where we left off. Besides, you must be famished. Your brother is already at one of our favorite restaurants waiting for you and there is a car downstairs to take you to him. Have a good evening and sleep well tonight, my nephew. I must retire for the evening so I can keep up with you tomorrow."

Paul stood to leave and his uncle leaned over and grasped his hand very tightly, looking up at him from his seated position. "I am very proud of you. I have always dreamed that you would be my replacement when my time comes. I see that I was right in my assessment of you, and if all you can be is a partial replacement for me that will be enough. Your brother is a wonderful human being but he is not you. He has a fabulous mind but it is equipped only for theory. Your brain is uniquely wired in not only theory but also in application of theory. Your thinking is very much like my own. I always suspected this and now after spending a day with you, it is very obvious that I was right. Thank you. Now go, you are late."

Paul looked back at his uncle who had always been larger than life to him. And now here sat a sick old man grasping for approval from his namesake.

Well, I will give it to appease him. But I will never mean it. Ever. And with those thoughts, Paul left.

Chapter 47

Outside the temperature had dropped considerably from the pleasant warmth of the morning. Paul breathed in the cool air to clear his head. In the town car he sat back in his seat and thought about the day's events. He wanted to call Sarina and fill her in, but he had the damn badge with him.

"I've been worried about you. How is everything?" Sarina sounded anxious.

He told her how unbelievable the city and the financial center were and that he was on his way to meet his brother for dinner. "I'll call you after dinner, if it's not too late."

"I don't need to sleep. I need to hear your voice. I'll be waiting. Have a wonderful meal with your brother. I love you. I love you very much."

"Ditto," he said as he hung up.

The opulence of the Italian restaurant was overwhelming. The maître d' escorted Paul to his brother's table, which was actually a private dining room. His brother stood up and Paul took note that Lewis was wearing a suit instead of his religious garb. It was obvious to even his plebeian eyes that this was a very expensive handmade Italian suit. Lewis noticed Paul looking at the suit and said "For your Christmas present I will have my tailor measure you for one."

"I don't want you wasting your money on something like that for me."

"No, it would give me a great deal of pleasure to have it made for you. I insist. My tailor will measure you on Saturday when we go sightseeing. It's done."

Paul got his bearings and took notice of his surroundings. The artwork was in the style of the French Impressionists. He was surprised to learn that they were not prints but the original oil paintings. Lewis explained that this restaurant was as much an art museum as it was a place to eat. Each private dining room had its own theme.

As soon they took their seats a waiter appeared with a basket of Italian bread.

"I remember how much you liked a fresh loaf of Italian bread when we were kids so I took the liberty of ordering a couple of loaves. But with one exception; these were actually made in the Pope's private bakery this afternoon and were brought here for this evening. I hope you like it."

Paul simply nodded.

The multi course meal was served in a dazzling array of various Italian courses. Paul was suitably impressed, but spoke very little. He knew his brother and knew he had brought him here to talk candidly.

Lewis pulled out his ID and motioned for Paul to give him his while putting his index finger across his lips, indicating that Paul should not speak. Lewis placed both badges in his suit jacket and when the waiter reappeared with another course, he asked him to please hang up their coats." Now, Paul understood Lewis had something to tell him without any unknown persons listening in.

"Our uncle is terminally ill. He hasn't said, but my guess is some type of cancer. It's very sad; I can't imagine my world without him. He's been a great mentor to me. Don't judge him by what he does in his personal life, but on what he has done for the church and its impact on today's society."

Again, Paul only nodded.

"He believes that you are the only person he can trust to refine and finish his work. He knows that you will never give up your secular life, nor would he want you to. But he needs you, and, believe me, the church will pay you handsomely for your services."

"I don't need their money," Paul interjected.

"That's not the point." Lewis continued, "This is an international business and they have the funds to reward effort that is expended on their behalf. Be careful little brother. They also destroy what gets in the way of their goals. Their allegiance is absolute. You're either for them or against them. It's black or white. There's no gray. I want to warn you before you get in too deep helping our uncle. His illness is weakening him in a lot of areas. I hope his judgment has not been compromised. He has an almost revered status in the Vatican. He has made the church an even greater force to be reckoned with. His predecessors laid the groundwork, but those in the know believe our uncle has gone way past any expectations that anyone had for the financial department. We both should be very proud of him."

"Can't anything be done to help him? If these are his last days on earth, why would he spend them at work, showing me his various systems?"

"What else does he have? Or more importantly, who else does he have to pass his life's work on to? He confided in me after the seminary that he has always believed that you were his successor for whatever reason. I believe him. You just need to help him any way you can. If not for him, then for our family, brother."

"That's the reason I came. No other. I had a feeling that this was coming, but I was hoping he was going to be better."

"I want you to rely on me. You can ask me about any questions or concerns you have. I have been here with him long enough to know how the system works. What one should do and not do." Lewis continued, "Do you have any idea how much they are going to pay you if you can fix the issues with their system and if you would be willing to go on retainer to help them when necessary? It is millions of dollars. Tax free dollars. Isn't that important to you?"

Paul could feel the anger building up within him listening to his idiotic brother trying to sell him on the premise that if they paid him enough money, he would do whatever the Vatican wanted. On the verge of exploding, Paul caught himself in time, realizing if he voiced his true feelings, it might jeopardize his plan.

After swallowing hard several times to compose himself, Paul coolly said, "Isn't it all about money? That's the true score on the scoreboard, brother."

Lewis's expression was telling. By the smile on his face, Paul understood that his brother had believed him.

Paul noted Lewis had set up this private meeting without the badges as if he was going to confide in him. All this staging was to confirm that Paul was willing to work for them as they hoped he would. They had a new Morgan convert in their cause, whatever that might be. Well, misery loves company and the more the merrier, Paul thought. He just never realized he was such a good actor. Or had he just given the performance of his life?

Chapter 48

PAUL WAS AWAKENED by the telephone in his room. A woman's voice announced his wake up call at five thirty in the morning and proclaimed that his town car would be at the front entrance in forty-five minutes. As she hung up the phone, the operator said his breakfast was waiting for him in the front room of the suite. He barely had time to consider that someone had let himself into his room while he slept. Paul opened the bedroom door and the aroma wafting into the room from the breakfast tray made his stomach growl. He ate as he readied himself. He knew today would be as intense and long as yesterday.

Paul made his way through the scanners and knocked at his uncle's office door. He found Fr. Paul already working. Paul took his position next to him. He watched and asked questions throughout the day and into the early evening. When he returned to his quarters his preselected dinner was served. This went on for the next couple of days. The work was intense, but Paul found it very interesting.

On Friday morning, Fr. Paul showed Paul a spreadsheet of accounts in a number of banks throughout the world. The numbers, with the commas in place to offset the number of zeroes, were staggering amounts to comprehend. Fr. Paul's dilemma was that the program could not tie all the accounts into a format of inflow and outflow that could easily be understood by an average accountant. There were other nuances he wanted to streamline as well.

Paul came up with a written diagram of what his uncle was looking for. He looked at his nephew with a smile and said, "Paolo, can a program be written to accommodate the number of accounts, transactions and disbursements? That is the ultimate question. Is it doable?"

With a smile on his face, Paul answered, "I believe with a little help I can design what you want."

His uncle, ever suspicious, asked, "How much help and by whom?"

"Relax, uncle, I can get Patrick Richie's code lab at UCLA to draw up a blue print of what I want and then I can bring it back to Rome and implement it. No one will be privy to the particulars except you."

"Can he and they be trusted?" his uncle questioned.

"Trust is not something that is needed here. It's a question of a blueprint for code. They won't know whether it's a system for monitoring church contributions or email contacts. It's a workflow system with many conduits in and out. Yes, it's complicated, but I think it can be designed and implemented."

Fr. Paul seemed to relax with his nephew's reassurance. "Well, nephew, let us not make this a late evening like the last few. We will recess for the day and take some libation in one of the world's most beautiful cities. It is time you see Roma in the daylight. I will tell my assistant to order my car and let your brother know we are on our way."

Paul straightened up their work area and his uncle turned off the computer system. He showed Paul the sequence in which the system was shut down. Fr. Paul warned him that any step that was done out of sequence would be an alarm or alert to security. Paul noted the sequence.

Paul folded the blueprint he'd drawn and put it in his suit jacket. He needed to refine it further and thought he would work on it that evening after dinner. They took the elevator down to the waiting car and as Paul passed through the second scanner the alarm went off.

He was immediately detained by two armed security guards who scanned his clothes. When the scanner came near his jacket pocket, the pulsating sensors went from blue to red. Paul was told to hold his arms out from his sides and one of the guards stuck his hand into his jacket pocket and pulled out Paul's blueprint outline. Fr. Paul stood in front of him. Paul explained that it was his code blueprint, which he was intending to work on over the weekend.

Fr. Paul told his nephew that nothing could be taken out of the building, paper or otherwise, unless granted special permission by him. He told the guards he would sign for its release.

Paul apologized for the ruckus.

"You couldn't have known, nephew. It's a safety precaution we initiated years ago. Haven't you noticed that no one going in or out of the building carries a briefcase or folder? The staff likes that they can't take their work home with them." Fr. Paul laughed.

As they got into the waiting car he turned to Paul. "Work on your blueprint over the weekend and I will let security know you are bringing it in with you on Monday. I am very excited that you think the design can be accomplished. If your friend Patrick, who impressed me at the graduation party, can help you with this, I will have the church pay him and make a donation to the University's code lab. We don't expect anything for free."

Paul knew how much Patrick would appreciate the extra income because he was enrolled in the master's program. It was good that his plan would be income to his friend, he thought.

"I expect we will finish with this phase on Wednesday and you will want to return to California as quickly as possible after that. When do you think that we can reasonably expect you to return to install and implement your code blueprint? I need to have an estimate in order to do all the preparation work and put together a time table for all those affected."

Paul thought for a moment and said, "I'll email Patrick with a rough idea of what we want designed—"

Fr. Paul raised his hand and interrupted him. "My nephew, it's obvious that you haven't tried to send an email or text from here as yet. All incoming and outgoing transmissions are restricted. Unless you have special clearance, nothing is sent or received electronically in the Vatican. All communications are intercepted and read for content and then either erased or forwarded to certain offices to be dealt with appropriately. I have a nearly sealed net around the Vatican when it comes to communication. You also haven't tried to use your cell phone within the confines have you? It is routed for content recording."

There is a large amount of paranoia sitting in this car with me, thought Paul.

"But enough of this security talk, it's time to celebrate in Roma, as Romans do."

At an impromptu reception, Paul met a number of security personnel who worked at the financial center. The department heads he had met on Monday were in attendance as well. Everyone seemed friendly enough, but he thought it was more out of respect for his uncle than for him.

Fr. Paul informed the chief of security that upon Paul's return to Rome, he wanted his nephew outfitted with a satellite telephone for his convenience. In glowing terms, Fr. Paul relayed that Paul was a partner in a major accounting firm in the United States and that he needed to be able to stay in contact with him.

Yes, the impenetrable, hack-proof satellite phone, along with my ID badge in my pocket that is being listened to at all times. Nice touch, Paul thought.

Within a couple of hours of arriving at the restaurant, Fr. Paul seemed to visibly tire. Lewis noticed him staggering. He immediately went to him, helped him to a chair, and gave him a glass of water so he could take the fistful of pills he carried in his coat pocket. Lewis motioned for Paul to come over.

They both helped him to his waiting town car. He thanked them and waived them off. "Now go back in there and keep up the Morgan tradition in Rome of being the last ones to close the place. I will be fine. I am just a little tired because my nephew has worked me so hard this week."

He winked at Paul. "Enjoy yourselves this weekend on your jaunt around the Italian countryside. And if you should get into trouble, call me. I can get you out of it." He slammed the car door and motioned for the driver and valet to drive on.

Paul had questions for his brother. "How bad is he? Do you have any idea how long he has? And why do all Vatican town cars have a driver and a valet?"

"In answer to the first two questions, I don't know, but it seems he grows visibly weaker day by day. All official Vatican vehicles are outfitted with this two-person team. Both the valet and driver are armed. They have implicit instructions to protect their occupants at all cost. It dates back when the church was in its beginning. The pontiff and his ranking religious were high profile targets of those whose design was unrest. What better way to make a statement than to assassinate a ranking member. From this grew the tradition of the two man team. Each team member is a certified marksman and is highly trained in the martial arts. On the local news, when anyone is found dead with a broken neck, people's first thought is, who attacked a Vatican car? They don't mess around here."

Paul just shook his head.

He didn't return to his hotel until one o'clock in the morning.

Chapter 49

THE WEEKEND STARTED very early Saturday morning with a wake-up call at six o'clock. Lewis had a full day of activities planned so Paul could have the complete Italian experience in a day. He and the town car were waiting downstairs at six thirty. They would spend the day traveling from major metropolitan areas to quaint countryside vineyards.

Throughout the day, the people they met were very welcoming and cordial. Lewis, the handsome young priest, was the object of much attention and anything he wished for was given to him by the locals. No one asked for or expected to be compensated for the glass of wine or bread or meal that Lewis and Paul consumed.

Lewis made sure the team that drove them was taken care of. The driver and the valet sampled everything their charges did, except the wine. There was a no-exception rule concerning that and not doing so was grounds for immediate dismissal.

There were a great number of beautiful girls who swarmed around the two of them whenever they stopped. Any young, attractive man appeared to be fair game for the ladies. Their flirting, especially with Lewis, was downright shameful.

"Why are the young women so forward, especially to a priest?" Paul asked Lewis.

Lewis laughed it off. "It's a different world here. A person who rides around in a town car, even with Vatican flags, must be important. Watch yourself little brother, you will be propositioned before the day is out.

"There is about a three to one ratio of women to men in this part of Italy. Many young women leave their small towns or rural surroundings to seek a better life in a world-renowned city like Rome. With that ratio, they go after any good looking guy, whether he is eligible or not. Being a priest doesn't stop them. They seem to know the celibacy clause is treated as an option."

"No kidding, brother. I thought you gave up women and now I come to find out you have a harem." They both laughed.

They continued their sightseeing until early evening. Lewis asked Paul if he had built up an appetite as yet.

"Oh yes, I'm starving."

"Great. It is time for dinner at one of my favorite places in the old town. It's not as fancy as the other night, but it's a lot more fun and the food is sensational." Lewis picked up the car phone and gave the name of the restaurant to the driver.

The Cafe Bistro in Rome was a hub of activity on Saturday nights. It was very popular with the young professionals in the city. The menu entrees were priced on the expensive side to attract a certain clientele. The live music on the weekends drew a cross section of the city, but very few ended up on the restaurant side. The live music side of the bistro was a haven for attractive young women looking for a young Mr. Right among the masses.

When the town car pulled up in front, the valet immediately jumped out to open the car door and ensure that Lewis and

Paul were escorted inside. There were a great number of people mingling on the street in front of the establishment.

The noise from the street combined with the noise from inside forcing Lewis to yell to Paul, "Hopping place, eh brother?"

Paul nodded and thought, I would never take Sarina to a place like this. He and Sarina enjoyed places offering live music occasionally, but with some semblance of order and decorum.

They were met by the owner and maître d', who Lewis introduced to Paul, but he didn't catch their names over the crowd noise and the band. They were escorted through two sets of large oak doors to the restaurant side with guards posted on each side. As soon as they passed through the second set of oak doors they were met with such a sudden silence it was as if someone pressed a mute button on a remote control. They were seated in a small private dining area with a curtain hanging in the entrance.

"It's a madhouse out there. Is every young person in Rome here tonight?" Paul asked Lewis.

"Little brother, have you become an old man before your time? I wanted you to see the hot side of this city on a Saturday night. This place used to be a tomb until new owners turned it into this establishment that is successful on both sides. The food is sensational."

They ordered the cafe's renowned pasta primavera with the clam sauce that the chef had built his career on and Paul excused himself to use the restroom. Outside of their private dining cubicle the valet stood guard.

Is it really necessary to take all of these precautions? I couldn't live like this if I tried, Paul thought.

After the meal and a couple of glasses of wine, Lewis suggested they move to the music side of the bistro so Paul could see how the younger set partied. Paul was not thrilled about this but he tagged along, followed by the valet.

"If you want to leave your jacket behind, it will be here when you get back. This place has great security." Lewis had removed his black sport coat and his clerical collar. Paul was surprised to see the collar and shirt front was some sort of dickey that covered up the polo golf shirt he was wearing underneath. His older brother now looked like some country club patrician who spent his whole day on the golf course, before coming to the bistro to party.

Once on the dance side, women swarmed them. Speaking in Italian and expressively gesturing, each female sought to entice Lewis and Paul to dance with them.

Forward doesn't begin to describe these women, thought Paul. He declined their invitations but his brother had no qualms about being out on the dance floor with a couple of young women. Both were scantily dressed and they danced in a very suggestive manner around Lewis.

What a damn hypocrite, Paul thought. But after seeing how Lewis had been pursued by young women all day when he wore his priest garb, it probably wouldn't have made any difference to these women anyway.

Paul could not envision Matt Whaley, the priest, behaving in this hedonistic manner. He thought back to all of the parish priests he'd known growing up and he couldn't imagine this in his wildest dreams or, more appropriately, his nightmares.

As soon as one dance ended, another set of dancers clamored for the chance to dance with the good father.

What would my family, especially my grandfather, think? Paul wondered. This spectacle was embarrassing to him, but it seemed to be nothing out of the ordinary for Lewis.

A server arrived with a fresh glass of wine as Paul sipped the last of his wine from the dining area. Paul inquired who had ordered it. The server pointed to Lewis saying, "Il Capo."

Paul wondered why they called his brother the boss and not padre or father.

After watching his brother cavort on the dance floor for about three more dances, Paul made his mind up to retreat back to the quiet sanctuary of the restaurant. The lights dimmed and the band took up a slow song. Curious, Paul turned to look at the dance floor. In the center, his brother was entwined with a stunning young woman. It looked more like a wrestling hold than a romantic embrace. Lewis had a hand on his partner's right buttock. It wasn't accidental as he visibly grasped it repeatedly. This went on for about thirty seconds before a man erupted from the spectators. He separated the couple with a violent push to Lewis and grabbed the woman's arm and pulled her violently with him.

In a flash, Lewis's valet descended on the man, grabbed his left arm, and violently pulled it up at an angle that a person's arm wasn't meant to be. The man immediately fell to the ground in pain, where his jaw met the valet's knee and he slumped forward unconscious. Two other men appeared from nowhere and picked up the man and disappeared.

The music had continued uninterrupted and within seconds, Lewis was back dancing with his partner as if nothing had happened. Paul stood for a moment, shocked not only by what he had just seen, but even more by the fact that no one in the crowd reacted, as if this kind of disruption happened all the time.

Paul retreated to the dining area to try to make sense of what he had just witnessed. He sat alone in the private cubicle for another half hour before Lewis appeared. His evening of dancing had left him soaking wet from sweating. He asked his brother what was up.

"I've got a headache. Do you mind if I take a taxi back to the condo?

"Forget the taxi. It is time for us to call it an evening anyway. We have a lot to do tomorrow. Let me take a minute to get cleaned up and I will return in five minutes. Little brother, I have ordered some of their New York style cheesecake. It's fabulous and it's flown here fresh from Manny's bakery in the Bronx daily. Try it. I will be right back." He spoke in Italian to the valet who picked up his cell phone and relayed his brother's message.

The dessert arrived and Paul, though not very hungry, picked at it while he waited for his brother. Ten minutes later, Lewis walked through the door. He was dressed in jeans and a sport shirt. He looked as if he had showered and his hair was dry. Obviously, he'd gone someplace to get cleaned up, but with a shower, new clothes, and who knows what else.

"The car is out front, let's go, Paul." Lewis grabbed his jacket as they left. The ever present valet followed Paul out the front of the bistro. The driver was waiting by the car door and looked suspiciously at every person who walked by. Paul jumped into the backseat and was surprised to find three of Lewis's dance partners sitting on the seat in front of him, including his slow-dance partner.

Lewis climbed in after his brother. "These young ladies needed a ride to their homes, so I decided to be charitable."

Paul glanced over at them and had another shock. They, too, had miraculously changed out the outfits they'd worn in the bistro, especially his brother's slow-dance partner. They were now even more scantily dressed.

One of the women persistently tried to get Paul's attention. When he glanced at her, she flirted openly with him. She leaned forward to reveal that she had nothing on under her top and let Paul know she was interested in him. Paul turned his head to look out the window in disgust.

Lewis interrupted the silence with, "How's your headache little brother?"

"Not good. I'm quite tired and want to go to my room if that's okay, Lewis."

"Sure."

Paul had seen enough of this behavior and just wanted the peace and quiet of his suite. And he wanted to call Sarina. He knew he couldn't mention what had just happened due to his ID badge, but he would definitely give her the sordid details when he got back the following Thursday. It couldn't come fast enough as far as he was concerned.

The town car pulled up to the condo entrance. Paul, sitting on the left side of the car, opened the door before the valet could get to it from the front seat. He wanted out of that car as fast as possible.

He turned back to say good-bye to Lewis and his brother said, "Get some rest. We're going to Mass tomorrow morning at ten o'clock. His holiness, the Pope, is saying the Mass. I have arranged a personal audience for you with him after the service. Good night, little brother."

Chapter 50

Paul was wide awake the next morning when his alarm went off at seven o'clock. He had hardly slept the entire night.

Images of his brother kept surfacing in his mind and when he did fall asleep it was as if they were part of a bad dream. He couldn't believe that Lewis was such a hypocrite. He was a walking lie as far as Paul was concerned and he couldn't escape from the questions swirling through his thoughts. Had he always been like this without Paul noticing, or had a new Lewis been born when he moved to Rome? What influence did his uncle have in his brother's hedonistic ways? These were questions that would not be easily or quickly answered.

Who was this person his brother had become? Paul's curiosity and disgust ran neck and neck with each other. He mulled this over and over in his mind. His breakfast had been silently delivered into the other room of the suite. He poured himself a cup of coffee and continued to ponder what he'd seen.

Paul knew he needed to refocus on Monday's task at hand. There were particulars in the accounting program he inquired about for code purposes that did not place any suspicion on his uncle or his security measures. But he needed to know more about the money. Where it came from and where it went. That part of the equation would give him clues as to what his uncle had been up to. He reasoned he needed another drinking episode with Fr. Paul to learn what was actually going on with his uncle. Because of Fr. Paul's weakened condition, this might prove more difficult than before, but Paul had a strategy to facilitate it.

The papal mass was an incredible experience for Paul. Though never seriously religious, he couldn't escape the feeling of awe and wonder that engulfed him at the Holy Father's Mass. He received communion from him personally, causing Paul to make himself a promise to be more involved in his faith when he returned home. He had never experienced anything remotely like this. He felt blessed and proud to be a Catholic.

This was in stark contrast to what he felt about his faith when he thought of his uncle and his brother. In his mind, he drifted back to happier times in his faith when he was young. Midnight Mass, Holy Communion and his confirmation. They were pleasant memories of a time when everything was right in the world and all of his family was there with him. But here in Rome he saw firsthand the polar opposites lived out before his eyes. Maybe Matt was right: It was the grass roots versus the corporate mentality.

Lewis, who had been a server during Mass, came up to him after the service. "What did you think?"

"No words can express what I just experienced and witnessed," Paul replied.

"Here, take this. It is a new zucchetto, or skull cap, to hand to the Pope when you meet him. It is customary because he is going to give you his as a token of thanks."

"Thanks, for what? I'm the one who is thankful to him."

Lewis smiled. "Decorum, nothing more. Go with it."

Paul was escorted into the side chapel where the man himself was seated in a high back chair. He looked much more relaxed than he had when saying Mass. His interpreter told Paul to approach His Holiness. Paul knelt in front of him and kissed the ring on the outstretched hand of the Pope, as he knew was the custom.

The Pope grabbed Paul's forearms and spoke to him in Italian.

The interpreter explained, "His Holiness is holding your forearms as a token of friendship. He would like you to sit down and talk with him."

Paul sat in the matching chair that mysteriously appeared behind him. The Pope spoke in Italian and the interpreter did his best to keep up with his rapid fire speech. He relayed to Paul the gist of the Pope's conversation. The Pope was happy he could attend Mass today. He was happy to have given Paul communion on this day. Paul's uncle had informed the Pope that Paul was assisting him and the Pope was especially grateful to Paul for the work he was doing for the church in the financial center of the Vatican.

According to the interpreter, the Pope went on to say that he knew Paul came from a good family that had dedicated their lives to the church. His uncle was a study in complete dedication and perseverance and his brother was following in his uncle's footsteps in a different area of the church's interests. His uncle had been in the Vatican long before he had been elected Pope and had served the Holy See and the Catholic religion with distinction.

"I am not a man of numbers, science or technology," The Pope continued. "God has made me the shepherd of billions of souls that I must lead to Him." The Pope laughed at himself good-naturedly as he said, "He knows better than anyone that He didn't create a business person in me, so He keeps me out of that side of our faith. We are fortunate that He brings us professionals like you to help us. Thank you, my son."

Paul didn't know what to say after that. He handed the Pope his new skull cap when prompted by the interpreter. His Holiness removed the skull cap from his own head and handed it to Paul. He stood and extended his hand to shake Paul's.

"Thank you," he said in broken English and left.

Paul stood dumbstruck until his brother grasped his arm and led him away. As they walked from St. Peter's Basilica and headed to a row of buildings that were of the same architecture as the main church Lewis asked his brother if he was okay.

Paul nodded in the affirmative.

"Well, my next surprise for you is that His Holiness has given you and me permission to have a private tour of the Vatican's artwork. As you can imagine, everything is closed on Sunday here. But in light of your busy schedule, it has been arranged for us to have an English speaking tour guide show us around. There are parts of the museums that I haven't had access to. So it's going to be a treat for me also. What do you think, brother?"

Paul had not yet recovered from his audience with the Pope and the impact of the experience had left him a little drained. He would revere every word the Pope had said to him for the rest of his life. He felt as though this experience came to him at the exact instant in his life that he needed it the most, to give him the strength and purpose to carry on with his plan.

They were met at the main entrance of the building that contained the Vatican's most treasured art by Sister Andrea, a nun who had been classically trained at the finest art universities and colleges in the world. She was attractive and very self-assured. Lewis, of course, cast flirting eyes on her, but she returned his look with a withering stare that said, "Not in this lifetime, nor any."

Shot down immediately, Paul thought as he laughed to himself. At first he was surprised that Sr. Andrea didn't react the way every other woman here did to his brother's charm. The fact that Sr. Andrea took her vows seriously was a reminder to Paul that just because his Uncle and brother were cynical, he didn't need to be.

She explained that she had been born in Oregon and knew very early in life what she wanted to dedicate her life to. She had entered the nunnery at the age of fifteen and had been in the structured service of Christ ever since. She had an easy manner about her that made them comfortable and that painted the tour with the brush of conversation rather than lecture.

Paul, intrigued by Sr. Andrea's background, asked her where she had studied.

She had received her doctorate from Oxford in England. Her undergraduate and master's degrees were from Harvard and she'd had the privilege of being a resident scholar at the Louvre in Paris. She went on to say that if she hadn't heard the calling from the Lord, she would have pursued the academic world as a professor.

Paul was rightly impressed. Sr. Andrea took them through the private preparation and restoration rooms in back and showed them the treasures not currently on display. She had significant insight and knowledge on the artists and their works of art that could only come from the in-depth study she had undertaken. Her passion for her work infused every aspect of her being and her enthusiasm and love for the work she did was evident.

One of the buildings housed artwork the Nazi's had stolen from Italy and parts of Germany during World War II. Her disgust for the Third Reich was crystal clear, not only of their world view, but of their treatment of some of the world's most priceless artwork. She lowered her voice as if in mourning for the numerous pieces destroyed by them.

After four and a half hours, which seemed more like thirty minutes, they were offered refreshments before beginning the next segment of their tour. Sr. Andrea looked at her watch and apologized profusely for taking so much of their time.

"We could go around again and not be bored for one moment. Thank you for sharing your love of the arts with us, Sister." Paul gave her a grateful smile.

After refreshments Sr. Andrea took them into the Sistine Chapel. No words were necessary. The only action required was to gaze in wonder at one of Michelangelo's crowning achievements. Paul was especially struck by the section of the ceiling where God's finger gave life to Adam. Nothing he had ever seen in any book or video had given him the full impact of this part of the ceiling.

They quietly passed to a foyer and abruptly came upon Michelangelo's Pieta. Its beauty and power were overwhelming. Paul stood in awe as he thought of the staggering amount of talent this artist possessed to have created such a glorious sculpture out of a block of marble. He truly depicted better than anyone before or after him, the indescribable bond between the mother and child, the Virgin Mary and her son Jesus. Michelangelo truly had been inspired by the divine.

These three stood motionless in front of the sculpture for what seemed to them to be several minutes. Their trance was broken by the tolling of a bell which indicated that the buildings would be locked down and secured in fifteen minutes. Sr. Andrea turned to the brothers and said, "Didn't it seem that just a few minutes passed while we viewed this marvel? We have been standing in front of it for almost an hour. Amazing."

Lewis and Paul stood speechless. All they could do was nod in agreement.

As they left the building, Lewis's cell phone rang. He shook hands with Sr. Andrea before hurrying to take the call.

Paul thanked Sr. Andrea profusely. He was floored by her next revelation.

She told him that they had a mutual acquaintance in Matt Whaley, who was a friend from their early high school days. Their common views on the church and its direction had placed them in a group with a similar philosophy. She went onto say that this group of soon-to-be religious neophytes was composed of not only Catholics, but of all faiths.

Sr. Andrea explained, "When I was asked about my religious ambitions for the future, my response struck a chord with the priests and nuns who interviewed me. Matt had had a similar experience. In fact, it was Matt who gave us the heads up on the true purpose of your trip."

So, Paul thought, Matt had known his true intentions all along. Paul wondered who else was aware of his plan.

"Please give Matt my regards when you next see him." Sr. Andrea extended her hand to shake his and in the palm of her hand was a business card that she passed to Paul.

"I know we will meet again. Call me from an unsecured line without the badge when you come back to Rome. You should know there are many here who have the same concerns as you do. Please help us if you can. By the way, your brother is a sleaze ball if you didn't already know it. As you can see, I always speak my mind to those I trust."

Lewis had just finished his phone call and was heading back to them.

Sr. Andrea hurriedly finished their conversation. "Another nun, Sr. Margaret, is arranging a meeting with you before you leave. Try to facilitate her if you can. She'll seem like a nut case to you, but it's important that you meet with her and listen to her. Her crazy act is just an act. Remember that."

Paul turned to see his brother coming, but when he turned back to Sr. Andrea she was gone.

Chapter 51

MONDAY MORNING'S WAKEUP call was unnecessary for by five thirty, Paul had been up and thinking for quite a while. He was attempting to come up with a plan to gather the information he needed without alerting the powers that be, and he had just three days left to secure it.

Paul was waiting at the front entrance of the condo when the town car pulled up. As he was driven to the financial center, he reviewed what he knew about the security. Any type of paper would be detected. What was there that wouldn't be? The car stopped at a traffic light and he watched a tourist taking photographs with his cell phone. Paul realized that his personal cell phone had never been examined going in or coming out through security.

Could that be it? He could use it to photograph files, drawings, schematics, operating systems, documents, and anything that could be photographed and take it back to Patrick to help them solve the mystery of his uncle and what he was up to. Paul had a thought about what would happen to him if he was found taking the photographs or if security found the photos on his cell phone. Would he live to return home? This was very dangerous. If caught, he could not possibly explain his way out of it.

Then, the idea came to Paul of taking a couple of generic photos of Fr. Paul's ultra-modern office to show his family in the US. He'd keep them as he entered and exited through security over the next thirty-six hours and see if his phone was ever scanned for photos of the building. He shot one of the front of the building when the car pulled up.

Fr. Paul was already at work when Paul arrived at his office. He looked a little better than when he'd left him Friday night, but he still was very drawn. They chatted about the code blueprint Paul had worked on over the weekend. Paul had pulled it out of his coat pocket before going through the scanners. Security was pleased to record the print going out last week and coming back today. All for one damn piece of paper, thought Paul. But he smiled at the guards because he was being a compliant little soldier and not trying to hide anything.

Paul asked his uncle to show him a few specific functions that he was interested in. He asked Fr. Paul why there was a need for conversion tables, whose function was to take certain data and change the figures into another system of numbers. Paul played dumb, even though he knew their purpose.

His uncle patiently explained that they were currency exchange conversion tables. They needed to know, in one currency, what the exact amounts of the inflows were.

Paul asked if there was a reverse table that reconverted them into the currency of their outflow or destination.

Fr. Paul nodded.

Paul innocently asked if they had ever considered using those funds to track inequities in various overnight international currencies. In other words, if the German mark went down, and the Chinese yen went up, they could employ a strategy that would sell currency on an overnight basis to profit from fluctuating currencies?

Fr. Paul laughed. "To make even more money by automating currency swaps overnight? A subtle form of arbitrage that is absolutely without risk. Brilliant just brilliant, my nephew. You know we are talking about hundreds of billions of dollars. I really like the innovation of your thinking. How would one employ such a strategy?"

"Hmm. I'll have to think about that for a while when I get back." He continued because he knew he had the big fish nosing around his baited hook. "With your permission, I will need to talk to Patrick about the code that is necessary for this function also. Is that okay, uncle?"

"By all means, yes. Do what you think is necessary to facilitate this. It's absolutely brilliant. I love it."

Paul knew right then that he had him. Money was the best bait for the greedy.

They continued into the late afternoon with only light refreshments and light lunch brought into the office. Fr. Paul began to visibly tire and Paul decided to call it a day. Not wanting to let his uncle know that it was because of him that Paul wanted to stop for the day, he told Fr. Paul that he was at a point where he couldn't keep his concentration. His brain was telling him that he had had enough.

Fr. Paul winked at him. "Maybe the weekend's festivities have caught up with you."

"It's quite possible, Uncle." And work was finished for the day.

The next two days passed very much as Monday had. Paul was getting a real feel for how the system worked and how the accounts and other data were coded. The key would be how to figure out the code.

Late Wednesday, as their work was wrapped up for the day, Paul innocently asked his uncle about the accessibility of information about departmental staff.

His uncle proudly announced that he was the only person who had total access to all such information. Each department head had a limited access equal to the scope of his particular work. However, no department head had total access but him.

Paul smiled. "Hey, since tonight is my last night for this trip, why don't the two of us go out and have a quiet dinner?"

"I thought you might want to do that so I have already taken the liberty of getting reservations at a nice quiet establishment that serves a very good continental fare. I have already asked your brother and he can join us for a short time before he has to get back to finish up a project tonight."

Paul, blatantly lying to his uncle's face, said, "I was hoping my brother could come." To himself, he thought, I'll bet the work he needs to do has something to do with his dancing friends from the other night. He hoped that Fr. Paul would consume enough wine for Paul to ignite his uncle into a rambling tirade like he did at the graduation reception.

Choosing to go straight from the office to dinner was practically an admission by Fr. Paul that he was tired. On the way to dinner Fr. Paul laid out the plans for the next day. He told Paul that he would be at the office at the regular time. They would meet and summarize what he expected on his next visit and clear up any questions Paul might have before leaving for the airport. "Have the valet bring your luggage to security in the morning and they will stow it on my helicopter. I want to give you an aerial view of Vatican City before meeting your plane tomorrow morning. I gave the pilot an approximate departure time of eleven o'clock."

The evening progressed just as Paul had planned it. Lewis had to excuse himself multiple times to take calls on his cell phone. Fr. Paul smiled and said, "Your brother inherited my work ethic. He never leaves his work. He is always on call."

Paul thought, if Lewis was in the antiquities department translating and interpreting ancient documents, then what the hell would be so urgent that multiple calls would disrupt his dinner? Maybe the ancient writings now wore a dress and wanted his attention.

Lewis made his apologies for having to leave and said he hoped he would see Paul tomorrow before he left, but he wasn't sure. He hugged Paul. "It was great to see you. Please come back soon. Uncle says you have some terrific ideas. Well, if I don't see you tomorrow then I will see you soon."

Paul got his uncle to match him glass for glass. He was subtle in his approach so his uncle wouldn't become suspicious. When Fr. Paul began to slur his words a little Paul moved in to light the fuse.

"So what do you think of these plagues that are showing up around the world? The Ebola outbreak seems to be especially deadly. What is your explanation for this uncle?"

Fr. Paul remained silent for a moment and a weird look came across his face. "It is punishment because the damn world is filled with sinners and non-believers, my nephew."

Here we go, thought Paul.

"God will humble and destroy those who don't keep his commandments. This is the way it's always been, since the creation of the earth. He gives man a clear path to follow as outlined in the Bible and waits for human arrogance and pride to interfere. Then He smites the offenders. He is very creative in the implements and instruments of His retribution."

Fr. Paul was on a roll now. He continued his tirade. "Do you think natural disasters are not by design? Only the Deity could cause such directed fury against those who have transgressed Him. Disasters and disease are manifestations of the wrong path being chosen by man. Mankind can be driven back to a need for Faith by the killing of the sinners. Of course, the innocent are not spared in the carnage, but this is meant to encourage survivors to pray and to reflect on the error of their ways. Fire and brimstone have always been an effective tool, but selective decimation can be even more effective as a punishment." He stopped and finished the rest of his glass of wine.

A waiter came in with a new bottle of his favorite wine and Fr. Paul tried to focus on him. He looked him up and down and asked, "Are you gay?"

"Yes." The waiter seemed proud.

"Give me that bottle you despicable sodomite. Get your fag hands off my bottle. You are going to burn in hell with all of your kind. Sinner! Call the manager to my table. Now!"

Paul was stunned by his uncle's outburst. Fortunately only a few heard him; their table was a private booth in the back of the restaurant. The manager appeared quickly. "Yes sir, what can I do for you Padre?"

Fr. Paul spoke viciously. "Fire that queer right now. I will not have his kind working in a restaurant that I own. Understand?" The manager nodded and disappeared quickly.

Paul noticed that the valet and driver were standing close by. Each had a hand in their jackets as if they were going to pull their weapons out to protect his uncle. Fr. Paul waved them away.

"The disease AIDS was brought to this earth to rid it of sodomites and free love. The Bible is very clear in its detesting of these abnormalities. Wipe them off the face of the earth and cast them down into hell for eternity. But before they go, give the ones around them something horrible to see before they are cast from this earth. Is there anything more devastating or horrible than that disease?" His head slumped forward as if he had passed out, but that was only temporary.

When his head snapped back, his eyes had taken on a look of pure evil. He seemed positively possessed. "Those science boys came up with something even more horrible than was originally designed. It was hard to fathom something that made a human being's last days on earth equal to what awaited him in hell. It was a perfect scenario and example for those who witnessed or heard of it. Complete devastation, nothing less." Fr. Paul's voice trailed off. He had slumped forward on the table, passed out.

The valet rushed to his side, pulled his head back, and gave him oxygen from a small tank. The driver grabbed his arm and gave him an injection which immediately brought Fr. Paul back to consciousness. "Nephew, it seems I can't hold my liquor as I did in the old days. I need to retire. There will be a car here to take you to your condo in a few minutes. Please accept my apologies for passing out, my nephew."

Paul was speechless. For a moment he thought he had killed his uncle with the wine. But his brain felt as if it was on fire. His uncle had just admitted to him that he'd had a hand in the design of the terrible disease, AIDS. He could not begin to understand or accept that. He had seen firsthand the terrible disease's victims when he was in high school. He had friends with older siblings that had contracted it. He was sick to his stomach thinking that his blood kin could be responsible for such evil. How could the church condone his actions?

Paul was still in a state of shock when he arrived at his condo. He had a sliver of hope that perhaps it was just a sick old man's drunken tirade about homosexuality, but the look in his eyes when he talked about it made Paul believe it was horribly true. He was sweating profusely. He needed to call Sarina, but he would wait until he regained his composure, if that would ever be possible again. What Paul had always suspected was confirmed, but he still had a hard time processing it. His uncle was no better than any other powerful lowlife on the planet. Hitler came to mind first and what he did to the Jews. It was as though his uncle was a modern day Hitler and he didn't even have to operate under the guise of a war.

Paul had never felt so ill in his entire life. Not just physically, but emotionally sick. And he was related to this devil incarnate.

Chapter 52

AFTER ANOTHER SLEEPLESS night, Thursday morning dawned. After his uncle's revelations of the previous night, Paul didn't think he could even speak to him without becoming sick to his stomach. As he packed his luggage and looked around his room, he thought of the tremendous number of ups and downs he had experienced during his time in Rome—from his papal visit to last night's horrible discovery. He needed to get out of this cauldron while he still could.

He knew that the real work of validating his uncle's story lay ahead. Even if he was able to prove that his uncle was the mastermind behind one of the most horrible diseases the world has ever known, what would he do? He pondered this dilemma and debated his options with himself until he remembered his town car was waiting outside.

At the financial center, two luggage valets waited to pick up his bags. He thanked his driver and tipped him for his services during his stay. Paul's luggage had already entered the security area and it was no great surprise that his suitcases were opened and the contents were being scanned and inspected.

Two priests stood at Fr. Paul's office door. They intercepted Paul and one of them said his uncle was not feeling well and he was unable to work with him today. All other plans remained the same. The helicopter would give him an aerial view of the Vatican and get him to his plane for his return to California.

They entered the office and a priest unlocked the computers so Paul could work for a couple of hours before his departure. The priests stationed themselves on the other side of the desk. Paul presumed they didn't have the security clearance to view financial records and were from another department.

Paul studied the code trying to decipher what he was looking at. The system wasn't that complicated in its mechanics, but the key to getting to the secured information eluded Paul. After a while, the two watchdogs excused themselves to use the lavatory and get some coffee. They asked Paul if he wanted anything. Paul declined, wondering if this was a set up or if he should continue his detective work.

Within moments of their departure, he decided to check for any type of surveillance in the office that he hadn't noticed previously. He got up to stretch and move around the spacious office as if he needed a break to clear his head. He noted the main entrance had a small camera at the door but it wouldn't show his uncle at his desk. Paul scanned the entire office before he sat back down. It was then he spotted the two micro cameras. One was on the bottom of one of the monitors with a view of him, and the other was on the table next to the desk with a view of the screen he was working on. Paul was sure he would have seen at least one of the cameras before so he deduced they were new and had been placed just so he could be watched.

There was a knock on the office door and Paul said, "Enter."

An elderly nun he hadn't seen before came in carrying a tray with coffee, tea and croissants. In broken English she said that these had been ordered to tide him over until he got to his plane later. Paul thanked her and she motioned for him to follow her to the office door. He followed.

She said, "There is a view of the Vatican from the window down the corridor that your uncle instructed me to show you before you left." She motioned to him out of view of the security cameras in a way that Paul interpreted as asking if he was wearing his ID badge. He shook his head no.

Paul obediently followed the nun as they walked down the hall toward a large window at the end. She pointed out various points of interest and then under her breath she whispered with greatly improved English, "Paul, my name is Sr. Betty. We were alerted to your coming by those who know your true purpose and we have an idea what you need. I don't expect you to trust me. I have only worked in this building a short time, but I have seen enough to know that what happens here is not good for the majority of people on this earth. Your uncle is a ruthless man if you hadn't already discovered. You need only to know one word to know whom to trust. The letters in this word must be contained at least once in a person's name. My name is Sr. Betty; the important letter to remember is the "B" in my name. Nod if you understand."

Paul nodded.

She seamlessly slipped back into her broken English tour of the Vatican. Moments later, she whispered, "The word is very simple and easy to remember. Our Lord was called a shepherd as you know. He tended most carefully to the lambs of the flock. Lamb is the word. The league of believers is called the Seal of the Lamb. You have already met the A and the B of the word."

She motioned for him to return to the office. She excused herself in broken English right in front of the office door. Paul knew there was a camera and sound there. He had left his badge on the desk when he went with Sr. Betty to view the window.

He went back to work thinking about the letters Sr. Betty had told him about. Then it dawned on him. The letter "A" was for Andrea—the nun who had given him and Lewis the tour of the Vatican art collection.

Now that he had met A and B, Paul wondered which letter he would encounter next? It wouldn't take long to have the answer. His uncle's personal helicopter pilot called his office and asked if he could introduce himself and talk about when he wanted to depart. The pilot knocked and entered Fr. Paul's office. He wore a dark blue jumpsuit with a name tag as its only form of decoration. It simply read "Lloyd."

Paul was ready to leave immediately. He called the security office and asked the officer in charge to have him logged out. Within thirty seconds, two security agents walked into the office. Paul knew very well they had been nearby watching the secret video monitors and had seen and heard everything. They logged him out.

Paul thanked them and proceeded to the helipad and his uncle's private helicopter. He took his suit jacket off and placed it with his luggage in the cargo hold. Lloyd handed him a small note that read:

Say nothing until we have left the pad. The helicopter blades and engine will make enough noise to prevent anyone from hearing.

Paul nodded his head.

The engine revved higher and higher and the blades rotated faster and faster; the helicopter lifted smoothly into the air. Lloyd politely asked, "Is this your first helicopter ride?" pointing to his ear to alert Paul that they were still in earshot of the helipad with the high powered directional microphones they sometimes employed.

"Yes. I've always wanted to ride in one."

The pilot got on the radio and informed control that they would be arriving at the terminal in about thirty minutes and to alert the airplane's pilot. As they swooped away, Lloyd turned to Paul and said in perfect English, "Now you've met the L of the word."

Lloyd went onto explain to Paul he had been a black hawk pilot for Special Forces in Iraq and Afghanistan. He applied for the position of his uncle's pilot about two years ago and won out over the other applicants. He had seen firsthand some of his uncle's ruthlessness. Your uncle wasn't aware that I'm fluent in several languages. Thinking that I only spoke English and Italian, he would converse on his satellite phone in French, German, and even Arabic."

Paul stared at him. "Who is behind this? Who employed or placed you in this position?"

"You don't need to know that. There are a number of people who have figured out what has been going on and want it ended. They also want to see an end to your uncle. He is a very bad man. You appeared on the scene at just the right time, but we knew you would. There are a lot of people hoping you can crack the damn code of the financial center's files to get the indisputable evidence we need against them. The world needs to know what these parasites have been doing."

Paul just gazed out the window as Lloyd began his tour monolog on the various points of interest they flew over. This was a completely different perspective from the terrestrial view of Paul's tour with Lewis. Paul was looking out his side of the window when Lloyd announced they would be landing in about five minutes.

Paul looked at him and Lloyd said, "You will meet 'M' when we land. She is a very powerful woman in Rome. Her mother designed a foolproof plan so she would not come to any harm.

Unfortunately for her mother, she didn't have such a good plan for herself. Everyone at the Vatican is afraid of this woman you're about to meet for what she could expose about them. Don't underestimate her. The crazy act is just that, an act."

Paul tried to remember who Sr. Andrea had said that about. She had said Sr. Margaret. The M is for Margaret, Paul realized.

The helicopter was on the ground. Paul thanked Lloyd and said. "I hope to see you when I come back."

Lloyd nodded, adding something that puzzled Paul, "You will. It is already planned."

The private jet terminal was on the other side of the airport, and Paul expected a cab or car would take him there. A public cab pulled up as his luggage was unloaded. He started walking to the cab when the honking of a horn drew his attention to a red Ferrari with a nun in the driver's seat. At least Paul thought she was a nun, without her headgear. She leaned over the windshield and in quick bursts of Italian told the cabbie where to take the luggage. She would take Mr. Morgan to the airport. She motioned for Paul to get in. She accelerated the big red machine so fast that when he sat down, he thought he had suffered a whiplash.

She motioned, as Sr. Betty and Lloyd had done to see if Paul had his ID on him.

"No," Paul said. "It's in my suit jacket with the other luggage."

"Good."

Chapter 53

"I AM SR. Margaret if you haven't guessed already. We are glad you finally have come to the Vatican. I can only tell you about pieces of the puzzle. I have to protect a number of other 'patriots,' as I will call them. We have about ten minutes to talk before arriving at your plane."

"Everyone seems to know I was coming and that I am returning. Do I need to know how, or better yet, why?"

"No. The people you have met under the Seal of the Lamb will be instrumental in getting you and the information that you seek out of the Vatican when you crack the code."

Paul looked around the very expensive car she was driving and asked. "Is this the latest financial enticement they give to get nuns to join?"

She laughed. Her voice was very high and her laugh sounded like that of a child. "No, you get this when you tell them you want it, in my case. I should give you a brief history.

My real father was the highest ranking member of the church's clergy. He knocked up my mother, his secretary, and wanted her to have an abortion. She refused, fled, and went into hiding. The Seal of the Lamb found her and kept her safe. She gave birth to me and to make a very long story short, my father wanted her back. No strings attached. She demanded DNA and other tests to validate my parentage. He agreed. A very complicated system was put into place so that if ever I was harmed in any way, the world would know who my real father was. Unfortunately, my mother took ill when I was young and passed away, but his Holiness would not chance anything happening to me. He told me that he loved my mother so much that he would have walked away from his position if she had asked him. It broke his heart when she died and he followed her in about a year.

"Now, my father faced the conundrum of what to do with me. I entered the convent to lend some sort of credibility to the reason I was raised in the private residence of the Vatican. A great number there know who my father was. I was sent to England to study at Cambridge and Oxford. My doctorate is in clinical psychology, and believe me, these bastards here could use my expertise.

"When I returned from Europe, I decided to be my own person. In other words, live a life that others could never dream of. The vows of a nun were not mine, but I found that with that cover, I could do anything I wanted and no one would have the guts to stand up to me. They know the evidence is just sitting there waiting to be exposed. It will rock the church's foundation when it is. Even that bastard, your uncle, gives me a wide berth. That's the way I prefer it."

Paul just stared at her in disbelief. Another hypocrisy to chalk up for the Vatican.

"Don't look so shocked. The knowledge you seek is desperately needed to help the church return to what it was meant to be."

They pulled up to the airport's private terminal. Paul lifted himself out of the low slung car and Sr. Margaret came around to his side of the car.

"Thanks for the ride to the airport." He extended his right hand to shake hers.

She engulfed him in a hug. She was tall and her hair was long and disheveled from the ride in the convertible. She winked and said, "My pleasure. Just figure out a way to get the information; the rest will be taken care of for you. Safe trip home. Ciao."

She was gone in a blink of the eye. The taxi cab pulled up with his luggage and immediately two valets appeared to load his luggage. One of them came forward to hand Paul his suit jacket.

Paul declined. "Just place it with the stowed luggage."

He grabbed a small duffle bag that contained his jeans and a sport shirt. He didn't want to get off the plane dressed like an undertaker. He wanted to be in his usual casual attire when he hugged and kissed the most important person in his world.

Chapter 54

UPON PAUL'S RETURN, there was an avalanche of questions about Fr. Paul, Lewis and the Vatican from Sarina, Ashley and family members, which he deflected with some success. Those closest to him gave him the wide berth that he seemed to need. His brain tried to process all he had seen and learned. More importantly, he needed to take this information and come up with a plan of what to do when he returned to the Vatican.

Getting back to work was a welcome respite. There were client issues to confront and resolve. Large, successful client firms were the main targets of the Internal Revenue Service.

Larry often said, "Money attracts parasites and thieves. We are the barrier between them and our clients. Audits, re-filings, and amendments to returns are the daily fare of our chosen profession. What clients interpret as a nuisance and invasion of their privacy, we look at as a financial windfall."

Sarina, Ashley and Tom knew he was dealing with inner turmoil from his trip. He would eventually confide in them, but he didn't have a clear plan or, for that matter, a feeling of how to even proceed. With these thoughts in his head he went to see one of his confidants and his new-found confessor, Fr. Matt Whaley. They exchanged pleasantries and Paul talked about his trip to the Vatican.

He recounted his trip from start to finish. At times, Fr. Matt just bowed his head or shook his head from side to side. Occasionally, his face showed disgust. Paul finished his lengthy recap and they both sat quietly for a long while.

Paul eventually broke the silence. "I guess the first place to start is with Patrick. I need to know what he thinks he can do with rewriting the codes in the accounting program that my uncle wants changed."

Fr. Matt nodded. "You can trust Patrick. We have had him vetted and he is not connected to the other side."

Paul had an astonished look on his face. "You did what?"

"We had to. To protect you and our cause."

Fr. Matt looked at him and said, "Okay, I should have told you about some of my friends whom you met there. There are a lot of us who have devoted our lives to the church and have seen or know of people and things that shouldn't be. My group represents the vast majority of those who have dedicated their lives to the church. Many have very full lives trying to bring salvation to those souls who have been entrusted to our influence and teaching. A few, like me and some of those you met on your trip, are dedicated to stopping the other side of the church in their special agendas. I took the liberty of alerting some of those people about you and what you are trying to do. All those approached readily offered their support in helping you."

Paul interrupted, "Yes, and for that I am grateful. So how do you know them?"

Fr. Matt explained. "I transferred and played football at UCLA as part of that plan. I was recruited to the group my first year in high school. That is where I met Andrea. The group knew of your disgust with your uncle and, subsequently, of your brother's very public exit to be with Fr. Paul. We knew you were not like them. We thought it would be only a matter of time before your uncle would reach out to his namesake to enlist his help to update the financial center's computer programs. People like him and your brother are more predictable than you think. Patrick was not recruited by the Seal of the Lamb, but we did a very thorough investigation of him."

"You know I think my uncle is involved with the spread of horrible diseases like AIDS for their own profit and agenda."

"That is known. What we need is irrefutable evidence that ties your uncle's group to their own special agenda. Don't take this wrong, but if you focus on getting the information that is needed then the rest will take care of itself. I have faith that all concerned will be led in the direction that the Lord wants."

"I hope you're right because I don't have any idea how to break into their system at this point."

"Believe and He will lead you."

* * *

Patrick and Paul met in a little park off of Sunset Boulevard across the street from the university computer lab. Paul related to him the details of what he had seen and any other particulars that he could remember. They both knew designing the code for his uncle was their first task. Paul explained the currency exchange mechanism that his uncle was so proud of.

Patrick whistled. "That is some really serious amount of money you are talking about. But just as important are the outflows and where they are going. The arbitrage idea of overnight money was a stroke of genius. That can be accomplished in the code schematic. Let me work on it and get back to you. A timeline to do this is about three to four months.

It's complicated but can be accomplished. When were you thinking of returning to visit?"

Paul thought for a moment and said, "I haven't thought about it yet. There is business at the firm I need to attend to before I can take off again. I am thinking after the second tax filing extension period in October."

"Good. That should give us plenty of time including a fudge factor. The main concern I have is how you're going to get access to your uncle's password. That's no small task. Did you happen to count the number of key strokes when he logged in?"

"I counted nine keystrokes and noticed it was made up of letters followed by numbers."

"Well, it's a start. Between us, we'll crack it or my nickname isn't the safecracker!"

Patrick continued, "Do you think it would raise suspicion if I went with you to help implement the new code?"

"I don't think that's a good idea for two reasons. First, they're very suspicious. You can tell from their security protocols that they're not going to let any information leave the financial center. Second, I'm not going to risk your life. This is my baby and I'll be the only one put at risk. No one else. I insist."

Patrick thought for a moment. "Okay then, we'll have to come up with a way to communicate without them being aware of it. I have some ideas. They don't know that they're dealing with a couple of Rose Bowl and National Championship winners, do they?"

Chapter 55

PAUL THREW HIMSELF headlong into his work. The accounting firm was just what he needed to distract him. It seemed his only sanctuary in addition to the firm, was the time he and Sarina spent alone.

Fr. Paul contacted him two weeks after Paul returned and asked him if he had enjoyed his trip.

Paul assured him that he had and thanked him again for making his trip to Rome so wonderful. He proceeded to give his uncle updates on what he and Patrick were working on for the new accounting program. Paul inquired after his uncle's health.

"Not well, but that is beside the point," Fr. Paul snapped. "The only thing I want you to focus on is the design. Then I need you to get back here to implement the changes. Neither my health, nor anything else, should distract you. What kind of timetable are you and Patrick looking at to finish this project?"

Paul said he was looking at the latter part of October.

After a moment, his uncle cleared his throat. "Well, all you need to do is to give me or your brother notice and we will arrange for your travel within a couple of days." He started coughing. "This needs to be done whether I am here or not. Understand, Paul? Here or not."

"Yes, uncle," Paul answered. The phone was disconnected on the other end.

This was unexpected. He thought about how he had used his dislike of his uncle to fuel his desire to discover what he was up to. Now, it sounded like Fr. Paul was on his way to the eternal punishment he so richly deserved. It gave him a twinge of remorse. But when he remembered his uncle's venom-filled rants, he immediately refocused on his plan to discover what it was that his uncle was involved in.

Patrick's and Paul's timetable was unexpectedly extended until the end of November when Ashley and Tom announced that their wedding would be on Thanksgiving weekend. It was good as far as Paul was concerned, because he and Patrick had thought all along that the holidays and the holy season could be a welcome distraction in Rome and quite possibly lessen the scrutiny of the computer programmer installing the system.

"Seasonal distraction" was the code name for what the fellow programmers called their plan. Paul didn't want to miss Thanksgiving because it had always been his favorite holiday. Besides the great food, it was a time when he reflected on what he had in his life and to whom he was grateful. Excluding his responsibilities in Rome, he was fully aware of how blessed he was to have achieved what few others of his age could. He had a great relationship with Sarina, a fabulous career, and the love and respect of all those in his life. In a moment of reflection, he thought about his life, smiled, and looked toward the heavens. "Thank you."

His sister and best friend's wedding plans were set. The ceremony would be presided over by Fr. Matt. They would be married in a small church where he had just been named the head pastor. Tom asked Paul to be his best man.

The big day came and there was one notable absence. Lewis sent his congratulations, but was unable to attend due to some church business in Rome. Paul was actually happy that he wouldn't be there. He still had a bad taste in his mouth when he thought about his brother. Our sister doesn't need a hypocrite attending her wedding, Paul thought.

Paul watched Ashley walk down the aisle with their father and thought she had never looked more beautiful in her life. She didn't look like the sister who had been his dearest friend. She was a mature woman who was marrying his best buddy and they would produce the first grandchild for Charles and Angeline Morgan. And to top it off, he would be the baby's godfather.

The ceremony progressed to the exchange of rings. After the bride and groom kissed, Fr. Matt introduced Mr. and Mrs. Fogerty to the assembled.

Fr. Matt raised his hand for silence. "I, or we, have an additional ceremony to perform before the celebration begins. Paul Morgan would you please come forward." Paul proceeded across the front of the sanctuary and knelt down in front of Sarina, who was Ashley's maid of honor.

Paul took Sarina's hands. Between choking on his words and tearing up he managed the words, "Sarina, would you like to make this a double ceremony?"

She began to cry and said, "With all my heart."

Ashley took off her bridal veil and put it on Sarina's head as Paul and his bride took their places in front of Fr. Matt. Paul slipped Tom, his best man, Sarina's wedding ring and handed a ring to his sister Ashley, Sarina's maid of honor.

The wedding guests cheered and Fr. Matt laughed. "This is going to be my shortest wedding ceremony ever."

The wedding reception was doubly grand. Paul's grandfather explained it this way: it was like thinking you were having one baby and the unexpected twin shows up. Now the Morgans, the Fogertys and the Burkes were all related. It was a great day for all.

Paul leaned over to Sarina and said, "I figured I better trap you while I had you near the altar."

She turned to him with tears in her eyes and said, "You had me at 'hello.'"

Chapter 56

MONDAY AFTER THE wedding Paul called his uncle's cell phone and was forwarded to Lewis's phone. Paul left a voice message saying the new program was ready. He received a call back from his brother's administrative assistant telling him that he would be picked up at Burbank Airport at nine o'clock on Wednesday morning.

As Sarina and Paul drove home after dinner, she voiced her concern for Paul's safety. As her eyes welled up with tears, she asked her husband, "What prevents them from taking you out after you've given them what they want? What's driving you to do this? What do you think will be accomplished? What will happen afterward?"

The questions came at Paul at a rapid fire pace. He let her run out of bullets before answering. Finally her tears overcame her. She waited for him to answer. He leaned over and kissed her. "You have nothing to worry about, my love. Every contingency has been taken into account. Nothing will ever stop me from being with you. Nothing."

When he boarded the plane a couple of days later, he had the same crew. However, this time, he was well rested and alert for any situations like the shower episode from his first trip.

The papal town car was waiting to drive him to the Vatican as before, but this time it was his brother's driver and valet. That's strange, Paul thought, everything else is unchanged.

A light rain fell. About a half-mile before reaching the Vatican, the valet called Paul on the car phone. "Your brother wants us to bring you to meet him. He has something he wants to show you before taking you to the Vatican."

Paul wondered what his lowlife brother wanted to show him. It all seemed very odd.

The town car pulled through the gate of a very ornate cemetery. Lewis stood at the entrance holding an umbrella. When Paul got out of the car, the valet handed him an opened umbrella.

"Don't ask. Just follow me, little brother."

They walked on a gravel pathway through the large burial plots. Every tomb stone was adorned with some sort of cross. Ornate marble buildings sat on the back row bordering the edge of the cemetery. Halfway down the path, Lewis turned into one of the largest of them. Paul froze when he looked up saw on the classic Greek architecture, the script Morgan.

He turned to Lewis. "What is this?"

"He didn't want you to know. He didn't want to interrupt your work on the code and program. He knew you would stop and come to pay your respects. He knew how your mind works because you two were very much alike.

"When we came to visit, he always knew how you would react to him before we even arrived. He told me before he died that you, not me, should have been the servant of the church, because you couldn't be bought. Your heart and your beliefs are what make you the man that everyone loves and wants to follow. He was very annoyed with me over my shortcomings. He admitted that I might have inherited some of his worst qualities. The ones that you were spared."

Paul was lost, not knowing what to do or say. He felt like all the oxygen had been sucked from his lungs. He was angry and sad. Angry he was not told, and sad because Fr. Paul was his flesh and blood, no matter how disgusted it made him feel.

Lewis pulled out a key and unlocked the thick etched glass door to his uncle's burial house. The marble slab on which his uncle's body lay occupied the center of the room. Paul looked around the chamber and noticed several burial shelves set in the walls. Lewis said, "Before you ask, you need to read this letter that he wrote to you."

My nephew Paolo, I am sorry that you were unable to attend my funeral. It was better you didn't. The good Lord took me before you came back to spare you the vision of a very sick old man. I recall how you looked at me on your visit; your shock was plain to see. I didn't want you to remember me how I became after you left.

Paul looked up at the mausoleum wall before him to view the inscribed Latin names. From what he could remember from his high school Latin, the names appeared to be a cross section of male and female names by the fact that the last names began either with "O" or "A." He turned his attention back to his uncle's letter.

Do not judge me on what you know or are going to learn. Some things need to be told by me. First, my model and patron saint for my religious career was St. Augustine. In him, I found the type of person who is sometimes called to follow our Lord in a way that is more ambitious than sanctified. He was a bishop who was devoted to his faith through his writings and his administration of his flock. He also took his vows very loosely. His life was one of academic excellence combined with wine, women and song. He didn't ask for forgiveness or understanding. He was the way he was. So he became my model. I never thought of women as *a temptation. I thought that if I gave, as Augustine had given of himself, my transgressions against the misguided law of celibacy for priests in the Roman Catholic Church would not be judged against me. If they are, then so be it.*

Do not judge me. Know that I did the best I could for my church. Yes, it made me a wealthy man, but you must know my first priority was the church. The walls around you hold my deceased children. Two of the crypts hold two of their mothers. All were lost at childbirth. It seems the Lord gave and then took from me. Some may take that as a sign of punishment for my sinful ways.

Know that I am proud of you and grateful for what you are going to do for our church. – Fr. Paul.

Paul closed the letter and looked around the room. There must have been eight or nine crypts. He bowed his head and wondered what kind of self-possessed soul his uncle must have been. The tears streamed down his face. They were not for his uncle, they were for the innocent people whose lives he destroyed.

Chapter 57

ON THE WAY to the Vatican, Lewis broke the silence. "I am sorry. He gave me strict orders not to tell any of the family. He didn't want to put a damper on Ashley's wedding, nor did he want to disturb your work for the church."

Paul remained silent.

"He left us, his brother's children, the bulk of his estate. He was very successful in his outside business pursuits. He was very generous to us. I don't know if you were told that he owned some restaurants here. He wants those maintained and continued. All told, he left the Morgans a little over two million dollars each. He left our mother and father about three million dollars so they could have an easier 'time of it' as he said in his will."

Lewis stared at Paul and then continued. "He stipulated that he wanted you to tell the family of his passing and of what he left them. Do you have anything to say little brother?"

Moments passed and finally Paul spoke. "Take me to my condo. I have a great deal of work to do to prepare for tomorrow."

Nothing else was said. Lewis thought that his brother must be very upset.

Paul was stopped at the entrance because he wasn't wearing his ID. He went to one of his suitcases and pulled it out and put it dutifully around his neck. He went to his suite which happened to be the same one he had before. He thought for a moment, turned around, and went back down stairs and asked to be placed in another room. Reluctantly the desk clerk obliged him.

Paul fumed over the recent course of events. His head was spinning as he entered his new suite. He called Sarina and told her how much he loved her and said he was going to get his work done there as soon as possible so he could get back to her. He had to get out of this hell hole he had agreed to come back to.

The next morning, the wakeup call came and the waiting car was where it had been on his last trip. When he arrived at the financial center, the head of security was waiting to greet Paul and take him to his late uncle's office. In the elevator, he told Paul in broken English how sorry he was about his uncle and what a good servant to his faith he had been. Paul wanted to puke. He was escorted to his uncle's office. Nothing had changed since his last visit.

The head of security noted that nothing would be moved or changed until his work was done. He said, "All of the people at the Vatican are grateful for such a great man as your uncle. To work with him and to have him teach you was a supreme accolade. I know you are very proud of him. He was proud of you. He spoke of you as if you were his son."

Paul fumed. "What does the term Padrone mean?" he asked his high ranking escort.

The man looked puzzled. "It means owner, proprietor. To really know one's job." The head of security logged Paul into the computer. He looked away in order to show no interest whatsoever in the password, but Paul watched his reflection of the office window. He counted the keystrokes: nine.

The security chief looked up from the computer. "Every day I will log you in. Then you will take this login code and login again to get specific access to what you need." He handed Paul a slip of paper with the letters and number: ABCDEF123. "If by chance you cannot get access to what you need, please call me and I will expand your access downstairs. Is that clear?"

Paul nodded.

Paul dove in, working very long hours over the next week. His energy and focus were unlimited, or so thought his watchers. To rewrite the program he needed to back up to discs in case there was an error in the new installation. The discs were supplied and members of security watched as he handed them over after their completion.

It was the season of advent, and in Vatican City every day held some sort of celebration or remembrance of the journey to Bethlehem and Jesus' birth. Paul's long hours, as planned, played havoc with the members of the security team's family life. This was the time of year when fathers went to children's plays at school and other functions that centered on their church. Paul was unrelenting in keeping them looking after his work.

One day he intentionally placed a stack of books in front of the side camera to his right. It blocked the view of his watchers. It took them ten minutes to arrive at the office and nonchalantly move the books out of the camera's way.

Paul took opportunity after opportunity to run into a snag or require additional access. Unknown to the head of security, Paul timed his calls for assistance to his arrival. The closer it got to Christmas, the more time elapsed before he arrived at his uncle's office.

Paul wandered down the corridor Sr. Betty had shown him on his last visit, and looked out the window at the end of the hall. He noticed tables situated along side of the building.

One day out of the blue, Paul's lunch was brought in by Sr. Betty. Paul was in the habit of placing his badge on the entry table of the office when he came in, and picking it up on leaving, which was getting later and later, much to the chagrin of the security staff. On the tray was a one word note: Window. He grabbed his pita bread and followed her to the window at the end of the hallway.

"It's beautiful this time of year with Christmas coming isn't it, Paul?" she asked.

He nodded and she said it was safe to speak.

"What are the tables outside for?"

"All of the employees at the financial center have a celebration on Christmas Eve. They invite their families and there is food and wine for everyone. The children are entertained by dressed up characters. It's very festive. You should come if you can."

"I might just do that."

"If there is anything you need or want, just ask. God is with you. Know that."

Paul smiled at her gratefully.

He returned to his office and, amazingly, no one arrived or called to ask why he wasn't wearing his ID.

His daily coded calls to Patrick became very routine, occurring around the same time every day. In code he gave prompts and numbers that were prearranged and scrambled to look like nothing but an account number. Patrick was progressing in unlocking the system but the only way he would be able to ascertain the real meaning of the particulars of the programs would be by total access. Access that could only be had if they could determine his uncle's password.

Early the next morning, when the security head was unlocking the computer, he told Paul that he must come up with a new personal password in order to log in. The letter and numerical code that was given to him had expired. He suggested Paul should make it something simple that he could easily remember because it would be his permanent code.

Joking with Paul, whom he had gotten to know, he said, "Make it something that you don't mind spelling out every day. We had a guard whose code was his ex-wife's name. She became his ex-wife after she cheated on him with a priest. Can you imagine the insult in that?"

He was laughing hysterically as was Paul. "He had to look at her name and birth date every damn day he worked here. He tried to have it changed, but the system wouldn't recognize it. Your uncle teased him that it was cuckold123."

They laughed even harder. He said, "If you need anything Paul, let me know."

Paul was still laughing. "I will. You have been very helpful and I don't even know your name to properly thank you."

"We never tell visitors our names, even our first names. It's badge number so and so. You are working very hard for your dead uncle. That is something to be admired. Off the record, it's Augustine. Just don't refer to me as cuckold 123!" The laughing continued as he left the office.

Paul realized he had the breakthrough that he desperately needed. He looked around the office in the dawning of a new day and realized both the mini cameras were gone. He tried to remember the last time he placed books there and when someone came to move them. Was it yesterday or the day before? No matter, they were gone.

His first order of business for the day was changing his password. It came to him easily. Sarina224; her name and birth date of February 24. He typed in the new password and repeated it. He waited and in disbelief saw the message: This password is not available. Please try another.

Paul stared at the screen for what seemed like an eternity.

He came out of his trance and realized many things. He would address those later. He carefully typed his brother's name, LewisMorgan, and then typed Sarina224. Success. Paul now had access to his brother's computer. Paul's heart pounded. He was close, so close, to what he had spent the last three weeks working on.

Now, Paul took his most daring chance. He logged out of Lewis's account. The moment was at hand. He felt himself start to perspire and his heart was racing in his chest. He needed this. He really needed this. He looked up at the ceiling as if his eyes were penetrating the roof of the office building and thought, please, help me.

His hand shook as he typed PaulMorgan for the user and then as he held his breath, he typed in the password Morgan512 and the computer opened to his uncle's account. He was in! He waited until one minute had elapsed on his chronograph stopwatch. He logged out and began to breathe again.

No alarms, no security rushed into the office, no buzzer, and no blinking lights. If he had stayed in longer would it have triggered the alarm? He made a mental note to experiment with longer access times.

Paul wanted to scream, he was so happy. Now was the time to call Patrick and tell him in code that he had gotten in. He would joke with him later that he was the new safe cracker, but that celebration would have to wait.

According to their plan, they wouldn't go live until they got what they wanted from the system, so there continued to be issues for Paul to work on. Patrick and he figured that the security staff's vigilance would wane with each passing day, and the holidays were almost upon them.

He made his call to Patrick in code and shared the happy news. Paul then decided to take a calculated risk. He broke code and told Patrick that he hoped to finish in the next three days and be home for his first Christmas with Sarina.

"Plus, I need to rest up for the Rose Bowl." The Rose bowl was between UCLA and Penn State, and Paul had given twenty points to Penn State.

He told Patrick about the Christmas Eve festival he wanted to attend in Rome, leaving for home right after the festival. If it could be arranged he would arrive in California in time to surprise Sarina Christmas morning."

Patrick was confused by Paul's slipping out of code. Unsure, Patrick confirmed some of Paul's message, slipping in and out of code himself. "So you think you can finish in time for the festival? What time does it start?"

"It runs from four o'clock in the afternoon until seven o'clock in the evening. I checked the weather and it's supposed to be clear for the next three evenings. There may be a storm coming in Christmas afternoon, but I don't think that will be an issue for my travel plans."

Paul continued, now in code. "How long do you think it will take to make sure the system works with the usual three or four test runs?"

Patrick replied, "Probably twenty minutes from start to finish. The same damn number you gave against my old team, you bastard." They both laughed.

Paul got serious, and slipping out of code, said, "I have to finish this on time. I don't want to impose on any of the security team to babysit me through Christmas. We must get it right."

"We will," Patrick assured him. "Let's make as many phone calls as we need so we can have everyone home for Christmas."

Paul said, "Let's do it, brother, let's do it."

The head of security hung up his phone at the same time as Paul and Patrick. He had listened to every call on that phone since Paul had arrived. Augustine smiled to himself and thought how this Paul was nothing like his uncle. He'd been his chief of security for over twenty years. That dead bastard would purposely work through Christmas, just to inconvenience his staff. He didn't care about others' family relationships. Only what suited him, the bastard.

Augustine immediately called his wife and gave her the good news that he would be home for Christmas. They might just skip the festival and have a nice dinner with some wine and amore at home after the kids went to bed. He thought, I like this nephew, Paul. Too bad he wasn't in charge the last twenty years.

Chapter 58

Paul and Patrick knew that all of their conversations were monitored and took the appropriate measures to speak in code, with the exception of the day Paul had discovered his uncle's password where Paul slipped in and out of code. He had lengthened the duration of time that he was logged into his uncle's account to nearly thirty minutes. Paul had located the correct directory and files and in code told Patrick what was needed to copy the files.

Patrick surmised that there was an anti-copy protocol on his uncle's computer and instructed Paul, step by step, how it could be disabled. They both worried that even though the system showed the anti-copy was deactivated, they wouldn't be certain until they tried to copy a file. Paul was just finishing up their work session when there was a knock on the office door.

"Come in."

Sr. Betty entered with his lunch. Uncertain if there were any surveillance devices still hidden in the office, she said that if there was anything else he needed she would be happy to bring it to him. When she set his lunch tray in front of him he noticed a small folded piece of paper. She pointed to it and he nodded that he had seen it.

He thanked her and she winked back at him. As he ate, he slid his hand over the note and discretely placed it in his pants pocket.

After lunch, he went down the hallway to the window that Sr. Betty had shown him. He stood looking out at the last minute preparations for the festival and opened the piece of paper. *Tonight, 8 p.m., Cafe Monet. Reservation under the name of Mr. Claude. Come alone.*

He put it carefully back into his pants pocket and left to use the restroom. In the restroom stall enclosure, he wadded the paper up and bent over as if to spit in the toilet bowl. He dropped the paper in and flushed it immediately.

The rest of the afternoon was split between calls to Patrick and a couple to Sarina. He also called the firm and got updates from Tom on how the business was going and how Ashley was feeling. Paul wondered if the person listening on the other end was bored by the chit chat. In the back of his mind he pondered who had sent the note, but since it was carried by Sr. Betty and Christmas Eve was the next day, he surmised it might just be the final installment of how he would get out of there and how the files would be copied.

Paul called to have his car ready at seven thirty. He had googled the cafe and had a very good idea where it was located. He gave the driver the address of a cafe that was about a half-block away. The valet and driver wanted to follow him but he told them he had private business to attend to and that he wished them to stay by the car. He wouldn't be long.

The other cafe was large, more like a cabaret then a cafe. Paul went to the men's room and took off his badge and hung it under the toilet's water reservoir. He exited out the cafe's back entrance and he walked down the alley to the entrance of Cafe Monet.

He approached the hostess and asked for the reservation for Mr. Claude. She led Paul to a private booth with a curtain across the entrance. A short while after he was seated two women entered the booth and shut the curtain. Paul recognized Sisters Margaret and Andrea. He hadn't known them at first because they were not dressed in the traditional nun's attire but were dressed as wealthy socialites. Sr. Margaret spoke first in her high register voice, "Great disguises, eh?"

The two nuns explained what would happen the next day and advised him to act his part. Sr. Andrea went on to describe tomorrow's Christmas Eve festival. She also pointed out that the camera on the heliport could not be disabled without sounding an alarm, so they had prepared a performance for the benefit of the surveillance camera.

"Paul, it is important that you act normally during this performance. The more convincing you are in trying to resist abduction tomorrow, the better the chance that you will escape unharmed. We will not give you too many details so this will play out on tape as naturally as possible. Do you understand?"

"Yes."

"You better get going."

"In case I don't see you again, I want to thank you for everything you both have done."

Sr. Andrea laughed. "Oh, you are going to see us before you leave tomorrow."

As they stood to leave, Sr. Margaret handed Paul a package.

"What's this?" Paul asked. "A Christmas gift?"

"No," Sr. Andrea replied. "It's your costume for the festival. It's very important that you wear it tomorrow. Everyone at the festival will be dressed in costume. This is your life-line out of Rome."

Paul left first. He retraced his steps, picked up his badge, and went to his waiting car with his package in hand. He instructed his driver to take him back to his condo.

In his suite, he opened the package. It was a donkey costume. He wondered if all of the character's costumes had something to do with the nativity.

Chapter 59

Paul's sleepless night reminded him of Christmas Eves when he was a boy growing up in California. The tree, the gifts, and the holiday feeling were what he really loved about Christmas as a youth. But now he couldn't sleep on the night before Christmas Eve wondering what would happen at the financial center. He hoped that they would carry off their plans without a hitch. He reminded himself to be prepared for the unexpected because it was the contingencies that they hadn't planned for that would be their downfall.

He had grown tired of the process of getting into his uncle's files and the subsequent testing of the security system. He just wanted to go home and be with his wife and family, not stuck in a damn foreign country in his dead uncle's office. It was time to return to the real world, the business world he loved and enjoyed and a career that brought him satisfaction and gave the financial stability to live the lifestyle he had dreamed of as young boy.

For an hour Paul performed the final testing in partnership with Patrick, who was on the phone from California. They implemented bogus run-throughs as the head of security listened in.

The head of security hoped that Paul would follow through on his previously stated wish to finish in time for the staff to spend Christmas Eve with their loved ones. He wanted be home for a romantic Christmas Eve with his wife. He was rooting for the success of the new computer program almost as much as Paul was.

Paul thought he was prepared, but the first of many surprises hit him a couple of hours after he arrived at the office. Augustine called to let him know that Lewis and an attorney were downstairs and wanted him to come down to the lobby. When Paul got off of the elevator, his brother was standing with his hands up in the air in front of one of the scanners. Lewis had apparently forgotten he was carrying a semi-automatic pistol. He wasn't about to give it up and the guards weren't letting him proceed.

The guards had their guns drawn amid a cacophony of Italian being rapidly fired at one another. When Augustine saw Paul he asked him, "Do you know this man? He claims to be your brother."

Augustine was following the protocol set in place by their uncle in all cases of firearms being discovered at the security scanners.

"Yes he is."

Augustine instructed his men to put down their firearms. "Fr. Morgan you may lower your arms but do not put your hand anywhere near your weapon. Please walk around the scanner and all will be well. I apologize for the misunderstanding. Fr. Morgan, I regret to inform you that you may not take your weapon into the building. And Paul, your brother doesn't have security clearance to go to your office. The three of you can make yourselves comfortable in our lobby conference room. My apologies, again."

Lewis shook his head as he, Paul, and the lawyer were led into the conference room by a guard. "Brother, I hear you burn the midnight oil as much as our uncle did. You and I inherited that work trait from the Morgan side of the family. I was hoping that while you were here, we would have a chance to go out to dinner and visit, but no such luck. I understand that you plan to finish this afternoon and that uncle's jet is going to take you home in time for Christmas. I will be serving Midnight Mass tonight in a small chapel outside of the city. I wanted you to attend, but it seems you have other plans.

"I brought uncle's solicitor to read the will. It is stipulated that you and I are to be present when the will is officially read, though I have made you privy to some of our uncle's previously stated wishes."

"Hello, Mr. Paul Morgan. My name is Julius Ernesto. I was your uncle's solicitor. Let me start by expressing my deepest sorrow on his passing. He was an employee of the Vatican, so he is absolved of any type of estate tax that is levied by Italy or the United States. He was very wise with his money. At the time of his death he still had a great deal of the money he made working for the church."

Ernesto continued, "Your uncle left the majority of his estate to his brother's four children. He did leave a trust fund for a number of women and children for whom he was a benefactor."

The bastard's common law wives and children, Paul thought.

"The properties and restaurants are to be managed by your brother Lewis and the net profits will be passed on to the four of you. I have four cashier checks drawn on the Banco de Swiss in Zurich, Switzerland in the amount of two million dollars each for Lewis, Paul, Ashley, and Claire Morgan. I understand that you are to return tonight, so I am entrusting the delivery of your sisters' checks to you, if that is agreeable with you, Mr. Morgan."

"Yes. I—"

Lewis interrupted. "Isn't this a great Christmas present for each of them? Fr. Paul was just the kind of person who always thought of his family. He was very generous."

Paul felt sick to his stomach listening to his brother's speech.

The lawyer continued. "He also left a three million dollar inheritance to his brother and sister-in-law that has already been electronically deposited, as of this morning, in their California bank account. Do you have any questions?"

Paul shook his head and Lewis said, "Thank you, from all of our family."

He turned to Paul and asked if he had time for lunch.

"No. I need to get back to work. I'm sorry."

Paul went straight to Augustine's office. "May I take this envelope through the scanner?" He held out the envelope containing the checks.

"I am sorry, but that is not permitted. You can pick it up on the way out this afternoon. We will safeguard it for you."

Paul nodded and proceeded through the scanners aware that his brother and the solicitor were watching him as he made a beeline to his office.

On his way back to his uncle's office, Paul realized that when he had gone down to the lobby, he had inadvertently left his uncle's account open. Thankfully, there were no alarms or alerts. Paul now felt confident that his mission would come to a positive conclusion in a couple of hours, although he still needed to figure out the finer details of how he was going to get his hands on the discs for copying the files.

At four o'clock in the afternoon, Augustine called Paul and inquired if he was close to finishing because the festival was beginning.

Patrick and Paul had the new system up and running. Paul told Augustine that he would be right down to pick up his envelope and package.

Paul reopened his donkey outfit right in front of Augustine and other four security guards. They all laughed, because three of them had the exact same costume. They donned their costumes and walked out of the building together, with Augustine and the three guards laughing the entire way. Augustine wore his traditional shepherd's costume that he had worn for the last twenty years. They all used their badges to clock out of the building, leaving one security guard at the financial center alone.

The festival was held in close proximity to the financial center, and nearly everyone in the square wore a costume. As Augustine walked with Paul, his attention was drawn to a woman walking toward him with four children in tow. Augustine embraced his wife and children, and introduced them to Paul. His wife said something to him in Italian and he smiled and all the children bowed their heads as they were introduced.

Augustine invited Paul to experience the festival with him and his family if he liked.

"Thank you, but I have other plans before I leave for my plane. Thank you for everything that you have done to help me while I was here."

Augustine looked at Paul fondly and embraced him. "You are a good man, Paul Morgan. God be with you."

Paul melted into the thick crowd looking at the many booths. It reminded him of his school carnivals, which he'd never particularly enjoyed. He strolled toward the fountain in the middle of the square that he had viewed from the window at the end of the office corridor. He sat down on the edge of the fountain and watched the costumed people walk by.

Someone sat down very close to him and began to speak. He recognized a woman's voice, but couldn't quite place it. He glanced up to see a donkey costume that was identical not only to his, but to many such costumes filling the plaza.

"We gave you the most popular costume to afford you the anonymity that you will need. Secretly pass me your ID so no one sees you. You will get it back. I will take your town car back to your condo with the valet and driver and check you out of the facility. I have a voice activator that mimics your voice when I speak."

She touched the side of her neck and Paul had the experience of sitting next to himself and speaking to himself.

"Tricky." Paul grinned at the woman.

She laughed. "A wide variety of technology is developed here, but not all of it is for the good of mankind. You will find that out soon enough. When you see a donkey costume with the wearer having the red plastic wristband the AIDS Foundation sells, follow him. I will see you in a bit. Be safe."

Now he realized Sr. Margaret had been sitting next to him. He hadn't recognized her because her voice was not as high-pitched as he remembered. Then he recalled the voice activator she spoke about. Very clever, he thought.

Chapter 60

PAUL CALLED HIS town car and requested to be picked up in front of the festival. Sr. Margaret was waiting for the car in her donkey costume. Thinking it was Paul, the driver and the valet drove Sr. Margaret to the condo. She used Paul's ID to check out and had the valet remain to load Paul's luggage and take it to the private airport terminal. She told the valet that she would be at the terminal in about an hour. She said she had some stops to make before leaving.

She grabbed Paul's duffle bag and the small photograph of Sarina that was by his bed. The rest would be loaded into the taxi.

The town car was directed to the restaurant where Paul had met Lewis and Fr. Paul on his first visit. Sr. Margaret told the driver if she wasn't out in five minutes to come in and help with the bakery goods that she was buying to take home as gifts for the family.

"Yes sir, Mr. Morgan."

The bakery was nearing closing time. When five minutes had elapsed, the driver came in and Sr. Margaret asked him to step into the back and help carry the pastry boxes. As he followed her instructions he was met by a pistol blow to the back of the head. He fell limp to the ground, unconscious. The restaurant and bakery owner, a woman known as Colleen B, had been waiting on Sr. Margaret. Colleen came around the counter with a large syringe and stuck the fallen driver in the neck.

Colleen took over and ordered her men to dispose of the garbage on her store's floor. One of the men requisitioned the driver's firearm at the same time as someone who could have been the original driver's twin arrived dressed in the same uniform.

He loaded the pastry boxes into the car and Sr. Margaret and he continued on their trip. As she climbed out of the car, she left Paul's badge on the back seat. She told the driver where his next stop was.

In the meantime, Paul sat by the fountain for about twenty minutes before another person in a donkey costume sat down next to him. He spotted the red plastic AIDS Foundation bracelet.

Paul cleared his throat and remarked on what a nice festival this was to get people in the mood for Christmas tomorrow.

The stranger nodded and said, "We will be long way from here by the time the sun rises on Christmas."

Again, Paul recognized the voice but its owner eluded him. Something nagged at the back of Paul's mind.

After sitting silent for a while the stranger cleared his throat and pointed at the building directly across the street. "I am going around the corner of that building. Wait a moment and then follow. When you see me, I will be dressed as the Virgin Mary. Embrace me and act as though you have been waiting for me. Got it?"

"Yes."

Paul waited a couple of minutes before following the donkey with the red bracelet. As soon as he rounded the corner, the Virgin Mary ran toward him and hugged him. He couldn't see her face but the body shape and smell of her perfume was that of his favorite person on earth.

Sarina whispered, "Don't react to who I am. They think we are being watched. I had to see you and be with you.

Paul couldn't believe that she was here with him. He was giddy with delight and itched to hug and kiss her. When he told her as much she giggled and said that would happen soon enough.

They had walked for a block when she grabbed Paul's hand and pulled him into the darkened alcove of a building. "Please kiss me," Sarina entreated.

Joyfully, Paul followed her instructions.

He had barely tasted her lips when a double appeared out of the darkness and Sarina disappeared. The double took his hand and they resumed their walk. They made a left hand turn and the woman finally spoke. It was Sr. Andrea.

"In about a hundred feet, we are going to hug and you are going to take off your donkey head and kiss me on the cheek. Anyone who is watching will see that it is you. I will get into a waiting taxi and you will walk down to the garage, third building on the left, where the delivery office light is on. Go inside. They are expecting you."

Paul entered what looked like an old aviation hangar near the Vatican. He was surprised to see his uncle's helicopter. An elderly man escorted him toward the rear of the helicopter. Waiting for him with a big smile on his face was his helicopter pilot, Lloyd.

"Once everyone is in position, we will move on to the next phase of the operation. Can I get you anything to drink?"

Paul paused for a moment. "I feel like I'm in some altered state, on a ride at an amusement park, and I am not quite sure whether everything that is happening is real."

"It is." Lloyd smiled as Paul noticed the red AIDS bracelet on his right arm.

"Yeah, it was me, my fellow donkey. I wear it for my brother who died from that horrible disease. I decided to devote my life to his memory. That is why I am a member of the Seal of the Lamb. Sit down. The best part is yet to come."

Chapter 61

THE TOWN CAR arrived with Sr. Margaret and her new driver. It was dark but the profile of her driver was very familiar to Paul. He knew this person. It was his brother-in-law Tom, who held his index finger to his lips as he handed the ID badge back to him. Sr. Margaret handed Paul a script to read and he nodded that he understood.

There was a physical scuffle between Paul and a couple of assailants, who were apparently trying to abduct him.

Paul yelled out, "What are you doing?"

Sr. Margaret, in a very deep man's voice said, "If you want to live to see California, shut up and get in."

She pushed him into his uncle's helicopter. Paul said nothing. She directed him to his script and again he nodded. Sitting in the co-pilot seat was another person dressed in an identical donkey suit which all four passengers wore. Nothing was said as the helicopter went airborne from the old aviation hangar and away from the Vatican, made a big loop and came in from the opposite direction that they had taken off from. Paul thought it took about ten minutes to make the loop.

They landed on the helicopter pad on top of the Financial Center. Margaret grabbed him and in deep manly voice ordered

Paul to get out. He then realized she was pointing a gun at him. The co-pilot got out with a gun drawn as well and had the pilot shut off the engine and get out with his hands up. Paul looked up and saw the red light on the motion sensor camera so he knew the camera was recording. One of the others in a donkey suit swiped the door with a key card and they stepped inside the elevator and again used the key card. His uncle's office was dimly lit and one of the kidnappers stood guard by the office door. They bolted it.

The computer was exactly how Paul had left it. He didn't want to have to wait for it to go through the start-up motions, so to save as much time as possible he'd left it in sleep mode. Sr. Margaret supplied a satellite phone and Paul called Patrick in code. Paul logged in as Paul Morgan, password Morgan512. It opened immediately and he went to the file folder that he had consolidated during his intermittent accesses to his uncle's account over the last few days.

One of the donkey suits holding a gun on him produced a memory stick for him to copy the file. Nothing needed to be said. Paul inserted it into the port and disabled the copy alarm as Patrick had previously instructed him to do. The download started immediately. No alarm or warning appeared. In the meantime, one of the donkey suits put a cord into another port and started the download on his laptop. This slowed the first memory stick slightly, which was going almost at full speed.

When the first memory stick was complete, Paul inserted another one and began downloading again. He looked at his watch; nearly five minutes had elapsed. The laptop finished and the speed on the second memory stick picked up. Paul was sweating under his donkey outfit and wished he could take the head unit off. Though the time was under the plan, he didn't want to see what would happen after twenty minutes. That was the time that Patrick had calculated that some sort of mainframe alarm would go off.

Copying to the third memory stick was underway and moving well. Soon it finished and number four was inserted. The building's electricity took a momentary drop in power. That was a common problem in Vatican City and for that matter, Rome. At peak times there could be a drop in current anywhere from a few seconds to a couple of minutes. Paul had experienced this phenomenon many times.

This caused the fourth memory stick to slow its download to almost a crawl. It had only reached fifty percent complete as the time quickly approached the twenty minute mark. With a sick feeling in his stomach, Paul watched as the time hit the twenty minute mark and passed it. When nothing occurred he breathed a sigh of relief.

The drop in electrical current lasted about thirty seconds, after which there was a surge up to full strength, bringing the download back on its normal pace.

Paul's eyes grew wide as he noticed that the screen was blinking red in the corner. He felt sick again at the realization that an alarm had been triggered. The download continued but another window appeared: *Warning. Unauthorized copy of classified material.* This was followed by yet another window: *Please login and use your password to continue.*

When the number four stick was at eighty percent, one of the kidnappers wrote a note to Paul that said: Forget it. *Let's go with what we have.*

Paul shook his head and logged on again as his uncle. *Unauthorized.* The stick was at ninety percent. The next window to appear read: *This computer will be shut down and be locked in ten seconds. To unlock, contact your administrator.*

The kidnapper grabbed Paul's arm and motioned to leave. Paul shook his head no. The stick was at ninety-five percent. The clock was down to six seconds and as the seconds counted down so did the percent of the download. As soon as it read 100 percent of download, Paul grabbed the stick out of the port. At the same instant the computer shut down and smoke exited the port that he had just removed the stick from.

A red light flashed at the base of the computer and they saw a light flashing by the office door. The four walked to the elevator and took it up to the roof. Outside the door, a red beacon flashed. As they climbed into the helicopter, Sr. Margaret turned and shot out the surveillance camera which now had a couple of flashing lights going off around it.

As the helicopter props began to rotate, Sr. Margaret motioned to Paul for him to hand her his badge. She opened her door, leaned over and entwined it around the bottom of what looked like a three foot by five foot drone that was suspended under the helicopter. The kidnapper in the back of the helicopter had a console with which to control the drone. He released the drone and sent it in the direction of the private airport terminal. The blinking red light on the drone was similar to the helicopter's but much smaller. The helicopter took off in the opposite direction of the drone. The drone's path would take it over the city and out over a lake that bordered the private airport terminal.

The red light flashed in the chief of security's office, but the lone security guard who was unfortunate to have duty on Christmas Eve, was busy having his own private party in the adjacent office with his new girlfriend. She had told him that her name was "Tracy A" and that she was a model from the States who was in Rome for a huge New Year's Eve fashion show. The guard couldn't believe his good fortune to meet such a beautiful woman who was willing to sneak into the financial center so he wouldn't be alone on Christmas Eve.

In a matter of minutes the alarm went from silent to sounding a horn. The guard jumped up thinking there was an intrusion in the building. He immediately notified the chief of security.

Augustine was enjoying wine and foreplay with his wife on their couch. The children had been put to bed and Augustine's evening was just getting started when the guard phoned. Augustine retrieved his computer from his home office to find its light blinking. He alerted two guards who were still at the festival and they were at the building's door in less than a minute.

Meanwhile, the lone guard instructed his new girlfriend to hide in an adjacent office until the guards got into the elevator and to let herself out. He told her he would call her, even though he was never successful in reaching her on her cell phone. The guards boarded the elevator and the door closed. Tracy put on a donkey costume, exited the building, and strolled into the thinning crowd.

When the guards got off the elevator on Fr. Paul's office floor they ascertained where the break in had occurred. The guards proceeded cautiously not knowing if the intruders were still in his office. They reported to the chief, that all was secure.

In the interim, Augustine pulled up the surveillance video from the helipad. As he reviewed the video, he struggled to understand what the hell was going on until he saw the intruder point a gun at the camera and the feed abruptly stopped. The chief tried to shake his wine-induced euphoria and focus on the break in.

He checked the badge entry log and stared at the screen in disbelief. He must be mistaken. This was not possible. Both the elevator ID and the computer login belonged to his deceased boss, Fr. Paul Morgan.

He groaned out loud. "Son of a bitch, the bastard is still alive."

He picked up the helicopter tracker on the drone, believing that Fr. Paul Morgan and his nephew, Paul, were on board the helicopter. Augustine thought for a moment how he had liked Fr. Morgan's nephew. He knew what he had to do. When he thought about Paul, it saddened him, but he delighted in the thought of taking out his former boss, who must have faked his own death.

Using his computer, he located the coordinates and alerted the intercept department head to get a missile "hot" for an outbound maverick. Within seconds, the coordinates were picked up by the intercept department and Augustine ordered, "Take them out over the lake by the private air terminal."

Within seconds, the missile was launched, hitting its target. When questioned later, the tower was convinced by the beacon signal that it was a private helicopter of the Vatican, although it seemed to produce a very small explosion. Even though the tower had expected a larger impact, it was confirmed that the helicopter was destroyed. Mission accomplished.

Augustine called his guards and released them to go back to their families except for the lone sentinel. He would deal with this tomorrow after Mass and when all the Christmas gifts had been opened. Augustine went back to the festivities awaiting him on his living room couch.

Chapter 62

THE HELICOPTER CARRYING Paul continued away from the private air terminal. Ten minutes later, the helicopter slowly began to lose altitude. Paul motioned to the pilot about the helicopter going down and the pilot gave him the thumbs up sign. They were now traveling just above the rooftops. To Paul's eye the buildings were very old and vacant. Soon they were hovering above a vacant field where he noticed a truck exposed by the helicopter's landing lights. The vehicle flashed its headlights three times.

When the helicopter landed they were met by two men with faces covered who handed keys to the pilot. Paul, Sr. Margaret, and the other mysterious occupant in a donkey costume, exited the helicopter with the pilot and headed to the waiting UPS truck with its motor running. They climbed into the back where large shipping crates had been loaded.

As they removed their donkey heads, Sr. Margaret spoke first, "Damn, I am glad to get that off of my head so I can breathe."

Sitting next to her was Sr. Andrea, as Paul suspected. The pilot was Lloyd. After they had shed their disguises, Sr. Andrea commented that everyone looked like drowned rats after being in the costumes for so long.

Lloyd spoke up, saying they could freshen up at the warehouse where they were headed. He donned a UPS driver shirt and coat. He'd worn the matching pants under his donkey outfit.

Sr. Andrea spoke up. "Before we get started, does everyone have their own memory stick? Good. Keep them secure. They are the keys to a new beginning." Sr. Andrea produced the laptop that had been used to copy the files at the financial center.

Paul and the two nuns rode in the back of the truck, sitting on three large wooden crates. The door behind Lloyd was closed. Sr. Margaret outlined to Paul what was going to happen. Before he could ask she explained, "Sarina and Tom are waiting at the warehouse to see you. I'm sorry we couldn't let you in on what was going to happen."

They arrived at what looked like a UPS terminal that backed up to an airport. Paul wondered if they were going to get them out on a commercial freight plane.

Lloyd used a remote control to open the warehouse door. He drove the truck in and closed the door behind him.

The door behind the driver's seat was opened and they all piled out into the dimly lit warehouse. Paul saw a very familiar outline walking quickly toward him. He smiled at his wife. "I sure didn't think we would be spending Christmas Eve in some parcel warehouse."

Sarina rushed into his arms. "I love you. You are unbelievably brave and I am very proud to be Mrs. Morgan."

His eyes fixed on a dim shape coming his way.

"Yo, bro. I didn't know that you were in some sort of James Bond scene. Glad I could be a part of it. Oh, your sister told me to tell you she is fine and will see us tomorrow for Christmas at the folks. She is getting really big with your godchild."

Paul was directed to a bathroom with a shower and was

handed the small duffle bag he had packed with his travel clothes. He showered, dressed and walked out of the bathroom to a waiting crowd. His other three cohorts had done the same, also changing into casual clothing.

Lloyd said, "Paul we need you to make a call to the private airport terminal and let them know you are still alive and want your luggage shipped to your California address. Tell them you met someone and you are staying in Rome for a couple of extra days. You will no longer need their services as other travel arrangements have been made for you."

Paul dutifully followed Lloyd's instructions to the letter. The surprise and disbelief was evident in his uncle's pilot's voice. He said he was very surprised to hear from him and asked what happened after he left the festival.

Paul read from the script he was handed. "I went into a bakery to purchase some bread and cakes for gifts for my family and when I walked out to the town car, it was gone. I called from my cell phone but no one answered. I called a friend I met at the Bistro and she came and picked me up. What happened to my driver and car?" Paul sounded like an innocent victim.

The airline pilot cleared his throat. "I think there must have been a miscommunication between you and the driver. I apologize on his behalf. We will make sure your luggage is delivered to your home address. I think it might be a couple of days."

"No problem. I am in no hurry. I have plenty of clothing here with me. Thank you for all that you and your staff have done for me."

The pilot smirked and thought the apple doesn't fall far from the tree. Paul is no different from his uncle and brother with their various women scattered all over the place. He then came to his senses and made a phone call to the Chief of Security.

The chief was irritated when his phone began to vibrate. He

and his wife were happily ensconced on the couch in amorous delight. "Don't answer it," pleaded his wife.

"I must. It's the damn pilot. I will hurry. Don't lose the mood."

The pilot repeated his conversation with Paul.

Augustine could not comprehend what he'd heard. "Who called you?" he yelled into the phone.

His wife nudged him to keep his voice down with the children sleeping upstairs. Augustine held his hand up and nodded that he had taken due notice. The pilot repeated his story.

"Go home to your family for Christmas, we'll figure it out tomorrow."

Augustine hesitated for a moment and decided, screw it, this will wait until tomorrow. He resumed his tryst with his wife on the couch.

Chapter 63

LLOYD HAD CHANGED into a UPS airline pilot's uniform. Tom said, "You really look like the official thing. Are you going to fly the big 747 parked outside?"

Lloyd nodded. "With a lot of help from Captain Sutherland."

A tall, auburn haired woman came toward the group. She walked with a regimented gait which foretold her military background. When she came into the light of the hanger, she was a stunning individual who just happened to be dressed in an airline Captain's uniform. Before she even spoke, her presence commanded respect. She had an air about her that said she tolerated no foolishness up in the air or down on the ground. She extended her hand to shake Paul's and introduced herself. "I am Captain Sutherland. I will be flying the cargo ship back to California, taking you and your party home."

"Thank you. Nice to meet you, Captain Sutherland."

"Please, call me Jodi. It is what everyone calls me." She continued, "From what my copilot Lloyd tells me about you, I should be thanking you for your heroic efforts."

She noticed Paul eyeing her quizzically. "You are very perceptive, Paul. Yes, I was one of the donkeys that you passed in the festival courtyard. Wasn't everyone dressed in a donkey costume?" They all laughed and the mood lightened.

Sr. Andrea briefed Paul and his group on how they were going to make their exit from Italy. "The wooden crates will be used to get you onto the cargo plane. The crates will be inspected by customs here and then you will embark on your journey. After you've left this place, the airplane will land in about an hour at another Italian airport. There you will change planes to a faster private jet that Jodi and Lloyd will pilot. You will arrive home twice as fast and be much more comfortable. Does anyone have any questions?"

She and Sr. Margaret would accompany them on the first leg of the trip. They were supposed to be at a retreat in Northern Italy for the holidays. No one was aware they had left the retreat and this plan allowed them to be present for morning prayers and Christmas Mass tomorrow. No one would be the wiser and who would believe them if they tried to explain? Sr. Margaret laughed.

Everything went exactly as planned and the California travelers were soon in the wooden crates and through customs inspection, which was virtually non-existent on Christmas Eve, and sitting in passenger seats in the area behind the cock pit.

Jodi invited each one of them to take a turn in the copilot's seat to experience the process of flying a jumbo jet filled with cargo. Paul was very impressed with the complexity of the control panel and the intricacies of the job. Tom, on the other hand, was more like a kid on a ride at Disneyland. They kidded him that they would have to get him his own junior pilot's wings.

The nuns left the entourage at the small Northern Italy airport. Sisters Andrea and Margaret shook everyone's hand except Paul's.

For him it was hugs from both. Each whispered nearly identical words. "You are a hero in my eyes. Thank you for what you have done for me and countless others. God bless you."

The private jet was larger than the Vatican jet he'd flown on previously, with four master suites in the rear of the plane. Tom summed up the surroundings in the plane with his customary, "Now, that's what I'm talking about."

Paul and Sarina retired to one of the suites and were instantly asleep. Tom followed the same course.

When Paul's phone woke him six hours later it was Lloyd. They would be landing in California in about two hours. The plane's two attendants wanted to prepare them breakfast before their arrival, or dinner if they preferred.

"That will be fine, Lloyd. Shall we say in about thirty minutes? And would you let Tom know, please?" He wanted to get cleaned up before eating. He told Sarina what was going on and stepped into the lavish bathroom adjacent to their suite for a much needed hot shower.

Moments later he was joined by Sarina, who simply said, "I know you're used to having company when you shower on these private flights. Just know that the one who is showering with you now is the only person you will ever shower with." They laughed and embraced. The shower took a little longer than usual.

Chapter 64

LARRY AND DIANNE met them in a town car. Ellen DePaolo, the defense attorney who had helped Paul when the police tried to arrest him at the Stanford game, was waiting in the car.

After pleasantries were exchanged, Ellen spoke up. "Paul, we have taken some preventive legal measures in case an extradition order back to Italy is invoked against you by an Italian court of law. You need to know that it will be blocked and you will not be forced to return to Italy or the Vatican for that matter. Do you have any questions or concerns?"

Paul shook his head as he handed an envelope to Tom.

"What's this?"

"Something the pilot asked me to give to you."

Tom opened it and out dropped a pair of junior pilot's wings to pin on his coat. As laughter filled the car, Paul thought how good it was to be back on California soil.

"You guys sure know how to get great pilots to fly you around on Christmas," said Larry after he got his laughter under control.

"What do you mean?" asked Paul.

"Those pilots, Jodi and Lloyd, are the pilots who landed Navy Seal Team Six in Pakistan when they took out Osama bin Laden."

"No shit," Tom said. "Well I got my wings from two international war heroes. You guys can laugh all you want. I am wearing these and then framing them." The laughter continued all the way home.

* * *

Mid-morning Christmas day, Paul received a call from Patrick. They agreed to meet at the advanced computer lab around the corner from the accounting office. Paul had memory disk four in his coat pocket. It was an unseasonably cool day in Westwood and the two of them joked that the East coast must have shifted to California. Patrick said, "The only thing missing is the Delaware snow."

In the lab, Paul handed over his memory stick. Patrick ran a scan of it. He tinkered with it for a couple of minutes getting readings.

"Is this the last stick that almost got vaporized when the system locked up?"

"Yes. Why?"

"I already have the first three sticks and the laptop, and have scanned them. This stick has more gigs of data than the others. It's a good thing you stayed and got this one copied.

"How can this stick have more data on it?"

I think I know how it happened, and I'm very happy that it does."

Paul smiled to himself. He remembered when the clock's countdown started, how something drove him to keep downloading and not give up. It was another one of those unexplained feelings that seemed to guide him through most of his perilous adventures. He couldn't explain it, he just went in the direction his feelings led him. Rarely was his gut feeling incorrect.

Paul often felt he must have a guardian angel watching over him, but with his escape from the Vatican the day before, he realized there were other guardian angels walking this earth helping him. He looked up at the sky and thanked God with a smile on his face.

"Well, I'll let you get to it." Paul stood up to leave.

"Before you go, I want you to meet someone who is going to help us with the deciphering."

They walked down the hall from his personal lab and Patrick introduced him to Tyler Molvig. He was also in the master's program at UCLA. They exchanged pleasantries and Tyler resumed his work. Patrick walked Paul out of the maze of offices to the main entry of the building.

"Call me when you have a handle on what we've got."

"I will, brother," was all that Patrick said.

Chapter 65

ON HIS WALK back to the firm, Paul called Sarina, who had decided to sleep in. He told her that he was going to look at his mail and then he would call her again. They could have a late lunch together after they stopped by his parents' house.

The office was closed until after New Year's and Paul was the only occupant today. He opened the mountain of mail that lay on his desk. It was actually smaller than he thought it would be. He opened and systematically delegated each piece to its appropriate pile; more often than not, the trash can under his desk. Much of the mail around this time of year asked for donations and contributions to various charities and causes. He worked his way through them.

He opened one that caught his eye. He felt compelled to read the entire mailer. It pictured an undernourished and sick child standing barefoot in front of a falling down shack and was from the AIDS Foundation of Los Angeles. He studied it and made note of the address on the return envelope. He folded it and slipped it in his jacket. He quickly finished and he and Sarina met all of the family at his parents' house.

After everyone was through hugging and telling each other how happy they were to be back together, Paul stood up and took two envelopes from his jacket pocket. He handed one to Ashley and one to his mother Angeline, telling his youngest sister Claire that their mother would take care of her gift from Fr. Paul. His father stood to say something and Paul held his up hand to stop him.

"I already know what has been done for you and Mom. I'm very thankful to Fr. Paul for looking out for you."

He turned his attention to Ashley, who in the weeks that he had been gone had flourished in her pregnancy. As she opened the envelope her eyes seemed to come out of her head. Tom was sitting on the arm of the chair by his wife as she opened her envelope. Speechless, they both looked at Paul. Ashley stammered, "I don't know what to say."

"There's more than enough there for whatever you need." Paul was all smiles as he looked around the room at the people who were so dear to him.

Sarina, who was watching the festivities, was probably the only person in the room besides Claire who didn't know what was going on.

Paul noticed her puzzled expression. "I'll explain over lunch."

They dined at a Mexican restaurant that was right across the street from St. Charles, the Catholic grammar school all of the Morgans had attended. After ordering and some small talk, Paul explained what was in the envelopes and what had been wired to his parent's account.

Sarina took a moment to absorb all that Paul had told her. "Did you receive the same amount as your sisters?"

He nodded and said nothing.

As their lunch was served, he broke the silence, "The tacos and burritos look great after eating nothing but Italian food for the last few weeks."

Sarina stared at him.

"It's not my money. I've had time to think about what needs to be done with it. Ever since Lewis handed those checks to me, I've felt that there is too much sorrow and suffering associated with that money. I don't know why I feel that way, but I do right now. Maybe it will change with the passage of time. I don't know." They discussed his thoughts about his uncle's gift.

Sarina nodded her head with a smile on her face. Paul leaned over and kissed her. For a moment, he contemplated bringing up his discovery of his brother's password being her name and birth date. Then he thought further and decided to tell her another day.

"I wish that Patrick would call so I can relax," Paul said between mouthfuls of Spanish rice, one of his favorites. His cell phone began to vibrate as soon as the words were spoken. "It's Patrick, how's that for service?"

The conversation was brief and Paul said, "I'm on my way right now."

He hung up and glanced at his wife. "I'll drop you off before I go to Patrick's lab."

"No you will not drop me off. I am going with you." Her expression told him that there was no alternative.

Chapter 66

Paul and Sarina arrived at Patrick's lab, expecting the good news that they had cracked the code. The expressions on the faces of Patrick and his assistant Tyler told a much different story

Paul stared at them. "What's wrong, did we not get the information? What went wrong?"

Patrick appeared to have aged visibly in the hours since Paul had dropped off his memory stick. He shook his head and sat down on a stool as if all the life had been drained out of him.

Paul looked at Tyler, whose reddened eyes looked as if he had been crying. He had an expression on his face that you see on survivors of a terrible catastrophe. Paul thought he looked like one of the survivors in the photographs of the aftermath of Hiroshima.

"What is it, brother? What the hell is in the data files?"

Patrick motioned for Paul to sit down in front of his two computer monitors.

"In a nutshell, the screen on the left shows inflows into various Vatican accounts. The Bank codes and the account numbers were easy to ascertain because while you were in the

Vatican, Tyler and I were decoding various branch codes and accounts throughout the world."

Paul looked over his shoulder at Sarina as Patrick continued. "The decoded cash inflows were from various cities and countries located all over the world, primarily the capital city of the country or province. Interestingly enough, in almost every other secondary entry associated with the capital city of the country was a secondary city that usually was the central headquarters or main office of a particular religion.

"Don't you understand what's going on here? The inflow list is composed of just about every major country in the world and their various religious organizations. These countries and religious institutions are sending vast sums of money into the Vatican. Anyone would ask why."

Patrick went on. "Note also that there are some strange bedfellows in the groupings. Tyler came up with a pairing chart of religions and their locations in all of these countries. Let me show you those." He clicked the mouse and another window came up. Paul stared in disbelief when he saw radical Islamic countries aligning their inflows with those from completely conflicting faiths. Buddhists with Christian. Muslims with Jews.

Paul turned his head toward Patrick. "What does this mean?"

Patrick answered shakily, "They are all playing out of the same purse. What the public is led to believe is that these contributing governments and religions are diabolical enemies, but in truth, they contribute large sums of monies together to the Vatican."

Paul was getting angry. "Again, what does it mean?"

"Look at the screen on the right. Do you really want Sarina to see this, brother?"

Paul looked at her and read her facial expression. She was staying put.

"This screen shows the outflows of the monies. The Vatican's multiple accounts located all over the world were used to conduit billions of dollars of various currencies to accounts of many companies and subsidiaries."

Leaning over Paul, Patrick used the mouse to click on a drop down menu and pulled up a sub-chart of accounts.

Paul stared at the entries on the list and what their known function was thought to be, and then the actual function in the last column. His eyes scanned across the columns of the table. XYZ lab located in Germany. World renowned for its research in children's diabetes. Its actual function was the development of various viruses that were distributed by table entry Subsection A. When he clicked on Subsection A, it showed the various clinics, physicians, and terrorist organizations that were paid distribution fees. Billions of dollars were paid by a laboratory to distribute viruses to the general public.

"For what purpose?" Paul screamed. The silence was oppressive.

Tyler finally spoke with tears in his eyes. "For control, for fear, and for unmitigated obedience to church and state. There's another entry when you click on the delivery system that gives the amount of bonuses paid to certain factions and individuals for a job well done. If you look, there was a bonus of a currency equivalent to twenty million dollars paid to a clinic for its above average infant death rate in New Guinea from scarlet fever."

Paul's eyes welled up. He turned to look at Sarina whose face was wet with tears.

Tyler continued. "Now this drop down arrow shows the percentile increase in various churches and faiths' collections. As the disease impacts and kills more people, so the increases in revenue rises. Note also, government receipts grow at almost the same percentile increase." Tyler was sobbing as he spoke. What he saw overcame him and everyone in the room.

They stared at the screen for a time before Paul broke the silence. "Can you put this together in an easy to comprehend format with all of the drop down boxes opened so the average person can understand it? Can this be done?"

Patrick and Tyler looked at each other and nodded.

"Then do it," Paul snapped, more angry than sad.

"Just a moment, brother," Patrick said. "I want to take you to a historic parameter. You need to see this especially in light of some of your uncle's comments. I think it will give an even better insight into who he was."

"Show me."

A couple of clicks brought the historical data up that dated back almost to the inception of Fr. Paul's file. Before continuing, Patrick said, "Before I show you these early entries, you must realize there are links to historical data that can be used as reference points for what the user needs for a course of action. If you click here, the historical reference for what I am about to show you pulls up the inside information, the bubonic plague for instance.

"Note the historical references to various people, places, and other relevant facts. The bubonic plague was ordered by such and such Pope in such and such country to curb what was described as religious waywardness. It gives the reason the plague was started and then it explains in detail all the other factors involved."

Paul could only stare at the screen.

Patrick went on. "The screen I'm opening now shows when your uncle was put in charge of his division, which was the late 1960s. There was a cultural revolution by various counter-culture groups that were advocating the dissolution of marriage, church, and state. It seems your uncle, by his use of historical data factors and links to two German labs involved in viral research, transacted large sums of monies that were transferred to the labs' various accounts throughout the world. The research was noted as being hyper-funded to get the results that were needed as soon as possible. Note the outflows of the lab were sent to various affiliates located in Africa, notably West Africa."

Tyler took up the commentary. "Also note where various monies were deposited in business and personal accounts. We traced some to clinics, newspapers, doctors, and if you can believe it, houses of prostitution."

Paul broke in. "You're showing me the beginnings of the AIDS epidemic, aren't you?"

"Yes," Tyler said in almost a whisper.

There was a palpable sadness in the room. The awful secret was in plain sight. They struggled to wrap their heads around the truth of what they'd been shown, while their hearts told them it couldn't be so.

How was it possible for any person or organization to invent, track, and profit from the pain of so many? The devil himself paled in comparison to what these religious and governmental groups had done to the human race for two things. Control and money.

The last screen showed the real world numbers of the AIDS epidemic. Thirty million deaths. Geographically, Africa was the most decimated continent with over one-half of the casualties.

Tyler started to bring up another screen and Paul said, "Stop, no more. I've had enough."

He stood up abruptly almost hitting Sarina with his shoulder. He turned and kissed her. "I'm sorry. I'm just numb. I need time to think. Patrick, put together an easy-to-read format of this data for worldwide distribution. Make it so that even a dummy can understand the numerical facts. I need time to think. Thanks, brother." They hugged.

As Paul was leaving, Patrick said, "We can have that formatted in about two to three hours. I'll call you." Paul nodded as he took Sarina's arm and they left the building.

"I need some time to grasp what we've just seen. I knew that my uncle was a ruthless bastard but I never dreamed that he was the harbinger of death for millions and millions of people."

As they climbed into Paul's car, his cell phone began to vibrate. He looked at the number. It was Fr. Matt Whaley.

Very quickly, Matt detected that Paul now knew what many had suspected. "Come over to the church and let's talk. I have always found His house is the best place to make decisions, especially big decisions." After a little more prodding, Paul and Sarina headed to Fr. Matt's church.

He greeted them at the front door of the church and led them to the front pew. The late night was even more calming in this house of worship. All three sat in silence with their thoughts. Paul was the first to speak.

"Matt, I don't know where to start. The truth is so much more horrific than I think any of us could have imagined. I am sick. Mentally and physically sick. I can't believe what those bastards have been doing to humanity as if the world was theirs to manipulate."

Fr. Matt nodded, "Paul, you were chosen by Him to bear this cross. Jesus didn't want to go through with the crucifixion. He went to Gethsemane to ask His Father to spare Him. After prayer and reflection, He knowingly went to His death for the salvation of man's soul. You are being asked to do something very similar. Go where your heart is directed. Follow it, you will not be led astray."

"You know what was on those memory sticks."

"Paul, the Seal of the Lamb just didn't come about because of your uncle. It has existed for hundreds of years. Various members of churches and governments formed the Seal of the Lamb to try to get to the bottom of what they believed was taking place. The insiders knew some of what was going on but had no tangible proof. You have discovered the irrefutable truth. Now you need to decide what to do with the information."

Paul was deep in thought with his eyes closed. After many minutes, he looked up and cleared his throat. "I am asked to reveal information that could dismantle the Catholic Church with the world watching. I don't think I can do this."

Fr. Matt looked at him and then at Sarina and slowly said, "Don't kid yourself, my brother. He knew when He chose you that you would do what is right. Your choice is between humanity's wellbeing and the church, and by the church I mean all of the religious institutions and government states party to these atrocities. Without humanity, there can be no religions and governments. Humanity is the ultimate reason for their existence."

Paul stood up and walked to the old wooden railing that separated the faithful from the altar. He knelt down and prayed for guidance. Sarina and Fr. Matt sat in silence.

As Paul knelt, he heard the church custodians in the back of the sacristy cleaning. They had a radio on and the song that played was familiar. The chords of the acoustic guitar sounded like an updated version of one of his classic rock favorites.

Paul listened to the lyrics from a song about being true to one's self and not complicating one's life with distractions. Find love and remember there is someone looking out for you "up above."

When the music stopped, Paul rose slowly and walked back to them. He had a peaceful expression on his face. Fr. Matt knew that he had been given the answer.

"Before you tell me what I think we already know, I need to confide in you. The Seal of the Lamb has known for many years of your uncle's despicable activities. When the development of Ebola started to unfold, we knew that he must be stopped. Those around him began to slowly end his reign of tyranny. He was not dying of a disease. He was slowly being poisoned so as not to evoke any suspicion."

"The members of the Seal of the Lamb recruited others to help them and you. Some were your friends and others were members of the secret society enlisted to help you. Our friend Patrick Michael Richie and his assistant, Tyler Molvig. Sisters Betty, Andrea and Margaret at the Vatican. Even your pilot Lloyd and me. Their names had at least one of the letters in the word LAMB, which told others in the society that they were members also. People from all faiths and nationalities have always made up the membership of the Seal of the Lamb.

"You walked into the equation totally unexpected and gave us the chance to prove where all this was going and to maybe be given the chance to bring the truth to the world. That's all I have to say, except for God bless you."

Paul started to speak but his cell phone was vibrating in his pocket. It was Patrick.

"Everything you asked for is ready. I've sent a link to your email for worldwide distribution of the file to television, print media and new agencies. Paul, you are the bravest and best friend I have ever had. I love you." Patrick ended the call.

Paul looked at Sarina. Knowing what he was going to ask, she nodded. Words were not necessary at this point. He looked at his phone and his email and opened the link. He thought for a moment and then he realized that his hand was being directed to start the download. Peace and calm unlike anything he'd ever experienced descended over Paul as he pressed Send to start the download. It was done.

The sun was rising. It was the dawn of a new day. Paul asked Fr. Matt to join him and Sarina for breakfast at a small diner. He opened the church door for Sarina and Matt. He hesitated a moment and Sarina turned back. Paul looked at her as he pulled the envelope out of his coat pocket. They stared at each other and Sarina nodded.

A smile crept across Paul's face. He looked down at the envelope addressed to the AIDS Foundation of Los Angeles. It contained the check for two million dollars that Fr. Paul had left him as his inheritance. Sarina and Paul had discussed the money and came to the decision that they didn't want anything from Fr. Paul.

Paul walked to the mailbox in front of the church and placed the envelope with the endorsed check in it.

In the car the radio was on. The news media was already discussing the impact of what was now known around the world. The truth had finally been brought to the masses. Paul changed to a music station. The song playing was so on point that he knew again that his hand had been directed to find and play it.

Run, don't stop
Don't look back.
If you must, look in the rearview mirror
Then hit the gas
Hit it hard.

~ Excerpt from *Adieu* by
H. Schaffer / Beyond Classy Music

Acknowledgements

I want to thank everyone who helped with this project or were supportive of it.

My "real" life friends and family, who lent me their persona so a novice writer could add "believability" to the characters.

Patrick Richie and family, Tyler Molvig, Jodi Sutherland, Ellen DePaolo, Tom Fogerty, Matt Whaley, Lisa Storey, Angie G., Colleen B., Tracy A., Andrea, Betty, Margaret, Ashley and Lisa. Thanks for giving me the dialogue I needed.

Larry V. - It wasn't hard to imagine what you would say in certain circumstances.

Jade and Jeff...next time you bastards will sign and return the releases.

Wes and Leah Foutch for the "spark" of focus, Dr. Cheri Neal, Patty Eason, Robin Neal, Jessica Sanchez, Joe Brown, Les and Colleen Beller, Laura and Kevin Stewart, Annette and Mike Gaddis.

Additionally Bernard (great catering), Sara Gelter, Corey Schroeder, Fred Slick and Dr. Jonathan Alvarez for "unkinking" my neck weekly. Our weekly meetings helped me in this endeavor more than you will ever know.

Much gratitude to my longtime friend and mentor, Rosalie Ramsey. You are perhaps the best "barometer" on what real life is all about.

Special thanks to Kiki Schomp for the original cover concept. You are a friend and a great sounding board. Those "appointments" that we had made me believe that to write this book was the right thing to do.

Dr. Joanie Coffey, my Wednesday morning breakfast partner, thank you for the final edit and the insight.

I want to extend my warmest appreciation to my editor, Peggy Petersen of Peak Editing. Your input was concise and precise and you made me appreciate your craft much more than I ever thought. This could have never come to fruition without you.

When I needed publishing skills, Joe and Jan McDaniel of BookCrafters appeared as if by magic. You both, in addition to Peggy Petersen, helped take this project to its culmination. For that I am most appreciative.

My sisters, Betty Subith and Susan Walker, thanks for the comments and thoughts.

In memory of Bill Howe, your friendship and mentoring came along in my life at the exact instant it was needed the most.

My "special and most longtime mentors" Jim and Ilene Roper...I found the best way to honor a person that was there from almost the beginning would be to utilize their alma mater. Your words and thoughts are always remembered as we recounted recently.

A great thanks to my best friend of forty plus years, Russell Drake. You have been there through thick and thin. You are the embodiment of the definition of a best friend.

Finally, what can you say about more than fifty years?

A rag tag boy of sixteen meets a girl the first day of the eleventh grade and they are together for the next forty years. That's more of an unbelievable story than Morgan 512.

It was great when you used to tell people to ask me about the first moon landing to alert them as to how "crazy" I was in my saying it was filmed in a B western movie studio.

The funny thing that happened with the original idea of this book was you didn't think it was so "out there." You let me ramble about it until it began to have some form and shape.

After you left this earth, I heard your voice when I would hit a snag or hiccup in my writing. There were times when the written text could have passed for yours and not mine. Yes, I am still pissed off about you getting better grades in English composition in high school.

Nerys, you always liked finishing first or being first. Our weekly Saturday night chess matches were a testament to that. British sportsmanship, my eye.

Enter the second "administration," Roxanne. I will never forget the day you came back to Oregon from Colorado after I spent four days and nights, round the clock writing and rewriting the damn outline to this book. When you asked me what I intended to do with it and I told you "it would make a movie." You told me they only base movies on books not five page outlines. That was the wellspring for my "discovery" of wanting to write.

You knew the right "buttons" to push to get me to proceed. I enjoyed your shock when you read the first manuscript and accused me of having a "writer" writing this book for me. Your "Jersey Girl" tact made this all possible. Thank you and love you.

Additional thanks for editing to Marianne Leiby, Roxanne Morgan and my "sister," Jane Morgan.

To all victims of AIDS and other horrible diseases, my thoughts and prayers are with you. May God bless you.

About the Author

H.C. Schaffer, former horseman, financial services professional, musician, songwriter and writer. I approached this topic as you would a chess match. Find the ultimate goal and work backwards from it. One of my early mentors told me to take a macro-view of a subject. Clearly identify the opposing forces and realize that in most cases their ultimate goal is either money or power or both.